The Collected Supernatural and Weird Fiction of Barry Pain Volume 1

The Collected Supernatural and Weird Fiction of Barry Pain Volume 1

Seventeen Short Stories & Two Novels of the Strange and Unusual Including 'The Tree of Death', 'The Moon-Slave', 'Locris of the Tower', 'The Magnet', 'An Exchange of Souls' and 'Going Home'

Barry Pain

LEONAUR

The Collected
Supernatural and Weird
Fiction of
Barry Pain
Volume 1
Seventeen Short Stories & Two Novels of the Strange and Unusual Including 'The Tree
of Death', 'The Moon-Slave', 'Locris of the Tower', 'The Magnet', 'An
Exchange of Souls' and 'Going Home'
by Barry Pain

FIRST EDITION

Leonaur is an imprint of Oakpast Ltd

Copyright in this form © 2022 Oakpast Ltd

ISBN: 978-1-915234-54-4 (hardcover)
ISBN: 978-1-915234-55-1 (softcover)

http://www.leonaur.com

Publisher's Notes

Contents

Linda

My elder brother, Lorrimer, married ten years ago the daughter of a tenant farmer. I was at that time a boy at school, already interested in the work which has since made me fairly well known, and I took very little interest in Lorrimer or my sister-in-law. From time to time I saw her, of course, when I paid brief visits to their farm in Dorsetshire during the holidays. But I did not greatly enjoy these visits. Lorrimer seemed to me to become daily more morose and taciturn. His wife had the mind of a heavy peasant, deeply interested in her farm and in little else, and only redeemed from the commonplace by her face. I have heard men speak of her as being very beautiful and as being hideous. Already an artist, I saw the point of it all at once: her eyes were not quite human. Sometimes when she was angry with a servant over some trivial piece of neglect, they looked like the eyes of a devil. She was exceedingly superstitious and had little education.

Our guardian had the good sense to send me to Paris to complete my art education, and one snowy March I was recalled suddenly from Paris to his deathbed. I was at this time twenty-two years of age, and of course the technical guardianship had ceased. Accounts had been rendered, Lorrimer had taken his share of my father's small fortune and I had taken mine. But we both felt a great regard for this uncle who, during so many years, had been in the place of a father to us. I found Lorrimer at the house when I arrived, and learned then, for the first time, that our uncle had strongly disapproved of his marriage. He spoke of it in the partially conscious moments which preceded his end, and he said some queer things. I heard little, because Lorrimer asked me to go out.

After my guardian's death Lorrimer returned to his farm and I to my studies in Paris. A few months later I had a brief letter from Lorrimer announcing the death of his wife. He asked me, and, indeed, urged me not to return to England for her funeral, and he added that she would not be buried in consecrated ground. Of the details of her death, he said nothing, and I have heard nothing to this day. That was five years ago, and from that time until this last winter I saw nothing of my brother. Our tastes were widely different—we drifted apart.

During those five years I made great progress and a considerable sum of money. After my first Academy success I never wanted commissions. I had sitters all the year round all the day while the light lasted. I worked very hard, and, possibly, a little too hard. Of my engagement with Lady Adela, I will say nothing, except that it came about while I was painting her portrait, and that the engagement was broken off in consequence of the circumstances I am about to relate.

It was then one day last winter that a letter was brought to me in my studio in Tite Street from my brother Lorrimer. He complained slightly of his health, and said that his nerves had gone all wrong. He complained that there were some curious matters on which he wished to take advice, and that he had no one to whom he could speak on those subjects. He urged me to come down and to stay for some time. If there were no room in the farmhouse that suited me for my painting, he would have a studio built for me. This was put in his usual formal and business-like language, but there was a brief postscript—"For Heaven's sake come soon!"

The letter puzzled me. Lorrimer, as I knew him, had always been a remarkably independent man, reserved, taking no one into his confidence, resenting interference. His manner towards me had been slightly patronising, and his attitude towards my painting frankly contemptuous. This letter was of a man disturbed, seeking help, ready to make any concessions.

As I have already said, I had been working far too hard, and wanted a rest. During the last year I had made twenty times the sum that I had spent. There was no reason why I should not take a holiday. The country around my brother's place is very beautiful. If I did work there at all, I thought it might amuse me to drop portraits for a while and to take with my first love—landscape. There had never been any affection between Lorrimer and myself, but neither had there been any quarrel; there was just the steady and unsentimental family tie.

I wrote to him briefly that I would come on the following day, and I hoped he had, or could get, some shooting for me. I told him that I should do little or no work, and he need not bother about a studio for me. I added: "Your letter leaves me quite in the dark, and I can't make out what the deuce is the matter with you. Why don't you see

8

a doctor if you're ill?"

It was a tedious journey down. One gets off the main line onto an insignificant local branch. People on the platform stare at the stranger and know when he comes from London. In order to be certain where he is going, they read with great care and no sense of shame the labels on his luggage. There are frowsy little refreshment rooms, tended by frowsy old women, who could never at any period of their past have been barmaids, and you can never get anything that you want.

If you turn in despair from these homes of the fly-blown bun and the doubtful milk, to the platforms, you may amuse yourself by noting that the farther one gets from civilisation, the greater is the importance of the railway porter. Some of them quite resent being sworn at. I got out at the least important station on this unimportant line, and as I gave up my ticket, asked the man if Mr. Estcourt was waiting for me.

"If," said the man slowly, "you mean Mr. Lorrimer Estcourt, of the Dyke Farm, he is outside in his dogcart."

"What's the sense of talking like that, you fool?" I asked. "Have you got twenty different Estcourts about here?"

"No," he replied gravely, "we have not, and I don't know that we want them."

I explained to him that I was not interested in what he wanted or didn't want, and that he could go to the devil. He mumbled some angry reply as I went out of the station. Lorrimer leant down from the dogcart and shook hands with me impassively. He is a big man, with a stern, thin-lipped, clean-shaven face. I noted that his hair had gone very grey, though at this time he was not more than thirty-six years of age. He shouted a direction that my luggage was to come up in the farm cart that stood just behind, bade me rather impatiently to climb up, and brought his whip sharply across his mare's shoulder.

There was no necessity to have touched her at all, and, as she happened to be a good one, she resented it. Once outside the station yard, we went like the wind. So far as driving was concerned, his nerves seemed to me to be right enough. The road got worse and worse, and the cart jolted and swayed.

"Steady, you idiot!" I shouted to him. "I don't want my neck broken."

"All right," he said. He pulled the mare in, spoke to her and quieted her. Then he turned to me. "If this makes you nervous," he said, "I'd better turn round and drive you back. A man who is easily frightened wouldn't be of much use to me at Dyke Farm just now."

"When a man drives like a fool, I suppose it's always a consolation to call the man a funk who tells him so. You can go on to your farm, and I'll promise you one thing—when I am frightened, I will tell you."

He became more civil at once. He said that was better. As for the driving, he had merely amused himself by trying to take a rise out of a Londoner. His house was six miles from the station, and for the rest of the way we chatted amicably enough. He told me that he was his own bailiff and his own housekeeper—managed the farm like a man and the house like a woman. He said that hard work suited him.

"You must find it pretty lonely," I said.

"I do," he answered. "Lately I have been wishing that I could find it still lonelier."

"Look here," I said, "do you mind telling me plainly what on earth is the matter?"

"You shall see for yourself," he said.

The farmhouse had begun by being a couple of cottages and two or three considerable additions had been made to it at different times; consequently, the internal architecture was somewhat puzzling. The hall and two of the living-rooms were fairly large, but the rooms upstairs were small and detestably arranged. Often one room opened into another and sometimes into two or three others. The floor was of different heights, and one was always going up or down a step or two. Three staircases in different parts of the house led from the ground floor to the upper storey. The old moss-grown tiles of the roof were pleasing, and the whole place was rather a picturesque jumble.

But we only stopped in the house for the time of a whisky-and-soda. Lorrimer took me round the garden almost immediately. It was a walled garden and good as only an old garden can be. Lorrimer was fond of it. His spirits seemed to improve, and at the moment I could find nothing abnormal in him. The farm cart, with my luggage, lumbered slowly up, and presently a gong inside the house rang loudly.

"Ah!" said Lorrimer, pulling out his watch, "time to dress. I'll show you your room if you like."

My room consisted really of two rooms, opening into one another. They seemed comfortable enough, and there were beautiful views from the windows of both of them. Lorrimer left me, and I began, in a leisurely way, to dress for dinner. As I was dressing, I heard a queer little laugh coming apparently from one of the upper rooms, in the passage. I took little notice of it at first; I supposed it was due to one of the neat and rosy-cheeked maids who were busy about the house. Then I heard it again, and this time it puzzled me. I knew that laugh, knew it perfectly well, but could not place it. Then, suddenly, it came to me. It was exactly like the laugh of my sister-in-law who had died in this house. It struck me as a queer coincidence.

Naturally enough, I blundered on coming downstairs and first opened the door of the dining-room, I noticed that the table was laid for three people, and supposed that Lorrimer had asked some neighbour to meet me, possibly a man over whose land I was to shoot. One of the maids directed me to the drawing-room, and I went in. At one end of the room a log fire flickered and hissed, and the smell of the wood was pleasant. The room was lit by two large ground-glass lamps, relics of my dead sister-in-law's execrable taste. I had at once the feeling that I was not alone in the room, and almost instantly a girl who had been kneeling on the rug in front of the fire got up and came towards me with hands outstretched.

Her age seemed to be about sixteen or seventeen. She had red hair, perhaps the most perfect red that I have ever seen. Her face was beautiful. Her eyes were large and grey, but there was something queer about those eyes. I noticed it immediately. She was dressed in the simplest manner in white. As she came towards me, she gave that little laugh which I had heard upstairs. And then I knew what was strange in her eyes. They also at moments did not look quite human.

"You look surprised," she said. "Did not Mr. Estcourt tell you that I should be here? I am Linda, you know." Linda was the name of my dead sister-in-law. The name, the laugh, the eyes—all suggested that this was the daughter of Linda Estcourt. But this was a girl of sixteen or seventeen, and my brother's marriage had taken place only nine years before. Besides, she spoke of him as "Mr. Estcourt." I was making some amiable and some more or less confused reply when Lorrimer entered.

"Ah!" he said. "I see you have already made Miss Marston's acquaintance. I had hoped to be in time to introduce you."

We began to chat about my journey down, the beauty of the country, all sorts of commonplace things. I was struck greatly by her air, at once mysterious and contemptuous. It irritated, and yet it fascinated me. At dinner she said laughingly that it would really be rather confusing now; there would be two Mr. Estcourts—Mr. Lorrimer Estcourt and Mr. Hubert Estcourt. She would have to think of some way of making a distinction.

11

"I think," she said, turning to my brother, "I shall go on calling you Mr. Estcourt, and I shall call your brother Hubert."

I said that I should be greatly flattered, and her grey eyes showed me that I had no need to be. From this time onward she called me Hubert, as though she had known me and despised me all my life. I noticed that two or three times at dinner she seemed to fall into fits of abstraction, in which she was hardly conscious that one had spoken to her; and I noticed, moreover, that these fits of abstraction irritated my brother immensely. She rose at the end of dinner, and said she would see if the billiard-room was lit up. We could come and smoke in there as soon as we liked. I gave a sigh of relief as I closed the door behind her.

"At last!" I said. "Now, then, Lorrimer, perhaps you will tell me who this Miss Marston is?"

"Tell me who you think she is—no, don't. She is my dead wife's younger sister, younger by many years. Her father took the name of Marston shortly before his death. I am her guardian. My wife's dying words were occupied entirely with this sister, about whom she told me much that would seem to you strange beyond belief; and at the time she gave me injunctions, wrested promises from me which, under certain conditions, I shall have to carry out. The conditions may arise; I think they will. I don't mind saying that I'm afraid they will."

"Why does she bear her sister's name? Why does she address you as 'Mr. Estcourt'? And why do you address her as 'Miss Marston,' when she introduces herself to me simply as 'Linda'?"

"Her mother had three daughters. The eldest was called Linda. When she died, the second, who was my wife, took that name. When my wife died the name descended to the third of them. There has always been a Linda in the family. The rest is simply Miss Marston's own whim. She has several."

"Who chaperons her here?" I asked. He smiled. "That question is typical of you. She is little more than a child, and she has an almost excessively respectable governess living here to look after her. Only I can't be bothered with the governess at dinner quite every night. Does that satisfy you?"

"No; well, perhaps yes. I suppose so."

"It may make your rigid mind a little easier if I tell you—and it is the truth—that if I had my own way I would turn Miss Marston out of this house tomorrow, and that I would never set eyes on her again; that I have a horror of her, and she has a contempt of me."

"And of most other people, I fancy. Well, anyhow, what's the trouble?"

"I haven't the time to tell you a long story now; she will be waiting for us. Besides, you would merely laugh at me. You have not yet seen for yourself. What would you say if I told you of a compact made years and years ago with some power of evil, and that this girl was concerned in the fulfilment of it?"

"What should I say? Very little. I should get a couple of doctors to sign you up at once."

"Naturally. You would think me mad. Well, wait here for a few weeks, and see what you make of things. In the meantime, come along to the billiard-room."

The billiard-room was an addition that Lorrimer himself had made to the house. We found Linda crouched on the rug in front of the blazing fire; I soon found that this was a favourite attitude with her. Her coffee cup was balanced on her knees. Her eyes stared into the flames. She did not seem to notice our entrance.

"Miss Marston," said my brother. There was a shade of annoyance in his voice. She looked up at him with a disdainful smile. "Do you care to give Hubert a game?" he asked.

"Not yet. I want to watch a game first. You two play, and I'll mark."

"What am I to give you, Lorrimer?" I asked. "Thirty?" He was not even a moderate player. I had always been able to give him at least that.

"You had better play even," said Linda. "And I think you will be beaten, Hubert."

I looked at Lorrimer in astonishment. "Very well, Miss Marston," he said, as he took down his cue. I could only suppose that during the last few years his play had improved considerably. And even then, I did not see why Linda had interfered. How on earth could she know what my game was like?"

"This is your evening," I said to Lorrimer after his first outrageous fluke."

"It would seem so," he answered, and fluked again. And this went on. His game had not improved; he did the wrong things and did them badly, and they turned out all right. Now and again, I heard Linda's brief laugh, and looked up at her. Her eyes seemed to have power to coax a lagging ball into a pocket; one had a curious feeling that she was controlling the game. I did my best with all the luck dead against me. It was a close finish, but I was beaten, as Linda said I should be.

Linda would not play. She said she was tired, and suddenly she looked tired. The light went out of her eyes. She lit a cigarette, and went back to her place on the rug before the fire. Lorrimer talked about his farm with me. The quiet of the place seemed almost ghastly to a man who was used to London. Presently Linda got up to go to bed. "Goodnight, Mr. Estcourt," she said, as she shook hands with my brother. Then she turned to me: "Goodnight, Hubert. You shouldn't quarrel with ticket-collectors about nothing. It's silly, isn't it?" She kissed me on the cheek, and ran off laughing. She left me astounded by her words and insulted by her kiss.

Lorrimer turned out the lights over the billiard-table, and we sat down again by the fire.

"What did you think of that game?" he asked.

"It was remarkable."

"Nothing more?"

"I never saw a game like it before. But there was nothing impossible about it."

"Very well. And did you have a row with that ticket-collector?"

"Not a row exactly. He annoyed me, and I may have called him a fool. I suppose you overheard and told her about it."

"I could not have overheard. I was outside the station buildings and you were on the farther platform."

"Yes, that's true. It's a queer coincidence."

"I tried that, too, at first—the belief that things were remarkable, but not impossible, and that queer coincidences happen. Personally, I can't keep it up any more."

"Look here," I said. "We may as well go to the point at once. Why do you want me here? Why did you send for me?"

"Suppose I said that I wanted you to marry Miss Marston?"

"I thought that at the time of my engagement with Adela I wrote and gave you the news."

"You did. The artistic temperament does sometimes do a brilliant business thing for itself. Lady Adela Marys—"

"We won't discuss her."

"Then suppose we discuss you. You are half in love with Linda already."

"Very well," I said, "let us carry the supposition a little further. Suppose that I or anybody else was entirely in love with her, what on earth would be the use? The one thing that one can feel absolutely certain about in her is that she has an amused contempt for the rest of her species, male and female. It's not affected, it's perfectly genuine.

14

Even if I wished to marry her, she would not look at me."

"Really?" said Lorrimer, with a sneer. "She seemed fond enough of you when she said goodnight."

"That," I said meditatively, "was the cleverest kiss that ever was kissed. It finished what the interchange of Christian names began. It settled the situation exactly—that I was the fool of a brother, and she the good-natured, though contemptuous sister."

"You needn't look at it like that. It is important, exceedingly important that she should be married."

"Marry her yourself—it won't be legal in this country, but it will in others, and I don't know that it matters."

"No, I don't know that it matters. On the day I wrote to you I did ask her to be my wife. She replied that it was disagreeable to have to speak of such things, and that they need not be allowed to come to the surface again, but that, as a matter of fact, *au fond* we hated one another. It was true. I do hate her. What I do for her is for my dead wife's sake, for the promises I made, and, perhaps, a little for common humanity. There are others who would marry her. The man whose pheasants you will be shooting next week would give his soul for her cheerfully, and it's no use. Very likely it will be of no use in your case."

"What was the story that you had not time to tell me after dinner?"

The door opened, and a servant brought in the decanters and soda-water and arranged them on the table by Lorrimer's side. He did not speak until the servant had gone out of the room, and then he seemed to be talking almost more to himself than to me.

"At night, when one wakes up in the small hours, after a bad dream or hearing some sudden noise in the house, one believes things of which one is a little ashamed next morning."

He paused, and then leant forward, addressing me directly. "Look here; I'll say it in a few words. You won't believe it, and that doesn't matter a tinker's curse to me. You'll believe it a little later if you stop here. Generations ago, in the time of the witches, a woman who was to have been burned as a witch escaped miraculously from the hands of the officers. It was said that she had a compact with the devil; that at some future time he should take a living maiden of her line. Death and marriage are the two ways of safety for any woman of that family.

"The compact has not yet been carried out, and Linda is the last of the line. She bears the signs of which my wife told me. One by one I watch them coming out in her. Her power over inanimate objects, her mysterious knowledge of things which have happened elsewhere, the terror which all animals have of her. A year or two ago she was always about the farm on the best of terms with every dog and horse in the place. Now they will not let her come near them. Well, it is my business to save Linda. I have given my promise. I wish her to be married. If that is not possible, and the moment arrives, I must kill her."

"Why talk like a fool?" I said. "Come and live in London for a week. It strikes me that both Linda and yourself might perhaps be benefited by being put into the hands of a specialist. In any case, don't tell these fairy stories to a sane man like myself."

"Very well," he said, getting up. "I must be going to bed. I am out on the farm before six every morning, and I shall probably have breakfasted before you are up. Miss Marston and Mrs. Dennison— that's her old governess—breakfast at nine. You can join them if you like, or breakfast by yourself later."

Long after my brother had gone to bed, I sat in the billiard-room thinking the thing over, angry with myself, and, indeed, ashamed, that I could not disbelieve quite as certainly as I wished. At breakfast next morning I asked Linda to sit to me for her portrait, and she consented. We found a room with a good light. Mrs. Dennison remained with us during the sitting.

This went on for days. The portrait was a failure. I have the best of the several attempts that I made still. The painting's all right. But the likeness is not there; there is something missing in the eyes. I saw a great deal of Linda, and I came at last to this conclusion, that I had no explanation whatever of the powers which she undoubtedly possessed. I also learned that she herself was well acquainted with the story of her house. She alluded to the fact that neither of her sisters was buried in consecrated ground; no woman of her family would ever be.

"And you?" I asked.

"I am not sure that I shall be buried at all. To me strange things will happen."

I had letters occasionally from Lady Adela. I was glad to see that she was getting tired of the whole thing. My conduct had not been so calculating and ignoble as Lorrimer had supposed. She was a very beautiful woman. It was easy enough to suppose that one was in love with her—until one happened to fall in love. I determined to go to London to see Lady Adela, and to give her the chance, which I was sure she wanted, to throw me over. I promised Lorrimer that I would only be away for one night. Lady Adela missed her appointment with

16

me at her mother's house, and left a note of excuse.

Something serious had happened, I believe, with regard to a dress that she was to wear that night. But really, I do not remember what her excuse was. I went back to my rooms in Tite Street, and there I found a telegram from Mrs. Dennison. It told me in plain language, and with due regard to the fact that each word cost a halfpenny, that my brother, in a fit of madness, had murdered Linda Marston and taken his own life. I got back to my brother's farm late that night.

The evidence at the inquest was simple enough. Linda had three rooms, opening into one another, the one farthest from the passage being her bedroom. At the time of the murder Mrs. Dennison was in the second room, reading, and Linda was playing the piano in the room which opened into the passage. Mrs. Dennison heard the music stop suddenly. Linda was whimsical in her playing, as in everything else. There was a pause, during which the governess was absorbed in her book. Then she heard in the next room Lorrimer say distinctly: "It is all right, Linda. I have come to save you." This was followed by three shots in succession. Mrs. Dennison rushed in and found the two lying dead. She was greatly affected at the inquest, and as few questions as possible were put to her.

Sometime afterwards Mrs. Dennison told me a thing which she did not mention at the inquest. Shortly after the music had stopped, and before Lorrimer entered the room, she had heard another voice, as though someone were speaking with Linda. This third voice, and Linda's own, were in low tones, and no words could be heard. I thought this over, and I remembered that Lorrimer fired three times, and that the third bullet was found in another part of the room.

Lady Adela was certainly quite right to give me up, which she did in a most tactful and sympathetic letter.

The Tree of Death

1

In the cool of the evening, I always saw her. She came up from the river with the other women. That was a great moment when she, who all the day had been in my heart, came at last into the sight of my eyes. Sometimes she would be soon lost to me, going into her father's house. Sometimes she would crouch with the others on the steps by the wall of a brown hut listening to the old storyteller, and it was wonderful to see the story reflected in her eyes as she heard it, like the image of the palm-tree in the deep river. Sometimes even she would walk by my side and speak with me, and those were evenings to be long remembered for rapture and for sorrow.

And one day I went to the storyteller. He was dark-skinned and not of our race, and he had come from a far country, travelling for many months alongside the river. Some said that he had fled for his life.

"This evening," I said to him, "I beg that you will come out and tell your stories to us."

He waved his hand at me in refusal, saying that he would not. But when I showed him the gift, I had brought for him, then he consented. And I did this because my eyes ached for the sight of her, and I could not bear that this evening she should pass quickly by me.

And when the man began to draw with his stick in the sand, and tell stories of that distant country from which he had come, she was among those that gathered round to listen. And I gazed at her as one tortured with thirst who sees far off the water he would drink.

He told us of a tree that is called the tree of death. He said that the seed was like bright silver to look at and of the size of a man's fist. If you set that seed in the ground, for two years nothing would appear, and then came the miracle, for betwixt sunrise and sunset the tree came to full maturity, growing with incredible rapidity to twice the height of a man, and died again. And in those short hours of life that tree sought to drink the blood of a man sending out a heavy fragrance that brought sleep and death, and lashing its victim with long, writhing tendrils. And each tendril was covered with sucking mouths like the mouth of a leech.

And thereon he told us a story of a faithless woman and of a man's deferred vengeance. Secretly, by night, the man planted the seed of the tree of death in the garden of his wife's lover. But when in two years the tree came to being, it slew the woman for whom the lover had deserted the wife.

They found her white body in the morning, buried beneath the dead and decaying ruin of the tree, and they found, moreover, the three silver seeds that the tree had produced.

"And in the whole earth," said the man, "there are but those three seeds left, and because the tree is so evil, those seeds have not yet been planted." Twice he stretched out the fingers of both hands and closed them again. "Yes, twenty times since then the river has risen and fallen. And for five years more the silver seed must be kept and guarded. And then the power of life, which is the power of evil, will have left those seeds and they will be harmless toys, and never any more will man or woman behold the great magic of the tree of death."

I give his story in a few words. He told it in many words, making it a living picture, so that we seemed to see all as it happened and to hear the very words that were spoken. And all the while my eyes were fixed upon the woman whom I loved in vain. She was as one entranced, breathing deeply, and her fingers tore to pieces the flowers of scarlet hibiscus that she carried, the petals dropping on the sand as drops of blood. The sunset, too, was blood-red that evening.

As he finished speaking, we heard a jackal far away in the desert. And then a boy, laughing, said that the man told many lies.

"Son of a dog, I lie not," said the man, with sudden fury. "I tell you what I have seen and known. In this hand—this very hand—I have held the silver seed of the tree of death. Yes, yes." He rose and stood erect, and his voice dropped to a whisper. "Was it not I, myself," he said, "who planted that seed in the garden of my wife's lover?"

We were all silent, and he turned and left us. And then for the first time that evening the woman looked at me and her hand made a little sign. So, I followed her down to the river bank, and there for a while we sat and talked in the light of a great burnished moon.

2

"You praise me and say that I am very beautiful," she said. "It may be and it may not be, but it is rather pleasant to hear. You bring many gifts to my father's house, and again it is pleasant to receive gifts. I think you paid the old storyteller, for clearly, he showed more deference to you than to others. And that is the best of all. For one day is as another, and we go the same round continuously, like the ox with bandaged eyes that draws up the water for the garden; but to the hearing of stories, we live many lives and are ever changing. But then—then—you pour out your love to me, and would have me give you mine. How can one give who has it not? Others also speak of love to me and have the same answer. It may be that I am still too young, for I am very young, and that one day the fire will burn up in me. But now, when you speak of love, it is as though I gazed at the writing of a scribe having no skill to read it. And yet—yet—there was something I would say."

"Speak on. Your voice is sweet to hear."

"It is of the story that we have heard. I think there is truth in it, even if it be not all true. I will tell you why, and I have told no other of this. Two years ago, an old woman lay dying in her house, and those that should have tended her had fled in fear. And I brought up water for her from the river. She drank eagerly of it, for the fever was on her. And then she bade me pour a little of the water in the hollowed palm of my left hand and hold it so that she might gaze into it. She looked long into it, so that my little hand shook. And then she said words that I have never forgotten and never yet told. These are the words: 'The eyes of the dying have seen beyond, and as I say it shall be. The man of your love shall come to you holding in his hand a ball that is not of silver but of the colour of silver, and in that ball, there shall be life and death.'

"Tonight, I knew that the ball must be the seed of the tree of death. I know not where the seed is. The old man said it was guarded. It may be that one must go a long and perilous journey, and that blood must be shed, and that a great price must be paid. But this I know—on the day that you come to me holding in your hand a seed of the tree of death, I shall be so filled with love for you that my head will droop and my eyes will faint, and my body and my soul will be yours."

And in a voice that had become suddenly hoarse I said: "And you have told no other of this?"

"Have I not said it? Also, if you swear you will get for me the silver seed, I shall tell no other until it is clear that you have failed. I chose you for many reasons. You are gentle, and when my beauty is gone and you cease to love me you will not then begin to beat me. You are not so wealthy as some of those that seek me, but neither do you hold your wealth with so hard a grip as they do. Did you not also pay the storyteller for my delight?"

"For your delight and for the delight of my eyes in you."

"It is as I thought. And without that I might never have heard of the tree of death or understood the secret of my future. And though I do not now love you—not in the very least—yet I come to you first. But if you think it too hard and hazardous for you, then—"

"Ah, wait!" I said. "Believe me that not for a moment has there been a doubt in my mind. If anywhere on earth there be that silver seed, I swear that I will find it, and bring it to you, and nothing save death shall stay me."

"It is enough," she said. "And when will you bring it?"

"I do not know how long it will be. Will you wait for me for a year if need be?"

"Yes, for a year. But I have seen love run away as water. If, when you hold the seed in your hand, you no longer love me, then bring it not to me, lest you bring sorrow with it."

I pointed to the river at our feet. "The river runs forever," I said, "but the river is ever there. So is my love for you."

And as we parted I said to her: "Then you wish to have this seed of the tree?"

"To me," she said, "it is no more than a sign of destiny. If you bring it, then I shall love you. But if you are not destined then another will bring it, and I shall love him. But for the seed itself, since it is evil, it shall be fuel for the fore. Or haply—" she looked at me with steady eyes—"I may keep it till it has no more power to harm, and then it may serve as a toy for the children that I bear."

That night I slept ill, my thoughts going backward and forward between joy and sorrow like a ball that is struck by the hands of the players. It was joy that she had spoken to me seated close by my side, that she had trusted me with a secret, that of her own will she had given me the chance to gain her love.

It was sorrow that she loved me not yet, and that if I failed in the adventure, she would never love me and would love another. Nay, the man had said that there were three seeds of the tree of death. It might be that if I found one of them, another man also might find one, and he, going more swiftly or by shorter road, might take from me my beloved.

Moreover, though in this adventure I might risk all, yet if I were not destined, I should fail; and if I were destined, then, though I sat quietly in my house and risked nothing, the unseen hand would place in mine the silver seed of the tree. And so, I came back to the wisdom that is old and strong and cruel as granite rock—that which is written, is written, and that which will be, will be.

And yet what pleasure could I have of gold dust and gems, of herds and fertile land, if I had not this woman? Without her, life itself was worthless. So, I was determined to risk all. Had I not seen this myself, and had I not heard of it in many stories—that he who of his own will makes a great sacrifice shall in the end have his reward?

3

I found the old man, as I had expected, stretched upon his bed, though for some hours the sun had been up. He was ever idle, though he still had strength to work. Those that by chance listened to his stories would bring him small gifts. But if one would command a story, as I had done, then the gift was greater; and so, he lived.

And at first, as I came in from the bright sunlight, the hut seemed dark. But presently I saw him well, and I knew who had given him the robe that he wore and who had given him the loose slippers that lay on the ground beside him.

And after our words of salutation, I said to him: "I have in my mind a great matter of which I would speak with you, desiring your help. If you can help me, then in return I will give many and very rich presents. Come into my garden, where we may talk quietly, and there is pleasant shade, and the fruit of last year still hangs upon my orange-tree."

So, he said courteously that I was without doubt of divine descent and that he was my servant. And, rising from the bed, he thrust his feet into his slippers and came shuffling after me.

Seated under the orange-tree, he sipped the coffee that was brought out to him, but the oranges that I gave him he wrapped in a fold of his robe for another time.

"Last night," I said, "you told us of the tree of death."

"And for that reason," he said, "a woman brought me this morning bread and coffee, but the coffee was less good than this."

"She was beautiful?"

"She was a song of love, but unfortunately I am now old. When I had eaten and drunk, I went out and found that son of a dog who said that I lied, and beat him with my slipper until he howled. For I had told him of things that have been and still are. True, I have also stories of things that might be, and these are more beautiful. What of it? Shall the young insult the old? But this matter in which you need my help, I beg you to tell me of it."

"I go to seek one of the three silver seeds of the tree of death. As beside that, my life and such wealth as I have are nothing. I must have that seed. You can tell me whither I must go and what I must do to attain it."

"If a man travel with the utmost rapidity and sparing nothing, he may make the journey in four months."

"Then in four months I will accomplish it."

"There are perils of the road—robbers and dangerous beasts."

"I fear them not." And I showed him the dagger that I carried.

"But you will come to a country where the stranger is suspect, and in the place where the silver seed lies guarded no stranger may enter at all; and the guard is threefold—a circle, and within it a second circle, and within that a third circle. You may stain your skin till it is as dark as mine, but you cannot speak in the tongue of that people, neither do you know their ways. And if you would attain your end by violence, you will be one man against a myriad of men. So, that if you go, two things are certain. The first is that you will never even see the silver seed, and the second is that you will die very soon."

"Have you no better help for me than this?"

"There may be another way. You said truly that this is a great matter. It is one that must be weighed well with long thought. I will, if you please, go back now and ponder upon it. And tomorrow at this time I will come again to you."

So, I gave him a present and let him go, his robe curiously swollen with many oranges that he carried.

And next day he came back to me and said: "There is one way, and one only. It may bring you what you seek but it is not sure. If you would take it, two things will be necessary. The first is that you must trust me utterly, more than most men will trust their brothers. Secondly, the cost will be great, so that of all your possessions there will be but little left to you."

"You are sure that it is the only way?"

"It is the only way."

"Then I will take it. Tell me of it."

"You cannot go, but I can go for you. Also, I am very willing to go. Twenty years have I been a stranger in this little place, and my own country calls me. I know the tongue of the people and all their ways. Moreover, I myself have been of the innermost guard of the temple, and know much which is hidden from most men of my race. If there is any man on earth who can get the seed of the tree of death, then I can get it. But I must be able to buy men, and they are such that a small present will not tempt them."

"When will you return?"

"In the ninth month from that day that I can start you should have the silver seed either at my hand or at the hand of a sure messenger."

"If I trust you whom at least I know, that may be well. Must I trust also as messenger whom I do not know?"

"You may do so without fear. For he will not receive the last half of his reward until he has delivered the seed into your hands. Moreover, he will know that if he is treacherous, his own life and the life of his dearest that he leaves behind him will be forfeited."

"It is a great journey, and you are old."

"I still have strength, not having spent myself with too much labour. Moreover, there are two that travel speedily—the young man that goes to his beloved and the old man that returns at last to his native country."

"You have no fear that you will be robbed? For you will carry with you much wealth."

"If I went with a train of laden camels, travelling as a rich merchant, then the danger would be great. But my wealth will be hidden in a belt about my body and I shall seem to be a poor man. There is indeed the chance that death one way or another may overtake me, but both you and I must take that chance."

"How do you know that you will find the silver seeds? Since it is known that they are evil, may not they have been destroyed?"

"No, for it is know that the evil must die of itself, and they who would destroy it will make yet worse evil that shall fall on their own heads."

"When you yourself planted that seed in the garden of your wife's lover, was it then guarded in the temple? And if that be so, how came you to be able to make these great gifts and so get possession of it?"

"The temple was triply guarded, and I myself was of the innermost guard. But the seed was not there then neither was the nature of it known—save to me only—until two years after I had planted it. In quite another way did I obtain that seed, and I beg that you will not ask of it, for it was shameful to me."

Many other questions did I ask of him, and to all he had a ready answer. But I showed little judgment, my mind being filled with thoughts of my beloved. And in all things, I did as he bade me.

Then for many days I sold my possessions until the man said: "It is enough," and afterwards I journeyed with him for three days to a town where there was a great bazaar, but our business was not in the bazaar, but at the house of the principal merchants. For we bought diamonds, emeralds, and pearls. And among the pearls there were two that were twins, being perfectly alike in size and shape, in weight and colour. And when he secured this treasure into the belt that he would wear, he left out one of these twin pearls and placed it in my hand, bidding me to keep it with the utmost care.

"For," he said, "I am an old man and it is more likely that I shall choose to die in the land of my fathers. The messenger that I send with the silver seed will take the great oath of my people, swearing that he will be guilty of no negligence, and no treachery, and no disobedience. If any man takes this oath and breaks it, then in the whole earth there is no place where he may hide from swift and terrible vengeance. For this reason, no man of my people will take this oath unless for a great reward."

"It is justice," I said.

"Therefore, I give him one of the twin pearls when he sets forth. And when he arrives and places in your hands the silver seed, you will give him the other. Then he will return and show me the two pearls, and that will be the sign that he has performed his oath, and I shall have written for him quittance of it. So, he will sell the pearls and get himself a wife and a house, and I myself may die in peace."

And he found a brown-sailed boat that went up with a favouring wind to the next village carrying sugarcane. And making a small payment to the owner of the boat, he stretched himself upon the sugarcane and so was carried out of my sight.

All the day he would sleep in the boat and at night he would leave the boat, and purchase an ass, swift and sure-footed, and ride all night. And so, he would go on, by this way and that, taking the best that chance offered or his wit could devise, until he came to his journey's end.

26

4

On the day that the man went I made my computation. My house and my walled garden were left to me, and there was enough for another month. All else—herds and fertile land, and the treasure that I had of my fathers—was changed into little stones and these stones were being carried away from me round the belly of a man whom I should never see again. In another month it seemed that I who had hired others to work for me must myself work for hire.

To most men these would have been black thoughts, and they would have rent their garments and cursed their own folly that had brought such ruin upon them. But to me all this was a source of joy. "Now truly," I said, "of mine own will have I made a great sacrifice, and in the end, I shall have my reward."

And that evening, as my custom was, I waited to see my beloved come up from the river. And as she passed me, she made a sign that I should wait. And having set the water-jar down in her father's house, she came back to me.

It was the first time she had spoken with me since the night when we heard of the tree of death and afterwards sat by the river together. True, I might have spoken to her, but I feared lest by being too importunate I should lose such favour as I had in her eyes.

"These last days," she said, "I have heard much foolish talk about you and about the old storyteller. Those that know a few things, yet have not the key of them, must always guess wrongly. But I have the key; would you hear what I know?"

"Your words are to me the sweetest music."

"Some say that the man has gone to tell his stories in other villages, that for one story he may receive many gifts. Others say he pays a visit to his own country, and others say that he goes to examine for you some house or land that you are minded to buy in place of that which you have sold. Certainly, he is gone, and another will sleep in his hut this night. It is true that he has gone to his own country, but I know that he goes to get for you the silver seed, though you declared to me that you would go yourself, even if it cost you your life, so great was love for me."

And then I told her all, as I have set it down, explaining that I had indeed been willing to go and why that could not be. And she said:

"If a man risk his life for a woman, that is his greatest praise of her. But if he buy another man to risk his life, that is a greater wisdom for him. Yet in other respects you have not acted wisely. For the old

27

man may die, or he may be a thief; and even if he live and be worthy of trust, he may fail to get the silver seed; and even if he gets it, he may fail to render it to you. So that if the measure of your folly be the measure of your love for me, I am still commended, though with a lesser praise. Meanwhile, there will be none to tell me a story, making the cool evening pleasant for me. Moreover, that which you have given to get me you cannot give again to keep me. Also, my father has scolded me, and—"

Here she stayed, and her brow cleared, and she laughed.

"Take no heed of these words. If you are destined for me, I shall certainly love you very much. It is this heavy air that makes me say bitter things to you. Nor is it I alone who am troubled by it. The river itself is troubled—fretting and tossing—and there is anger in the setting sun. Somewhere tonight there will be havoc and great misery."

And therein she spoke the truth. For that night the earthquake came, awakening me from a deep sleep. Scarce can the fringe of it have touched the village. In my house two jars were shattered and I felt the earth move under me; but three mud-huts were brought down in ruins, so that there was much praying and screaming until the dawn came.

I judged that the full force of the earthquake had spent itself in the desert, so when the dawn came, I saddled an ass and rode into the desert to see what had befallen. And since the air was now fresh and serene, the ride was pleasant to me. And presently I saw that the outline of a great rock had changed from what it was aforetime. So, I rode up to it. And then I saw that the rock had split, revealing the entrance to a tomb.

I dismounted and went in a little way, but it was so dark within that I could distinguish nothing. And I went back to my house and said nothing of what I had seen, lest some others should forestall me.

And that night, when the village slept and all was at peace, again I rode out, taking with me a spade and a good lantern. And all the night I spent in the tomb.

I think it was the tomb of one of royal blood. It had many chambers with marvellous paintings on the walls, ranged on each side of the entrance hall, and from thence were fine wide steps that led downwards, but somewhat encumbered with sand and fallen fragments of the rock. And never had I seen such treasure—cups and platters, rings and figures, all of the purest gold. And there were also ornaments of precious stones.

Much of this treasure I had buried that night in another place, marking the spot in a way that none save he who set the mark could have the skill to see. And on many of the nights that followed I buried further treasure. And I had none to help me, for I could trust none.

So, once more it became necessary for me to go to that great town. By night I loaded two camels with treasure, hiding it so that it would appear that they carried forage only. And even so I travelled in great fear, with my dagger ever ready to my hand, and urging the camels to their greatest speed.

But it was appointed that I should arrive safely. And I was well received in the houses of the principal merchants with whom I had traded before, and so disposed of my treasure.

Thus, by chance all that which I had given up, in order that I might have the silver seed and thereby the heart of my beloved, was restored to me again, and at first, I was well content.

But afterwards my eyes were opened, and in great anguish I saw what had befallen me. For of my own free will had I made sacrifice and it had not been accepted, and that which I had given was returned into my hands again. What reward then, could I hope?

"Without doubt," I said, "the earthquake overtook the old story-teller as he went through the night and he is buried beneath fallen rocks or is drowned in the river. And the desire of my heart is taken from me,"

And that very night I spoke with a man who, as he was travelling towards the village on the day of the earthquake, had met the old man. Thus, vainly do we fit our keys to the door that is ever locked. That which is written, is written, and that which will be, will be. So that now I no longer dared to forecast either my happiness or the manner of my suffering. I folded my hands and waited.

Once more in the evening my beloved spoke to me.

"They speak of you in the village after this manner," she said. "They say that you sold much and that now you buy much, and that in the difference of the price you have your advantage. This is the wisdom of fools who speak, not having the key. But I have the key. I know that, when you sold, the old man took it away with him, so that I even marvelled if my father would willingly give me to one who had become poor. Whence, then, have you the means now to buy so much? Either you lied to me, and the old man bore no wealth of precious stones in his belt, or you have worked some great magic. And if it be the first, then he will not send you the silver seed, for it was not his habit to do much for little, nor are you destined for me. But if it be the second, then I beg that you will show me how to work the same magic, that I may make my father very content and also buy for myself a new robe and bracelet of gold."

"Neither have I lied to you, nor have I worked any magic. Since you gave me your secret, and have kept close in your own heart what I have told you so far, I will trust you yet again. It was destined that I should find a great treasure, making up for all that I had bestowed on the old man. Ask me no more of this now, but tell me why you wish for a new robe and a bracelet of gold?"

"I have a cousin, and she is beautiful, but not so beautiful as you think I am. Also, the time has come that she must be married. Neither she nor I know who her husband will be, but she is obedient and will leave the choice to her father. Undoubtedly, he will choose a rich man, and there will be a very great festival of the marriage, lasting all the night through, with music and dancing girls. Surely I shall be bidden to the festival, and I would not be ashamed there. But my father is not rich, neither does he ever find anything."

"Then it is you who must find."

"What shall I find?"

"A purse hidden in a basket of pomegranates. And this basket of pomegranates I will send to your father's house soon after the hour of sunrise tomorrow."

"Listen," she said. "Your love for me is as the desert, and my love for you is not even yet as one grain of sand. Will you still send this gift?"

"I will still send it."

She said that, if it were known, the tongues of the malicious would speak evil of her, and, therefore, it would be a secret. And she was pleased, just as a child may be pleased with a little gift. She had said truly that she was still very young. She laughed and played with the maidens of her age. And neither for me nor for any other man had she one thought of love.

Yet even then love slept deep in her calm eyes, as the fish with golden scales lies sleeping at the bottom of a deep pool. And the time of awakening was near.

5

He that enjoys knows how swift the passage of time may be. But at last, eight months had passed since the departure of the old storyteller, and he had said that in the next month—the great month of fruition—I should receive the silver seed of the tree of death—if, indeed, I ever received it.

So now in every footstep I seemed to hear the sound of an approaching messenger, and in every sound to hear my name called. My blood grew hot as with a fever and my sleep left me, so that for the greater part of the night I paced I my garden alone.

All night on the ninth night of the month I heard in the distance the sounds of music and revelry. It was the wedding of the cousin of my beloved, and there was a great festival. But towards dawn the sounds died away, and I paced to and fro in my garden. And suddenly, as I passed the door in the wall of the garden, I heard a little sound, and I was called by my name. But it was not the voice of any messenger that called. It was the voice of my beloved.

I opened the door and bade her enter. She came in without a word, wearing the new robe and the golden bracelet. And in the grey and awful light of dawn her face seemed still wondrous beautiful, and yet changed.

"You are weary?" I said.

She made a sign of assent.

"Yes," I said, "the marriage festival was long. All night I heard the music. Your eyes tell of your weariness." And I spread a silken carpet for her under a tree that she might rest, greatly wondering that she should come to me in this way.

She knelt on the carpet, bending her body and covering her face with her hands.

"I have not been at the festival," she said. "Oh, I have much to say and there is not one word of it that you can ever forgive. Yet promise to hear me to the end, and then—then do with me as you will."

Then my heart fainted and doom sang in my ears. And there was a long silence before I could say: "I will hear you to the end."

And now she stretched herself at full length on the rug, her hands clasped behind her head. And she spoke like a tired child that repeats a long lesson.

"Yesterday," she said, "at sunrise I went down to wash myself in the water of the river. And when I had put on my garment again and risen up, I was aware that a youth came towards me riding upon a white ass that was bedecked with silver ornaments. And he dismounted and looked long at me. He was darker than we are, yet not so dark as the old storyteller. And I read in his eyes that which I have read in yours and in the eyes of other men. I knew that he desired me. Every day a

31

beautiful woman may read that language. Yet it moved me not, and it was as if there was a mist before my eyes.

"He named you and asked me where he might find you, speaking in our tongue but slowly, as one but newly accustomed to it.

"I said: 'If you follow me, I will take you to him.'

"'And afterwards?' he said. 'For you are more beautiful than any woman on this earth, and it is for you that my love has waited.'

"I laughed, for there was still the mist before my eyes. Besides, such a speech was daring and sudden, since he now saw me for the first time. 'Afterwards,' I said, 'will be as it will be. Meantime what seek you with this man?'

"He turned his eyes from me, as if he feared to look on me. 'It is forbidden to me,' he said, 'so much as to speak of it.'

"Now, whether you believe it or not, it is true that in the next words which I said I had no intent but to vex him a little. Was not the mist still before my eyes, so that I could not judge aright? Was I any more than the thistle-seed caught in the wind of destiny?

"I said, still laughing: 'You love me, and yet you refuse the first thing that I ask of you?'

"And now he looked long at me again, breathing deeply, and suddenly he thrust his hand into his robe and drew forth something that glistened.

"'Since you ask it,' he said, 'behold! I go to render this to him'

"And so he stood before me, holding in his hand a ball that was not of silver but of the colour of silver, and in the ball there was life and death. Thus, was it determined in the beginning, before the stars were set and before the earth was shaped. The mist passed from my eyes and I saw that there was no beauty like his beauty. And when he spoke his voice was dearer to me than any that I have ever heard. And never had there been such love as now burnt my whole being.

"'See!' he cried. 'I have broken the great oath, and for that death will come soon upon me. My hours are numbered, and yet if they be hours of love, the price is small. Do I not love you? Do I not worship you?'

"My head drooped and my eyes fainted and I sank down on my knees. 'Lord of my heart!' I said. 'Lord of my life.'"

And now she turned over on her face, and her whole body was shaken with weeping.

For a few moments I remained silent, and then I said: "Have you ended that which you would say to me?"

32

"No, no!" she cried. "No, no!"

"Speak on then," I said, "and I would beg you to speak quickly."

Now she rose to her feet, and thereafter she spoke standing, holding to the trunk of the tree as if for support.

"He had come by the way of the desert, and the night before he had come to the great rock. And finding a great tomb in the rock, he had rested there for the night, and there he had left his gear, setting forth with the white ass to find you, and so to complete his mission.

"Little thought had he now of that mission. And since already people were astir in the village, he took me back with him to the tomb in the rock. I rode and he ran by my side, and in less than an hour we were there alone with our love in the cool dusk of the tomb.

"And when it drew near to the evening, I was afraid lest my father should send out on all sides to seek me, and haply I should be found with my lover. So, I arose and went to my father's house, and when he demanded why I had been away so long, I said I had been helping in the preparation for my cousin's festival. Moreover, I put on my new robe and the gold bracelet on my arm, and said to him that I now went to her wedding. And he was content, and disposed himself to sleep, for he is old and feeble and unsuited to a night of revelry.

"And so, in breathless haste I went back to my lover, knowing that our hours were but few, and that eternity could scarce contain our love. Until an hour ago I was with him, and then it was necessary to see you. And I came near the latticed door of your garden, and, hearing your step, I called to you. And so, I come to the very heart of the matter."

Here, pausing, she looked intently at me. And presently she went on speaking.

"There is neither anger nor mercy in your eyes. They have become like the eyes of a stone image in a temple—eyes that change not and see not. Hear me now to the end.

"He has broken the great oath, and the punishment is sure. One will come to him—he knows not when, but it will be very soon—and will say to him: 'show me the twin pearls that are in all things alike, for this is the proof that you have fulfilled your oath.' And if he has them not, then must he be slain instantly. And, further in that far country from whence he came the life of his mother will be forfeited, for she was the surety for him in the great oath. And shall not his death be also mine?

"He has but one of the twin pearls, and the other is in your keeping. So that you now hold in your hand three lives.

"It may be that you will say to yourself that I was very young, and that when I tempted him to break his oath, I knew not what I did. And you may say further that your hatred is against destiny, and not with these thistle-seeds that the wind of destiny has swept together. If that were so, and you gave me the twin pearl and let us depart with it to his own country, then in all the words of praise there is none, that is worthy of such a great nobility.

"But in that I ask, it may be, more than any man can give. So, if you still desire me, I will remain here. And if you would have me as a wife or as a slave, I will be ever faithful and obedient. And I ask no reward but that by some instant messenger you will send the twin pearl to my lover, that he may go in peace. And I myself will see him no more at all. Do with me as you will, but let not his blood be upon my head. The fault was mine. Moreover, he has in part fulfilled his oath, for by me he sends to you the seed of the tree of death. I pray you to answer me."

It is very truth that until then I knew not what I would answer. But as she spoke, she drew from her garment that silver glistening ball, and held it out to me, and I took it. It was still warm with the warmth of her beautiful body.

In a moment I had buried my dagger deep in her body. She fell at my feet, and a shudder went through her, and she was dead.

I became quite calm again, and my mind was as clear water, and my heart beat steadily and quietly. I knew just what I would do.

I dug a deep grave for her in a corner of my garden. Then I drew forth the dagger, wrapped her in the silken carpet, and so buried her and the silver seed with her.

I made the earth smooth over her, and cleaned my dagger. And at last, it was all so ordered that the garden looked even as it looked the morning before, and there was no trace of that which had been done. Neither had any eye beheld it.

And then I rode forth to the tomb that I had found in the great rock, and that the woman's lover had also found. But there, even as I feared, I came too late, and my work had been done for me.

The man lay dead in the entrance to the tomb with a knife in his throat. The bundle of fodder that he had carried for the ass had been spread out like a couch, and beside it were a jar of water and a brass cup. But the white ass bedecked with silver ornaments was no longer there; and I supposed that the man who had slain him had taken it, but he had not taken the twin pearl, for that lay on the open hand of the dead man. There I left it. And I left the dead man to the vultures and jackals. And I saw that all the time the messenger journeyed from that far country another had travelled close behind him, watching to see if he fulfilled his oath, and with the power to slay him if he broke it.

And after that I went back to my own house and lay on my bed, preparing for myself that which I believed should be my last sleep, merging itself in the end in death. But the drug that I took failed me. Sleep, indeed, I obtained, but at noon on the following day I waked again. And in my sleep, it was revealed to me that not at this time, nor after this manner, should my death be. There were to be yet two years of waiting for me, while the silver seed woke to life where I had set it, even in the very heart of death.

6

It was said in the village that my beloved had fled with a man of another race—for the two had been seen together—thus bringing shame upon her father's house. It was also said by others that the river had taken her, for she was accustomed to wash herself in the water of the river. And some said one thing and some another, but none said the truth, nor did any accuse me.

And as the tale of the months grew, I became greatly changed. No longer could the beauty of any woman move me, nor could any enterprise attract me. Had fabulous wealth been within my reach I would not have put out my hand to it. I was almost without wishes, save the wish to be alone. Never was there a guest in my house, nor the sound of music, nor laughter. Long and sweet sleep at night had left me, and I slept fitfully at strange hours, haunted always by dreams that seemed so real, that waking I scarce knew whether I was awake or slept, nor which was the substance and which the shadow.

Waking or sleeping, the thought of her whom I loved was ever present with me. I longed to call her up from death that I might tell her how nearly I had come to forgiveness, and how slight a thing in the end had driven me to madness. It grieved me that she would never know that. There was no longer any jealousy or rancour in my heart towards her. She had been ever as she had said, as thistledown caught in the wind of destiny.

After the first year of waiting, I sometimes saw her as I walked in my garden in the cool of the evening. She came and vanished again, like smoke scattered by the wind. And as the second year drew on, the vision came more frequently and remained longer with me. Even I heard her speak. She stood beneath my orange-tree, and she opened her robe wide and pointed to the wound in her breast.

"You have hurt me," she said. "How could you hurt her whom you loved?"

And at last, the day came when the tree of death should rise to twice the height of a man, and should drink my blood, and should die again, and all betwixt a sunrise and a sunset.

The sun was not fully risen when I examined the earth over her grave. None other but myself was permitted to come into that part of the garden, and it was with my own hands that I had kept it free of all chance growth. And I saw now that there were in the earth crevices like the picture of the sun's rays, and through the centres of these something hard pushed its way. It was rounded at the top, and it was dark green and crimson intermingled, and on the surface of it were little drops of moisture as though it sweated with the struggle to get through.

Then I went back through the empty garden to the empty house, for on the day before I had sent forth those that waited on me. And I bathed myself and put on a white robe, and then I saw to it that the doors were securely locked, and came back to the tree of death. It had risen now to the height of my knee, and it was still a single shaft tapering upwards, and it seemed to me that a light vapour came from it. And sitting down I watched this great miracle.

When it was the height of a man many stems separated themselves from the main stem save at the base where they were joined to it, and these lolled outwards and grew no more. But from these side stems a shower of tendrils began to descend, writhing in the air as if they had been serpents. And looking closely I saw that each of them was covered with little mouths that opened and shut continuously. But the centre stem grew upwards tapering still, but carrying at the summit a curious mass. This increased in size, and I knew that from it would come the flower of the tree.

It was the hour of noon. I withdrew myself a little and watched. From the side stems the rain of tendrils descended continuously, and they covered the ground so that over the place where I had laid her here was a moving sea of green and crimson. And shortly after noon the heavy mass at the head of the stem separated into three pods; the skin of them was like clear, thin silk, and they had veins like the veins of a man. I could see them swelling more and more, and that something white seemed to be struggling within them, and the top of the stem rocked to and fro a little as if in agony.

So far all had gone on in silence. But suddenly the skin of one of these pods was rent fro end to end, and in the rending, it made a sound like a woman that is hurt. From the burst pod there leapt a white flower of gorgeous beauty, greater than I have ever seen, and from the flower there fell a cloud of gold dust, sparkling in the sunlight, and the perfume of it, even at the distance where I stood, was of almost intolerable richness.

Then I cried aloud the words that came to me:

"O tree of love!" I cried. "You whose roots have devoured and taken into your being all that I have loved on earth, now take me also, that at the last we may be mingled together, and after the anguish and evil of life there may be peace. O tree of love and death, I come to you!"

And I went forward slowly and knelt beside the tree, looking upwards. And twice I heard that cry as of a woman that is hurt as the second and third flower burst forth. The clouds of gold dust blinded my eyes, and the heavy scent suffocated me. I fell at full length among those ramping tendrils whose little mouths sought my blood. And the last sleep came.

★★★★★★★★★★★★

I have written this, I who have been long dead, so that my bones are dust and for countless years my name has been forgotten. And I have written in a strange language and in a strange land, and by the living hand of one whom I know not.

The Bottom of the Gulf

Three hundred and sixty-two years before Christ a chasm opened in the Roman Forum, and the soothsayers declared that it would never close until the most precious treasure of Rome had been thrown into it. It is said that a youth named Mettus (or Mettius) Curtius appeared on horseback in full armour, and before a very fair audience, exclaiming that Rome had no dearer possession than arms and courage, leaped down into the gulf, which thereupon closed over him. This incident, like most of the legendary history of Rome, has been subjected to severe criticism. Those who too hastily disbelieve in it will reconsider their opinion on reading the account, not previously published, of what took place at the bottom of the gulf.

Curtius and the horse fell in the order in which they had started, with the horse underneath. After a few minutes' rapid passage, the horse stopped falling somewhat suddenly, broke most of itself, and died. Curtius, who, though a little shaken, was uninjured, sat up on his dead horse and looked round to see if he could discover the nearest way back. As he looked upward, he saw the top edges of the cavern close together, and the daylight shut out. But a curious greenish light still lingered in the cavern in which he found himself, and from one of its recesses came a voice which startled Mettus considerably. It said interrogatively:

'Did you hurt yourself?'

'Not much,' replied Curtius. 'I didn't know there was anybody down here. You quite startled me. Do come out and let me see you.'

'No, thanks,' said the voice. 'Did you really believe that you would die when you jumped down the gulf?'

'Certainly, I did.'

The voice laughed, a mean little snigger.

'So, you will, too. You'll die of suffocation, slowly, when the air in this cavern is exhausted.'

'Then we'd better get to work at once,' said Curtius. 'I have an excellent sword here and a couple of daggers. I put them on for the occasion. I didn't fall so far as I expected, and if we both of us work hard we shall be able to cut our way out.'

'Thanks,' said the voice, 'but I'm not going to do any work. I'm not of the same kind as yourself. I don't need the air of the outer world. In fact, I don't think much of the outer world, even its best specimens. That's why I live down here. You've got to die. Sorry, but there's no help for it. I've set my trap, and I caught you, and if you're the best specimen they can provide on top, my low opinion of them is confirmed.'

'What do you mean by the "trap"?' asked Curtius.

'Well, it was I who caused the chasm to open, knowing the kind of tomfool thing your soothsayers would remark about it. I sat here wondering what I should get. Shouldn't have been surprised at a brace of vestal virgins. They would have exclaimed, "Purity and devotion," instead of "Courage and arms," amid loud applause, of course. Or it might have been an elderly matron, with a good old tag that Rome held nothing more precious than the tender love of her mothers. It might have been a soothsayer, it might have been anything. As it is, it's you, and I think very little of you. Arms? Of what use do you think all those tin-pot arrangements which you have hung about you are likely to be? Courage? Why, man alive! you've got no courage at all.'

'I have,' said Curtius stolidly; 'I fully expected to die, and I was willing to die.'

'Just for one moment,' said the voice, 'when you had got all that mob of howling fools around applauding you. Applause is an intoxicant, and you got drunk on it. Now you are sober again, and you don't want to die at all. The man who can die alone, slowly and terribly, is courageous. But you've got no more courage in you than a piece of chewed string. You're as white as chalk.'

'That's the effect of the green light,' interposed Curtius.

'Rubbish!' replied the voice, 'green light doesn't make a man shake all over, does it?'

'That's just the shock from the fall,' said Curtius. 'But I can't stop here arguing with you; I'm off to explore the cavern. There must be a way out somewhere.'

'There isn't,' said the voice; 'but you can explore.'

'I can't die like a rat in a trap,' said Curtius, whimpering.

And off he went on his exploration. He looked in at the recess

40

from which the voice had proceeded and found nothing. The cave was enormous. For many hours he tramped on and on, and never through one tiny chink in the roof did he see the light of day. Exhausted and ravenous, at last he flung himself down on the floor of the cave, and almost immediately the voice, which had been silent all this time, began again. First of all came that faint, mean little snigger; then it said:

'Hungry?'

'Worn out with hunger,' sobbed Curtius; 'I'm thirsty, too. My mouth is so parched that I can hardly speak, and there doesn't seem to be one drop of moisture in this damned cavern.'

'There isn't,' said the voice, 'nor one crumb of food either, with the exception of your horse, and I don't think you will be able to find that again. You can try back if you like. Now I come to think of it, you won't die of suffocation, but of starvation. Cuts my entertainment rather shorter than I had hoped, but I must put up with that.'

'I can't die like this,' sobbed Curtius.

'Courage and arms,' replied the voice, 'are the things which Rome holds most precious. Go on, my boy; you'll last sometime yet.'

Then Curtius drew his sword, and went to look for the proprietor of the voice in order to slay him. But he didn't find him. He resumed his explorations.

In a few hours he was too weak to walk any further. He fell into a kind of doze, and when he woke again his arms had been taken from him.

'Where is my sword?' he exclaimed.

'I've got it,' replied the voice, this time from the roof of the cavern; 'what do you want it for?'

'Want to kill myself,' said Curtius.

'If I give you your sword, will you own that you were merely a drunken theatrical impostor?'

'Yes.'

'And that you are a coward, and are dying the death of a coward?'

'Yes.'

The sword clattered down from the roof on to the floor of the cavern at the feet of the hero.

He picked it up and set his teeth.

The Missing Years

Sylvia Hetheril, was the only daughter of James Hetheril, solicitor of Iddenside. She had one brother, Charles, seven years older than herself, who had been articled to his father and after his admission had continued to work in his father's office. The family lived together in a picturesque old house half a mile outside the town; the garden, in which Mr Hetheril took a great interest, sloped down to the banks of the River Idden. Every weekday morning at half-past nine the father and son walked into the town to their office. They did not always return together. Sometimes Mr Hetheril would return an hour or two earlier, to work in his beloved garden, leaving his son in charge.

Sylvia was beautiful and intelligent, and she thought a great deal more of her intelligence than she did of her beauty. Her father, whose ideas were a little old-fashioned, had not permitted Newnham. But Sylvia subscribed to a library in London which specialised in works of science, and studied hard. The science master at the big school in Iddenside helped her, and she was by far his most advanced pupil.

Somebody said one day to Sylvia's mother that Sylvia was perfectly charming.

"Well," said Mrs Hetheril, "Sylvia's a good girl and a good daughter, but I do wish she were rather more like the other girls. I don't want her to be vain, but really, she never seems to think about clothes at all. Shopping actually bores her. If she hadn't me to see after her, she'd be—well, she'd be an absolute scarecrow. Books, books, books! She works too hard. She prefers to play tennis with somebody who can just beat her. If she takes the punt out, it's to see how far she can get in a given time. Too strenuous altogether—I tell her so."

"She's the picture of health in spite of it," said the friend. "And she's very much admired."

"What's the use of it? It's my belief that she will never marry. She will be quite friendly with a man—till he falls in love with her. Then

43

she's finished with him. I've seen it time after time."

One evening in June Sylvia's brother Charles, shortly after his return from the office, came into the library and found his sister at the writing-table.

"Sweltering evening," said Charles. "I'm going down to get a bathe before dinner. Coming along?"

"Don't think so," said Sylvia. "I had a swim this morning, while you were snoring. I was going to finish this library list and then stroll down the road and post it."

Charles produced a letter from his pocket.

"Good," he said. "Then you might stuff this into the box for me. I meant to give it to the boy to post with the office letters, and forgot the damned thing."

"Right-o," said Sylvia cheerily.

Charles passed out through the open French windows, and went down the garden towards the boat-house, whistling away.

Suddenly a change came over Sylvia. She put her arms down on the table and rested her head on them. Her eyes closed. She was not asleep, but she was in a daydream. It was delightful and new. Nothing of the kind had ever happened to her before. She was filled with happiness. She had forgotten library lists, and letters, and the room in which she sat. It seemed she was in a wood at twilight with a crescent moon above her. For nearly twenty minutes she remained motionless.

And then she suddenly started up, a little frightened. What on earth had happened to her? Feverishly she finished her library list. There would be just time to get to the pillar-box and back before she went up to dress for dinner. She put on the hat and gloves that lay on the table beside her, and snatched up the letters. Was there anything else? Yes, there was an envelope with banknotes in it—a quarter's dress allowance. Her father would be annoyed if she left it lying about. She put it in the little bag she carried.

And then she hurried out of the house, expecting to be back again in five minutes.

Her father, mother, and brother sat down to dinner without her. It was not a very unusual occurrence, for Sylvia was sometimes a little unpunctual. It was expected that she would enter any moment, breathless, smiling, and apologetic.

As he finished his soup her father said, rather peevishly: "Where's Sylvia? I mean to say. What's she doing? She knows the dinner-hour. Reason in all things."

A maid was dispatched to find Miss Sylvia. Miss Sylvia was not to be found. There was definite evidence that she had not gone up to her room to get ready for dinner.

"She told me she was going down the road to post some letters," said Charles. "Probably she met some friends and they've collared her for dinner. She'll be telephoning directly."

By the end of dinner Sylvia had not returned nor had she telephoned. Her mother began to grow anxious.

Mr Hetheril said it was really too bad of Sylvia. Charles telephoned the Ingates and the Morrisons. Sylvia was not there, but Mrs Morrison had seen her posting letters and had spoken to her. Sylvia had seemed quite well and happy. A little later Mr Hetheril went to the police-station. At ten news came of her. She had gone up to London by the 7.20 train. The booking-clerk knew her by sight, and could describe the dress she was wearing. She had no luggage with her, and had to hurry to catch the train. There were two down trains that night by either of which Sylvia might return. Charles met them both, but she was not in either train.

Two days later the portrait of the missing girl appeared in the principal London newspapers with a full description. Several people wrote and claimed to have seen her on the evening of her departure, but none of the claims would stand investigation. Mr Hetheril then offered a reward of £1,000 for information which would lead to her recovery. This also produced nothing but a great number of unsatisfactory letters. Some weeks later the body of an unknown woman was taken out of the Thames, and it was thought by the police that is answered to the description that had been given them. Charles went up to London and saw the body. It was not his sister.

At the end of a year Sylvia's father and mother had practically given up hope. Their loss had aged them both considerably. Charles was still optimistic. He said that Sylvia had no troubles, that she was in excellent health, and that if she pleased, she was quite well-equipped to earn her own living as a teacher. She had always been independent in character, and might have chosen this way to see how she could get along by herself. It was pointed out to him that it was unlike Sylvia to do anything so cruel, and that if she had done it, she would most certainly have been seen and recognised by scores of people.

But when Sylvia had been away two years, Charles was astounded one morning to receive a letter addressed to him in what seemed to be her handwriting. He tore the envelope open and took out the letter, expecting to find that after all the similarity of the handwriting had been merely a coincidence.

But the letter was from Sylvia. It was written from a London hotel and was very short. She said that she was perfectly well, and that she was returning home late that evening. She thought it better for Charles to break this news to her father and mother. She could not tell them where she had been, or what she had been doing during the last two years. She had absolutely no recollection of it. She hoped that they would not ask her about it, because it worried her.

After a family consultation it was decided that her father and mother should go to London to fetch Sylvia back, and a telegram was sent to her to tell her to expect them.

Sylvia could tell them very little. Four days before she had found herself in London, without luggage, without anything, except for the clothes she stood up in, and with a handbag in which she found money. There was nearly £100 in notes, considerably more than she had in her possession when she left home. At one of the big London stores she had bought everything she required, had it packed in a couple of suitcases, and had then taken her room at the hotel. She wanted time to pull herself together, time to decide what was the best course to take. She had finally decided to write to her brother. She was perfectly well, and she did not think she had been ill or unhappy during her absence. Her mother noticed that Sylvia was well and expensively dressed, and asked if she bought those things in London.

"No," said Sylvia, "I was wearing them when I came to London. Please don't ask me any questions. I would tell you if I could remember. It's all gone. Those two years have been missed out of my life."

Her eyes filled with tears and the subject was immediately changed.

But Sylvia had not told her parents quite everything. On her arrival in London, she had noticed that she was wearing a plain gold wedding-ring. She had taken this off and hidden it. Later, she buried it in the garden.

She was not distressed with any further questions. This was in accordance with advice given by the family doctor. It had been, he thought, a case of secondary personality in which all recollection of the first personality had been lost. It was to be hoped that this secondary personality would not return, and meanwhile it would be better that her mind should be as undisturbed as possible, and that some sort of unobtrusive watch should be kept over her.

Mrs Hetheril made two little discoveries that she did not mention to Sylvia. The dress that she had been wearing on her return bore the mark of a fashionable draper in Helmstone, and the linen was embroidered with a monogram, and the monogram was quite distinct S.M.

Sylvia quickly took up again the threads of her normal life. There was much talk about her in Iddenside, which she detested, but gradually the wonder of her absence and her return was forgotten. She continued her scientific studies as before. She acted as bridesmaid at her brother's wedding, and she herself refused two offers of marriage. At the age of thirty-two she died of pneumonia, following on influenza.

★★★★★★★★★★★★

It chanced that the letter which Charles Hetheril gave to his sister to post was addressed to a business acquaintance temporarily resident at a hotel in Helmstone. As Sylvia walked to the post, she knew that she must hurry in order to be back in time for dinner. The feeling that she must hurry still persisted, but she had quite forgotten why. It really annoyed her a little that Mrs Morrison met her and delayed her. As she dropped the letters in the pillar-box the word Helmstone caught her eye, though she would not have said that she had noticed it. She knew now that she must hurry because she was wanted. It was something important. She had not the least hesitation as to the direction she should take. It seemed to her that she knew it without thinking about it. She took the road to the railway station and just caught an up train.

Helmstone, she said to herself in the train. You went to it from Victoria in ten minutes. She felt that she really ought to have looked up a train for Helmstone. But she supposed she must take her chance. Again, chance aided her. She had not to wait five minutes. Of course, when she reached Helmstone, she would not be at her journey's end, but she could take a taxi most of the way.

"Where to, miss?" said the driver at Helmstone station.

"Go up to the sea front, turn to the left, and drive on till I tell you to stop."

"Will it be far, miss?"

"Five or six miles, perhaps. I'm not sure. I shall tell you when we get there."

Sylvia sat back in the cab, a little impatient to be at her journey's end. Taking no notice whatever of the streets of Helmstone. Presently Helmstone was left behind. A little later the lights of a village blinked at her through the windows of the car. At intervals she could hear the constant murmur of the sea.

Suddenly she sat up and tapped the glass in front of her sharply.

The driver pulled up on the near side, a little surprised, for there was no habitation in sight.

"This is as far as I can go by taxi," said Sylvia in explanation. "I have to walk the rest of the way. It's not far."

Sylvia had impressed the driver strongly. He would have remembered her face and the dress she was wearing. He would have seen the portrait of her which appeared in the newspapers. He would have communicated with the Hetherils. But on his return journey to Helmstone his car collided with another and he was thrown out and killed.

Sylvia went up across the downs. Soon she saw in front of her the wood for which she had been looking. It covered about two acres of ground and there was a high palisade round it. She found the gate in this palisade without any difficulty. There was a notice-board by the gate, but it was too dark for her to read it, and she did not trouble about it. The board stated that the wood was private property and that the public was not admitted. It also gave a warning that the dogs at large in the wood were dangerous. Sylvia entered, closing the gate behind her. She had gone a few steps when a great mastiff leapt from a thicket and came slowly towards her, growling.

"Don't be so silly," said Sylvia to the dog. "I'm not going to hurt you. Just you come here at once."

It almost seemed as if the dog had recognised her voice. The growling ceased. He came up to her, sniffing suspiciously. Then he pushed his cold nose into her hand, and wagged his tail.

"That's right," said Sylvia, patting his head and then taking hold of the loose collar on his neck. "Now then. You take me by the nearest way up to the house."

Sylvia and the mastiff went on together by a grassy track to a clearing in the middle of the wood where stood a big brick-built bungalow. At some distance behind it there were outbuildings.

Sylvia rang, and the door was immediately opened by a manservant. At the sight of the man the dog began to growl again.

"Be quiet," said Sylvia to the dog, patting him on the head.

"You are Miss Sefton?" said the man anxiously.

"No," said Sylvia, "I——"

Suddenly a door into the hall opened and a man came out whom Sylvia had expected to see. He was young and very dark, and his expression was tragic. He was in evening dress with a short jacket and black tie. Sylvia turned to him at once.

"I had to come to you," she said. And then a wave of trouble passed over her. "I've lost my memory," she stammered. "Will you help me?"

"Of course, I will," said the man quietly. "Come in here, won't you?" He turned sharply to the servant. "Carter, see that a room is got ready for this lady at once."

The room into which Sylvia was taken was furnished as a library, brightly lit with electric lights. The top drawer of a bureau was open and the man went quickly to it and closed it. He made Sylvia sit down on a couch, and drew up a chair beside it.

"Now then," he said, "you're quite all right here, aren't you? I did not expect you and yet you came just in time." He looked at her steadily. "Almost exactly the same," he said in a low voice. And then addressing her again: "My name is Richard Mordaunt, you know. I wonder if you can remember what yours is."

"My first name is Sylvia. I'm quite sure of that, but I do not know what the second name is. I think I've travelled a long way to get here. I had to come to you. You looked just as I expected. But you'll be happier now, won't you?"

"Of course, I shall. I suppose you've not dined?"

"I don't remember. But I'm not a bit hungry. I'm rather tired."

"That's all right," he said in his pleasant musical voice. "You shall go to bed early. Mrs Carter and her daughter Alice will look after you. But I think we must have some supper first. You see, I did not dine this evening."

He touched the bell.

"That was very foolish," said Sylvia, looking up at him and smiling. "Why not?"

"It didn't seem worthwhile. The condemned man does not al-ways——"

He broke off as Carter entered. "Carter," he said, "supper in the dining-room as soon as you can."

"Very good, sir. I was already preparing it. Mrs Carter thought it would be required."

"Sensible woman. And the room?"

"Alice is seeing to it."

"That's right. Send Alice here as soon as the room is ready."

As Carter left, he turned again to Sylvia and pointed to the big mastiff who had followed her in and was now asleep on the hearthrug.

"You know, Sylvia," he said, "you're rather a miracle. The dog does not allow anybody but myself to touch him. A tripper from Helm-

49

stone was foolish enough one day to disregard the notice I put up and to come into my wood, and he got pretty badly mauled before I could get to him and take the dog off."

"He was quite gentle with me," said Sylvia. "He really showed me the way to the house."

Alice, a ruddy-cheeked, healthy-looking damsel, entered and said that the room was ready.

Mordaunt's eye caught the monogram S.H. on Sylvia's handbag, and he made up his mind quickly.

"That's right," he said to Alice. "Miss Harding has lost her luggage. But you'll do the best you can for her, won't you?"

When Sylva had gone from the room Mordaunt stood for a moment or two in deep thought.

"An absolute miracle," he said aloud.

He crossed over to the bureau and opened that drawer again. In it were two letters which he had spent the day in writing. One of them was to a Miss Sefton, and the other was addressed to his solicitors. On the top of them lay a revolver. He removed the cartridges from the revolver. They would not be wanted now. He tore the two letters across. Though the evening was warm there was a small fire smouldering in the fireplace before which the dog lay.

Mordaunt touched the dog with his foot. "Get out of the light, Leo," he said.

The dog rose obediently, and moved a few steps away. Mordaunt threw the torn letters on the fire and smiled as he watched them burn. The dog looked up at him inquiringly, obviously asking a permission.

"Yes," said Mordaunt, "you can go back. You ought to be out in the wood looking for people, instead of behaving like a pampered spaniel. But you've done a good work this evening, and you shall have your own way for once."

Soon after dinner Sylvia retired for the night. Mordaunt called to the dog, took a short stroll through the wood, and then he also went to his room. In the servants' quarters the event of the evening was being discussed by the Carter family. Mr Carter smoked a cherrywood pipe and enjoyed a bottle of stout. Mrs Carter and Alice listened to him as to the fount of wisdom.

"I don't pretend to understand it," said Mr Carter, "but I'm glad of it. If things had gone on as they were going on, in another week my gentleman would have been either in his coffin or in a madhouse."

"And who do you take it that she is?" asked Mrs Carter.

"Ah, there you're asking something. When I opened the door, I felt certain she was Miss Sefton come back again. She's pretty well the image of her to look at. Then she comes into the hall, turns to him, and says she's lost her memory, and will he help her? Yet that dog behaved as if he'd known her all his life. She was pulling him about in a way that none of us would like to do. When I waited on them at dinner he and she were talking exactly like old friends. What's more, he called her by her Christian name all the time. First time I've heard him laugh or seen him eat a meal as if he enjoyed it for many a long month. Why, he's a changed man. But if you ask me to explain it, I can't. One thing doesn't seem to fit with another."

"Well, George," said Mrs Carter, "I'll tell you an idea that has crossed my mind. The bit about her losing her memory and wanting him to help her may have been some sort of private joke between them."

"Don't you believe it, my dear. I saw her, and heard her, and she wasn't joking. What's more, he didn't expect her, or the room would have been ready. I suppose she didn't happen to say anything to you, Alice?"

"Well," said Alice, "she was very pleasant and talked quite a good deal. But she didn't seem to tell me anything, and of course, I couldn't ask."

"I wonder now," said Carter, "as a point of etiquette, if it's alright for her and him to be staying alone together in a house like this."

"You seem to forget there's us. Of course, if we weren't here, I should give notice instantly—what I mean to say is, I shouldn't approve of it."

Richard and Sylvia, to neither of whom the "point of etiquette" had occurred, met at breakfast next morning. Sylvia said that she had slept perfectly.

"And you?" she asked.

"I also slept well," said Richard, "for the first time for four months."

"I'm glad. And what are we going to do today?"

"If you don't mind, I'd like to drive you into Helmstone. You see, you arrived without luggage. You will have to buy heaps of things."

"That will be lovely," said Sylvia. "I find I've got some money in my handbag, though I've no notion where it came from."

"Oh, you will have to let me be your banker while you are here. I shall enjoy the drive too. For four months I've not been outside my wood."

"Four months again," said Sylvia meditatingly.

"Yes, I shall tell you all about that very soon, I think."

"And after we've bought everything?"

"Then I suppose we must go to the police-station and try to find out who you are, and see if you can be restored to your relatives again."

Tears came into Sylvia's eyes.

"No," she said, "I don't want that. I don't know anything about my relatives. Perhaps I have none. It must have been something bad that made me go away. I won't do anything to find out who I was. I'm content to be what I am. You must promise me that you won't do anything either."

"Well," he said hesitatingly.

"I don't want to be a bother to you. If you don't want me here, I'll go away, of course. But I'm not going back again to the place I came from."

"You cannot guess how very much I want you here."

"Then promise you won't try to find out who I am."

And after some persuasion he gave his promise. He knew it was all wrong, but he would have promised her anything and kept his word if it had been humanely possible.

For Richard had fallen very much in love with Sylvia, and she with him. It had happened instantaneously—at first sight.

Sylvia's mother had said quite truly that Sylvia did not care for shopping and was careless about dress. But the new Sylvia that had come into being enjoyed her shopping immensely and was particularly careful to choose things that would suit her. They lunched together at a hotel in Helmstone and drove back with the little car laden with packages. More were to be sent out later.

Sylvia was seen that morning by many shop assistants and by waiters at the hotel, but no description of her had yet appeared in the newspapers. It was not till three days later that her portrait was published.

Newspapers were delivered regularly at the house in the wood. For four months Richard had never looked at them because he had lost his interest in the world. He never looked at them now because he was too much interested in Sylvia. But Carter was careful to keep himself well informed. A really good murder was a great satisfaction to him. He would retail the newspaper account afterwards to his wife and daughter with his own theory of the case, and his astonishment at the ineptitude of Scotland Yard.

On the morning that Sylvia's portrait was published, Carter held a consultation with his wife and then brought the newspaper to his master.

"I don't know if I'm doing right, sir, but we thought I should show you this. Christian name is the same and there seems to be some likeness."

Richard looked at the portrait, glanced over the letterpress, and laughed.

The portrait in the newspaper had been taken from a bad and not very recent photograph of Sylvia. It was very hurriedly and badly reproduced. Richard honestly did not believe that this was the Sylvia he knew.

"Not a bit like Miss Harding," he said to Carter. "Thousands of girls have got *blond-candré* hair and blue eyes. Thousands of girls are just about that height. Thousands of girls wear a dark blue coat and skirt. Besides, if the Christian names are the same, the surnames are different. Yes, it's all right to have shown it to me, but don't bother Miss Harding about it. Just put the idea out of your mind. You're too romantic, Carter."

Neither Carter, nor Mrs Carter, nor Alice was quite convinced. There were certainly many points of coincidence, but when they looked at the portrait again, they could see that it was quite possibly a portrait of somebody else, and decidedly it was not for them to interfere.

It was after dinner that night that Richard Mordaunt told Sylvia something of his history. He was, so far as he knew, without a relative in the world. His income was derived principally from house property that he had inherited from his father. He owned several houses in Helmstone, and was rather sardonic about them. He employed an agent to look after his property and had himself very little taste for business. Six months before he had met Mabel Sefton at a friend's house. At the end of a month, they became engaged, and the engagement lasted one more month. Then Mabel Sefton threw him over.

The four months which followed had been a period of increasing melancholy, depression, and insomnia. He had shut himself up alone in his house, seeing nobody except his servants, and taking every precaution that his solitude should be uninterrupted. On the night of Sylvia's arrival, he had decided to make an end of it all, and that life was not worth living. He had the revolver in his hand when Sylvia rang at the front door.

"And now?" said Sylvia.

"Oh, Mabel was quite right. I can see that now, of course."

"What was she like?"

"She was very much like you. Wonderfully like you. But you're better. Mabel was just a little bit metallic."

The night was hot and they strolled out through the French windows, taking the grass path through the wood. Suddenly Sylvia stopped short.

"Ah," she said.

"What is it?" said Richard.

"I've been here before. The wood was just like this with that crescent moon above. The line of the trees against the sky was just like that, and I was very happy."

"And you're very happy now?"

She did not speak, but pressed her lips together and bowed her head in assent.

"I too," he said. He paused and quoted:

"What are we waiting for, O my heart?"

And in an instant, he held her in his arms.

★★★★★★★★★★★★

They were married by license as soon as possible in the village church. Sylvia's name was given as Sylvia Harding, and her age as twenty-two. She had no idea at this time what her real age was. A honeymoon of three months was spent in Switzerland, and when they returned again to England to the house in the wood the search for Sylvia Hetheril had been practically given up.

Richard had several men friends whom it now seemed that he had neglected too long. Besides he was very proud of Sylvia. He wished to show the treasure that he possessed. And so, for the next month or two, there were generally men staying in the house. Richard knew there would be questions, and he was quite capable of dealing with them.

"You know, Richard," said an old friend of his one evening as they sat over their port after dinner, "you always were a curious sort of cuss, and you've sprung a great surprise on us with this sudden marriage of yours. If I am any judge, you are very much to be congratulated on it. But may I ask you one question?"

"Anything you like," said Richard.

"Let's see. Your wife's maiden name was—"

"Harding," said Richard—"Sylvia Harding."

"When did you first meet her?"

"We first met," said Richard, "under very romantic circumstances, about which"—he paused and smiled humorously—"we are both of us determined not to say one word to anybody."

"Ah, well," said his friend, as he refilled his glass, "you always were unsatisfactory and mysterious, and I suppose you always will be."

Sylvia's baby, a girl, named after her, was born just about one year after Sylvia Hetheril left her home. The younger Sylvia was a very gay and healthy baby, receiving much devotion from the entire household. Alice Carter became the baby's nurse having developed a natural genius in that direction, and another maid was engaged to take Alice's place.

One evening, when the baby was about six months old, Richard said to his wife at dinner: "Sylvia, you don't look very happy this evening. Are you worried about something?"

"Not worried exactly. But I've been thinking about something. You remember Mabel Sefton?"

"Good old Mabel," said Richard. "She did me a good deal better turn than she ever imagined."

"Yet when she left you, you grew melancholy. You were even on the point of suicide."

"You remind me of past follies. But you remind me too that it was you who saved me."

"If I died, or if for any other reason I went out of your life, would you again be tempted to do that?"

"I might be tempted. I should be as unhappy as a man could be. But I should never do it. Not now. I've got the baby Sylvia to look after, you know."

"Yes, I've thought of that."

"And apart from death, what reason could there possibly be that you should leave me?"

"When I came to you, you know, I had forgotten everything that had happened before. It seems to me that I had changed in some way, that I was not quite the same person. I did not want to go back. I did not want to be the person that I had been before. I made you promise, you remember."

"Yes, I remember."

"Well, the thing that has been haunting me is that something of the kind may happen again. I might suddenly remember the girl I used to be, and quite forget the woman that I am now. Possibly somewhere or other, I have a father and mother living, and should want to

55

go back to them. If that ever happened, I want you to promise not to look for them."

"You ask a hard thing, Sylvia—an impossible thing. Why do you ask it?"

"Because I dread the conflict between the two people—the girl I was and the woman I am. The circumstances of neither would fit with the other. I should be confused. I think I should go mad. If you love me, promise it, Richard."

"Then I must promise it. It will probably never happen. I do not believe you can ever forget me. I do not believe you can ever forget the baby Sylvia. Still, there's the chance that the thing that happened once may happen again. I must see what ought to be done."

A few days later he brought her £100 in banknotes.

"I'd like you, Sylvia," he said, "to put those in some pocket of that little bag you always carry. I don't believe you're ever going back to—to wherever you were before you were sent to me. But if you do, the change may come suddenly when you are alone, and you must have money with you."

When the baby Sylvia was just a year old, Sylvia came out of the house one morning with two letters in her hand, invitations for the weekend. She found Richard reclining at full length in a comfortable chair on the verandah. He had been reading a newspaper, but had found the exertion too much, and had put it down. He was very nearly asleep.

"Richard," said Sylvia, "who is the laziest man on earth?"

"Can't say. I'm not in the first tree. I cut a tree down yesterday. Where are you off to?"

"Just going to the pillar-box in the road to post these."

Richard pulled a somewhat crumpled letter from his pocket.

"You might post that as well," he said. "I carried the damned thing about all yesterday and didn't remember to post it. Hurry up or you'll be late for lunch."

"Right-o," said Sylvia.

It was as she posted the letters that the change came. Victoria Street was the address on one of them, and it caught her eye. She went straight on in the direction of the village. She must certainly hurry, for her father was always annoyed if she was late for dinner. Suddenly she pressed her hand to her forehead. Where was she? This was not Iddenside. She must get back to Victoria at once. In the village she took the motor omnibus into Helmstone She felt dazed and horrified. She looked at her clothes. That was not the dress she had been wearing when she went away. How long had she been away? It was not until she reached Victoria that her mind became clear at all. She knew now that she had been away for two years, but she did not know what she had been doing. Of her baby and her husband, she had no recollection whatever.

★★★★★★★★★★★★

Shortly after her death, Dr Norton, who attended her in her illness, sat one evening talking over things with his partner.

"You knew poor Miss Hetheril, didn't you?" said Norton.

"Slightly. Didn't she go away in a mysterious way years and years ago?"

"She did. And I now know why she went."

"You don't mean to say—"

"I have not the slightest doubt of it. This is between ourselves, of course. Her people don't know. And it was not part of my duty to tell them."

Dr Norton's partner knocked out his pipe in the fender. "And she seemed such a nice quiet girl," he said meditatively. "One never knows."

Sylvia was thirty-two years old when she died. Her age in the newspaper announcement of her death, and also on her tombstone, was given as thirty. This was done at her express request. There were, so she said, two years of her life that had been missed out. She had never had them. Somebody had taken them from her.

The Case of Vincent Pyrwhit

The death of Vincent Pyrwhit, J. P., of Ellerdon House, Ellerdon, in the county of Buckingham, would in the ordinary way have received no more attention than the death of any other simple country gentleman. The circumstances of his death, however, though now long since forgotten, were sensational, and attracted some notice at the time. It was one of those cases which is easily forgotten within a year, except just in the locality where it occurred. The most sensational circumstances of the case never came before the public at all. I give them here simply and plainly. The psychical people may make what they like of them.

Pyrwhit himself was a very ordinary country gentleman, a good fellow, but in no way brilliant. He was devoted to his wife, who was some fifteen years younger than himself, and remarkably beautiful. She was quite a good woman, but she had her faults. She was fond of admiration, and she was an abominable flirt. She misled men very cleverly, and was then sincerely angry with them for having been misled. Her husband never troubled his head about these flirtations, being assured quite rightly that she was a good woman.

He was not jealous; she, on the other hand, was possessed of a jealousy amounting almost to insanity. This might have caused trouble if he had ever provided her with the slightest basis on which her jealousy could work, but he never did. With the exception of his wife, women bored him. I believe she did once or twice try to make a scene for some preposterous reason which was no reason at all; but nothing serious came of it, and there was never a real quarrel between them.

On the death of his wife, after a prolonged illness, Pyrwhit wrote and asked me to come down to Ellerdon for the funeral, and to remain at least a few days with him. He would be quite alone, and I was his oldest friend. I hate attending funerals, but I *was* his oldest friend, and I was, moreover, a distant relation of his wife. I had no choice and

I went down.

There were many visitors in the house for the funeral, which took place in the village churchyard, but they left immediately afterwards. The air of heavy gloom which had hung over the house seemed to lift a little. The servants (servants are always very emotional) continued to break down at intervals, noticeably Pyrwhit's man, Williams, but Pyrwhit himself was self-possessed. He spoke of his wife with great affection and regret, but still he could speak of her and not unsteadily.

At dinner he also spoke of one or two other subjects, of politics and of his duties as a magistrate, and of course he made the requisite fuss about his gratitude to me for coming down to Ellerdon at that time. After dinner we sat in the library, a room well and expensively furnished, but without the least attempt at taste. There were a few oil paintings on the walls, a presentation portrait of himself, and a land-scape or two—all more or less bad, as far as I remember. He had eaten next to nothing at dinner, but he had drunk a good deal; the wine, however, did not seem to have the least effect upon him. I had got the conversation definitely off the subject of his wife when I made a blunder. I noticed an Erichsen's extension standing on his writing-table. I said:

'I didn't know that telephones had penetrated into the villages yet.'

'Yes,' he said, 'I believe they are common enough now. I had that one fitted up during my wife's illness to communicate with her bed-room on the floor above us on the other side of the house.'

At that moment the bell of the telephone rang sharply.

We both looked at each other. I said with the stupid affectation of calmness one always puts on when one is a little bit frightened:

'Probably a servant in that room wishes to speak to you.'

He got up, walked over to the machine, and swung the green cord towards me. The end of it was loose.

'I had it disconnected this morning,' he said; 'also the door of that room is locked, and no one can possibly be in it.'

He had turned the colour of grey blotting-paper; so probably had I. The bell rang again—a prolonged, rattling ring.

'Are you going to answer it?' I said.

'I am not,' he answered firmly.

'Then,' I said, 'I shall answer it myself. It is some stupid trick, a joke not in the best of taste, for which you will probably have to sack one or other of your domestics.'

'My servants,' he answered, 'would not have done that. Besides, don't you see it is impossible? The instrument is disconnected.'

'The bell rang all the same. I shall try it.'

I picked up the receiver.

'Are you there?' I called.

The voice which answered me was unmistakably the rather high *staccato* voice of Mrs. Pyrwhit.

'I want you,' it said, 'to tell my husband that he will be with me tomorrow.'

I still listened. Nothing more was said.

I repeated, 'Are you there?' and still there was no answer.

I turned to Pyrwhit.

'There is no one there,' I said. 'Possibly there is thunder in the air affecting the bell in some mysterious way. There must be some simple explanation, and I'll find it all out tomorrow.'

✴✴✴✴✴✴✴✴✴✴✴✴

He went to bed early that night. All the following day I was with him. We rode together, and I expected an accident every minute, but none happened. All the evening I expected him to turn suddenly faint and ill, but that also did not happen. When at about ten o'clock he excused himself and said goodnight I felt distinctly relieved. He went up to his room and rang for Williams.

The rest is, of course, well known. The servant's reason had broken down, possibly the immediate cause being the death of Mrs. Pyrwhit. On entering his master's room, without the least hesitation, he raised a loaded revolver which he carried in his hand, and shot Pyrwhit through the heart. I believe the case is mentioned in some of the text-books on homicidal mania.

The Celestial Grocery

A Fantasia

It is precisely one year today since the incidents happened which I
am going to record. Since that time, I have been waiting for developments. But no developments have taken place. I find myself, in consequence, so completely at a loss what to do or what to think, that I
venture to state the case plainly, and to ask for advice.

Thomas Pigge, my old college friend, had sent me a stall-ticket for
the play. It was not often that I went to a theatre at all; and I had never
sat in the stalls before. Pigge said in his letter that he had been meaning to come with me, but had been prevented by a sprained ankle. I
found afterwards that this was quite untrue. Pigge, as a matter of fact,
had bought the ticket by a mistake. He had been told that *The Dark
Alley* was having a great success. About a week afterwards he saw the
advertisement of *Fair Alice*, and as his memory is notoriously weak, he
confused the two plays, and ordered a ticket for the wrong one.

Soon afterwards he discovered what he had done, and learning
that *Fair Alice* was a dismal failure, he offered his ticket first to his aunt
and then to his tailor, both of whom refused it. It was then—and only
then—that he sent it on to me. I do not think this was very nice of
Thomas Pigge. I half suspected something of the kind at the time, and
I was careful to make the few words of thanks that I sent him rather
cold. I do not suppose he noticed it.

When I had dressed for the evening, I rang the bell—partly to
tell my landlady that she need not sit up for me, but also with the
intention of letting her see that, although I lived in inexpensive lodgings, I was familiar with the mode of life of English gentlemen. She
surveyed me admiringly, and asked me if I would like a flower for my
button-hole. "No, thank you," I said, with a smile: "they are not worn."
I noticed with pleasure that these few authoritative words had their
proper effect. However, as I was walking down the Strand on my way

to the theatre I saw a man, in evening dress, who was wearing a rose in his coat, and thinking that it would be safe to follow his example, I spent sixpence on a gardenia with some maidenhair. The circumstance would be trivial were it not for its bearing on after-events.

I cannot say that I enjoyed the piece altogether. The house was by no means full. The few young men in the stalls seemed mostly to know one another, and none of them knew me. The two who came in after me had those hats that shut up; mine was an ordinary silk hat that I had worn for a year. This fact served to make me feel more lonely. My fine sensibilities render me peculiarly liable to this sort of thing; but they also do me good service by making me notice for imitation slight shades in the manners of the best people, which those of a coarser mind entirely miss. For instance, I had observed that the *habitués* of the stalls generally look a little careless—not reckless precisely—but with an air of taking everything for granted. I copied this expression throughout the evening.

A man's surroundings have a great effect upon his character; I felt myself perceptibly refined by my presence in the stalls. My position as an under-master in a private school seemed unworthy of me. "It is not," so I thought, "the profession for a gentleman. I shall change it." I must have known perfectly well that it was impossible to change it; but it pleased me to say so to myself. My old tendencies towards economy vanished. I felt that I must have a cab to take me home. It would cost two shillings probably, but that would be better than an incongruity. My aesthetic principles positively forbade me to walk home after having sat in the stalls.

So, I hired a four-wheeler, as I always mistrust hansoms. "After all," I said to myself as I put up the window, "what is money? We assign a value to it, but it is relative and transitory. We don't know what anything's really worth. What is money? What is money?" The words repeated themselves over and over again, in time with the rattling of the cab—"What is money?" Such a repetition is liable to send one off to sleep. I am not sure that I might not have fallen into a doze myself, if I had not suddenly been startled into wakefulness by the stopping of the cab. I felt certain that the man could not have driven to my lodgings in the time, but I jumped out.

To my amazement I found myself in an empty street. On one side of it ran a low stone wall, on the other there were houses; the darkness hid them to a great extent; but the house at which my cab had stopped was brightly lighted up, and appeared to be some kind of a shop. There

64

was nothing set out in the windows, but over the door were the words "Joseph, Grocer." The street itself was paved with blocks of crystal, and in the air there sounded the wildest music. I turned to my cabby, utterly at a loss as to where I was, or why I was there. He sat absolutely motionless; his hands still held the reins, but his eyes were shut. "Now then, cabby!" I cried, "where have you taken me to?"

He made no answer, and gave no sign of having heard me but the horse turned its head and looked at me. As it did so, the music ceased.

"You're starring," the horse remarked.

I remember perfectly well that one of the young men with the shut-up hats had made the same remark about some actress, and I had then wondered what he meant. "This is very confusing," I said. "It was the cabman that my remarks were addressed to."

"Look over that parapet," answered the horse.

I could not help thinking how extraordinary it was to hear a horse speak. All my life long I had been accustomed to regard a horse as a poor dumb animal. It might, of course, be all very well in fables to—

"Shut up!" shrieked the horse.

"I never said anything," I replied, indignantly.

"No, but you thought."

"Well, I can't help thinking."

"Can't you? If you think like that again, I'll kick this cab to splinters. I was shod yesterday. Why can't you look over the parapet, and do as you're told?"

I gave in. I had an indistinct idea that I was going mad, but I walked carefully across the polished street, and leaned over the low stone wall. Certainly, it was a marvellous and beautiful sight. Far down, as far as my eye could reach, there was darkness; and the darkness was strewn with myriad golden stars. I heard the horse's voice behind me: "The smallest of those is the world you've just left, and this is the world you've come to."

I knew perfectly well that this was impossible and quite unscientific, and as I leaned over the wall, I formed my conclusions. I had been terribly overworked lately, and probably part of my brain had given way—

"Never had any!" yelled the horse, and went into a roar of unmannerly laughter.

I took no notice whatever of this, but went on thinking. These delusions must have arisen from some such partial failure of brainpower. It was to be hoped that it was only temporary. Probably rest and medical advice would soon set me up again. I would step across to the grocer's, and inquire where the nearest doctor lived. As I crossed the street, I noticed that the horse was humming the National Anthem. I pushed open the door of the grocery and entered. There were counters and shelves, but nothing on them. After waiting a little while I ventured to tap on the floor with my foot. A voice from the other side of the counter said:—

"What may we have the pleasure of doing for you?"

I looked, but I could not see anyone, and I ventured to say so.

"No, you can't see me. It doesn't really matter, but I think I left it downstairs. James," the voice called to some invisible person at the farther end of the shop, "what did I do with my body? I had it only this morning."

The answer came in a boyish voice: "You left it in the cellar, Joseph, when you were packing up the nightmares."

"So, I did, so I did. You're right, James."

"But," I said, "I can't see James's body either."

"No, you see James has only got one. You're very inquisitive. If you must know, his body's gone to the wash. You wouldn't have him wear it dirty?"

"I generally wash my own," I said mildly.

"Well, we don't. This is a grocery, not a laundry."

"You must excuse me," I pleaded, "I'm quite a stranger in these parts." I saw it was no good to inquire for a doctor. If the grocery was part of the delusion, as it seemed to be, it would be absurd to make the inquiry there. If, on the other hand, the grocery really existed, then probably I did not require the doctor's services. But I felt very muddled about it. "I suppose you're Mr. Joseph?" I said.

"I am Joseph, and I should take it as a favour if you would tell me with what I can serve you."

"Well," I said, "judging from the state of your counter and shelves, I don't see anything you can serve me with."

"Of course, you don't see," he answered, a little snappishly. "You can't see the abstract. I'm not a grocer in the concrete. Kindly shut that door. There's a draught keeps coming down the back of the place where my neck would have been, and that's a thing I can't stand."

As I shut the door, I felt more bewildered than ever. An abstract grocer was beyond me, and I said so. "What, for instance, is abstract sugar?" I asked.

"Sugar's concrete," was the reply, "and if you abstract it, you get spanked. We've got no sugar here. If you'd like a Pure White, Crystallised, Disinterested Love, we keep that, although there's not much demand. They mostly use the coarser kinds. They say they're sweeter."

"Ah!" I cried, "you deal in abstract nouns then."

"That's more like it. It's a clumsy way of putting it, but it's fairly right. We supply, or, to speak more accurately, we groce, all the Emotions to the Solar System, and trade's very slack just now in that branch. We are doing rather better in States of Being, and we've just got a new assortment of Deaths. Now, once for all, do you intend to buy anything?"

I remembered with joy that I had a couple of sovereigns and some loose silver in my pocket. All my life long I had suffered from want of emotional experiences. I had always regretted the want of variety, the general flatness and dullness. If the delusion or reality—I neither knew nor cared now which it was—would only last, I was determined, to gratify to the full my fine perceptions. Especially was I struck with the mention of the Pure White Love.

I may confess at once that I never got on much with women. I have a natural dignity and reserve that is sometimes mistaken for nervousness. I fancy it sets women against me. Somehow, I am never able to say to them quite what I want to say. I have often looked at a young girl, and thought that if she could only know me as I really was—if she could once regard me as apart from wretched circumstances, my poverty, my shabby clothes, my unfortunate reserve—she might abate something of her pretty scorn.

"Certainly, I intend to buy something," I said. "To commence with, I should like to see some samples of that peculiar Love you mentioned."

"Dear me!" broke in Mr. Joseph. "How many more times am I to tell you? You can't *see* samples. You can feel them if you like. James!"

"Yes, Joseph," answered the boyish voice from the further end of the shop.

"Let's have some of the 'Pure White,'—look sharp."

"Right."

"Now then," continued Mr. Joseph. "Take that chair. Adopt an easy, natural position. Don't cross the legs. If you find the light too strong, you can blink the eyes once or twice, it won't make any difference. Head a little more this way. You're frowning. That's better. Now then, we're ready. Steady, please."

The light certainly was too strong. A sudden flash blinded me, and when I recovered my sight, I was apparently no longer in the Grocery. I was in a dimly-lighted conservatory and the middle of a sentence. I have never been able to find out what could have been the beginning of it.

". . . which it is not, and never was," I was saying. "I am content only to have told you, and now I relinquish you. Let this be my fare-well, my goodbye to you before I sail from England. In books that we read, a man would have asked you for one clasp of the hands, or even one kiss, but I neither ask nor wish for that."

I looked up, and saw the girl to whom I was speaking. I had certainly never seen her before, but yet the figure was familiar. She sat in her white dress, shaded from the light by some tropical plant. It was with passionate and hopeless adoration that I looked at her, and yet I was full of a strange content; it seemed to be enough to have loved her. I saw that her head was slightly turned away from me, and that she was sobbing.

"I am sorry," I went on, "that I have made you cry. I want you to be happy, and I know there is only one way."

"I never knew it was going to be like this," she said tremulously.

For the matter of that, neither had I when I first ordered the first sample pure white. But it struck me as being all quite natural. Some of that peace which must come to men of a great soul, had come to me.

"Goodbye," I said. "I am not going to do anything desperate, any-thing that could cause you regret. It is enough for me to have loved you, and to feel that in comparison the rest of my life is one . . ."

Just as I had begun in the middle of a sentence so I ended in the middle of a sentence. The dim-lit conservatory and the maiden van-ished, and I found myself once more in the Celestial Grocery.

"Do you like it?" asked Mr. Joseph's voice.

"Yes," I said, hesitatingly, "it is grand, it is sublime. But I don't think I could stand very much of it. How much is it a pound?"

"We don't sell it by the pound; we sell it by the spasm."

"Then," I said, "I'll take six spasms."

"James, six of the pure white."

"Right," said the voice of James.

For a moment I tried to recall the beautiful girl in white whom I had just seen. I wondered how my first sentence began and how my last sentence would have ended. I seemed to have walked for a while upon those heights of love that reach beyond the fires of passion, and on which lie the snows of perpetual purity. I felt that my self-respect had considerably increased in consequence. Here I was interrupted by Mr. Joseph.

"What will be the next order?"

"I have often longed," I replied, "for a little real happiness."

"Yes," said Mr. Joseph. "But that is a blend. You buy the ingredients and you blend them yourself. Unfortunately, we do not provide Incomes. We have a Literary Fame which gives great satisfaction. 'Political Success' is in considerable demand. Then there's 'Religious Exaltation'—not much asked for lately, I'm afraid. 'Requited Love' is not expensive, but we've had complaints that it doesn't wear well. Of course, there's Death by Drowning, Death by—"

"Stop, Mr. Joseph," I cried, "I have no desire to die." I had already decided what should be my next experiment; for even under-masters have their ambitions. "I think," I said, "that I should rather like to try the 'Political Success.'"

Mr. Joseph took my order with alacrity, and the same process as before was repeated. Once more I seemed to have left the grocery. I was standing on a balcony, my hat in my hand, and below me in the street there was a surging mass of people. As far as my sight could reach, I could see eager, excited faces upturned. I was just concluding a speech, and, as before, was in the middle of a sentence.

"... not derogatory to the national sense—(cheers)—of what is the fittest, the truest, and the best way—(renewed applause)—of proving to those who at one time may have thought otherwise, that, in spite of all preconceived opinions, which, if they are not praiseworthy—and I do not say they are so—yet may with some show of justice—(hear, hear)—be asserted to have had their origin in a sentiment felt by humanity at large, and more especially by the English-speaking races, and to which we tonight, with the generosity of the conquerors towards the conquered—(loud cheers)—can well afford to extend our fullest indulgence. It is not only in the family but in a man's public capacity; not only by the fireside, but also beneath that fiercer light that beats upon the high offices of this nation—(loud and prolonged cheering)—not only with the ..."

I would have given anything to have gone on a little further. I do not even know what my politics were, although I am inclined to form an opinion from internal evidences in my speech. But I never in all my life felt such a delightful sense of exhilaration, triumph, and power. When I came to, I found myself seated on the floor of the grocery, perspiring profusely.

"Oh, that was good," I exclaimed, "very good!" I picked myself up, and inquired eagerly what the price was, and how it was sold.

"It is expensive," said Mr. Joseph, solemnly, "very expensive; and we sell it in bursts."

I did not like to ask for further details. I expected that Mr. Joseph would give me a reasonable amount of credit, and with the literary fame that I intended to buy I thought that I should soon be able to pay for everything. But I thought it wise to order only two bursts of the "Political Success."

"Mr. Joseph," I said, "I hardly know what to order next. I should like to have a price-list, and a week to think it over. I never bought anything abstract before. At present I've got only some 'Disinterested Love' and some 'Political Success'; do you think you could let me have some Literary Fame, Musical Ability, Personal Charm, Popularity, and Contentment?"

"It's a large order," said Mr. Joseph, "but we will do our best to execute it. James, will you see about those articles?"

"I will," said James.

"And when shall I have them?"

There was no answer.

"I should like to know when I can have them," I continued. "I don't want to hurry you. Any time in the course of a year would do. I can give you a reference if you like. The master of St. Cecilia's knows all about me. But as I did not imagine I was coming here tonight, I have brought hardly any money with me. However, if you would not object to taking two pounds on account—"

I pulled out my two sovereigns, and laid them on the counter. As I did so I looked up. I had ceased to be capable of surprise, or I think I should have been surprised. Before me, on the other side of the counter, stood a young girl. Perhaps I should more accurately describe her as a young angel, except that she had no wings or halo. She was dressed in some loose, white garment, which looked like the apotheosis of a nightgown. I could not say within a year or two how old she was, but she seemed to be on the verge of womanhood. Her figure was tall and slight. Her small white hands were clasped before her.

Her face was, perhaps, a little wan and pale, but full of the most spiritual beauty. The expression upon it was one of sweet, calm seriousness. Her eyes seemed to be looking sadly at something far off. Her hair was long and dark, and fell loosely about her shoulders. I gazed at her a long time before I could speak.

"Mr. Joseph?" I stammered out, questioningly.

"Joseph and James," she said, in a low musical voice, "have gone downstairs to feed Joseph's body. They sent me up here to wait on you. What are these?"

She took up the two sovereigns I had placed on the counter.

"A mere trifle," I said. "I thought that, perhaps, it would be better to pay a trifle on account. If I had known that I was coming here, I would have brought more—I would, indeed."

"Will you please put them away?" she said, slowly. "They have no value. I will tell you about it soon. I have known you for a long time—known you so well."

I was entranced by her beauty, and could hardly find words to speak, but I muttered the usual commonplaces. It was very stupid of me, but I did not seem to recall her face. I did not even remember her name.

"No," she replied, "you have never seen me before. You will know my name one day, but not yet. I have watched you for years, and sometimes I have been with you. I am glad that you came here tonight, for I have often wished to speak with you."

It is possible that I may have looked a little incredulous, for she fixed her eyes full upon mine, leaning across the counter, and whispered something to me. I do not see that I am called upon to write down what she said. It was quite personal and private. If I did record it, it would probably be misunderstood. But it answered its purpose. It made me feel that she knew me indeed, that here I had no impression to make and none to mar. There was no longer any barrier of reserve between us.

"And at last, you have come to me," she said. "No one can overhear us; we are quite alone."

My cheeks were flushed and my voice trembled. "You do not talk," I said, "as the women I met on earth, nor as Joseph and James did. No earthly woman that I know would have whispered to me the things that you did."

"You are not angry with me for it?" she said.

I loved her for it, but I could not tell her so. For a moment or two I gazed at her in a kind of rapture. "You are very beautiful," I said at last.

"Yes; but that is not of any real consequence here. Here the body is always beautiful, because the spirit never spoils it. Would that I could alter your nature and make it like ours! But they told me that you would look at me as on your earth a man looks at a woman. I do not understand that. I do not know your way—ah, do not look at me so."

"I cannot help it; you draw my eyes towards you."

"Do not say that!" she cried, in a distressed voice. "Do not think of it. I can think, and speak, and love when I am not in the body. I almost wish that I had not come to you like this. If I had been only a voice, I should still have desired you."

Like most people of a shy disposition, I have an occasional access of boldness. "Do you mean that you do not understand the kind of attraction that a woman has for a man? Do you not know what flushed cheeks, and longing looks, and trembling voice mean? And yet I could believe that the earthly love would be possible to you."

"The lower is always possible for the higher," she said. "But that is not what I want. I long tonight to teach you the other love. But now that I am face to face with you, I have no words. There are none in any language that will tell you. I want names for things of which you know nothing—things which with men and women of your world do not exist. I should feel no shame in speaking to you of it, for there is no shame in our love. Your love is full of shame. That was why at first, I whispered to you. That was why I told you that no one could hear us. It was for your sake, not mine." She stopped and sighed.

"Why do you sigh?" I asked.

"Because I cannot say what I want."

"Try," I said.

"No, it is no use now. What have you been buying?"

I gave her a list of my purchases, and she went over them, as it seemed to me, a little sadly. "You have not bought the best things," she said. "But they will cost you all that you have here, one gardenia and a sprig of maidenhair."

"Is that flower really worth more than the two sovereigns that I offered you?"

"Yes, we have none here, and flowers are the only purity on your earth."

"But this will die in an hour."

"No," she said, "it would have died there, but here it will never die." As I laid it on the counter, I noticed that even the maidenhair was quite fresh.

"If I had only known," I said, "I would have loaded my cab with flowers. Can I not come back again?"

"No—never."

"Then let me change the things that I have bought. They seemed

72

high and noble, especially the White Love."

"Yes, you shall change them. You did not value the Love because it was noble, but because it made you feel noble."

"And what shall I buy for myself?"

"Nothing. If you had kept the goods that you ordered, you would have made a little flutter on an indescribably small portion of a rather insignificant world. You would have been called the great poet, the eminent statesman, and it would not have helped you any further it would not have raised you any higher. Your nature would still have been bounded on the earth by earthly possibilities. No, you shall buy nothing for yourself. There is only one step that you can take that will bring you nearer me. There is only one thing that you can do that has a real value."

"You mean self-denial," I said. "I will obey you. I surrender all that I had bought. You shall give me instead the best thing for someone else—for whom?"

"For your own father."

I bent my head in shame. It was a subject of which I could hardly bear to speak; but she with great tenderness, laying one of her little hands softly and caressingly on mine, dropped her voice almost to a whisper.

"Yes, for your father. My poor boy, there are no secrets between you and me. There is to be no shame between you and me. I know all. In the same asylum where your grandfather died your father now lies. His reason is gone. A horrible darkness has come over his mind. He lies there moaning and—"

"Stop!" I cried. "For pity's sake say no more. You are right. Give me the best thing for him."

"It shall be so," she said. "And now the end of your time here grows near. But you have taken the first step. You and I have advanced a little further towards the sacred unity of the new love. Come, let us go and look down at the stars, and I will tell you about them."

She came round to my side of the counter, and we passed through the door together. Her bare feet trod lightly on the crystal blocks with which the street was paved. I gazed at her in an ecstasy of adoration. The cab was still standing there, and the horse looked round at us. He grinned horribly, showing his yellow fangs.

"Oh my! ain't it sweet!" he called out.

"You vulgar beast!" I said to him angrily, "if you say another word, I'll take that whip and simply flay you."

73

"You needn't distress yourself," he answered, "because you'll be asleep in two minutes."

I saw that she had taken no notice of the unmannerly animal. She had crossed the street, and was leaning over the low stone wall, with her beautiful head supported on one hand; I saw that my most dignified course was to follow her, and I did so.

"Yes," she said, pointing downwards with her finger, "those are the other worlds. They were put there to be a heating and lighting apparatus for the most insignificant of them—at least that is the prevalent creed, for the most insignificant. Do not believe it. On each one there is life, and for each one there is a purpose; all are part of one scheme that—"

The horse was quite right. At this point, I rested my head on my arms as I leaned over the parapet, and went fast asleep. I can never forgive myself for it, but I was powerless to prevent it. I do not know how long I slept, but I woke suddenly. She was no longer leaning over the parapet; she stood on the pathway, gazing upwards, with a strange light in her eyes. Of course, she was in the middle of a sentence. That was only part of the generally unsatisfactory nature of everything.

"——would get new experiences, new data. You would think and imagine new things. You would know what the new love means. I can only speak to you as a woman to a man, but I do not look at you as a woman would. She would see only a poor little schoolmaster, not very beautiful, rather sleepy-headed, in a dress-suit much too tight for him. I too can see that. But I see also a life that long ago came out into the darkness hand-in-hand with mine. Had you been placed in this world, you would have known as I know; but I came here, and you were sent elsewhere. Out of the same clay the potter makes two vessels, one to honour and one to dishonour."

"And that is extremely unjust," I said.

"It would be quite impossible for you to think otherwise; but you are wrong. You will soon know that you are wrong."

"When?" I asked.

"On the day that you know my name, when the earthly love that you feel for me is changed to the new love of which it is the shadow, when we come back together, you and I, out of the darkness into the light."

"Where is the light?"

"Look upwards. There are no more stars, and above all seems dark. And the darkness flows on like a river, on and on. But the river will run dry at the last, the darkness will have passed at the last, and then we shall enter into the light."

"And now," said the voice of the unconscionable cab-horse behind us, "I will ask you to join with me in singing the last hymn on the paper."

"What on earth," I exclaimed testily, "is the point of making that perfectly idiotic remark?"

"Mere absent-mindedness," the brute answered. "I thought from the general style of the conversation that I was at some missionary meeting. That's all."

"At any rate," I said, "you need not interrupt a—a lady."

"Lady! S'help me! That high-toned, female grocer's assistant, a lady!" The beast positively shrieked with laughter. "Get into the cab, you little fool, and let's get home. There's no place like home."

I sprang at the cab, seized the whip, and determined to take my revenge. But I never got it. The agile beast waltzed round and round with amazing rapidity in the middle of the street. I struck out wildly; but though I occasionally hit the cab, I never succeeded in hitting the horse. All this time the cabman remained motionless. Suddenly the brute stopped, and backed the cab right into me. I fell down on the pavement by the low wall. I picked myself up and gazed around.

She was no longer there.

I staggered across the road. The lights were out in the grocery. I tried the door, but it was locked. I shook it, and called loudly, but no answer came. Once more I turned savagely on the horse, but at the first stroke the whip broke in my hands.

"Now then," he yelled, "you little fool, get into the cab, and let's enter into the Light!"

For a moment I stood there helpless. I felt weak and sick with my fall. Then I flung down the broken whip, and got into the cab, which started instantly at full speed. I buried my face, in my hands, and burst into tears.

When, after a moment, I looked up again, there was the roar of the London streets about me, and we were within a hundred yards of my lodgings. The cab stopped at them, and I got out. It was evident that the cabman knew nothing about what had happened; he looked cheery, comfortable, and commonplace. I saw that there would be no use in speaking to him about it. I merely paid him three times his proper fare, to compensate him for the loss of his whip, which, by the way, he did not seem to have noticed.

I was very tired, and soon went off to sleep. I had lost fame, and I had gained for my father a return to sanity. It was worth the sacrifice. He should come to London, and live with me. It was years since I had been able to speak to him. Then slumber interrupted my thoughts.

As soon as I woke in the morning I sprang from my bed, and took up my dress-coat. No, it was no dream. The gardenia and maidenhair were gone, and my father had regained his reason. Would that I could see her once more, and thank her.

There came a tap at my door.

"All right, Mrs. Smith," I cried. "I'm getting up."

"There's a telegram for you, sir."

It was pushed under the door. I opened it. It was from the doctor at the asylum where my father was placed, and it read as follows:—

"Your father died suddenly early this morning. Please come at once."

There have been no further developments, and I do not know what to do. I feel that I must see her, and ask her.

I cannot understand. And, alas! I cannot get to her.

✸✸✸✸✸✸✸✸✸✸✸✸

Since writing the above, I have had a letter from my Principal. He wants my resignation. He says something about "strangeness of man-ner—medical advice—real kindness to me—hope for recovery." Mrs. Smith has asked me, with tears in her eyes, to leave my apartments. She says that I have been most regular in my payments, and in every way showed myself to be a perfect gentleman; but the other lodgers are frightened of me, and I frighten her sometimes. She can feel for me, because she had a cousin who once went off like that; but would I mind going?

Well, I have resigned my post, and tonight I leave my lodgings. I am very lonely.

The Diary of a God

During the week there had been several thunderstorms. It was after the last of these, on a cool Saturday evening, that he was found at the top of the hill by a shepherd. His speech was incoherent and disconnected; he gave his name correctly, but could or would add no account of himself. He was wet through, and sat there pulling a sprig of heather to pieces. The shepherd afterwards said that he had great difficulty in persuading him to come down, and that he talked much nonsense. In the path at the foot of the hill he was recognised by some people from the farmhouse where he was lodging, and was taken back there. They had, indeed, gone out to look for him. He was subsequently removed to an asylum, and died insane a few months later.

★★★★★★★★★★★★

Two years afterwards, when the furniture of the farmhouse came to be sold by auction, there was found in a little cupboard in the bedroom which he had occupied an ordinary penny exercise-book. This was partly filled, in a beautiful and very regular handwriting, with what seems to have been something in the nature of a diary, and the following are extracts from it:

June 1st.—It is absolutely essential to be quiet. I am beginning life again, and in quite a different way, and on quite a different scale, and I cannot make the break suddenly. I must have a pause of a few weeks in between the two different lives. I saw the advertisement of the lodgings in this farmhouse in an evening paper that somebody had left at the restaurant. That was when I was trying to make the change abruptly, and I may as well make a note of what happened.

After attending the funeral (which seemed to me an act of hypocrisy, as I hardly knew the man, but it was expected of me), I came back to my Charlotte Street rooms and had tea. I slept well that night. Then next morning I went to the office at the usual hour, in my best clothes, and with a deep band still on my hat. I went to Mr. Toller's room and knocked. He said, 'Come in,' and after I had entered: 'Can I do anything for you? What do you want?'

Then I explained to him that I wished to leave at once. He said:

'This seems sudden, after thirty years' service.'

'Yes,' I replied. 'I have served you faithfully for thirty years, but things have changed, and I have now three hundred a year of my own. I will pay something in lieu of notice, if you like, but I cannot go on being a clerk any more. I hope, Mr. Toller, you will not think that I speak with any impertinence to yourself, or any immodesty, but I am really in the position of a private gentleman.'

He looked at me curiously, and as he did not say anything I repeated:

'I think I am in the position of a private gentleman.'

In the end he let me go, and said very politely he was sorry to lose me. I said goodbye to the other clerks, even to those who had sometimes laughed at what they imagined to be my peculiarities. I gave the better of the two office-boys a small present in money.

I went back to the Charlotte Street rooms, but there was nothing to do there. There were figures going on in my head, and my fingers seemed to be running up and down columns. I had a stupid idea that I should be in trouble if Mr. Toller were to come in and catch me like that. I went out and had a capital lunch, and then I went to the theatre. I took a stall right in the front row, and sat there all by myself. Then I had a cab to the restaurant. It was too soon for dinner, so I ordered a whisky-and-soda, and smoked a few cigarettes. The man at the table next me left the evening paper in which I saw the advertisement of these farmhouse lodgings. I read the whole of the paper, but I have forgotten it all except that advertisement, and I could say it by heart now—all about bracing air and perfect quiet and the rest of it. For dinner I had a bottle of champagne. The waiter handed me a list, and asked which I would prefer. I waved the list away and said:

'Give me the best.'

He smiled. He kept on smiling all through dinner until the end; then he looked serious. He kept getting more serious. Then he brought two other men to look at me. They spoke to me, but I did not want to talk. I think I fell asleep. I found myself in my rooms in Charlotte Street next morning, and my landlady gave me notice because, she said, I had come home beastly drunk. Then that advertisement flashed into my mind about the bracing air. I said:

'I should have given you notice in any case; this is not a suitable place for a gentleman.'

June 3rd.—I am rather sorry that I wrote down the above. It seems so degrading. However, it was merely an act of ignorance and carelessness on my part, and, besides, I am writing solely for myself. To myself I may own freely that I made a mistake, that I was not used to the wine, and that I had not fully gauged what the effects would be. The incident is disgusting, but I simply put it behind me, and think no more about it. I pay here two pounds ten shillings a week for my two rooms and board. I take my meals, of course, by myself in the sitting-room. It would be rather cheaper if I took them with the family, but I do not care about that. After all, what is two pounds ten shillings a week? Roughly speaking, a hundred and thirty pounds a year.

June 17th.—I have made no entry in my diary for some days. For a certain period, I have had no heart for that or for anything else. I had told the people here that I was a private gentleman (which is strictly true), and that I was engaged in literary pursuits. By the latter I meant to imply no more than that I am fond of reading, and that it is my intention to jot down from time to time my sensations and experiences in the new life which has burst upon me.

At the same time, I have been greatly depressed. Why, I can hardly explain. I have been furious with myself. Sitting in my own sitting-room, with a gold-tipped cigarette between my fingers, I have been possessed (even though I recognised it as an absurdity) by a feeling that if Mr. Toller were to come in suddenly I should get up and apologise. But the thing which depressed me most was the open country. I have read, of course, those penny stories about the poor little ragged boys who never see the green leaf in their lives, and I always thought them exaggerated.

So, they are exaggerated: there are the Embankment Gardens with the Press Band playing; there are parks; there are Sunday-School treats. All these little ragged boys see the green leaf, and to say they do not is an exaggeration—I am afraid a wilful exaggeration. But to see the open country is quite a different thing. Yesterday was a fine day, and I was out all day in a place called Wensley Dale. On one spot where I stood, I could see for miles all round. There was not a single house, or tree, or human being in sight. There was just myself on the top of a moor; the bigness of it gave me a regular scare. I suppose I had got used to walls: I had got used to feeling that if I went straight ahead without stopping, I should knock against something. That somehow made me feel safe.

Out on that great moor—just as if I were the last man left alive in the world—I do not feel safe. I find the track and get home again, and I tremble like a half-drowned kitten until I see a wall again, or somebody with a surly face who does not answer civilly when I speak to him. All these feelings will wear off, no doubt, and I shall be able to enter upon the new phase of my existence without any discomfort. But I was quite right to take a few months' quiet retirement. One must get used to things gradually. It was the same with the champagne—to which, by the way, I had not meant to allude any further.

June 20th.—It is remarkable what a fascination these very large moors have for me. It is not exactly fear any more—indeed, it must be the reverse. I do not care to be anywhere else. Instead of making this a mere pause between two different existences, I shall continue it. To that I have quite made up my mind. When I am out there in a place where I cannot see any trees, or houses, or living things, I am the last person left alive in the world. I am a kind of a god. There is nobody to think anything at all about me, and it does not matter if my clothes are not right, or if I drop an 'h'—which I rarely do except when speaking very quickly. I never knew what real independence was before. There have been too many houses around, and too many people looking on. It seems to me now such a common and despicable thing to live among people, and to have one's character and one's ways altered by what they are going to think.

I know now that when I ordered that bottle of champagne I did it far more to please the waiter and to make him think well of me than to please myself. I pity the kind of creature that I was then, but I had not known the open country at that time. It is a grand education. If Toller were to come in now, I should say, 'Go away. Go back to your bricks and mortar, and account-books, and swell friends, and white waistcoats, and rubbish of that kind. You cannot possibly understand me, and your presence irritates me. If you do not go at once I will have the dog let loose upon you.' By the way, that was a curious thing which happened the other day. I feed the dog, a mastiff, regularly, and it goes out with me.

We had walked some way, and had reached that spot where a man becomes the last man alive in the world. Suddenly the dog began to howl, and ran off home with its tail between its legs, as if it were frightened of something. What was it that the dog had seen and I had not seen? A ghost? In broad daylight? Well, if the dead come back, they might walk here without contamination. A few sheep, a sweep of heather, a grey sky, but nothing that a living man planted or built. They could be alone here. If it were not that it would seem a kind of blasphemy, I would buy a piece of land in the very middle of the loneliest moor and build myself a cottage there.

June 23rd.—I received a letter today from Julia. Of course, she does not understand the change which has taken place in me. She writes as she always used to write, and I find it very hard to remember and realize that I liked it once, and was glad when I got a letter from her. That was before I got into the habit of going into empty places alone. The old clerking, account-book life has become too small to care about. The swell life of the private gentleman, to which I looked forward, is also not worth considering. As for Julia, I was to have married her; I used to kiss her. She wrote to say that she thought a great deal of me; she still writes. I don't want her. I don't want anything. I have become the last man alive in the world. I shall leave this farmhouse very soon. The people are all right, but they are people, and therefore insufferable. I can no longer live or breathe in a place where I see people, or trees which people have planted, or houses which people have built. It is an ugly word—people.

July 7th.—I was wrong in saying that I was the last man alive in the world. I believe I am dead. I know now why the mastiff howled and ran away. The whole moor is full of them; one sees them after a time when one has got used to the open country—or perhaps it is because one is dead. Now I see them by moonlight and sunlight, and I am not frightened at all. I think I must be dead, because there seems to be a line ruled straight through my life, and the things which happened on the further side of the line are not real.

I look over this diary, and see some references to a Mr. Toller, and to some champagne, and coming into money. I cannot for the life of me think what it is all about. I suppose the incidents described really happened, unless I was mad when I wrote about them. I suppose that I am not dead, since I can write in a book, and eat food, and walk, and sleep and wake again. But since I see them now—these people that fill up the lonely places—I must be quite different to ordinary human beings. If I am not dead, then what am I? Today I came across an old letter signed 'Julia Jarvis'; the envelope was addressed to me. I wonder who on earth she was?

July 9th.—A man in a frock-coat came to see me, and talked about my best interest. He wanted me, so far as I could gather, to come away with him somewhere. He said I was all right, or, at any rate, would become all right, with a little care. He would not go away until I said that I would kill him. Then the woman at the farmhouse came up with a white face, and I said I would kill her too. I positively cannot endure people. I am something apart, something different. I am not alive, and I am not dead. I cannot imagine what I am.

July 16th.—I have settled the whole thing to my complete satisfaction. I can without doubt believe the evidence of my own senses. I have seen, and I have heard. I know now that I am a god. I had almost thought before that this might be. What was the matter was that I was too diffident: I had no self-confidence; I had never heard before of any man, even a clerk in an old-established firm, who had become a god. I therefore supposed it was impossible until it was distinctly proved to be.

I had often made up my mind to go to that range of hills that lies to the north. They are purple when one sees them far off. At nearer view they are grey, then they become green, then one sees a silver network over the green. The silver network is made by streams descending in the sunlight. I climbed the hill slowly; the air was still, and the heat was terrible. Even the water which I drank from the running stream seemed flat and warm. As I climbed, the storm broke. I took but little notice of it, for the dead that I had met below on the moor had told me that lightning could not touch me. At the top of the hill I turned, and saw the storm raging beneath my feet. It is the greatest of mercies that I went there, for that is where the other gods gather, at such times as the lightning plays between them and the earth, and the black thunderclouds, hanging low, shut them out from the sight of men.

Some of the gods were rather like the big pictures that I have seen on the hoardings, advertising plays at the theatre, or some food which is supposed to give great strength and muscular development. They were handsome in face, and without any expression. They never seemed to be angry or pleased, or hurt. They sat there in great long rows, resting, with the storm raging in between them and the earth. One of them was a woman. I spoke to her, and she told me that she was older than this earth; yet she had the face of a young girl, and her eyes were like eyes that I have seen before somewhere. I cannot think where I saw the eyes like those of the goddess, but perhaps it was in that part of my life which is forgotten and ruled off with a line. It gave one the greatest and most majestic feelings to stand there with the gods, and to know that one was a god one's self, and that lightning did not hurt one, and that one would live for ever.

July 18th.—This afternoon the storm returned, and I hurried to the meeting-place, but it is far away to the hills, and though I climbed as quickly as I could the storm was almost passed, and they had gone.

August 1st.—I was told in my sleep that tomorrow I was to go back to the hill again, and that once more the gods would be there, and that the storm would gather round us, and would shut us from profane sight, and the steely lightnings would blind any eye that tried to look upon us. For this reason, I have refused now to eat or drink anything; I am a god and have no need of such things. It is strange that now when I see all real things so clearly and easily—the ghosts of the dead that walk across the moors in the sunlight and the concourse of the gods on the hill-top above the storm—men and women with whom I once moved before I became a god are no more to me than so many black shadows.

I scarcely know one from the other, only that the presence of a black shadow anywhere near me makes me angry, and I desire to kill it. That will pass away; it is probably some faint relic of the thing that I once was in the other side of my life on the other side of the line which has been ruled across it. Seeing that I am a god it is not natural that I can feel anger or joy any more. Already all feeling of joy has gone from me, for tomorrow, so I was told in my sleep, I am to be betrothed to the beautiful goddess that is older than the world, and yet looks like a young girl, and she is to give me a sprig of heather as a token and—

★★★★★★★★★★★★

It was on the evening of August 1 he was found.

The Glass of Supreme Moments

Lucas Morne sat in his college rooms, when the winter afternoon met the evening, depressed and dull. There were various reasons for his depression. He was beginning to be a little nervous about his health. A week before he had run second in a mile race, the finish of which had been a terrible struggle; ever since then any violent exertion or excitement had brought on symptoms which were painful, and to one who had always been strong, astonishing. He had felt them early that afternoon, on coming from the river. Besides, he was discontented with himself. He had had several men in his rooms that afternoon, who were better than he was, men who had enthusiasms and had found them satisfying. Lucas had a moderate devotion to athletics, but no great enthusiasm. Neither had he the finer perceptions. Neither was he a scholar. He was just an ordinary man, and reputed to be a good fellow.

His visitors had drunk his tea, talked of their own enthusiasms, and were now gone. Nothing is so unclean as a used tea-cup; nothing is so cold as toast which has once been hot, and the concrete expression of dejection is crumbs. Even Lucas Morne, who had not the finer perceptions, was dimly conscious that his room had become horrible, and now flung open the window. One of the men—a large, clumsy man—had been smoking mitigated *Latakia*; and *Latakia* has a way of rolling itself all round the atmosphere and kicking. Lucas seated himself in his easiest chair.

His rooms were near the chapel, and he could hear the organ. The music and the soft fall of the darkness were soothing; he could hardly see the used teacups now; the light from the gas-lamp outside came just a little way into the room, shyly and obliquely.

★★★★★★★★★★★★

Well, he had not noticed it before, but the fireplace had become a staircase. He felt too lazy to wonder much at this. He would, he thought, have the things all altered back again on the morrow. It would be worthwhile to sell the staircase, seeing that its steps were fashioned of silver and crystal. Unfortunately, he could not see how much there was of it, or whither it led. The first five steps were clear enough; he felt convinced that the workmanship of them was Japanese. But the rest of the staircase was hidden from his sight by a grey veil of mist. He found himself a little angry, in a severe and strictly logical way, that in these days of boasted science we could not prevent a piece of fog, measuring ten feet by seven, from coming in at an open window and sitting down on a staircase which had only just begun to exist, and blotting out all but five steps of it in its very earliest moments.

He allowed that it was a beautiful mist; its colour changed slowly from grey to rose, and then back again from rose to grey; fire-flies of silver and gold shot through it at intervals; but it was a nuisance, because he wanted to see the rest of the staircase, and it prevented him. Every moment the desire to see more grew stronger. At last, he determined to shake off his laziness, and go up the staircase and through the mist into the something beyond. He felt sure that the something beyond would be beautiful—sure with the certainty which has nothing to do with logical conviction.

It seemed to him that it was with an effort that he brought himself to rise from the chair and walk to the foot of that lovely staircase. He hesitated there for a moment or two, and as he did so he heard the sound of footsteps, high up, far away, yet coming nearer and nearer, with light music in the sound of them. Someone was coming down the staircase. He listened eagerly and excitedly. Then through the grey mist came a figure robed in grey.

It was the figure of a woman—young, with wonderful grace in her movements. Her face was veiled, and all that could be seen of her as she paused on the fifth step was the soft, dark hair that reached to her waist, and her arms—white wonders of beauty. The rest was hidden by the grey veil, and the long grey robe, that left, however, their suggestion of classical grace and slenderness. Lucas Morne stood looking at her tremulously. He felt sure, too, that she was looking at him, and that she could see through the folds of the thin grey veil that hid her face. She was the first to speak. Her voice in its gentleness and delicacy was like the voice of a child; it was only afterward that he heard in it the under-thrill which told of more than childhood.

"Why have you not come? I have been waiting for you, you know, up there. And this is the only time," she added.

"I am very sorry," he stammered. "You see—I never knew the staircase was there until today. In fact—it seems very stupid of me—but I always thought it was a fireplace. I must have been dreaming, of course. And then this afternoon I thought, or dreamed, that a lot of men came in to see me. Perhaps they really did come; and we got talking, you know—"

"Yes," she said, with the gentlest possible interruption. "I *do* know. There was one man, Fynsale, large, ugly, clumsy, a year your senior. He sat in that chair over there, and sulked, and smoked *Latakia*. I rather like the smell of *Latakia*. He especially loves to write or to say some good thing; and at times he can do it. Therefore, you envy him. Then there was Blake. Blake is an athlete, like yourself, but is just a little more successful. Yes, I know you are good, but Blake is very good. You were tried for the 'Varsity—Blake was selected.

"He and Fynsale both have delight in ability, and you envy both. There was that dissenting little Paul Reece. He is not exactly in your set, but you were at school with him, and so you tolerate him. How good he is, for all his insignificance and social defects! Blake knows that, and kept a guard on his talk this afternoon. He would not offend Paul Reece for worlds. Paul's belief gives him earnestness, his earnestness leads him to self-sacrifice, and self-sacrifice is deep delight to him.

"You have more ability than Paul Reece, but you cannot reach that kind of enthusiastic happiness, and therefore you envy him. I could say similar things of the other men. It was because they made you vaguely dissatisfied with yourself that they bored you. You take pleasure—a certain pleasure—in athletics, and that pleasure would become an enthusiastic delight if you were a little better at them. Some men could get the enthusiastic delight out of as much as you can do, but your temperament is different. I know you well. You are not easily satisfied. You are not clever, but you are—" She paused, but without any sign of embarrassment.

"What am I?" he asked eagerly. He felt sure that it would be something good, and he was not less vain than other men.

"I do not think I will say—not now."

"But who are you?" His diffidence and stammering had vanished beneath her calm, quiet talk. "You must let me at least ask that. Who are you? And how do you know all this?"

"I am a woman, but not an earth-woman. And the chief difference between us is that I know nearly all the things you do not know, and you do not know nearly all the things that I know. Sometimes I forget your ignorance—do not be angry for a word; there is no other for it, and it is not your fault. I forgot it just now when I asked you why you had not come to me up the staircase of silver and crystal, through the grey veil where the fire-flies live, and into that quiet room beyond. This is the only time; tomorrow it will not be possible. And I have—" Once more she paused.

There was a charm for Lucas Morne in the things which she did not say. "Your room is dark," she continued, "and I can hardly see you."

"I will light the lamp," said Lucas hurriedly, "and—and won't you let me get you some tea? He saw, as soon as he had said it, how unspeakably ludicrous this proffer of hospitality was. He almost fancied a smile, a moment's shimmer of little white teeth, beneath the long grey veil. Or shall I come now—at once?" he added.

"Come now; I will show you the mirror."

"What is that?"

"You will understand when you see it. It is the glass of supreme moments. I shall tell you about it. But come."

She looked graceful, and she suggested the most perfect beauty as she stood there, a slight figure against the background of grey mist, which had grown luminous as the room below grew darker. Lucas Morne went carefully up the five steps, and together they passed through the grey, misty curtain. He was wondering what the face was like which was hidden beneath that veil; would it be possible to induce her to remove the veil? He might, perhaps, lead the conversation thither—delicately and subtly.

"A cousin of mine," he began, "who has travelled a good deal, once told me that the women of the East—"

"Yes," she said, and her voice and way were so gentle that it hardly seemed like an interruption; "and so do I."

He felt very much anticipated; for a moment he was driven back into the shy and stammering state. There were only a few more steps now, and then they entered through a rosy curtain into a room, which he supposed to be "that quiet room beyond," of which she had spoken.

It was a large room, square in shape. The floor was covered with black and white tiles, with the exception of a small square space in the centre, which looked like silver, and over which a ripple seemed occasionally to pass. She pointed it out to him. "That," she said, "is the glass of supreme moments." There were no windows, and the soft light that filled the room seemed to come from that liquid silver mirror in the centre of the floor. The walls, which were lofty, were hung with curtains of different colours, all subdued, dreamy, reposeful. These colours were repeated in the painting of the ceiling.

In a recess at the further end of the room there were seats, low seats on which one could sleep. There was a faint smell of syringa in the air, making it heavy and drowsy. Now and then, one heard faintly, as if afar off, the great music of an organ. Could it, he found himself wondering, be the organ of the college chapel? It was restful and pleasant to hear. She drew him to one of the seats in the recess, and once more pointed to the mirror.

"All the ecstasy in the world lies reflected there. The supreme moments of each man's life—the scene, the spoken words—all lie there. Past and present, and future-all are there."

"Shall I be able to see them?"

"If you will."

"And how?"

"Bend over the mirror, and say the name of the man or woman into whose life you wish to see. You only have to want it, and it will appear before your eyes. But there are some lives which have no supreme moments."

"Commonplace lives?"

"Yes."

Lucas Morne walked to the edge of the mirror and knelt down, looking into it. The ripple passed to and fro over the surface. For a moment he hesitated, doubting for whom he should ask; and then he said in a low voice: "Are there supreme moments in the life of Blake— Vincent Blake, the athlete?" The surface of the mirror suddenly grew still, and in it rose what seemed a living picture.

He could see once more the mile race in which he had been defeated by Blake. It was the third and last lap; and he himself was leading by some twenty yards, for Blake was waiting. There was a vast crowd of spectators, and he could hear every now and then the dull sound of their voices. He saw Vincent Blake slightly quicken his pace, and marked his own plucky attempt to answer it; he saw, too, that he had very little left in him. Gradually Blake drew up, until at a hundred yards from the finish there were not more than five yards between the two runners. Then he noticed his own fresh attempt. There were some fifty yards of desperate fighting, in which neither seemed to gain or lose an inch on the other. The voices of the excited crowd rose to a roar. And then—then Blake had it his own way. He saw himself passed a yard from the tape.

"Blake has always just beaten me," he said savagely as he turned from the mirror.

He went back to his seat. "Tell me," he said; "does that picture really represent the supreme moments of Blake's life?"

"Yes," answered the veiled woman, "he will have nothing quite like the ecstasy which he felt at winning that race. He will marry, and have children, and his married life will be happy, but the happiness will not be so intense. There is an emotion-meter outside this room, you know, which measures such things."

"Now if one wanted to bet on a race," he began. Then he stopped short. He had none of the finer perceptions, but it did not take these to show him that he was becoming a little inappropriate. "I will look again at the mirror," he added after a pause. "I am afraid, though, that all this will make me more discontented with myself."

Once more he looked into the glass of supreme moments. He murmured the name of Paul Reece, the good little dissenter, his old schoolfellow. It was not in the power of accomplishment that Paul Reece excelled Lucas Morne, but only in the goodness and spirituality of his nature. As he looked, once more a picture formed on the surface of the mirror. It was of the future this time.

It was a sombre picture of the interior of a church. Through the open door one saw the snow falling slowly into the dusk of a winter afternoon. Within, before the richly decorated altar, flickered the little ruby flames of hanging lamps. On the walls, dim in the dying light, were painted the stations of the Cross. The fragrance of the incense smoke still lingered in the air. He could see but one figure, bowed, black-robed, before the altar. "And is this Paul Reece—who was a dissenter?" he asked himself, knowing that it was he. Someone was seated at the organ, and the cry of the music was full of appeal, and yet full of peace: "*Agnus Dei, qui tollis peccata mundi!*"

Then the picture died away, and once more the little ripple moved to and fro over the surface of the liquid silver mirror. Lucas went back again to his place. The veiled woman was leaning backward, her small white hands linked together. She did not speak, but he was sure that she was looking at him—looking at him intently. Slowly it came to him that there was in this woman a subtle, mastering attraction which he had never known before. And side by side with this thought there still remained the feeling which had filled him as he witnessed the supreme moments of Paul Reece, a paradoxical feeling which was half restlessness and half peace.

"I do not know if I envy Paul," he said, "but if so, it is not the envy which hurts. I shall never be like him. I can't feel as he does. It's not in me. But this picture did not make me angry as the other did." He looked steadfastly at the graceful, veiled figure, and added in a lower tone: "When I spoke of the travels of my cousin a little while ago—over Palestine and Turkey, and thereabouts, you know—I had meant to lead up to a question, as you saw. I had meant to ask you if you would put away your veil and let me see your face. And there are many things which I want to know about you. May I not stay here by your side and talk?"

"Soon, very soon, I will talk with you, and after that you shall see me. What do think, then, of the glass of supreme moments?"

"It is wonderful. I only feared the sight of exquisite happiness in others would make me more discontented. At first you seemed to think that I was too dissatisfied."

"Do not be deceived. Do not think that these supreme moments are everything; for that life is easiest which is gentle, level, placid, and has no supreme moments. There is a picture in the life of your friend Fynsale which I wish you to see. Look at it in the mirror, and then I shall have something to tell you."

Lucas did as he was bidden. The mirror showed him a wretched, dingy room—sitting-room and bedroom combined—in a lodging house. At a little rickety table, pushed in front of a very small fire, Fynsale sat writing by lamplight. The lamp was out of order apparently. The combined smell of lamp and *Latakia* was poignant. There was a pile of manuscript before him, and on the top of it he was placing the sheet he had just written. Then he rose from his chair, folded his arms on the mantelpiece, and bent down, with his head on his hands, looking into the fire. It was an uncouth attitude of which, Lucas remembered, Fynsale had been particularly fond when he was at college.

When the picture had passed, Lucas looked round, and saw that the veiled woman had left the recess, and was now standing by his side. "I do not understand this," he said. "How can those be the supreme moments in Fynsale's life? He looked poor and shabby, and the room was positively wretched. Where does the ecstasy come in?"

"He has just finished his novel; and he is quite madly in love with it. Some of it is very good, and some of it—from merely physical reasons—is very bad; he was half-starved when he was writing it, and it is not possible to write very well when one is half-starved. But he loves it. I am speaking of all this as if, like the picture of it, it was present;

although, of course, it has not happened yet. But I will tell you more. I will show you, in this case at least, what these moments of ecstasy are worth.

"Some of Fynsale's book, I have said, is very good, and some of it is very bad; but none of it is what people want. He will take it to publisher after publisher, and they will refuse it. After three years it will at last be published, and it will not succeed in the least. And all through these years of failure he will recall from time to time the splendid joy he felt at finishing that book, and how glad he was that he had made it. The thought of that past ecstasy will make the torture all the worse."

"Perhaps, then, after all I should be glad that I am commonplace?" said Lucas.

"It does not always follow, though, that the commonplace people have commonplace lives. There have been men who have been so ordinary that it hurt one to have anything to do with them, and yet the gods have made them come into poetry."

Once more Lucas fancied that a smile with magic in it might be fluttering under that grey veil. Every moment the fascination of this woman, whose face he had not seen, and with whom he had spoken for so short a time, grew stronger on him. He did not know from whence it came, whether it lay in the grace of her figure and her movements, or in the beauty of her long, dark hair, or in the music of her voice, or in that subtle, indefinable way in which she seemed to show him that she cared for him deeply. The room itself, quiet, mystical, restful, dedicated to the ecstasy of the world, had its effect upon his senses.

More than ever before he felt himself impressed, tremulous with emotion. He knew that she saw how, in spite of himself, the look of adoration would come into his eyes.

And suddenly she, whom but a moment before he had imagined to be smiling at her own light thoughts, seemed swayed by a more serious impulse.

"You must be comforted, though, and be angry with yourself no longer. For you are *not* commonplace, because you know that you *are* commonplace. It is something to have wanted the right things, although the gods have given you no power to attain them, nor even the wit and words to make your want eloquent." Her voice was deeper, touched with the under-thrill.

"This," he said, "is the second time you have spoken of the gods— and yet we are in the nineteenth century."

"Are we? I am very old and very young. Time is nothing to me; it does not change me. Yesterday in Italy each grave and stream spoke of divinity. '*Non omnis moriar,*' sang one in confidence, '*Non omnis moriar!*' I heard his voice, and now he is passed and gone from the world."

"We read him still," said Lucas Morne, with a little pride. He was not intending to take the classical tripos, but he had with the help of a translation read that ode from which she was quoting. She did not heed his interruption in the least. She went on speaking:

"And today in England there is but little which is sacred; yet here, too, my work is seen; and here, too, as they die, they cry, 'I shall not die, but live!'"

"You will think me stupid," said Lucas Morne, a little bewildered, "but I really do not understand you. I do not follow you. I cannot see to what you refer."

"That is because you do not know who I am. Before the end of today I think we shall understand each other well."

There was a moment's pause, and then Lucas Morne spoke again:

"You have told me that even in the lives of commonplace people there are sometimes supreme moments. I had scarcely hoped for them and you have bidden me not to desire them. Shall I—even I—know what ecstasy means?"

"Yes, yes; I think so."

"Then let me see it, as I saw the rest pictured in the mirror." He spoke with some hesitation, his eyes fixed on the tiled floor of the room.

"That need not be," she answered, and she hardly seemed to have perfect control over the tones of her voice now. "That need not be, Lucas Morne, for the supreme moments of your life are here, here and now."

He looked up, suddenly and excitedly. She had flung back the grey veil over her long, dark hair, and stood revealed before him, looking ardently into his eyes. Her face was paler than that of average beauty; the lips, shapely and scarlet, were just parted; but the eyes gave the most wonderful charm. They were like flames at midnight—not the soft, grey eyes that make men better, but the passionate eyes that make men forget honour, and reason, and everything. She stretched out both hands toward him, impulsively, appealingly. He grasped them in his own. His own hands were hot, burning; every nerve in them tingled with excitement. For a moment he held her at arm's-length, looking at her, and said nothing. At last, he found words:

"I knew that you would be like this. I think that I have loved you all my life. I wish that I might be with you forever."

There was a strange expression on her face. She did not speak, but she drew him nearer to her.

"Tell me your name," he said.

"Yesterday, where that poet lived—that confident poet—they called me Libitina; and here today, they call me Death. My name matters not, if you love me. For to you alone have I come thus. For the rest, I have done my work unseen. Only in this hour—only in this hour—was it possible."

He had hardly heeded what she said. He bent down over her face.

"Stay!" she said in a hurried whisper; "if you kiss me you will die."

He smiled triumphantly. "But I shall die kissing you," he said. And so, their lips met. Her lips were scarlet, but they were icy cold.

★★★★★★★★★★★★

The captain of the football team had just come out of evening chapel, his gown slung over his arm, his cap pulled over his eyes, looking good-tempered, and strong, and jolly, but hardly devotional. He saw the window of Morne's rooms open—they were on the ground-floor—and looked in. By the glow of the failing fire, he saw what he thought was Lucas Morne seated in a lounge-chair. He called to him, but there was no answer. The old idiot's asleep," he said to himself, as he climbed in at the window. "Wake up, old man," he cried, as he put his hand on the shoulder of Lucas Morne's body, and swung it forward; "wake up, old man."

The body rolled forward and fell sideways to the ground heavily and clumsily. It lay there motionless.

The Moon-Slave

The Princess Viola had, even in her childhood, an inevitable submission to the dance; a rhythmical madness in her blood answered hotly to the dance music, swaying her, as the wind sways trees, to movements of perfect sympathy and grace.

For the rest, she had her beauty and her long hair, that reached to her knees, and was thought lovable; but she was never very fervent and vivid unless she was dancing; at other times there almost seemed to be a touch of lethargy upon her. Now, when she was sixteen years old, she was betrothed to the Prince Hugo. With others the betrothal was merely a question of state. With her it was merely a question of obedience to the wishes of authority; it had been arranged; Hugo was *comme ci, comme ça*—no god in her eyes; it did not matter. But with Hugo it was quite different—he loved her.

The betrothal was celebrated by a banquet, and afterwards by a dance in the great hall of the palace. From this dance the princess soon made her escape, quite discontented, and went to the furthest part of the palace gardens, where she could no longer hear the music calling her.

'They are all right,' she said to herself as she thought of the men she had left, 'but they cannot dance. Mechanically they are all right; they have learned it and don't make childish mistakes; but they are only one-two-three machines. They haven't the inspiration of dancing. It is so different when I dance alone.'

She wandered on until she reached an old forsaken maze. It had been planned by a former king. All round it was a high crumbling wall with foxgloves growing on it. The maze itself had all its paths bordered with high opaque hedges; in the very centre was a circular open space with tall pine-trees growing round it. Many years ago, the clue to the maze had been lost; it was but rarely now that anyone entered it. Its gravel paths were green with weeds, and in some places the hedges, spreading beyond their borders, had made the way almost impassable.

For a moment or two Viola stood peering in at the gate—a narrow gate with curiously twisted bars of wrought iron surmounted by a heraldic device. Then the whim seized her to enter the maze and try to find the space in the centre. She opened the gate and went in.

Outside everything was uncannily visible in the light of the full moon, but here in the dark shaded alleys the night was conscious of itself. She soon forgot her purpose, and wandered about quite aimlessly, sometimes forcing her way where the brambles had flung a laced barrier across her path, and a dragging mass of convolvulus struck wet and cool upon her cheek. As chance would have it, she suddenly found herself standing under the tall pines, and looking at the open space that formed the goal of the maze. She was pleased that she had got there. Here the ground was carpeted with sand, fine and, as it seemed, beaten hard. From the summer night sky immediately above, the moonlight, unobstructed here, streamed straight down upon the scene.

Viola began to think about dancing. Over the dry, smooth sand her little satin shoes moved easily, stepping and gliding, circling and stepping, as she hummed the tune to which they moved. In the centre of the space she paused, looked at the wall of dark trees all round, at the shining stretches of silvery sand and at the moon above.

'My beautiful, moonlit, lonely, old dancing-room, why did I never find you before?' she cried; 'but,' she added, 'you need music—there must be music here.'

In her fantastic mood she stretched her soft, clasped hands upwards towards the moon.

'Sweet moon,' she said in a kind of mock prayer, 'make your white light come down in music into my dancing-room here, and I will dance most deliciously for you to see.' She flung her head backward and let her hands fall; her eyes were half closed, and her mouth was a kissing mouth. 'Ah! sweet moon,' she whispered, 'do this for me, and I will be your slave; I will be what you will.'

Quite suddenly the air was filled with the sound of a grand invisible orchestra. Viola did not stop to wonder. To the music of a slow saraband she swayed and postured. In the music there was the regular beat of small drums and a perpetual drone. The air seemed to be filled with the perfume of some bitter spice. Viola could fancy almost that she saw a smouldering camp-fire and heard far off the roar of some desolate wild beast. She let her long hair fall, raising the heavy strands of it in either hand as she moved slowly to the laden music. Slowly her body swayed with drowsy grace, slowly her satin shoes slid over the silver sand.

The music ceased with a clash of cymbals. Viola rubbed her eyes. She fastened her hair up carefully again. Suddenly she looked up, almost imperiously.

'Music! more music!' she cried.

Once more the music came. This time it was a dance of caprice, pelting along over the violin-strings, leaping, laughing, wanton. Again, an illusion seemed to cross her eyes. An old king was watching her, a king with the sordid history of the exhaustion of pleasure written on his flaccid face. A hook-nosed courtier by his side settled the ruffles at his wrists and mumbled, '*Ravissant! Quel malheur que la vieillesse!*' It was a strange illusion. Faster and faster, she sped to the music, stepping, spinning, pirouetting; the dance was light as thistle-down, fierce as fire, smooth as a rapid stream.

The moment that the music ceased Viola became horribly afraid. She turned and fled away from the moonlit space, through the trees, down the dark alleys of the maze, not heeding in the least which turn she took, and yet she found herself soon at the outside iron gate. From thence she ran through the palace garden, hardly ever pausing to take breath, until she reached the palace itself. In the eastern sky the first signs of dawn were showing; in the palace the festivities were drawing to an end. As she stood alone in the outer hall Prince Hugo came towards her.

'Where have you been, Viola?' he said sternly. 'What have you been doing?'

She stamped her little foot.

'I will not be questioned,' she replied angrily.

'I have some right to question,' he said.

She laughed a little.

'For the first time in my life,' she said, 'I have been dancing.'

He turned away in hopeless silence.

★★★★★★★★★★★★

The months passed away. Slowly a great fear came over Viola, a fear that would hardly ever leave her. For every month at the full moon, whether she would or no, she found herself driven to the maze, through its mysterious walks into that strange dancing-room. And when she was there the music began once more, and once more she danced most deliciously for the moon to see. The second time that this happened she had merely thought that it was a recurrence of her

97

own whim, and that the music was but a trick that the imagination had chosen to repeat. The third time frightened her, and she knew that the force that sways the tides had strange power over her. The fear grew as the year fell, for each month the music went on for a longer time—each month some of the pleasure had gone from the dance.

On bitter nights in winter the moon called her and she came, when the breath was vapour, and the trees that circled her dancing-room were black bare skeletons, and the frost was cruel. She dared not tell anyone, and yet it was with difficulty that she kept her secret. Somehow chance seemed to favour her, and she always found a way to return from her midnight dance to her own room without being ob-served. Each month the summons seemed to be more imperious and urgent. Once when she was alone on her knees before the lighted al-tar in the private chapel of the palace, she suddenly felt that the words of the familiar Latin prayer had gone from her memory. She rose to her feet, she sobbed bitterly, but the call had come and she could not resist it. She passed out of the chapel and down the palace-gardens. How madly she danced that night!

She was to be married in the spring. She began to be more gentle with Hugo now. She had a blind hope that when they were married, she might be able to tell him about it, and he might be able to protect her, for she had always known him to be fearless. She could not love him, but she tried to be good to him. One day he mentioned to her that he had tried to find his way to the centre of the maze, and had failed. She smiled faintly. If only she could fail! But she never did.

On the night before the wedding, day she had gone to bed and slept peacefully, thinking with her last waking moments of Hugo. Overhead the full moon came up the sky. Quite suddenly Viola was wakened with the impulse to fly to the dancing-room. It seemed to bid her hasten with breathless speed. She flung a cloak around her, slipped her naked feet into her dancing-shoes, and hurried forth. No one saw her or heard her—on the marble staircase of the palace, on down the terraces of the garden, she ran as fast as she could.

A thorn-plant caught in her cloak, but she sped on, tearing it free; a sharp stone cut through the satin of one shoe, and her foot was wounded and bleeding, but she sped on. As the pebble that is flung from the cliff must fall until it reaches the sea, as the white ghost-moth must come in from cool hedges and scented darkness to a burning death in the lamp by which you sit so late—so Viola had no choice. The moon called her. The moon drew her to that circle of hard, bright sand and the pitiless music.

It was brilliant, rapid music tonight. Viola threw off her cloak and danced. As she did so, she saw that a shadow lay over a fragment of the moon's edge. It was the night of a total eclipse. She heeded it not. The intoxication of the dance was on her. She was all in white; even her face was pale in the moonlight. Every movement was full of poetry and grace.

The music would not stop. She had grown deathly weary. It seemed to her that she had been dancing for hours, and the shadow had nearly covered the moon's face, so that it was almost dark. She could hardly see the trees around her. She went on dancing, stepping, spinning, pirouetting, held by the merciless music.

It stopped at last, just when the shadow had quite covered the moon's face, and all was dark. But it stopped only for a moment, and then began again. This time it was a slow, passionate waltz. It was useless to resist; she began to dance once more. As she did so she uttered a sudden shrill scream of horror, for in the dead darkness a hot hand had caught her own and whirled her round, *and she was no longer dancing alone.*

★★★★★★★★★★★★

The search for the missing princess lasted during the whole of the following day. In the evening Prince Hugo, his face anxious and firmly set, passed in his search the iron gate of the maze, and noticed on the stones beside it the stain of a drop of blood. Within the gate was another stain. He followed this clue, which had been left by Viola's wounded foot, until he reached that open space in the centre that had served Viola for her dancing-room. It was quite empty. He noticed that the sand round the edges was all worn down, as though someone had danced there, round and round, for a long time. But no separate footprint was distinguishable there. Just outside this track, however, he saw two footprints clearly defined close together: one was the print of a tiny satin shoe; the other was the print of a large naked foot—a cloven foot.

The Tower

In the billiard-room of the Cabinet Club, shortly after midnight, two men had just finished a game. A third had been watching it from the lounge at the end of the room. The winner put up his cue, slipped on his coat, and with a brief "Goodnight" passed out of the room. He was tall, dark, clean-shaven and foreign in appearance. It would not have been easy to guess his nationality, but he did not look English.

The loser, a fair-haired boy of twenty-five, came over to the lounge and dropped down by the side of the elderly man who had been watching the billiards.

"Silly game, ain't it, doctor?" he said cheerfully. The doctor smiled.

"Yes," he said, "Vyse is a bit too hot for you. Bill."

"A bit too hot for anything," said the boy. "He never takes any trouble; he never hesitates; he never thinks; he never takes an easy shot when there's a brilliant one to be pulled off. It's almost uncanny."

"Ah," said the doctor, reflectively, "it's a queer thing. You're the third man whom I have heard say that about Vyse within the last week."

"I believe he's quite all right—good sort of chap, you know. He's frightfully clever too—speaks a lot of beastly difficult Oriental languages—does well at any game he takes up."

"Yes," said the doctor, "he is clever; and he is also a fool."

"What do you mean? He's eccentric, of course. Fancy his buying that rotten tower—a sweet place to spend Christmas in all alone, I don't think."

"Why does he say he's going there?"

"Says he hates the conventional Christmas, and wants to be out of it; says also that he wants to shoot duck."

"That won't do," said the doctor. "He may hate the conventional Christmas. He may, and he probably will, shoot duck. But that's not his reason for going there."

"Then what is it?" asked the boy.

"Nothing that would interest you much, Bill. Vyse is one of the chaps that want to know too much. He's playing about in a way that every medical man knows to be a rotten, dangerous way. Mind, he may get at something; if the stories are true, he has already got at a good deal. I believe it is possible for a man to develop in himself certain powers at a certain price."

"What's the price?"

"Insanity, as often as not. Here, let's talk about something pleasanter. Where are you yourself going this Christmas, by the way?"

"My sister has taken compassion upon this lone bachelor. And you?"

"I shall be out of England," said the doctor. "Cairo, probably."

The two men passed out into the hall of the club.

"Has Mr Vyse gone yet?" the boy asked the porter.

"Not yet. Sir William. Mr Vyse is changing in one of the dressing-rooms. His car is outside."

The two men passed the car in the street, and noticed the luggage in the tonneau. The driver, in his long leather coat, stood motionless beside it, waiting for his master. The powerful headlight raked the dusk of the street; you could see the paint on a tired woman's cheek as she passed through it on her way home at last.

"See his game?" said Bill.

"Of course," said the doctor. "He's off to the marshes and that blessed tower of his tonight."

"Well, I don't envy him—holy sort of amusement it must be driving all that way on a cold night like this. I wonder if the beggar ever goes to sleep 'lit all?'"

They reached Bill's chambers in Jermyn Street.

"You must come in and have a drink," said Bill.

Don't think so, thanks," said the doctor; "it's late, you know."

"You'd better," said Bill, and the doctor followed him in.

A letter and a telegram were lying on the table in the diminutive hall. The letter had been sent by messenger, and was addressed to Sir William Orlsey, Bart., in a remarkably small handwriting. Bill picked it up, and thrust it into his pocket at once, unopened. He took the telegram with him into the room where the drinks had been put out, and opened it as he sipped his whisky-and-soda.

"Great Scot!" he exclaimed.

"Nothing serious, I hope," said the doctor.

"I hope not. I suppose all children have got to have the measles some time or another; but it's a bit unlucky that my sister's three should all go down with it just now. That does for her house-party at Christmas, of course."

A few minutes later, when the doctor had gone, Bill took the letter from his pocket and tore it open. A cheque fell from the envelope and fluttered to the ground. The letter ran as follows:

Dear Bill,—I could not talk to you tonight, as the doctor, who happens to disapprove of me, was in the billiard-room. Of course, I can let you have the hundred you want, and enclose it herewith with the utmost pleasure. The time you mention for repayment would suit me all right, and so would any other time. Suit your own convenience entirely.

"I have a favour to ask of you. I know you are intending to go down to the Leylands' for Christmas.

"I think you will be prevented from doing so. If that is the case, and you have no better engagement, would you hold yourself at my disposal for a week? It is just possible that I may want a man like you pretty badly. There ought to be plenty of duck this weather, but I don't know that I can offer any other attraction.—Very sincerely yours,

Edward Vyse.

Bill picked up the cheque, and thrust it into the drawer with a feeling of relief. It was a queer invitation, he thought—funnily worded, with the usual intimations of time and place missing. He switched off the electric lights and went into his bedroom. As he was undressing a thought struck him suddenly.

"How the deuce," he said aloud, "did he know that I should be prevented from going to Polly's place?" Then he looked round quickly. He thought that he had heard a faint laugh just behind him. No one was there, and Bill's nerves were good enough. In twenty minutes, he was fast asleep.

The cottage, built of grey stone, stood some thirty yards back from the road, from which it was screened by a shrubbery. It was an ordinary eight-roomed cottage, and it did well enough for Vyse and his servants and one guest—if Vyse happened to want a guest. There was a pleasant little walled garden of a couple of acres behind the cottage. Through a doorway in the further wall, one passed into a stunted and dismal plantation, and in the middle of this rose the tower, far higher than any of the trees that surrounded it.

Sir William Orlsey had arrived just in time to change before dinner. Talk at dinner had been of indifferent subjects—the queer characters of the village and the chances of sport on the morrow. Bill had mentioned the tower, and his host had hastened to talk of other things. But now that dinner was over, and the man who had waited on them had left the room, Vyse of his own accord returned to the subject.

"Danvers is a superstitious ass," he observed, "and he's in quite enough of a funk about that tower as it is; that's why I wouldn't give you the story of it while he was in the room. According to the village tradition, a witch was burned on the site where the tower now stands, and she declared that where she burned the devil should have his house. The lord of the manor at that time, hearing what the old lady had said, and wishing to discourage house-building on that particular site, had it covered with a plantation, and made it a condition of his will that this plantation should be kept up."

Bill lit a large cigar. "Looks like checkmate," he said. "However, seeing that the tower is actually there—"

"Quite so. This man's son came no end of a cropper, and the property changed hands several times. It was divided and sub-divided. I, for instance, only own about twenty acres of it. Presently there came along a scientific old gentleman and bought the piece that I now have. Whether he knew of the story, or whether he didn't, I cannot say, but he set to work to build the tower that is now standing in the middle of the plantation. He may have intended it as an observatory. He got the stone for it on the spot from his own quarry, but he had to import his labour, as the people in these parts didn't think the work healthy. Then one fine morning before the tower was finished, they found the old gentleman at the bottom of his quarry with his neck broken."

"So," said Bill, "they say of course that the tower is haunted. What is it that they think they see?"

"Nothing. You can't see it. But there are people who think they have touched it and have heard it."

"Rot, ain't it?"

"I don't know exactly. You see, I happen to be one of those people."

"Then, if you think so, there's something in it. This is interesting. I say, can't we go across there now?"

"Certainly, if you like. Sure, you won't have any more wine? Come along, then."

The two men slipped on their coats and caps. Vyse carried a lighted stable-lantern. It was a frosty moonlit night, and the path was crisp and hard beneath their feet. As Vyse slid back the bolts of the gate in the garden wall, Bill said suddenly, "By the way, Vyse, how did you know that I shouldn't be at the Leylands' this Christmas? I told you I was going there."

"I don't know. I had a feeling that you were going to be with me. It might have been wrong. Anyhow, I'm very glad you're here. You are just exactly the man I want. We've only a few steps to go now. This path is ours. That cart-track leads away to the quarry where the scientific gentleman took the short cut to further knowledge. And here is the door of the tower."

They walked round the tower before entering. The night was so still that, unconsciously, they spoke in lowered voices and trod as softly as possible. The lock of the heavy door groaned and screeched as the key turned. The light of the lantern fell now on the white sand of the floor and on a broken spiral staircase on the further side. Far up above one saw a tangle of beams and the stars beyond them. Bill heard Vyse saying that it was left like that after the death in the quarry.

"It's a good solid bit of masonry," said Bill, "but it ain't a cheerful spot exactly. And, by Jove! it smells like a menagerie."

"It does," said Vyse, who was examining the sand on the floor.

Bill also looked down at the prints in the sand. "Some dog's been in here."

"No," said Vyse, thoughtfully. "Dogs won't come in here, and you can't make them. Also, there were no marks on the sand when I left the place and locked the door this afternoon. Queer, isn't it?"

"But the thing's a blank impossibility. Unless, of course, we are to suppose that—"

He did not finish his sentence, and, if he had finished it, it would not have been audible. A chorus of grunting, growling and squealing broke out almost from under his feet, and he sprang backwards. It lasted for a few seconds, and then died slowly away.

"Did you hear that?" Vyse asked quietly.

"I should rather think so."

"Good; then it was not subjective. What was it?"

"Only one kind of beast makes that row. Pigs, of course—a whole drove of them. It sounded as if they were in here, close to us. But as they obviously are not, they must be outside."

"But they are not outside," said Vyse. "Come and see."

They hunted the plantation through and through with no result, and then locked the tower door and went back to the cottage. Bill said very little. He was not capable of much self-analysis, but he was conscious of a sudden dislike of Vyse. He was angry that he had ever put himself under an obligation to this man. He had wanted the money for a gambling debt, and he had already repaid it. Now he saw Vyse in the light of a man with whom one should have no dealings, and the last man from whom one should accept a kindness.

The strange experience that he had just been through filled him with loathing far more than with fear or wonder. There was something unclean and diabolical about the whole thing that made a decent man reluctant to question or to investigate. The filthy smell of the brutes seemed still to linger in his nostrils. He was determined that on no account would he enter the tower again, and that as soon as he could find a decent excuse, he would leave the place altogether.

A little later, as he sat before the log fire and filled his pipe, he turned to his host with a sudden question; "I say, Vyse, why did you want me to come down here? What's the meaning of it all?"

"My dear fellow," said Vyse, "I wanted you for the pleasure of your society. Now, don't get impatient. I also wanted you because you are the most normal man I know. Your confirmation of my experiences in the tower is most valuable to me. Also, you have good nerves, and, if you will forgive me for saying so, no imagination. I may want help that only a man with good nerves would be able to give."

"Why don't you leave the thing alone? It's too beastly."

Vyse laughed. "I'm afraid my hobby bores you. We won't talk about it. After all, there's no reason why you should help me?"

"Tell me just what it is that you wanted."

"I wanted you if you heard this whistle"—he took an ordinary police-whistle down from the mantelpiece—" any time tonight or tomorrow night, to come over to the tower at once and bring a revolver with you. The whistle would be a sign that I was in a tight place—that my life, in fact, was in danger. You see, we are dealing here with something preternatural, but it is also something material; in addition to other risks, one risks ordinary physical destruction. However, I could see that you were repelled by the sight and the sound of these beasts, whatever they may be; and I can tell you from my own experience that the touch of them is even worse. There is no reason why you should bother yourself any further about the thing."

"You can take the whistle with you," said Bill. "If I hear it I will come."

"Thanks," said Vyse, and immediately changed the subject. He did not say why he was spending the night in the tower, or what it was he proposed to do there.

It was three in the morning when Bill was suddenly startled out of his sleep. He heard the whistle being blown repeatedly. He hurried on some clothes and dashed down into the hall, where his lantern and revolver lay all ready for him. He ran along the garden path and through the door in the wall until he got to the tower. The sound of the whistle had ceased now, and everything was horribly still. The door of the tower stood wide open, and without hesitation Bill entered, holding his lantern high.

The tower was absolutely empty. Not a sound was to be heard. Bill called Vyse by name twice loudly, and then again, the awful silence spread over the place.

Then, as if guided by some unseen hand, he took the track that led to the quarry, well knowing what he would find at the bottom of it.

The jury assigned the death of Vyse to an accident, and said that the quarry should be fenced in. They had no explanation to offer of the mutilation of the face, as if by the teeth of some savage beast.

The Unfinished Game

At Tanslowe, which is on the Thames, I found just the place that I wanted. I had been born in the hotel business, brought up in it, and made my living at it for thirty years. For the last twenty I had been both proprietor and manager, and had worked uncommonly hard, for it is personal attention and plenty of it which makes a hotel pay. I might have retired altogether, for I was a bachelor with no claims on me and had made more money than enough; but that was not what I wanted. I wanted a nice, old-fashioned house, not too big, in a nice place with a longish slack season. I cared very little whether I made it pay or not. The Regency Hotel at Tanslowe was just the thing for me. It would give me a little to do and not too much.

Tanslowe was a village, and though there were two or three public-houses, there was no other hotel in the place, nor was any competition likely to come along. I was particular about that, because my nature is such that competition always sets me fighting, and I cannot rest until the other shop goes down. I had reached a time of life when I did want to rest and did not want any more fighting. It was a free house, and I have always had a partiality for being my own master. It had just the class of trade that I liked—principally gentlefolk taking their pleasure in a holiday on the river. It was very cheap, and I like value for money. The house was comfortable, and had a beautiful garden sloping down to the river. I meant to put in some time in that garden—I have a taste that way.

The place was so cheap that I had my doubts.

I wondered if it was flooded when the river rose, if it was dropping to pieces with dry-rot, if the drainage had been condemned, if they were going to start a lunatic asylum next door, or what it was. I went into all these points and a hundred more. I found one or two trifling drawbacks, and one expects them in any house, however good—especially when it is an old place like the Regency. I found nothing

109

whatever to stop me from taking the place.

I bought the whole thing, furniture and all, lock, stock and barrel, and moved in. I brought with me my own headwaiter and my man-cook, Englishmen both of them. I knew they would set the thing in the right key. The headwaiter, Silas Goodheart, was just over sixty, with grey hair and a wrinkled face. He was worth more to me than two younger men would have been. He was very precise and rather slow in his movements. He liked bright silver, clean table-linen, and polished glass. Artificial flowers in the vases on his tables would have given him a fit. He handled a decanter of old port as if he loved it—which, as a matter of fact, he did.

His manner to visitors was a perfect mixture of dignity, respect and friendliness. If a man did not quite know what he wanted for dinner, Silas had sympathetic and very useful suggestions. He took, I am sure, a real pleasure in seeing people enjoy their luncheon or dinner. Americans loved him, and tipped him out of all proportion. I let him have his own way, even when he gave the thing away.

"Is the coffee all right here?" a customer asked after a good dinner.

"I cannot recommend it," said Silas. "If I might suggest, sir, we have the Chartreuse of the old French shipping."

I overheard that, but I said nothing. The coffee was extract, for there was more work than profit in making it good. As it was, that customer went away pleased, and came back again and again, and brought his friends too. Silas was really the only permanent waiter. When we were busy, I got one or two foreigners from London tem-porarily. Silas soon educated them. My cook, Timbs, was an honest chap, and understood English fare. He seemed hardly ever to eat, and never sat down to a meal; he lived principally on beer, drank enough of it to frighten you, and was apparently never the worse for it. And a butcher who tried to send him second-quality meat was certain of finding out his mistake.

The only other man I brought with me was young Harry Bryden. He always called me uncle, but as a matter of fact he was no relation of mine. He was the son of an old friend. His parents died when he was seven years old and left him to me. It was about all they had to leave. At this time, he was twenty-two, and was making himself useful. There was nothing which he was not willing to do, and he could do most things. He would mark at billiards, and played a good game him-self. He had run the kitchen when the cook was away on his holiday. He had driven the station-omnibus when the driver was drunk one night. He understood book-keeping, and when I got a clerk who was a wrong 'un, he was on to him at once and saved me money.

It was my intention to make him take his proper place more when I got to the Regency; for he was to succeed me when I died. He was clever, and not bad-looking in a gipsy-faced kind of way. Nobody is perfect, and Harry was a cigarette-maniac. He began when he was a boy, and I didn't spare the stick when I caught him at it. But nothing I could say or do made any difference; at twenty-two he was old enough and big enough to have his own way, and his way was to smoke cigarettes eternally. He was a bundle of nerves, and got so jumpy sometimes that some people bought he drank, though he had never in his life tasted liquor. He inherited his nerves from his mother, but I daresay the cigarettes made them worse.

I took Harry down with me when I first thought of taking the place. He went over it with me and made a lot of useful suggestions. The old proprietor had died eighteen months before, and the widow had tried to run it for herself and made a mess of it. She had just sense enough to clear out before things got any worse. She was very anxious to go, and I thought that might have been the reason why the price was so low.

The billiard-room was an annexe to the house, with no rooms over it. We were told that it wasn't used once in a twelve month, but we took a look at it—we took a look at everything. The room had got a very neglected look about it. I sat down on the platform—tired with so much walking and standing—and Harry whipped the cover off the table. "This was the one they had in the Ark," he said.

There was not a straight cue in the rack, the balls were worn and untrue, the jigger was broken, Harry pointed to the board. "Look at that, uncle," he said. "Noah had made forty-eight; Ham was doing nicely at sixty-six; and then the Flood came and they never finished." From neatness and force of habit he moved over and turned the score back. "You'll have to spend some money here. My word, if they put the whole lot in at a florin we're swindled." As we came out Harry gave a shiver. "I wouldn't spend a night in there," he said, "not for a five-pound note."

His nerves always made me angry. "That's a very silly thing to say," I told him. "Who's going to ask you to sleep in a billiard-room?"

Then he got a bit more practical, and began to calculate how much I should have to spend to make a bright, up-to-date billiard-room of it. But I was still angry.

"You needn't waste your time on that," I said, "because the place will stop as it is. You heard what Mrs Parker said—that it wasn't used once in a twelve month. I don't want to attract all the loafers in Tanslowe into my house. Their custom's worth nothing, and I'd sooner be without it. Time enough to put that room right if I find my staying visitors want it, and people who've been on the river all day are mostly too tired for a game after dinner."

Harry pointed out that it sometimes rained, and there was the winter to think about. He had always got plenty to say, and what he said now had sense in it. But I never go chopping and changing about, and I had made my mind up. So, I told him he had got to learn how to manage the house, and not to waste half his time over the billiard-table. I had a good deal done to the rest of the house in the way of redecorating and improvements, but I never touched the annexe.

The next time I saw the room was the day after we moved in. I was alone, and I thought it certainly did look a dingy hole as compared with the rest of the house. Then my eye happened to fall on the board, and it still showed sixty-six—forty-eight, as it had done when I entered the room with Harry three months before. I altered the board myself this time. To me it was only a funny coincidence; another game had been played there and had stopped exactly at the same point. But I was glad Harry was not with me, for it was the kind of thing that would have made him jumpier than ever.

It was the summer time and we soon had something to do. I had been told that motorcars had cut into the river trade a good deal; so I laid myself out for the motorist. Tanslowe was just a nice distance for a run from town before lunch. It was all in the old-fashioned style, but there was plenty of choice and the stuff was good; and my wine-list was worth consideration. Prices were high, but people will pay when they are pleased with the way they are treated. Motorists who had been once came again and sent their friends. Saturday to Monday we had as much as ever we could do, and more than I had ever meant to do. But I am built like that—once I am in a shop, I have got to run it for all it's worth.

I had been there about a month, and it was about the height of our season, when one night, for no reason that I could make out, I couldn't get to sleep. I had turned in, tired enough, at half-past ten, leaving Harry to shut up and see the lights out, and at a quarter past twelve I was still awake. I thought to myself that a pint of stout and a biscuit might be the cure for that. So, I lit my candle and went down to the bar. The gas was out on the staircase and in the passages, and all was quiet. The door into the bar was locked, but I had thought to bring my pass-key with me. I had just drawn my tankard of stout when I heard a sound that made me put the tankard down and listen again.

The billiard-room door was just outside in the passage, and there could not be the least doubt that a game was going on. I could hear the click-click of the balls as plainly as possible. It surprised me a little, but it did not startle me. We had several staying in the house, and I supposed two of them had fancied a game. All the time that I was drinking the stout and munching my biscuit the game went on—*click, click-click, click.* Everybody has heard the sound hundreds of times standing outside the glass-panelled door of a billiard-room and waiting for the stroke before entering. No other sound is quite like it.

Suddenly the sound ceased. The game was over. I had nothing on but my pyjamas and a pair of slippers, and I thought I would get up-stairs again before the players came out. I did not want to stand there shivering and listening to complaints about the table.

I locked the bar, and took a glance at the billiard-room door as I was about to pass it. What I saw made me stop short. The glass panels of the door were as black as my Sunday hat, except where they reflected the light of my candle. The room, then, was not lit up, and people do not play billiards in the dark. After a second or two I tried the handle. The door was locked. It was the only door to the room.

I said to myself: "I'll go on back to bed. It must have been my fancy, and there was nobody playing billiards at all," I moved a step away, and then I said to myself again: "I know perfectly well that a game was be-ing played. I'm only making excuses because I'm in a funk."

That settled it. Having driven myself to it, I moved pretty quickly. I shoved in my pass-key, opened the door, and said "Anybody there?" in a moderately loud voice that sounded somehow like another man's. I am very much afraid that I should have jumped if there had come any answer to my challenge, but all was silent, I took a look round. The cover was on the table. An old screen was leaning against it; it had been put there to be out of the way. As I moved my candle the shadows of things slithered across the floor and crept up the walls. I noticed that the windows were properly fastened, and then, as I held my candle high, the marking-board seemed to jump out of the darkness. The score recorded was sixty-six—forty-eight.

I shut the door, locked it again, and went up to my room. I did these things slowly and deliberately, but I was frightened and I was puzzled. One is not at one's best in the small hours.

The next morning, I tackled Silas.

"Silas," I said, "what do you do when gentlemen ask for the billiard-room?"

"Well, sir," said Silas, "I put them off if I can. Mr Harry directed me to, the place being so much out of order."

"Quite so," I said. "And when you can't put them off?"

"Then they just try it, sir, and the table puts them off. It's very bad. There's been no game played there since we came."

"Curious," I said, "I thought I heard a game going on last night,"

"I've heard it myself, sir, several times. There being no light in the room, I've put it down to a loose ventilator. The wind moves it and it clicks."

"That'll be it," I said. Five minutes later I had made sure that there was no loose ventilator in the billiard-room. Besides, the sound of one ball striking another is not quite like any other sound. I also went up to the board and turned the score back, which I had omitted to do the night before. Just then Harry passed the door on his way from the bar, with a cigarette in his mouth as usual. I called him in.

"Harry," I said, "give me thirty, and I'll play you a hundred up for a sovereign. You can tell one of the girls to fetch our cues from upstairs."

Harry took his cigarette out of his mouth and whistled. "What, uncle!" he said. "Well, you're going it, I don't think. What would you have said to me if I'd asked you for a game at ten in the morning?"

"Ah!" I said, "but this is all in the way of business. I can't see much wrong with the table, and if I can play on it, then other people may. There's a chance to make a sovereign for you anyhow. You've given me forty-five and a beating before now."

"No, uncle," he said, "I wouldn't give you thirty. I wouldn't give you one. The table's not playable. Luck would win against Roberts on it."

He showed me the faults of the thing and said he was busy. So, I told him if he liked to lose the chance of making a sovereign he could.

"I hate that room," he said, as we came out. "It's not too clean, and it smells like a vault."

"It smells a lot better than your cigarettes," I said.

For the next six weeks we were all busy, and I gave little thought to the billiard-room. Once or twice, I heard old Silas telling a customer that he could not recommend the table, and that the whole room was to be redecorated and refitted as soon as we got the estimates. "You see, sir, we've only been here a little while, and there hasn't been time to get everything as we should like it quite yet."

One day Mrs Parker, the woman who had the Regency before me, came down from town to see how we were getting on. I showed the old lady round, pointed out my improvements, and gave her a bit of lunch in my office.

"Well, now," I said, as she sipped her glass of port afterwards, "I'm not complaining of my bargain, but isn't the billiard-room a bit queer?"

"It surprises me," she said, "that you've left it as it is. Especially with everything else going ahead, and the yard half full of motors. I should have taken it all down myself if I'd stopped. That iron roof's nothing but an eyesore, and you might have a couple of beds of geraniums there and improve the look of your front."

"Let's see," I said. "What was the story about that billiard-room?"

"What story do you mean?" she said, looking at me suspiciously.

"The same one you're thinking of," I said.

"About that man, Josiah Ham?"

"That's it."

"Well, I shouldn't worry about that if I were you. That was all thirty years ago, and I doubt if there's a soul in Tanslowe knows it now. Best forgotten, I say. Talk of that kind doesn't do a hotel any good. Why, how did you come to hear of it?"

"That's just it," I said. "The man who told me was none too clear. He gave me a hint of it. He was an old commercial passing through, and had known the place in the old days. Let's hear your story and see if it agrees with his."

But I had told my fibs to no purpose. The old lady seemed a bit flustered. "If you don't mind, Mr Sanderson, I'd rather not speak of it."

I thought I knew what was troubling her. I filled her glass and my own. "Look here," I said. "When you sold the place to me it was a fair deal. You weren't called upon to go thirty years back, and no reasonable man would expect it. I'm satisfied. Here I am, and here I mean to stop, and twenty billiard-rooms wouldn't drive me away. I'm not complaining. But, just as a matter of curiosity, I'd like to hear your story."

"What's your trouble with the room?"

"Nothing to signify. But there's a game played there and marked there—and I can't find the players, and it's never finished. It stops always at sixty-six—forty-eight."

She gave a glance over her shoulder. "Pull the place down," she said. "You can afford to do it, and I couldn't." She finished her port.

"I must be going, Mr Sanderson. There's rain coming on, and I don't want to sit in the train in my wet things. I thought I would just run down to see how you were getting on, and I'm sure I'm glad to see the old place looking up again."

I tried again to get the story out of her, but she ran away from it. She had not got the time, and it was better not to speak of such things. I did not worry her about it much, as she seemed upset over it.

I saw her across to the station, and just got back in time. The rain came down in torrents. I stood there and watched it, and thought it would do my garden a bit of good. I heard a step behind me and looked round. A fat chap with a surly face stood there, as if he had just come out of the coffee-room. He was the sort that might be a gentleman and might not.

"Afternoon, sir," I said. "Nasty weather for motoring."

"It is," he said. "Not that I came in a motor. You the proprietor, Mr Sanderson?"

"I am," I said. "Came here recently."

"I wonder if there's any chance of a game of billiards."

"I'm afraid not," I said. "Table's shocking. I'm having it all done up afresh, and then—"

"What's it matter?" said he. "I don't care. It's something to do, and one can't go out."

"Well," I said, "if that's the case. I'll give you a game, sir. But I'm no flyer at it at the best of times, and I'm all out of practice now."

"I'm no good myself. No good at all. And I'd be glad of the game."

At the billiard-room door I told him I'd fetch a couple of decent cues. He nodded and went in.

When I came back with my cue and Harry's, I found the gas lit and the blinds drawn, and he was already knocking the balls about.

"You've been quick, sir," I said, and offered him Harry's cue. But he refused and said he would keep the one he had taken from the rack. Harry would have sworn if he had found that I had lent his cue to a stranger, so I thought that was just as well. Still, it seemed to me that a man who took a twisted cue by preference was not likely to be an expert.

The table was bad, but not so bad as Harry had made out. The luck was all my side. I was fairly ashamed of the flukes I made, one after the other. He said nothing, but gave a short, loud laugh once or twice—it was a nasty-sounding laugh. I was at thirty-seven when he was nine, and I put on eleven more at my next visit and thought I had left him nothing.

Then the fat man woke up. He got out of his first difficulty, and after that the balls ran right for him. He was a player, too, with plenty of variety and resource, and I could see that I was going to take a licking. When he had reached fifty-one, an unlucky kiss left him an impossible position. But I miscued, and he got going again. He played very, very carefully now, taking a lot more time for consideration than he had done in his previous break. He seemed to have got excited over it, and breathed hard, as fat men do when they are worked up. He had kept his coat on, and his face shone with perspiration.

At sixty-six he was in trouble again; he walked round to see the exact position, and chalked his cue. I watched him rather eagerly, for I did not like the score. I hoped he would go on. His cue slid back to strike, and then dropped with a clatter from his hand. The fat man was gone—gone, as I looked at him, like a flame blown out, vanished into nothing.

I staggered away from the table. I began to back slowly towards the door, meaning to make a bolt for it. There was a click from the scoring-board, and I saw the thing marked up. And then—I am thankful to say—the billiard-room door, opened, and I saw Harry standing there. He was very white and shaky. Somehow, the fact that he was frightened helped to steady me.

"Good heavens, uncle!" he gasped. "I've been standing outside. What's the matter? What's happened?"

"Nothing's the matter," I said sharply. "What are you shivering about?" I swished back the curtain, and sent up the blind with a snap. The rain was over now, and the sun shone in through the wet glass—I was glad of it.

"I thought I heard voices—laughing—somebody called the score."

I turned out the gas. "Well," I said, "this table's enough to make any man laugh, when it don't make him swear. I've been trying your game of one hand against another, and I daresay I called the score out loud. It's no catch—not even for a wet afternoon. I'm not both-handed, like the apes and Harry Bryden."

Harry is as good with the left hand as the right, and a bit proud of it. I slid my own cue back into its case. Then, whistling a bit of a tune, I picked up the stranger's cue, which I did not like to touch. I nearly dropped it again when I saw the initials "J.H." on the butt. "Been trying the cues," I said, as I put it in the rack. He looked at me as if he were going to ask more questions. So, I put him on to something else.

117

"We've not got enough cover for those motorcars," I said. "Lucky we hadn't got many here in this rain. There's plenty of room for another shed, and it needn't cost much. Go and see what you can make of it. I'll come out directly, but I've got to talk to that girl in the bar first."

He went off, looking rather ashamed of his tremors.

I had not really very much to say to Miss Hesketh in the bar. I put three fingers of whisky in a glass and told her to put a dash of soda on the top of it. That was all. It was a full-sized drink and did me good.

Then I found Harry in the yard. He was figuring with pencil on the back of an envelope. He was always pretty smart where there was anything practical to deal with. He had spotted where the shed was to go, and he was finding what it would cost at a rough estimate.

"Well," I said, "if I went on with that idea of mine about the flower-beds it needn't cost much beyond the labour."

"What idea?"

"You've got a head like a sieve. Why, carrying on the flower-beds round the front where the billiard-room now stands. If we pulled that down it would give us all the materials we want for the new motor-shed. The roofing's sound enough, for I was up yesterday looking into it."

"Well, I don't think you mentioned it to me, but it's a rare good idea."

"I'll think about it," I said.

That evening my cook, Timbs, told me he'd be sorry to leave me, but he was afraid he'd find the place too slow for him—not enough doing. Then old Silas informed me that he hadn't meant to retire so early, but he wasn't sure—the place was livelier than he had expected, and there would be more work than he could get through. I asked no questions. I knew the billiard-room was somehow or other at the bottom of it, and so it turned out.

In three days' time the workmen were in the house and bricking up the billiard-room door; and after that Timbs and old Silas found the Regency suited them very well after all. And it was not just to oblige Harry, or Timbs, or Silas that I had the alteration made. That unfinished game was in my mind; I had played it, and wanted never to play it again. It was of no use for me to tell myself that it had all been a delusion, for I knew better. My health was good, and I had no delusions. I had played it with Josiah Ham—with the lost soul of Josiah Ham—and that thought filled me not with fear, but with a feeling of sickness and disgust.

It was two years later that I heard the story of Josiah Ham, and it was not from old Mrs Parker. An old tramp came into the saloon bar begging, and Miss Hesketh was giving him the rough side of her tongue.

"Nice treatment!" said the old chap. "Thirty years ago I worked here, and made good money, and was respected, and now it's insults."

And then I struck in. "What did you do here?"

I asked.

"Waited at table and marked at billiards."

"Till you took to drink?" I said.

"Till I resigned from a strange circumstance."

I sent him out of the bar, and took him down the garden, saying I'd find him an hour or two's work. "Now, then," I said, as soon as I had got him alone, "what made you leave?"

He looked at me curiously. "I expect you know, sir," he said. "Sixty-six. Unfinished."

And then he told me of a game played in that old billiard-room on a wet summer afternoon thirty years before. He, the marker, was one of the players. The other man was a commercial traveller, who used the house pretty regularly. "A fat man, ugly-looking, with a nasty laugh. Josiah Ham his name was. He was at sixty-six when he got himself into a tight place. He moved his ball—did it when he thought I wasn't looking. But I saw it in the glass, and I told him of it. He got very angry. He said he wished he might be struck dead if he ever touched the ball."

The old tramp stopped. "I see," I said.

"They said it was apoplexy. It's known to be dangerous for fat men to get very angry. But I'd had enough of it before long. I cleared out, and so did the rest of the servants."

"Well," I said, "we're not so superstitious nowadays. And what brought you down in the world?"

"It would have driven any man to it," he said. "And once the habit is formed—well, it's there."

"If you keep off it, I can give you a job weeding for three days."

He did not want the work. He wanted a shilling, and he got it; and I saw to it that he did not spend it in my house.

We have got a very nice billiard-room upstairs now. Two new tables and everything ship-shape. You may find Harry there most evenings. It is all right. But I have never taken to billiards again myself.

And where the old billiard-room was there are flowerbeds. The pansies that grow there have got funny markings—like figures.

The Magnet

(Subsequent to the inquest on the body of the Rev. Ingram Shallow, who shot himself in the churchyard of St. John's, Ilworthy, Bedfordshire, on the evening of October 14, the following paper was found at his lodgings in the village, and is here published for the first time. It will be remembered that at the inquest the usual verdict of temporary insanity was returned.)

Thursday, October 6.—The world is still ringing with the news of the ghastly accident to the express the night before last. The *Times* has a column and a half. Nothing else is spoken of in the village. Yesterday afternoon I went over on my bicycle to witness the scene of the accident. Of course, the more horrible traces of it had already been removed; the screams of the injured and dying and the sight of mangled bodies, about which we read in the papers, would have been too much for me.

The up line was already clear, and it was expected the down line would also be clear in the course of a couple of hours. There was a perfect army of men at work, with every kind of ingenious contrivance for removing the heavy obstacles. All along the embankment fragments of the *débris* are still strewn. At a distance of at least forty yards from the point where the accident actually happened, I found, among some wet grass and fern, a part of one of those plates they have up in the carriages, giving the number that the carriage is intended to carry. I have, often noticed, when standing in the station, the appearance of strength which locomotives and carriages on the fast trains always have.

Yet here one saw all this strength of no avail. The engine and the carriages were broken up just like a child's toys. I do most sincerely hope and believe that it was nobody in Ilworthy who was responsible for the disaster. Whoever it is, I do trust and pray that he may be discovered, and that he may pay with his own life for the lives of those hundreds his fiendish action has sent, without a moment of warning, into eternity.

Friday, October 7.—The Vicar came back with me to breakfast this morning after the early service. After some talk about the accident, I asked him if he intended to touch upon it on Sunday morning. He said that he would if I thought it necessary, but that his sermon was already written, being one of a series on the Gospels for the day, which he prepared some time ago. I said that undoubtedly the accident was a terrible event, and one which had sunk very deeply into the minds of everybody in Ilworthy. It was an event which might give point and weight to many a lesson, and it had been my view that Christianity was a practical religion, and the priest should, wherever possible, bring it to bear upon the events of the day.

At the same time, I did not insist; it was not for me to instruct him, the contrary was rather the case. He smiled good-temperedly, and said that since I seemed to be so full of the accident, and had taken such an absorbing interest in it, I could probably preach a better sermon on it myself, and I might use that as my subject for Sunday evening. I thanked him, and said that I would do so. I have spent the whole day over this sermon. I do not, like the Vicar, read my sermons, but I have written this out in full, and shall commit it to memory.

I have given what I think is really a somewhat vivid and impressive picture of the great express rushing at headlong speed to ruin; the obstacle just seen by the driver one moment before his engine crashed into it; the sudden darkness of the train through the extinction of the lights; the screams for help; the sight of the dead bodies laid out on the embankment.... I have worked myself up so much about this sermon that I have only to shut my eyes actually to witness the scene myself. I seem to be standing by the obstruction, and to see the long train crashing down upon me when it is too late to do anything.

I hope I am not exciting myself too much about it. It is already past ten, and I think I shall have a cup of hot cocoa quietly and go to bed. I notice that one of the illustrated papers in the reading-room has a magnificent full-page illustration of the accident. I have often thought, by the way, of writing a little for the papers myself I know I have some taste for the work, and I am inclined to think I have some little gift also. The supplement to one's income would be useful.

Sunday, October 9—I have just returned from church, exhausted.

I preached over forty minutes, without the least sign of impatience from any of the congregation. No coughing or shuffling of the feet, or anything of the kind. In the vestry afterwards, Mr. Johnson, our senior churchwarden, took me aside, and told me that it was one of the strongest and most impressive addresses he had ever heard delivered from that pulpit. I hope I did not appear to be unduly pleased at this; one must not think of self in these matters, and I strive against it. I was a little surprised that after this special effort of mine the Vicar should have said nothing at all. He is not a small-minded man, and I cannot believe him to be actuated by jealousy. He spoke of the accident again, and said in what seemed to be rather a patronising way that he was afraid I was letting it prey too much on my mind.

I tried to be humble, and I think I can submit to a rebuke when it is deserved. But really, this is nonsense. I still picture to myself at times the man standing by the obstruction and watching the express coming towards him. But for the awful wickedness of it, it would be, in a way, a magnificent moment. He would have the thought that he, a weak man, could at his will check the rush of a train, hurl it over, twist and break the strong iron as if it were cardboard, and avenge himself on hundreds of people; and then have all the police in the country hunting for him—and in vain. Exhausted though I am, I am afraid that I shall get no sleep tonight until I have been out in the fresh air a little.

The church was crowded, and oppressively hot. The whole village is asleep, and no one will be any the wiser. I think I will get on my bicycle and ride down again to the place where the accident happened. It is within a quarter of an hour to midnight, and so Sunday is practically over. Besides, there are many very good men who do not consider that cycling on Sunday is wrong.

Monday, October 10.—Today I have been beset by a terrible and most extraordinary temptation. I thank God that I have wrestled against it successfully; but the fact that such a temptation could even occur to me appals me.

Tuesday, October 11.—The Vicar called this morning. He will take both sermons next Sunday. He said that I looked ill, and that he thought I had been overdoing it, and was in want of a holiday. I think he is right. He is really a very kind man. I shall go away next week. Again, all day long, I have been subject to the same diabolical impulse. I was half tempted to speak to the Vicar about it, but shame prevented me. I get but little sleep now at nights, and if I do sleep, I am always haunted by the same dream. I see the lights of the express coming nearer and nearer. . . .

Wednesday, October 12.—It is done now. It had to be done, and it was no good to contend against it. I believe that it must have been the will of God that I should do it, for ever since the burden has been lifted from my mind, and I have been quite myself again. Late last night, or rather very early this morning, finding myself unable to sleep, I got up and went out. I did not take my bicycle. I ran all the way to that point on the line that I have always been thinking about. There is a stack of heavy sleepers there. It is at the bottom of a deep cutting, and you can see the train coming for some distance. I knew by the tables that I had not much time to spare.

I had got six of the heavy sleepers across the rails, when I thought I heard it coming, but I was mistaken. I dragged on another, and then I heard the roar; there was no mistake about it. I could see the lights flashing as I saw them in my dream. I am ashamed that I had not the strength of mind to wait until the last moment. I tried to, but I could not. I ran away up the embankment and crossed some fields. I saw some men coming and hid behind a hedge. I knew that detectives were about. I lay there panting, and was afraid they would hear me, but they passed on. I got back to my lodgings while it was still dark; nobody had heard me go out, and nobody heard me come back. That is all right.

Since writing the above I have been to the Wednesday evening service. The Vicar was to deliver an address. At the last moment I felt that I wished to preach on this awful accident and the lessons it must have for every one of us. I crossed over to the Vicar and asked permission to preach. He refused. I warned him that I intended to preach, and that if he attempted to occupy the pulpit he would do so at his peril. Then I suddenly seemed to see the matter in a different light and apologised to him.

However, I wish very much to address the village on the subject, and as I am not allowed to preach in church I shall call a public meeting on the recreation-ground. I must remember to get arrangements made as to the printing and posting of bills tomorrow.

This is All

It was a very hot summer day. The doctor's brougham had been waiting in the shade of the chestnut avenue leading to the big white house. Then a servant brought out a message.

'Morning, Jameson'—he knew the coachman. 'Stopping to luncheon—you're to go round to the stables.'

'I guessed as much. What—is he worse this morning?'

'No, not a bit of it.' Then, confidentially: 'Between ourselves, there's no more the matter with Mr. Wyatt nor there is with you nor me.'

'So, I've always supposed.' If you can be surprised at anything you will not make a good coachman. 'Well—see you again later.' And the wheels crunched slowly along the gravel.

In the meantime, Mr. Alexander Wyatt paced the entire length of his great library. He was lean, tall, bent in the shoulders. His hair was grey and rather too long; his face was clean-shaven and ashy in colour. He looked worried—hunted.

Dr. Holling watched him narrowly. The doctor was no younger, but his hair was black. He was a giant—his chest was broad and deep, and he stood six foot three in his socks. His face was slightly florid, and his figure showed some tendency towards corpulence. But he looked like a man of the world, and not like a mere sensualist—there was that distinction. Under the heavy brows were the eyes of a man who knows what he wants to know and is quite sure that he knows it. He looked confident and clever.

'My dear fellow,' said the doctor, 'the long and short of it is that you ought to have come to me long ago. I don't mean in Harley Street—I mean here at home. Of course, I wouldn't see any ordinary patient here; but an old friend like you—yes, really you ought to have come to me.'

'I might have gone up to Harley Street. It's only an hour away. You go there and back most days in the year, and I might have taken the

125

journey for once. I don't know why I didn't—I had thought of it—but you're always so busy.'

'Busy? Well, yes. But I don't let myself be so busy that I can't see a friend who's ill.'

Wyatt sighed heavily,

'And now you're spoiling one of your rare holidays for my sake. I say, old man, do take a fee—a proper fee—something in proportion.'

'Now, don't talk like that. If fees had had anything to do with it, could I have come to you and suggested that it might be as well if I just went over you? Besides, I wouldn't give up a day of my holiday for any fee. Why should I? I've already made more money than I shall ever spend. I'm not stopping because I've got a patient. I'm stopping because an old friend is ill.'

'It's very good of you—very, very good.'

'Come back to the point. Why didn't you send for me before—you must have known that you were ill?'

'I had my suspicions. I—I didn't want to think about it.'

'And so, you waited until, from mere casual observation, I also had my suspicions, and told you so. I think you were foolish. Come now: what were you afraid of? I haven't hurt you.'

'No, no,' said Wyatt. 'Of course not. But I didn't want to know that I was going to die.' There was a longish pause, and Wyatt's eyes grew rounder and stared. 'O, my God! O, my God!' he muttered to himself.

'Well?' said Dr. Holling.

He hated these exhibitions, but he spoke sympathetically.

'I can't die!' stammered Wyatt, 'It—it—it mustn't be.'

'You will find ultimately that you can die,' said Dr. Holling. 'We all shall. If you will persist in working yourself up into this condition of shivering cowar—of nervous panic, you will die rather sooner, or possibly very much sooner, than you otherwise would. Come, man, you may have another ten or a dozen years, if you'll avoid every kind of stress. You're wealthy, have no ambitions, have no hard work, are not passionately attached to anybody. It is highly unlikely that the stress will come upon you from the outside—take care that it does not come from yourself.'

'You're right, you're right. I shall pull myself together,' he said; but he still spoke excitedly. 'I—I only gave way for the moment. Ten or a dozen years at the least; with absolute moderation, quiet living, self-restraint, and so on, who knows that it might not be a score of years?'

The doctor looked at him curiously and said nothing.

'There, you see—I'm all right. I've faced the situation. And now tell me exactly what's the matter with me.'

'Heart,' said the doctor laconically.

'I know that,' Wyatt said irritably. 'I want to know the name of the disease, and if there's any complication.'

'Well, I shan't tell you. You'd try to look yourself up in your old edition of Roberts's "Theory and Practice of Medicine," and you'd find something more or less like yourself, and it wouldn't do you any good.'

'Some doctors would have told me.'

'Hang it! then, go and ask them,' said Dr. Holling quite quietly. 'Whomever else I meet in consultation, it's quite certain I won't meet my own patient.'

'Of course not. I only mentioned it. I'm not silly enough to go to any other doctor—never dreamed of it. Of course, I know very well that you're the first man on heart. I'm not so ignorant of medicine as you suppose.'

'Ah!' said the doctor cheerfully, 'I wish you were twice as ignorant, or else knew a thousand times as much as you do.'

Luncheon was announced. The doctor rose smiling. Poor Wyatt did what he could during luncheon to shake off the heavy depression that weighed on him, but he did not make much of a host. He could only talk of his own illness, and speculate on what death really was. On these subjects Dr. Holling had little to say, but he spoke of the rising value of land in the neighbourhood; and Wyatt was a landlord. Wyatt heard with a wretchedly simulated cheerfulness on his sad-eyed, sallow face. What would it profit him though he gained the whole world?

Wyatt had been in his day the brightest and best of companions; but when a man's material heart within him has taken on autumnal tints the man's spirits droop also. Both, the doctor knew, were symptomatic.

And he who knew this, and had known the old Wyatt, was patient; but when he was being driven away from the great white house, he became very sad.

★★★★★★★★★★★★

That afternoon Wyatt sat crouching in a big easy-chair in his library, alone. It was a hot day, but he had a shawl wrapped round his feet: latterly his feet had been always cold, as though already they felt the chill of wet earth. There was a pile of books on the table beside him, and on the floor. He turned avidly and restlessly from one to the other. There were comforting books of religion; there were terrifying books of religion; there were works of metaphysics; there were blasphemous diatribes; there was science conscious of its limitations.

Now he would take for company some drunken tinker jeering at the notion of a hereafter, repelling by its brutal ignorance but appealing by its complete self-confidence. And now again he would hear the calm voice of science: 'There are beautiful stories, but I dare not tell you that they are true. In some places, where it has been possible to test them, I have tested and found they were not true. As to the rest, those stories seem more beautiful than probable. I still wait for verification or disproof—not with folded hands, but working at other things.'

He had always feared death, and now for many long days and nights he had busied himself in this futile search for something certain about it. He heard a hundred voices all crying differently, and knew not to which he should listen.

He used to make attempts, from time to time, to pull himself together; he made one now.

'What does all this concern me?' he said aloud. 'I'm not going to die. Holling said so. Holling gave me twenty years, with reasonable care, and he knows what he is talking about.' He pushed the books aside contemptuously. 'Pack of nonsense!' He picked up instead a catalogue that his wine merchant had sent him. There was some port of a fairly recent vintage that he wished to put down. 'That's it,' he said, marking the catalogue with pencil, 'we'll say fifty dozen.' He rubbed his chilly hands together, and hummed a light tune.

At five his man Jackson brought him in a glass of whisky-and-water, carefully measured. Wyatt had got into the habit of drinking a good deal of strong tea in the afternoon while he pottered over his collections—one philatelic, the other eighteenth-century autographs. The doctor had forbidden tea, and Wyatt, even when he was pulling himself together, obeyed the doctor.

Holling had forbidden late hours also. Wyatt had induced—actually induced—the habit of insomnia. Before the doctor's interference he would never go to bed before two or three in the morning. After one of his own delightful dinners, or if he had been dining out, he would still sit up. He professed that these hours were of incalculable value— that he could not live in society unless for a little time each day he lived absolutely alone. All the lights were put out except in the library;

the rest of the house went to sleep. Wyatt smoked, read, thought about things. At intervals he sipped strong coffee. It was only when he found himself unable to keep awake that he lit his candle and went upstairs. Every night, or early morning, as his candle lit the long mirror on the landing, he saw himself reflected, and the reflection always came as a surprise. He never looked as he supposed that he looked; sometimes the reflection seemed almost unrecognisable.

'I can't sleep before three in the morning,' Wyatt had maintained to the doctor.

'Then it must be *morphia*,' said Holling.

He called that night with a hypodermic syringe, and that night Wyatt went up to bed at ten o'clock and slept at once.

'But I mustn't go on with *morphia*, of course,' said Wyatt knowingly.

'It won't be necessary,' said Holling. 'You see, after I've given it you for three nights, I shall have broken through your habit. Then you at once return to the normal state, and go to sleep at the ordinary time.'

The doctor reeled off this absolute nonsense with an air of the utmost gravity and conviction. He knew his patient. He had never given him any *morphia* at all—he had punctured the skin, but injected nothing. Wyatt's insomnia yielded completely to discreet and masterly humbug and the abolition of his after-dinner coffee.

Strong tea and late hours were quite given up now. Wyatt was positively anxious to give things up; in his mad terror of death, he had grown to regard it as a monster to be appeased by sacrifice. He had a notion—vague but deeply rooted—that the more he gave up the longer he would live. He was almost disappointed that the doctor did not forbid stimulants.

★★★★★★★★★★★★

Jackson, Wyatt's servant, had been with him for twenty years. When Wyatt was alone it was Jackson himself who made the after-dinner coffee—for on this point Wyatt mistrusted women. Jackson was a creature of habit. For over a week he had diligently remembered that coffee was forbidden. Tonight he forgot it; habit asserted itself, and twenty minutes after Wyatt had left the dining-room for the library, Jackson entered the library with the coffee. He was considerably startled at his reception.

Fits of deep depression sometimes alternate with fits of extreme irritation. Wyatt flew into a mad rage. He swore the wretched man was trying to kill him, ordered him out of the house, and abused him virulently, loudly, and at length. 'Go, go!' he shrieked finally.

Jackson conveyed the news to the kitchen that there was only one thing the matter with Mr. Wyatt—he was clean off his head, that was all.

As Jackson left the library Wyatt dropped into a chair, his face contorted, covered with sweat, bending forward, his hands tightly fixed against his chest. That awful anginal pain! No, it had never been like that before. It must mean death. Ah, if he could only get to that bell! He tried to call. The words, 'Dr. Holling. . . .at once,' came out in a whisper.

The pain ceased, almost suddenly. A strange calm came over him, and for the first time in many days he thought of other people. Dr. Holling? Of course, he would not send for him. It would be too bad, at that time of night—altogether too bad. Besides, it was his own fault. He had given way to temper, and had been punished for it. Why, he might have died. Upon his word, it would have served him right if he *had* died. Poor Jackson! It was the first time in his life he had spoken to Jackson like that. Well, when he came to die Jackson was remembered in his will, and would forgive him. After all, why live so long, at such care, with such trouble? Nature calls—obey cheerfully.

And the calm became drowsiness, and the drowsiness became sleep all very quickly. It was a lovely sleep, with a consciousness of well-being permeating its faintly-sketched dreams.

Jackson looked in at ten o'clock, at a quarter-past, at twenty-five minutes past, and at half-past.

Then he sought Mrs. Palfrey, the housekeeper.

'He's still asleep,' said Jackson.

'You're sure it's sleep?' said Mrs. Palfrey gloomily.

'Oh, I leave tomorrow, anyhow, whatever he says,' said Jackson. 'It's the responsibility I can't stand. It's wearing me. But come and see for yourself.'

They opened the library door cautiously and peered in.

'The top of his shirt-front's moving,' said Mrs. Palfrey in an undertone. 'He's asleep.'

'Don't he look awful? I 'on't wake him. I swear I 'on't wake him.'

'Better not. Put his candle on the table, by the lamp; cough, as if accidental, as you go out. Then if he wakes, so much the better. If not, we'll all go to bed, and you'll put the lights out, same as in the old days.'

Jackson shivered, and followed this advice carefully. The cough (as if accidental) was unavailing, and the lights were put out. Only in the library the lamplight fell on the gleaming shirt-front, still moving. And on the landing the full-length mirror waited, its eyes closed in the darkness, but ready to wake as the lighted candle came slowly up the staircase, and to reflect in a moment the figure of the master of the house, dishevelled, late, on his way to bed.

★★★★★★★★★★★★

He was awake. The lamp had burned itself out; the dawn, the early midsummer dawn, was already advanced; its light came, tempered yet sufficient, through the ugly Venetian blinds. From the garden and the country beyond came the shrill concert of innumerable birds. A heavy cart jolted and bumped to early work on some distant road. No, there was no need of the candle; he would go to bed by daylight, with that delightful sense of well-being, that firm conviction that there was no good in worry or argument, still comforting him.

Ah! how often at this hour he had trod the stairs, with a fantastic curiosity to see what he looked like in the tall mirror. By this time his head should have appeared in it, coming close to the Japanese cabinet. There in the mirror gleamed the pale gold of the cabinet, and there was the blue-and-white of the tall Oriental vase, and there were the masses of dark shadow beyond. Alexander Wyatt found all there but himself. Him only the mirror gave back no more. Back! back to the library as in a panic. Something has happened!

And there in the library the spirit of Alexander Wyatt, that the mirror saw not, found in the easy-chair the huddled body, dressed in clothes that no longer moved to the breathing.

'I am dead,' said Alexander Wyatt, 'and this—this—this is all.'

When That Sweet Child Lay Dead

It was quite a little room. The window looked out on a garden, on an orchard beyond it, and on the old quiet hills that had made the child understand what "far away" meant. She had heard, months ago, the bees monotonously, musically busy among the garden flowers; she had watched in the orchard the blossoms delicate with the fragile grace of immaturity, and when the autumn came, she had seen the boughs twisted and bent with their effort to do good, with their burden of fruit; she had strayed through the park-land; she had seen the sun set over the hills, when far up the sky went the touch of pale gold on clouds that were like angels' wings.

Her eyes had grown brighter, always, and her thoughts stranger as she watched; it had made her, the child of a musician, want to hear the music that in her serious moments had seemed to understand her best. She was not to see such things, nor hear them, nor understand any more. On this eve of the New Year, she lay motionless, arranged with white hands crossed, on the bed in one corner of the room; the trees in the orchard were gaunt and black, mocked by cruel winds; the snow drove and drove; the year's last day died out in darkness.

Everything in the little room—a little room in a great house—was very neat and orderly. Someone had taken away from the low table by the bedside the row of medicine bottles—grim reminders of futile effort—and had placed there an old blue-and-white bowl, full of Christmas roses. In the fireplace the logs burned brightly. She did not need the grace of the flowers nor the warmth of the fire any more. But someone had seen to these things—had done them from a sentiment; nearly all the best things that one does are done from a sentiment.

Flowers and fire were useless; but when that sweet child lay dead, to those in the great house all things had seemed useless. She had been very dear to all of them; they thought her lovelier, brighter, gentler than other children. Yet her chief charm was, perhaps, that she had returned their affection; she had loved people very easily—even unlikely people. Downstairs the servants who had waited on her were ludicrously pathetic; it was a chance whether one who had seen them would have laughed or felt like weeping. Two maids, who had known enmity from some jealousy about that child, now snuffled together in common sorrow, grotesquely genuine.

"And Mr. Richards feels it too," said one of them, "though it's little as Mr. Richards ever shows." Richards was the old butler, a stern man, made cynical possibly by too intimate a knowledge of the wine trade. He was in his pantry, polishing silver very briskly, almost jauntily; he caught sight of her cup, a christening gift; he recalled how she had once wrung from his sternness some slight concession about a new footman, really by no means up to his work; he began at once to whistle the gayest of tunes in a desperate whispered whistle, then stopped suddenly, made an involuntary curious sound in his throat, and went on polishing furiously. Later on, his manner grew icy.

From her room one could now have heard very faintly the sound of the organ being played in the wide gallery which ran from wing to wing of the house. It was her father, the great composer, who was playing. She had been his only child, and her mother had died in her babyhood. So, he was alone now. He had been saying that to himself during the day: "I am quite alone now." There were other people in the house, relations more or less near; but, as far as his sorrow was concerned, they were a hundred miles away. He had been happy, as some count happiness; he had loved his art and had been great in it; he had wealth, and could follow art for art's sake. Only he was human. and had not escaped human joys, nor the sorrows that follow them so closely; he had loved a wife and child, and he had lost them. That afternoon he had sat quite alone in his studio, thinking.

A salver, laden with letters, was brought into the room. He opened a few of the letters. They were all well-meaning; and yet so futile. He felt that he could read no more of them, and that he could not keep quiet and inactive any longer. He went up into the long gallery and paced up and down. Then he arranged the mechanism which blew the organ, and opened the instrument, and lit the candles on either side of it. The rest of the gallery lay in darkness. And then he sat down to play. The music was sorrow without consolation; religion without hope.

In the little room the flicker of firelight fell on the golden hair and delicate upturned face of that sweet child. Did it matter to the rest of the world—to things that are inarticulate, or even voiceless, and, as some think, inanimate? Were the flowers that she had loved sorry, or the winds that had played in her hair? Perhaps on that bleak eve of the New Year there was something said that one would not have heard as one hears a voice, which might through a dream have won its way to words. What did the Christmas roses think about it in that old blue-and-white bowl on the table by her side? Was it all nothing to them when that sweet child lay dead?

★★★★★★★★★★★★

It was sheer carelessness, of course, and had not been done with any evil intention at all. But that did not alter the facts of the case—his stem was not in the water, and he had felt a little wilted at the very outset.

Flowers choose their own names, and this one had called himself Wilkinson. He had seen the name on a scrap of newspaper that had been blown down the garden walk, and never ought to have been there, and was the under-gardener's fault. Wilkinson knew that owing to sheer carelessness his death would be hastened by some few hours; he did not mind the death (flowers, possibly from vanity, love to be cut and put in vases; and it is heaven to them to be worn in a girl's hair), but he did object to anything like carelessness. He liked people to do their whole duty. Even while selecting the name of Wilkinson, he had deprecated the untidiness of the under-gardener.

"Cut me and put me in a bowl, if you like," he remarked snappishly. "If you think me beautiful, you couldn't do any better. Only *do* it. Don't half do it. Don't leave me with my stem out of the water in this sickening way. If you do, you commit sin; and I can't bear to see it done." He was not addressing any of the other flowers in particular, he was merely soliloquizing on the subject of strict duty, which was an unpleasing habit that he had. No flowers care in the least about death, except the sweet violets, who have some mysterious love secrets of their own, never properly understood, which they do not like to be interrupted. Few flowers are quite so strict or quite so sharp-tempered as Wilkinson was.

"It wasn't *her* fault," pleaded a little bud, called Candor, who had been looking at the sweet child motionless on her bed.

"My dear child," said Wilkinson, rather patronizingly, "how very young you are! Anyone could tell you were a bud. Don't you know that sweet child's dead? She's no use—can't put flowers in water any more—so they'll throw her away. They ought to have thrown her away before, I should have thought; but human beings are always so careless and untidy."

"She's very pretty," said Candor; "very pretty indeed. I wish they had put me in her hair. Who was it placed us in this bowl? "

"Ah! yes. You were too young to remember it. It was Richards who put us here—and left my stem out of the water. How *mad* such thoughtlessness does make me! You're too young to be worn in a girl's hair. But Richards might perhaps have selected something-something a little more full blown. I don't refer to myself in particular, of course, although for the matter of that, as far as mature beauty is concerned—well, well, it's not for me to say."

"Death is very beautiful. Do human beings like to die?"

Wilkinson shrugged his petals impatiently. "What a perfectly bud-like remark! Death is *not* beautiful. Death is nothing. You simply stop, that's all. As you are generally feeling rather faded, you're not sorry to stop. But you're not particularly glad. It's pleasanter, of course, to die in a girl's hair than to live in a garden, especially where the under-gardener's so grossly untidy. I believe you have been talking to those violets," he added, rather sharply.

"No, really, I haven't. Why did you ask that?"

"They've got some sentimental ideas about death. No, I don't suppose human beings mind it. I don't see how they can mind a thing which is of absolutely no importance."

"They live longer than we do."

"They live an unconscionable time, most of them, especially under-gardeners. That is probably because they have not our advantages, and do not understand. That child has stopped rather early—yes, she is a sweet child. I can remember when I was quite a bud, she went past laughing. You should have seen the sunlight on her hair!"

There was a long pause. Candor spoke at last:

"Wilkinson, do you think anything *really* stops, or is it just seeming? She is so pretty, and you remember her laughter, and any flower would have been glad to die in that beautiful hair. It can't have all been to no purpose."

Wilkinson was distressed—deeply distressed. "You pain and grieve me more than I can say. The old faiths are all going. Have you not been taught to believe in the nothingness of everything? Why do you listen to the hideous voice of emotion?"

Candor grew almost passionate. "I *must*. If I did not listen, I should not know what to do for sorrow! She is lovely. She is an angel's dream—not dead, but come true at last. Sweet child, speak to me and tell me that I am right. Speak only once and tell me this trifling—this life and death-is not everything. Tell me that there is more beyond—beyond."

'You are sickly and heterodox," said Wilkinson sternly. "There is nothing beyond. I believe—nay, I know—that death is entire cessation. And I am going to drop."

He dropped fragmentarily. It is ordained that in its last moments even the tidiest flower shall be untidy. And Candor still waited; but all was silent in that little room.

★★★★★★★★★★★★

Now, the winds are spirits, lost spirits; they never rest, and they ever long for rest.

That night a great wind swept past the house, ice-cold and howling with misery. It beat on the windows of that little room until they shook; and then it went flying onward through the driving snow. After it came another, softly pattering, like the pattering of a child's feet as it shuffles through the crisp, fallen leaves. These two winds were spirits, without shape to human eyes; and yet a dreamer—a musician, perhaps, seated at the organ, alone with sorrow-might have imagined something. He might have seen them—the first like a gaunt woman, with flying robes and hair; the second like a girlchild, with an old man's malice and a devil's cruelty in her look, and to the dreamer their voices might have grown articulate.

"Perdita," said the young wind, as side by side they sped onward into the night, "did you not see as we went past the house? In one of the rooms a child is lying; a beautiful child, and she is dead; I shook the window to frighten her, but she never moved. Can I not do anything to hurt her? I hate all beautiful things."

"No, we can do nothing, Ira. I, too, used to hate as you hate, but with me it has worn itself out. I am tired, and cold, and miserable. But there is no rest—no rest anywhere. We can do nothing to hurt that child and nothing to help her. She is dead."

"I would help no one, but I would hurt her. Can we not reach her, even though she be dead? What is death?"

Perdita seemed now to be speaking to herself rather than Ira. It was a thousand years ago that they sent me here—they to whom a thousand years are but as a day. Beyond this world, beyond the tangle of which this world is a thread, I lived in broader space, in brighter light, in warmer, clearer air. I do not remember what it was that I did, but for my punishment they sent me here to roam forever up and down. For a thousand years I have never rested; I have seen the children of men grow up, and fall, and die; and I have found out many secrets; but I do not yet know what death is."

"I too," said Ira, "came from that place of which you speak. With me it was but a day ago; yet I, too, cannot remember what it was that I did. But I have been punished—punished until there is nothing left in me but hatred. I long to wreck the ships and tear down the trees. Nothing will make me happy any more, and I am most miserable when I destroy. Yet I cannot help longing to destroy."

"It does not matter," Perdita answered. "The longing will wear itself out. You may grow gentle and play with the flowers. That will not matter either. You will always be unhappy and you will never rest. Oh, if one could rest! If one could be still for a little while, only a little while!"

"In that great house the child that was dead was still—motionless. What is death?"

There was a pause—a long pause before the voice of Perdita spoke in reply:

"Can it be? Can it be that we are already dead? Can it be that the punishment of which we spoke was nothing else but death, and that death means the torture of endless unrest? Perhaps the spirit of that child is out in this lonely night, suffering as we suffer."

"I feared that you would say it," whispered Ira. "It is quite true. This night that child is with us. Did I want to hurt her? That was foolish of me." And Ira laughed savagely.

The two winds sped on together, past an iron coast, over a dark, desolate sea, and on and on. In the long gallery of the house the music was changed; into its sorrow had entered that tragic anger which knows its own impotence.

★★★★★★★★★★★★

The night had grown very quiet. The furious winds had passed; the sky had cleared. Over the wide lands lay the fallen snow. The child's father had risen from the organ and opened one of the windows. He stood there looking out. Perhaps it was because he thought of the gentleness of falling snow, or because its wonderful whiteness seemed almost like a conscious kindness; but as he looked out into the tranquil night his anger ceased. Far off he heard the flooded river sweep the base of the bridge, and the monotonous sound seemed to him like a consolation, like a consoling voice:

"I am glad because I draw near to the sea. I shall die, but I shall not be really lost. It is only change. I give myself to the sea, and in return I enter into its strength. The life of a man is but the bandage that blinds his eyes; and he shall never see the great secret until he himself is part of it. All the rivers run into the sea, and all the lives run into the life eternal. No gain is greater than that loss of self."

His own thoughts followed the voice of the river. Could it be that our identity, which we valued so much, was better lost? He had no patience to think the thing out, but he liked that idea of all the lives flowing into the life eternal. He found himself believing in the river's guess-work; or else he had grown tranquil under the tranquillity of the night; or else, perhaps, this quietness was but reaction following upon action, and the bitterness of sorrow had exhausted itself. He cared very little what the reason might be. He only knew that he was in some wonderful way consoled. Death was not annihilation. Death was not punishment. Death was just the loss of individuality and the gain of something far greater; something which possibly the saints thought when they spoke of perfect communion and of peace that cannot be understood.

He turned instinctively to symbolism and analogy. That thing for which lovers long—that total surrender of self to the beloved, which love ever desires and ever misses, is the gift that death has for us. By death we merge into that fulfilment which is past words.

And past music?

He turned once more to the organ—to that mysterious language that can be translated into no known tongue.

"And," said Richards, next morning, "as I stood at the fur end, he began to play. You won't believe me, Mrs. Smith, and I can't hardly believe myself, but it was one of the 'appiest toons I ever heard him play—regular light. Well, thinks I to myself, this is queer; and there, all of a sudden-like, 'e drops 'is 'ands and bends 'is 'ead low—this way—and begins sobbing-great, gaspin' sobs. I couldn't bear it. I come away. It was too awful!"

139

Locris of the Tower

1

I am by profession an architect. For the last eight years I have practised in my native town at Stannoke in Gloucestershire, at first in partnership with my father, and after his retirement alone and on my own account. The greater part of my boyhood was spent in Stannoke, and I have early recollections of the family solicitor William Locris.

Twenty years ago, I used to see Locris in church every Sunday morning. He sat with his wife, a rather heavy and plethoric woman, in the pew just in front of our own, accompanied by their son, a boy of my own age. Locris cannot have been more than thirty-five then, and his hair had not yet begun to turn grey. He assisted in the collection of the offertory, and throughout the service maintained an air of decent interest. His son sometimes fell asleep in the sermon, and so did I. My father always did, and, I think, made a point of it, but Locris was always wakeful and quietly attentive.

He had an office in the High Street and a villa outside the town—rather an abominable modern construction called "The Elms." He must have been fairly well off, for he had all the best of the business in Stannoke, but he was not reputed to be a rich man. He was regular in his attendance at business, and regular in taking walking exercise. He went away at the right time every year for his summer holiday at the seaside. If at that time, or indeed for many years afterwards, I had wished to express the quintessence of the commonplace, I should have described Locris.

I believe he was a fairly good, but not a brilliant, solicitor. He was honest and punctual and painstaking. He always discouraged litigation, and I owe him a debt of gratitude for having prevented my father from embarking on a very expensive and probably fruitless lawsuit.

I was quite a young man when Mrs. Locris died. I remember she was buried rather sumptuously, and that Locris and his son wore deep mourning for the prescribed time. I no longer saw him in church, for I had ceased to go to church, but I often saw him on his way there, carrying a prayer-book in his gloved hands. He wore black kid gloves, the most rancid form of gloves that has yet been devised. On weekdays I used to see him on his way to the office with the same loathsome gloves, but with a copy of the *Times* newspaper in place of the prayerbook.

Later, I came upon him two or three times in the course of business. I am inclined to think the man happy who seldom requires the services of a solicitor, and that good fortune was mine. When he had any work to do for me, I always found him able and practical, and his charges were fair enough.

Five years ago, when I was nearly thirty, and Locris must have been quite fifty, he called on me one morning at my office. He gave me a commission that was quite worth having, but it was of an extraordinary character. Looking at him now closely, I saw something in his eyes which seemed rather to belie the dull and even tenor of his life. I accepted the commission without hesitation, because, although the work was of a kind that I had never done before, I knew where I could get good advice. I had only to run up to London and see my old father about it.

2

My father had lived for by far the greater part of his life in a provincial town, but he preferred London. As soon as circumstances made it reasonable for him to retire and to hand over the business to me, he took a flat in Jermyn Street and went to live there. He had many friends in London and was a member of two clubs. He was glad enough to be free of routine work, but he was still interested in his profession, and was always glad to help me where his greater experience was useful.

We lunched together at his club, and then, in a retired corner of the smoking-room, he asked me what the trouble was.

"Well," I said, "I don't know that I should call it trouble. It's rather a nice little commission. But before we start on that I'd like you to tell me all you can about old Locris."

"Old Locris? Oh, damn it, James, he's not so very old. He's younger than I am. I've only known him professionally. We never had any social relations. He's all right, quite a solid man, I should say."

"Yes, I know that. You wouldn't call him romantic?"

"No, not now. There was a story when he was very much younger, before he married. He wanted to marry Sir Luke Mallow's daughter—Grace her name was. She was a pretty girl, with a lot of golden hair, the kind that you read about in story-books and never see in real life. They didn't think Locris was good enough, and I suppose from a social point of view they were right, though, for that matter, in spite of her beauty, it was not every man who would have married her. I wouldn't myself. The poor girl was short of one finger on her left hand. She smashed it up when she was a kid, and it had to be amputated."

"So, she chucked Locris?"

"No. She did not. He and Sir Luke were fighting it out together, and if Sir Luke did not give way, I fancy Locris meant to run away with her. He is an obstinate chap. However, while they were disputing, Grace settled the question for them by dying quite suddenly—diphtheria, I believe. There was a lot of it about at the time. And within a month Locris was married—daughter of a poor parson and very appropriate. So, it's Locris who has given you this commission, is it? Well, the money will be all right. He's never spent half his income. It's quite time he had a better house."

"And suppose I told you that Locris had gone mad?"

"Any man may. It's possible. In his case I should think it is extremely unlikely. Has he gone mad then?"

"Well, he says he has not. While he was talking to me, he made his scheme seem perfectly reasonable, but if he is not mad, he is at any rate extremely eccentric."

"Oh, come, come," said my father impatiently. "Let's have it. What is it the man wants?"

"Locris has bought land on the east coast not far from Aldeburgh. He wishes to do there what the old Duke of Portland did before him."

"I see. Rooms underground."

"Yes. One biggish room, forty by thirty, and a smaller anteroom communicating with it. From the anteroom is to be a flight of steps up to the surface, and the entrance is to be masked by a small tower with two or three living-rooms in it. Do you call that the project of a sane man?"

"If you wanted to do it yourself, I should certainly say you were insane. But I do not think so in the case of Locris. It is not unnatural in a man of a certain history who has come to his time of life. After all, there are days that one does not wish to see. Speaking frankly, the idea has occurred to my own mind before now. I have never done it, and never shall do it. But it is by no means without its fascination."

"That is very much the way in which he put it. In a year's time he means to retire and to leave Stannoke. And during that year this house is to be got ready for him."

"Is the construction to be secret?"

"I asked him that. He said he should make no effort at secrecy, as such efforts always attracted too much attention. He says that people will find their own explanation—that he wants an inordinately big wine-cellar, or something of that kind. In any case, before the tower had been built three years, people would have forgotten that there is this big room below it. I gather that he has chosen rather a lonely spot where he won't be troubled by many callers."

"Did he tell you in so many words what his reason was—why he is doing this?"

"No. But he said it was a thing which he had had in his mind for very many years past, and that he was glad now to have the opportunity to carry the idea out. You see, he is quite alone in the world. His wife's dead, and his son's away."

"The son," said my father, meditatively. "What's the boy doing?"

"Professorship of Greek in an Australian university—I forget which. I don't know what they'll make of him out there. He was an appalling prig."

"Yes," said my father. "I remember him. He was very, very Oxford. Well now, it seems to me you've got nothing to do but to go ahead. Excavation's a much easier job now than it was twenty years ago. I can't go into it now, because I've promised to play bridge. But we will dine at my flat and spend the evening over the plans afterwards."

"Oh, thanks very much, dad, that will suit me admirably. Meanwhile, I will go and have a look at the winter show at the Academy. Oh, by the way, on that question of secrecy—he did say that he didn't want the thing talked about in Stannoke, said it would be unpleasant to be bothered with questions, and that clients would regard him as a lunatic and leave him, and that this would have a bad effect on the value of his practice when he came to sell it. I don't think that anybody but myself knows that he means to leave Stannoke. Down in Suffolk, though, there is to be no secret about the excavation."

On my way to the Academy, I was greatly surprised to see Locris himself. He was coming out of a shop where they sell ecclesiastical furniture and vestments. He did not see me, but got into a cab and drove off. I wondered what he could be doing in a shop of that description, and reflected that it was quite possible that he intended to make some presentation to his parish church before leaving Stannoke.

3

During the next year I saw a good deal of Mr. Locris. He liked to be consulted about the details of the work which I had in hand, and he was not an unreasonable man; that is to say, he always gave me my own way in the end. His general principle seemed to be to spend as much money as possible on the underground rooms, and as little as possible on the tower, in which I presumed he would generally live. I did not ask him in so many words if there was any special purpose for which he needed these underground rooms. It might of course be an elderly man's weariness—the fact that, as my father put it, there were some days he did not wish to see, and another explanation also occurred to my mind.

I went up to "The Elms" one night to show Locris, at his own request, the estimates I had obtained for carrying out some elaborate metal-work. The servant, who showed me into the drawing-room, told me that Mr. Locris was in the laboratory. When he came in a minute or two later, I spoke to him chaffingly about this, and asked him if it was another new idea.

"Oh, no," said Locris. "Every man must have a hobby. The law is a very interesting profession, but it would interest me very much less if I did nothing else. I have been a student of chemistry for many years past in my leisure time."

"Going to invent a new poison?" I suggested.

"No," he said. "Something new, perhaps, but not a poison. Shall we get to business?"

In some ways Locris was a disappointment to me. He would not fit in at all with my preconceived idea of what a man should be like who builds himself an underground dwelling. I had to consult him about this time with reference to the renewal of the lease of my house. I wanted to get the renewal, and I did not want the rent to be put up. Locris managed it for me, showing tact and intelligence and all good business qualities in the negotiation. It was true that the law interested him. He would break off his examination of drawings of details for his new abode, in order to speak again of that lease. It contained one or two unusual clauses.

But at any rate I had this other possible explanation for his actions.

He was keen on chemistry and was expecting to produce some new discovery. Inventors are jealous people. He might perhaps think himself safer if his laboratory were underground.

He showed himself to be a kindly man. This was particularly the case with regard to poor old Simpson, the verger at the church which Locris attended. Simpson was a man of well over sixty, and incapable of doing any hard work. Rheumatism had compelled him to give up the grave-digging many years before. He was an intermittent drunkard. He had long spells of total abstinence, interspersed with brief bursts of intoxication. As a rule, he timed his breakdowns very carefully, so that they should not attract the attention of his employers. But on one occasion he had been found drunk in the churchyard, and he had now been guilty of a still more horrid delinquency. He had been found incapacitated by drink in the church itself, and had been promptly dismissed.

Locris was quite angry about it. He kept on repeating that Simpson was an old man and that there was no chance of his getting any other berth, and that it was a shameful thing to allow the one or two days when he had yielded to temptation to counterbalance his many years of faithful and effective service. It was plausible, but it did not prevail. Locris moved heaven and earth to get Simpson kept on, and Locris had a good deal of influence with the vicar. But the thing was too heinous, and the old man was turned out. It was expected, of course, that, as he had no one to support him, he would have to go to the workhouse. But Simpson did not go to the workhouse. He kept on his small cottage and worked in the scrap of garden which belonged to it. When questioned by the philanthropical or the curious, he maintained that he had private means. Most people guessed that Locris was allowing him a small pension.

In due course the work at Mangay near Aldeburgh was completed, and Locris sold his practice to a couple of young solicitors who were in partnership together. It was announced that he was about to leave Stannoke, and the vicar, in one of his sermons, made a very feeling and sympathetic reference to the impending departure. Locris found himself referred to as "one who has set such an excellent example, not only in the rectitude of his professional career and his private life, but also in his regular attendance at divine worship."

At the same time, the vicar did not know everything about Mr. Locris. He met me in the street one day and stopped me. "So sorry," he said, "you are to lose your friend Mr. Locris. He tells me that he is going to live in the country."

"That is so, I believe."

"But he did not happen in his conversation with me to mention what part of the country." "Oh," I said, "there's no secret about it, I believe. He's going to live in Suffolk."

I hurried on. Suffolk as a postal address is perhaps somewhat vague, but I do not like curious vicars. If Locris had meant to have told him everything, he would have done so himself.

4

For three years I never saw Locris and had no news of him. For a provincial architect I was doing fairly well in my profession. I specialised in bungalows and small houses, and had as much work as I could do. My father thought that I should leave Stannoke and come to London, and I was not altogether averse to making the plunge; but still, the local connection meant a good deal to me, and I did not want to lose it. Life at Stannoke went on with its customary placidity. Market-day was the one day in the week when we all of us seemed to be alive. And Sunday was the one day in the week when we all of us seemed to be dead. On the other days we were in a condition of mild lethargy.

In such a town very small things make a sensation. Sir Luke Mallow, son of the Sir Luke to whom my father referred, had an old cart-horse stolen from one of his fields. We talked about it for weeks, and our best policeman seemed practically to live on his bicycle. But neither he nor anybody else ever found the horse or the man who had stolen it. Then old Simpson sold his few sticks of furniture to a dealer one day, paid the three weeks' rent he still owed, and started off into the unknown. We talked a good deal about the fate of Simpson too. There were many theories, but alcohol and sudden death had their part in all of them. A week later, a touring company was unwise enough to visit Stannoke, and the sensation caused wiped out all recollections of Simpson.

And then a man, whose brother lived at Stannoke, decided to build himself a bungalow at Aldeburgh. I knew the brother, and I received the commission. I went down to Aldeburgh to spend some days over the business, and it occurred to me that I was within an easy drive of the tower where Locris lived. I managed to hire a dog-cart of sorts, and drove out there one afternoon.

I left my dog-cart at the one little inn in Mangay, and struck across the fields on foot towards the tower. I had mentioned at the inn that I was going to see Mr. Locris, and found that any interest which might have been taken in him, or his unusual dwelling, had entirely subsided.

"Nice old gentleman," said my landlord. "Wish I had his cellars. I could buy my winter coal in the summer then, and save a bit. There's a fine view, they say, from that tower of his. I suppose that's what he built it for."

"Do you see much of him?" I asked.

"Not to say much," the landlord admitted. "Sometimes when he's out for a walk he'll drop in here for a glass of bitter, but he's not been of late. He doesn't enjoy the best of health, they tell me, and—well, we're none of us so young as we were."

The tower had changed very little since I last saw it. As a piece of work I was not very proud of it. I could have made a good thing of it, but Locris had been very skimpy and ignoble about that tower. He would not let me have the materials I wanted. It seemed absurd enough too, when he was burying good black-and-white marble underground.

Greatly to my surprise the door of the tower was opened to me by old Simpson. He had resumed the suit of black broadcloth, with the boot-lace neck-tie, which had been his official costume as verger. He must have recognised me, but he gave no sign of it. He waited there like a stone image for me to speak. I asked if Mr. Locris was in.

"He is, sir," said Simpson, severely. "Kindly wait where you are. I'll enquire if he can see you."

He returned in a moment with the announcement that Mr. Locris would be pleased to see me, and showed me into one of the small living-rooms, where Locris sat writing at a cheap American desk. I noticed at once that he had aged very much in these last few years. He was more bent. He seemed to have shrunken.

He rose as I entered, and shook hands with me.

"It is strange that you have come," he said. "I had just written to you."

He showed me a sealed letter addressed to myself, which was lying on the desk, but he did not give it to me.

"The fact of the case is," he said, "that my son being out of England, I have made you the executor of my will. It will give you very little trouble. I hope you will not refuse to act."

I answered, of course, that I was quite willing to undertake the work, and made the usual banal observation that I hoped the time was still far distant for it.

"I should not say that," said Locris. "I am not well. I am far from well. Dr. Hanneford from Aldeburgh is coming up to see me tomorrow morning. However, I do not want to bore you about my health. I should perhaps tell you that by my will I am leaving you my land here."

"You will pardon me," I said, "but I don't think you should do that. I hope you will reconsider it. You have a son, you know, and I believe you have not quarrelled with him."

"I am on perfectly good terms with my son. I have been in communication with him on this very matter. He is quite content that it should be so. You must remember that these three acres represent a very small portion of my property, and that he will have the rest." He paused and looked at me very intently, as if he were trying to read my thoughts. "Are you wondering," he said, "what you will do with a house like this?"

He had guessed my thoughts exactly, but I told him that the idea had not occurred to me.

"I ask," he said, "because you will not have the house. You will have the land, but not the house."

"I don't understand," I said. "An explanation will be forthcoming. I may give it to you today perhaps—tomorrow perhaps—any day. If you have not received the explanation at the time of my death, it will be waiting for you in my writing. You will have the land, and you will not have the house."

At this moment Simpson brought in some very strong and bitter tea, and some untidy bread and butter. These are not things that I love precisely, but I partook of them meekly. I asked the old man if he found Simpson a useful servant.

"Simpson has been invaluable to me. From the domestic point of view, he is perhaps the worst servant that ever existed, but that is a matter of comparatively little importance. I am not a very particular man. Almost anything does. Nowadays I live principally on tea, and I fancy it is not very good tea, is it?"

"Since you ask me, it is a very low grade of Indian tea, and I should imagine that the continued consumption of it might have something to do with the ill-health of which you complain. Really, Mr. Locris, I think you ought to get yourself looked after better."

"I have thought so myself," said Locris, sadly. "Something perhaps must be done. But in any case, I must keep Simpson, because he is a faithful man and holds his tongue. You see? He goes down below with me, and he comes up with me, and he does what he is told, and no one hears anything about it. I am never bothered."

I could not quite make out to what he was referring. I suppose I looked puzzled.

"Yes," said Locris, suddenly. "Why not? Better perhaps on the whole. You shall have your explanation now. You shall come down with me."

I consented at once. I was human enough to be rather curious as to the use to which he had put these underground rooms. He rang the bell, and told Simpson to bring the lanterns. They were just ordinary candle lanterns of japanned tin. The spiral staircase which went up to the top of the tower also descended below the surface to the underground rooms. They were not very far down, the roof of them being twenty feet below the surface. We went through the iron gate and down the stairs together. Old Simpson went first with a lantern, and I followed him. Behind me came Locris with the other lantern.

The aspect of the anteroom seemed to show me that my conjecture had been right. It was fitted as a laboratory and looked as if it had been in recent use. Locris waved his hand towards the shelves and bottles. "What do you know about that kind of thing?" he asked.

"Nothing," I said. "It is not in my line. Is there anything very wonderful there?"

"Yes," said Locris, pointing to a bottle which seemed to contain some brown resinous powder. "That stuff in there is very wonderful."

I raised my hand to take it down and have a look at it, and found my arm struck down at once by old Simpson. Locris could see that I was angry, and hastened to apologise.

"Sorry," he said. "But Simpson was quite right. He had to do it in the interests of your safety."

"I don't see how my safety was concerned. It doesn't kill a man to touch a bottle. Did he think I was going to eat the stuff?"

"No, no," said Locris. "The thing is very simple. You asked me once if I was inventing a new poison. I told you that I was not. It would not interest me in the least. And besides, we have plenty of the old-fashioned poisons which do their work in a perfectly satisfactory manner. What I really have invented is a new explosive. There is a specimen of it in that bottle. Had you dropped the bottle, it would have been the end of all of us."

"Cheerful work," I said. "And the big room beyond? Is that a continuation of the laboratory?"

"Hush!" said Locris, impressively. "It is not. The room beyond is a tomb—a chapel of the dead. Come, Simpson, give me the keys. We shall show this gentleman everything."

I picked up one of the lanterns.

"We shall not need that," said Locris. "The chapel is always lighted."

Simpson was already pulling back the heavy sliding-doors between the two rooms, and I could see the bright light beyond. Simpson and Locris entered first. Locris went down on his knees on a fald-stool near the door, and Simpson, a grotesque figure, knelt on a hassock behind him. I myself stood for a moment in the doorway, astonished by the scene which I witnessed.

In the middle of this underground chapel there was erected a high *catafalque*, draped with gold and white. On the *catafalque* there lay in her white shroud the body of a young girl. Her hair, astonishingly golden and profuse, was loose about her shoulders. Her hands were clasped on her breast. As I looked at them, I saw what I had expected to see. The first finger of the left hand was missing. The face in profile, as I saw it, was very beautiful, and had not the yellowish waxy look of the face of a corpse. There was a tinge of colour in the cheeks. One could almost have believed that the girl was alive. On either side of the *catafalque* were three brass candlesticks, eight or nine feet in height.

Each of these candlesticks had seven branches. There were thick yellow candles in them, now burning low. The candle flames lit up the red jewels in a high cross that stood behind the head of the girl. A faint scent of incense still lingered in the air. The walls of the room were draped with white and gold, and but for those things which I have mentioned, the room was empty. Locris and the old verger remained kneeling in silence for perhaps five minutes, but it seemed to me a very much longer time. Then Locris arose, and both of them stepped backwards from the room, closing the heavy door behind them.

The silence was perfectly terrible. I wanted to speak, in order to break the spell of it, but found nothing to say. At last came the voice of Locris, almost in a whisper.

"Now do you understand?"

"Partly, I think. Let us come upstairs again."

As before each of the two men took a lantern, and I walked between them. Upstairs in the living-room, Simpson began to clear away the strong tea and the untidy bread and butter. I waited until he had gone, and then I turned to Locris. "How is this to end?" I said.

"Quite simple," said old Locris, rubbing his thin hands together.

"I shall know when my time has come, and it cannot now be long delayed. I shall go down to the chapel, and old Simpson with me. It is his own wish that he should not survive me. I shall have nothing to do then, but to start in the anteroom a little piece of clockwork apparatus. It is connected with that explosive which you have seen.

"In a few minutes, as we are kneeling there, the crash will come. All your good work will be spoiled, my friend. This tower will fall, and the rooms below it will be buried deep. You will have your simple explanation to give. You knew that I was interested in the chemistry of explosives, and that I worked at the subject in those rooms down there. You will say nothing more than this."

"Very well," I said. I was absolutely convinced of the man's insanity, and was wondering what was the best thing to be done.

"You see nothing unnatural in this, I hope," said Locris. "That, you know, is the only woman whom I have loved or can love. Life would have taken me from her, but I could have prevailed over the living. Death was too strong for me. When she died, I had no other aim in life but to do what I have done here. For that purpose alone, were all my years of work, and all the money that I made. For me there has never existed any other woman."

I ventured to remind him. "But you were married, Mr. Locris."

"Never," he said vehemently, "never! The man who passes as my son is not my son. I married his mother to save her from ruin, but there was in the marriage no more than the ceremony, and she understood that there never would be any more."

There were other questions which I might have asked him, but I thought it better to get away and take the necessary steps as soon as possible. I did not know, for instance, how he had managed to remove the body from the vault in the churchyard at Stannoke, but the strange alliance between him and the old verger might be at the bottom of this. The details of that removal I never did discover. But I learned that the body had been embalmed, and a doctor told me that the method of embalmment adopted would account for that slight tinge of natural colour in the dead girl's face.

****

I waited impatiently at the inn for my horse to be put in. My nerves were upset, and I left the man who was with me to do the driving.

"Back to the hotel, sir?" he said.

"No. You know where Dr. Hanneford lives? Drive there, and drive as fast as you can."

About two hours later Dr. Hanneford and three other men, of whom I was one, were driving in the direction of the tower. We had got within a little more than a mile of it when we heard the roar of the catastrophe. The horse in the cart shied violently and fell.

"We are too late," said Dr. Hanneford, as he got down to see to the horse.

The Woman in the Road

Henderson drove slowly. There were several small carts in the road, driven in the indolent, unintelligent, rustic fashion, and little groups of villagers. All were going in the same direction, turning in at the gates of the drive. Henderson had seen the notices of the sale by auction displayed on the outer walls of the garden. Everything apparently was to be sold, and everything included a motorcar. It might be worthwhile to look at it. Henderson wanted a more powerful car than the one he was driving, and there might be other things that he would like to buy. In any case these auction sales were frequently amusing.

A dealer came up to him as he stepped out of his car and asked if he could execute any commissions. He took Henderson to see the big motorcar. "Mr. Jasper only drove it about a month," said the dealer.

"Why is it being sold?"

"Everything is being sold. Mr. Jasper is a bankrupt and in prison now."

It was a modern, up-to-date, 36-h.p. car, and Henderson went over it with an engineer's critical eye and could find no fault. When his prolonged examination was finished, he decided that if it went for £400, he would buy it. He believed that it would fetch much more, but at these country sales one never knew.

He gave the dealer his instructions and the dealer bought the car for him for £95.

"Now then," said Henderson to the dealer, "tell me what's wrong."

"There is nothing wrong that a sensible person would take any notice of. These villagers get ideas into their heads. Mr. Jasper wasn't liked even before that thing happened, and—"

"Look here! What's this?" said Henderson. He unwound a few long black hairs that were entangled in the acetylene lamp.

"Bless my soul!" exclaimed the dealer. "They must have come from the woman that he killed."

"Ran a woman down in the road, did he? How was that?"

"He was bad-tempered always, and that day he was drunk too. I suppose she didn't skip out of the road fast enough for him."

"Why didn't you tell me all this before?"

"I supposed you knew it. Everybody about here knows it. Why, it was because of what she said just before she died that no one would bid today. She said that she knew she was going to die, but she was not done with that car yet. She was a gipsy, and some people think that gipsies can foretell things. It's all stuff and nonsense to my mind."

"It's absolute stuff and nonsense. Why didn't you buy the car yourself? You might have made money on it."

"Might, or might not. It's not my line of business. I know nothing about motors, and I've got no capital to put into a thing like that."

A few days later Henderson got his big car home. He was delighted with it. He liked to feel the great power under him and to compare the pace at which he could take the steepest hills now with what he had been able to do on the smaller car. This smaller car he sold for considerably more than he had paid at the auction, and on the whole he considered that it had been a very good day's work for him, and blessed the superstitions and prejudices of ignorant people.

★★★★★★★★★★★★

The rest of the story came out in the evidence which Henderson's driver, a Frenchman who spoke no English, gave at the inquest. The interpreter was asked more than once by the coroner if he was quite certain that he was giving the man's evidence correctly. The evidence was that Henderson was driving fast on a straight stretch of road with nothing in sight. There was a stone wall' on his left. Suddenly Henderson gave a loud cry, pulled the wheel hard over to the left, and dashed into this wall.

By some miracle the Frenchman was not injured in the least, and he did the best he could for his master, who lay unconscious. In a minute or two Henderson opened his eyes and spoke. He said, "Did we go over her?" The driver told him there had been nobody there. "Of course, there was," said Henderson. "She jumped out suddenly into the middle of the road, right in front of the car—a swarthy sort of woman, looked like a tramp." He tried to say more, but again became unconscious, and died in a state of unconsciousness an hour later,

Exchange

1—DORIS

There was once a girl-child named Doris who went out skating with her bigger brothers one afternoon over flooded fields in the Fen country. But her brothers played hockey with school-fellows, and Doris skated contentedly enough by herself. She was wearing Bob's skates, which she liked better than her own, and the man had put them on very well indeed. She went from one field through a gap in the hedge into the next, and then on into a third field. There were very few people here, and most of the ice was not swept; all of this was very pleasant to Doris, and made her feel adventurous. It was beautiful, too; and even children unconsciously understand a sunset with those old thin trees trembling black against the crimson disc, and everywhere bits of white brightness on a grey sea of fog. She skated as fast as she could, the wind helping her, feeling strangely and splendidly animated, when quite suddenly. . . .

★★★★★★★★★★★★

But this was not the Fen country. This was the north of Yorkshire. She had been here before on a visit to her cousins. Yonder was the top of Winder; she had climbed it on clear days and seen Morecambe Bay flashing in the distance. But it was night now—almost a black night, and it was very cold for Doris to be wandering over those hills alone. She had an irritating sensation that she had to go somewhere before the dawn came, and that she did not know where or why. It was lonely and awesome. "If I only had somebody to speak to, I shouldn't mind it so much," she said to herself. At once she heard a low voice saying, "Doris! Doris!" and she looked round.

In a recess of the ravine which a ghyll had made for itself as it leaped from the cold purity of a hill-top to the warm humanity of a village in the valley—a village no better than it should have been— a small fire of sticks was smouldering. Doris could just see that the person crouched in front of the fire-the person who had called her by her name—was an old, haggard woman, with her chin resting on her knees.

"Tell me, old woman," Doris said almost angrily, "what does this all mean? I was at Lingay Fen skating, and now I am wandering over the Yorkshire hills. It has changed from afternoon to night—"

"It generally does," said the old woman in a chilly, unemphatic way. Doris stamped her foot impatiently. "I mean that it has changed quite suddenly. Just a moment ago, too, I felt quite certain that I had to go somewhere, and I had forgotten where. Now I don't think I have to go anywhere."

"No—you have arrived," said the old woman softly.

At that moment a dry twig burst into flame, and lit up the old woman's face and figure for a second. She was hideous enough; her face was thin and yellow; her cavernous eyes sparkled to the momentary flicker. Her dress and cloak were torn and faded, but they had been bright scarlet.

"You naturally ask why," she continued, "because you are young and have not yet learned the uselessness of it. What has just happened to you seems very meaningless and foolish, but it is not more meaningless and foolish than the rest of things. It is all a poor sort of game, you know. Explain? No, I shall not explain; but it was I who brought you here. Sit down by me under the night sky, and watch."

"No, I will not," said Doris, and walked away.

She took about ten paces away, and then came back again and did the very thing which she said she would not do. She sat down by the old woman, and was a little angry because she could not help doing it. Then she began to grumble at the fire. "That's not half a fire," she said; "it just smoulders and makes smoke. I will show you what you ought to do. You put on some fresh sticks—so. Then you put your mouth quite close to the embers, and blow and keep—on—blowing. There!" She had fitted her actions to her words, and now a bright flame leaped out. It shone all over, on her dark hair and dark bright eyes, and on the grey furs of her dress. It shone, too, on the old woman, who was smiling an ugly, half-suppressed smile.

"Doris," said the old woman, "leave the fire alone. I do not want flame. I only want it to stream forth smoke."

"But why?"

"See now—there." The old woman made a downward gesture with both hands, and the flame sank obediently down again, giving place to a quick yield of black smoke. "Look at the smoke, Doris. That is what you have to watch." There was a little more energy in the old, quavering voice now.

Doris did as she was told; but suddenly she stopped and cried, half-frightened, "There are faces in it!"

"Yes, yes," said the old woman, almost eagerly; "and there are pictures of the future in it—of the future as it will be unless I alter it this night. I alone can alter it, you know. Are you not glad now that you came?"

"It is something like fortune-telling; did you ever have your fortune told?"

"No, I never did," replied the old woman. Her smile was very ugly indeed. "But how shall I know that it's true?"

"Why, you *do* know."

That was the strangest part of it. Doris felt certain without having a reason that she could give for it. "Show me my future," she said breathlessly.

"Watch the smoke, then."

So, she watched, and picture followed picture. At the first of them she made some little exclamation. "Ah!" she cried, "that is a splendid dress; and I *do* like those shoes. I wish I might have long dresses now—I'm sure I'm old enough; and I want to have my hair done up the proper way, but—" She stopped suddenly, because the picture had changed. "I look much prettier in this one," she said. "I have been dancing, I think, from the dress, and because I seem a little out of breath. There is a man with me, and now he—no, no! I would *not*. I should hate it. That picture cannot be right!" The third picture represented her marriage with great splendour. "Well," she said, "I do not mind that so much—just standing up and wearing a beautiful veil. But I don't want to be married at all. I like skating ever so much better."

There was a faint sound of laughter, muffled and bitter, from the old woman. "You like skating?" she said. "Where are your skates, then, Doris?"

Doris looked for them, but could not find them, and this distressed her. "Oh, what *shall* I do? They were not my skates; they were Bob's."

"Who is Bob?"

"Bob is my smallest brother—ever so much younger than I am; he's my favourite brother, too. He's got red hair, but he's a pretty boy."

"He must be a milksop if he can't skate."

"He *can* skate. He can do the outside edge backward; he skates bet-

159

ter than any of my three big brothers."

"Well, well—it's a pity that he's stupid, though."

"Stupid? Do you know why he lent me his skates? Because he was going to write a story this afternoon, and he's going to put me in it. Bob can do almost anything. He's wonderful. When he grows up, he'll very likely write a whole book, he says."

"Look at his future—Bob's future—in the smoke," said the old woman grimly, heaping on more sticks.

Doris looked reluctantly. The pictures came flashing past one after the other. Some she could not altogether understand, for she knew nothing of the vices of young men; but they were vaguely terrible. But even a child could understand the last picture of all. It was awful and vivid. She almost fancied that she could hear the report of the pistol, and the dim thud as the body fell awkwardly on the floor.

"You needn't cry," said the old woman, as Doris burst into tears.

"Oh! Bob is so splendid," sobbed Doris. "Don't let it be like that. Do alter it. You don't know him or you would change it. You said you could. I'll give you everything I've got if you'll stop it somehow."

"Will you give me your beauty—your youth—your life?"

"Oh, willingly—everything!"

"I want none of them—none of them," said the old woman fiercely and quickly. "But I want something else. Give it me, and I will alter it as you wish." She stretched out a lean finger and tapped Doris' forehead, and whispered a few words in her ear.

Doris turned white enough, but she nodded assent. "Then it will alter my future, too," she said with a little gasp.

"It will alter the future of everybody in the world—indirectly and in some cases very slightly. But you will give it me?"

"Yes, yes."

She paused a moment, and then added a torrent of questions: "Old woman, who are you? Why are you dressed in scarlet? Why did you have me brought here? I should like it to turn out to be a dream. Oh! why do you want it? Why are you so horribly—horribly cruel?"

But the old woman, and the fire, and the great dark hills grew dim and indistinct; and there was no answer.

★★★★★★★★★★★★

The two old men—one with a medical, the other with a military air—came slowly down the broad staircase from the bedrooms without speaking. The little red-headed boy was waiting for them as usual. "Is Doris any better, papa?" he asked eagerly. "Will she live?"

It was no good to keep it from him; he would have to know sooner or later.

"Yes, Bob," said the colonel, "she will live. But the—the injury to her head has—" He stopped with a gulping sound in his voice. The boy looked up at him wistfully with a scared face.

Don't, colonel," said the doctor; "you'd better leave it to me. I will tell the boy."

2—MAJOR GUNNICAL

Nobody ever denied in my presence that Major Gunnical was a capital shot and a good fellow. He went straight, and it was always imputed to him for righteousness. But the other day the only man of the world with whom I am acquainted accused the major of want of taste, and based his accusation on the fact that he took the liberty of dying in the country-house of a friend, not having been invited for that purpose. I might have pointed out that Major Gunnical knew Sir Charles quite well enough to take a liberty which would have been unpardonable in a casual guest; I might have added that it was one of those accidents which may happen to any man, and that it was unintentional and unforeseen on the major's part. But I prefer to give the facts of the case, which seem to me to explain everything.

On the evening which opened the night of his death, Major Gunnical had gone upstairs to dress sooner than the rest of them. He stood in his bedroom with his back to the fire, well knowing that if the back be warm the whole body is warm also. He was half-afraid that he had caught a chill, and chills affected him. There was nothing in his appearance to tell you that his heart was wrong. His body was large and muscular, and he looked a strong man.

His hair had only just begun to get a little grey. His complexion was pale, but it had been tanned by hot suns and seemed clear and healthy. His eyes were thoughtful grey eyes-quite out of keeping with the active look of the man. His best point was his simple directness; he could do right things, even when they were not easy, without thinking of them at the time or afterward. His worst point was his temper, which broke loose occasionally. At the present moment he was thinking about himself, which was not a usual occurrence with Major Gunnical, and his thoughts were depressing; so, he tried to dismiss them. "It's all nervousness and too much tobacco," he thought to himself; "but I will go up to town tomorrow and let old Peterson prescribe for me. I shall be all right in a day—probably only liver—no exercise, thanks to this cursed frost. Oh, yes, it's just liver—nothing else."

He paused once when he was fastening his collar, and said slowly and distinctly, "Damn presentiments." But he was not able to shake off a feeling of quietness: a desire to be at peace with men and a tendency to look at the sad side of things. When he got downstairs, he found only one man already in the drawing-room—a man called Kenneth, who wrote. Now there was a certain disagreement between Kenneth and the major. In the smoking-room the night before, the major had expressed his sincere admiration for a certain story of soldier life by a new writer, and Kenneth had explained to him that this admiration was wrong, because the story was not at all well-constructed.

"I own," he had said, "that it takes a critic to see the faults of the technique." This was a little vain of Kenneth. "Yes," said the major hotly, "and it takes a *man* to feel the merits of the story." This was a little rude of the major, for Kenneth was obviously an effeminate person. Kenneth put up his eye-glasses and looked at the major curiously. "Don't be so damnably affected," said the major. Then Sir Charles had interposed lazily.

Consequently, when the major entered the drawing-room Kenneth at once began to assume more dignity than Providence had made him able to carry easily. The major walked up to him and held out one hand. "Look here, Kenneth," he said, "I'm an old fool, and always thinking I know another man's business as well as my own. I'd no right to question your opinion last night and make an angry ass of myself. I'm sorry."

Kenneth's dignity came down heavily, and he took the major's hand at once. For a fortnight he loved him, and then he told publicly the story of how he had gone to the major and forced him to apologise. For there is a combination of imagination and vanity which nothing—not even kindness—can kill.

The major was very dull at dinner, but when his host's two children came in afterward, they seemed to find him very satisfactory. The major loved children. He did not stop very long in the smoking-room that night. He wanted badly to be alone.

For some time after he had gone to bed, he lay awake thinking. Maude, his host's elder daughter, reminded him in appearance of his own niece Doris. It seemed hard that Maude should be so bright and happy, and that Doris—owing to a skating accident—should be condemned to lose all her brightness, and her flow of talk, and her power to understand. Yet Doris never seemed actually unhappy; her eyes were vacant, as if the light behind them had gone out, but she did not seem to be suffering. During the first part of her illness, she had babbled about some woman, an old woman dressed in scarlet, who frightened her.

Thus thinking, the major fell asleep. It was long past midnight when he opened his eyes and saw a figure of a woman standing on the hearth-rug, and stretching yellow hands like claws toward the remnant of the fire. It startled him, but he did not want to wake up the rest of the house.

"What are you doing in my room?" he said in a rapid whisper.

The old woman turned round. He could hardly see her face, but the flicker of the fire showed him that she was dressed in rags of faded scarlet. Her voice was very gentle and low.

"Awake? Are you awake? I made a little noise to wake you on purpose. But generally, they go on sleeping when I come. I am the scarlet woman of whom Doris spoke. She has been taken."

"Dead? A merciful deliverance."

"No, she is not delivered yet. She has to go through life again in a lower form before she is delivered. I hate her. I will see that she is unhappy again before she is delivered."

"Why does this all seem real instead of seeming fantastic and absurd—as it ought to?"

"Because it *is* real; but they always ask me that, all those who see me. Doris shall become a caged bird, I think—one of those who are driven nearly mad by captivity and yet are so strong that they die slowly."

"You can't do that," said the major quickly.

"You know I can, and you know I shall," replied the old woman in the same soft whisper. I need not argue, or prove, or do anything of that kind. When I speak men *know* that all is as I say; but they do not often hear me, because they are nearly always asleep when I come."

"Where is Doris now?"

"She waits in dreamland, where nothing is real, until I get my opportunity, and she is born once more, and caught, and caged, and tortured."

As she said this, she seemed to grow a little more excited; and, as if in sympathy with her, the fire suddenly burned up more brightly, and showed her horrible, lean face, and deep, leering eyes.

"That's cruel," said the major. "And what shall I be when I die?"

"You will not have a bad time," she said, grinning. "You shall be a dear little white lamb that lives an hour and then is delivered. You will die tonight, by the way. But Doris shall beat her heart out against bars, because I hate her. You will see one another in dreamland, while you are waiting until I get the two right opportunities."

An idea occurred to the major. "Change us, Doris and myself."

The old woman trembled with agitation, and her voice rose shrilly. "I will not! I will not!" she cried.

But something bright and sure, like a steady light, seemed to fill the man's mind.

"But you will—you cannot help it," he answered very quietly.

The old woman strode quickly across the room, her face aflame with rage, and touched him on the heart. He fell backward, and did not speak any more.

"I must always come when they are asleep in future," said the old woman, as she went back to the fire. "It is too much to risk—I have lost by Doris and this man."

There was a long pause. "But I will torture him even more than I would have tortured Doris," she whispered gently to the fire.

☆☆☆☆☆☆☆☆☆☆☆☆

Two months afterward a white lamb was born, in a sheltered place, on a grassy fell. And in an hour, it died.

And on the same day a certain bird-catcher, resident in Whitechapel, went out early and had luck.

3—DORIS IN THE HEREAFTER

The release had come at last. To Doris it was an exquisite release; the years spent in darkness were over; the short, mystical period which followed her death was over; her spirit went out into the moonlit night—white, naked, beautiful. She could remember but little consciously of her earth-life. She had suffered—she could recollect that, and she had spoken with a grim woman an old woman dressed in rags of faded scarlet. She did not recollect what had been said, but she knew that it had been the beginning of the darkness which had fallen on her mind. Of her death she knew nothing; of a short strange time after her death, she knew a little, dimly and vaguely.

She was free, and it was enough for her. It seemed to her that she still kept the body which had been called Doris during its earth-life, but that now it was light as the air, stronger than before, and far more beautiful. She stood, a childish figure, graceful and erect, on a shred of dark cloud which a steady night wind blew past the hill-tops and over the valley. Below her she could see the flooded river, angry with its old stone bridges, crying itself to sleep in long, still reaches, with the mists rising white all about it. She saw, too, much that the living do not see.

In a lonely cottage, low and roughly built, some young spring flowers had just died; she saw their souls—their fragrance, as she had been used to call it—pass upward; and as they passed, they changed and became a handful of ghost-lilies in the garden-land of dreams. And all night long she went on her way, seeing beautiful things. She could never be tired anymore; and the rain and the dew did not hurt her; and the cold wind did not seem cold her.

And when the morning came, a little baby breeze came up to her with a message. It was so young and forgetful that it had not got the exact words of the message. But it remembered the drift of it. "He said you were to go and look for sorrows," it whispered in her ear. It lingered for a moment, playing with her hair, and then it went down below and tried to blow a dandelion clock. And not being strong enough, it sat down and sulked; for it had not yet learned that the only things worth doing are the things one cannot do.

Then Doris went on about her work, very happy, singing little songs that she remembered. And first of all, she went to a great house where a proud and beautiful lady lived. But the proud lady sat huddled up and quite undignified in her own room, crying till her nose was red and she was not pleasant to see. And all because someone or other—I think it was her husband—was dead, and was going to be forever happy! Doris laughed contemptuously, and passed on.

She next went to a nursery where there was a little freckled girl with sandy hair. And the little girl was unhappy because of a bad accident to a ninepenny doll, which was her most intimate friend. There was a small hole in the doll's neck and a possible escape of sawdust. It was only by holding the doll wrong way up and shaking it that you could make the sawdust come out; and the little girl did not want the sawdust to come out at all, for it caused her agony when it came out; and yet she held the doll upside down and shook it. For this was the kind of girl that, when she grows up, becomes a woman. Doris was sorry for her, and whispered in her ear, "You had better get a little piece of stamp-paper and stick it over the hole in the doll's neck—but it won't last long."

The child thought Doris was a beautiful idea, and went radiantly to the study and opened the despatch-box. There was no stamp-paper. There was one penny stamp, and she knew that it was wicked to take it. So, she compromised—which was feminine of her—and tore the stamp in two and only took half of it. Then she went back to the nursery, and fixed the half-stamp as Doris had suggested. Doris, who had watched her, was horrified. "You ought not to have taken that stamp," she said to her. "You had better confess what you have done, and say that you do not wish to tell a lie." Then the little girl supposed Doris was conscience—for, of course, Doris was invisible—and did not think quite so much of her. Neither did she confess. Doris was not very unhappy about it, knowing that children are always forgiven and occasionally forgotten.

She saw many other sorrows and she thought very little of them. People, she perceived, always exaggerated the importance of death, and money, and love. Yet she saw a wind—a venomous wind—snap the stalk of the very loveliest daffodil, and nobody wore black clothes for it, or had sherry-and-biscuits, or showed any of the signs of sorrow. She had only been for a few hours in the Hereafter, and yet she already felt herself to be out of touch with humanity.

And it happened that she came to a great dirty city, and she stopped where a cage of wicker-work was hung outside a grimy shop in a grimy street. There were several things in the cage: a yellow glass for water with no water in it; a blue glass for seed with no seed in it; something which had once been a turf and now looked like a badly cooked brick; and something which panted on the floor of the cage in the corner—it was all that was left of a bird, a soaring bird that loved the upper air and the sunlight, but was now reduced to plain dying and high thinking. Now none of the other sorrowful persons had seen Doris; but the bird saw her and called to her, but she did not understand the language. She went into the shop and whispered to the man in charge, "Your bird outside wants attention; it's ill."

"Bless my soul! and I gave a shilling for it!" So, he took the bird some water and something to eat which was not good for it. The bird chirped. "It knows me and loves me already," said the man. It was really saying, "Would you kindly wring my neck, and end this?"

"I am sorry for it," said Doris, as she passed on. "I am glad I was never a pet. She would have been more sorry if she had known all the history of that bird.

An Exchange of Souls

CHAPTER 1

I met Daniel Myas first in the winter of 1905, at Hamilton's house, in Paris. Hamilton married a Frenchwoman, and they lived in Paris for the greater part of the year. They were both terribly musical, and musicians of many nationalities came to the house. Conversation, on the days when *Madame* received, was tryingly polyglot for a plain Englishman like myself.

As often happens at a first meeting, one received an impression which was in part erroneous and in part short of the truth. Until he spoke to me, I thought that Myas was a Frenchman. His necktie was aggressively French. It was bulgy and droopy and black silk. He used a little gesture. He had been speaking French to my hostess, and with a perfection that in an Englishman was almost unpatriotic. But he spoke English to me, and as only an Englishman can ever hope to speak it. It was not only a question of a perfect accent; he knew the latest phrases of the society in which he was moving.

His talk with me was principally on the subject of the Paris restaurants; he seemed to have made a special study of the art of dining, and as a result of the experimental work he had slightly sacrificed his figure. He gave me the impression that I had much to learn. He was rather under the medium height and powerfully built. His eye was vivacious and his expression kindly. I noticed his hands particularly; they were rather too white and well-shaped.

Just as I was leaving, I had a few words with my hostess about him. *Madame* was always amusing, but not always accurate. She told me that I had been talking to a great savant. No, he was not always so sweet-tempered as he appeared. For example, he always swore at his manicurist; but then he sent her sweets from Rumpelmayer's to make up for it. If he interested me, would I not meet him at dinner there on the following Wednesday? It further appeared that somebody with a name like a tropical disease would be playing the 'cello.

I accepted, and in this way began an acquaintance which I wish that I had never made. I say that deliberately. I liked Myas. I hope that this story will show that when he became my friend, I accepted the duties of friendship. But he led me into, a track where I was mazed and lost.

In the course of the next month, I saw Myas frequently. He knew Paris well, and showed me much that I had not seen before. He was generally interesting, and sometimes astounding. One day he happened to speak, with a flash of that temper which *Madame* had led me to expect, of the extreme narrowmindedness of medical men.

"Well, you are a medical man yourself, aren't you?"

"Oh yes," he said. "As a matter of fact, I am an M.D. of London, and at one time had a practice—a beastly practice in a beastly Somersetshire village. But as soon as I was in a position to give it up, I did so, and that was two years ago. I came into some money on my father's death."

"I see," I said. "And as soon as you became independent, your interest in medical science ceased."

"Goodness, no! You might almost say that was when it began. It is that which has kept me wandering round the foreign hospitals for the last two years. Research is absolutely lovely work. As a rule, it leads to nothing; when it does lead to anything, you get punished for it. You think you have found out something, you send a communication to the scientific press, and you metaphorically get your head bashed for your pains by your distinguished and learned colleagues. But don't try to look as if you were interested in science. You can't be, you know. You belong to the leisured classes. Come along, and we will lunch at Ledoyen's."

"If I belong to the leisured classes, that is more my misfortune than my fault. I'll tell you all about that one of these days. What was your line of research, and who jumped on you?"

"Somebody or other on the *Lancet*. I should imagine from the style and knowledge displayed, that the office-boy is allowed to do a little reviewing in his spare time. Well, well, it's a lesson to me. Never show children or fools half-finished work—there's no better proverb than that."

He was by way of making a joke of it, but it was quite obvious that in reality he was very sore about it, and for this reason I did not press him further on the subject.

168

It was my last day in Paris, and as we were smoking the post-luncheon cigarette, Myas asked me when we could meet again.

"Don't know. Soon, I hope. Do you ever come to London?"

"Of course. Everybody does. I am not quite sure, but I think my work will send me there in the spring."

We arranged that he should come to see me then at my little flat in St. James's Place.

"And by that time," he said, "I may be able to answer you more explicitly about my work."

"Quite likely," I said. So far, of course, he had not answered me at all.

The day after my return to London, I happened to meet at the Club an old friend of mine, Dr. Habaden. He is a mighty physician, with a right to put a decoration on his evening coat on suitable occasions. I asked him if by any chance he knew a Dr. Myas.

"Daniel Myas.?"

"That's him," I said, with the usual disregard of grammar.

"Yes, I know of him. As a student he did rather brilliantly. Got a resident appointment at his hospital. Quarrelled with everybody about everything, and had to go. Then he bought himself a practice, and that was how I came across him. He brought a patient up from Somersetshire to see me. I don't mind telling you that it was a devilish difficult case, and I found that Myas had diagnosed it correctly and treated it correctly."

"Did the patient recover?"

"No; died. But that's got nothing to do with it. He impressed me at the time as a very able man, quite beyond the run of the ordinary general practitioner. He's given up practice and taken up research now, and he's gone absolutely off the lines. You should see the kind of stuff that he's been writing. A ghoulish business, I call it."

"Ghoulish? How do you mean? What is it he does?"

"Dr. Daniel Myas is making a special investigation of the moment of death. You understand? He makes observations of dying people. When the thing is practically over, and a decent man would go away, down swoops Myas with his ophthalmoscope and his electro-cardiograph and all the rest of his bag of tricks, like a scientific vulture. I should suppose he's watched more deaths than any man living. Does his work abroad principally. And if the truth's told, he has tried some rum-funny experiments, too—things that would never be tolerated in any hospital this side of the Channel."

"I met him in Paris, you know, just the other day. He didn't tell me that he was interested in death, and I should have said he was much more interested in his dinner. In fact, he didn't impress me as a ghoul at all."

"Oh, I don't say he's a ghoul in ordinary life. He probably wouldn't talk shop to you. It's the man's work that is ghoulish."

"I thought that science had declared all research to be good, and that in the sacred cause of truth nothing was to be considered horrible or disgusting?"

"Yes, that may be so if the research is directed to any useful end. But what good do you suppose Myas is doing? He is simply wasting time. We know what life is and what death is."

"Do we?" I asked.

I knew the question would irritate Dr. Habaden, and it did.

"If you think you're going to lure me into one of your profit-less metaphysical discussions, you're mistaken, my friend. The medical man knows when life ends and death begins, and in the case of a patient who is past remedial aid that is all he needs to know. There is plenty of good work to be done, and as Myas has the time and the means he might just as well devote himself to it. What is the aetiology of disseminated sclerosis? What's the morbid anatomy of paralysis agitans? That's the kind of thing he ought to be telling us. Cancer isn't settled yet. I could name fifty things that might employ him usefully. He prefers to worry the last moments of poor devils for whom neither he nor anybody else can do anything. It's sheer perversity, and I hate to see a man of his abilities so much misled."

"Well," I said, "Myas will be coming to town in the spring, and I shall be seeing him. Shall I tell him what you think about him?"

"Do. Mind, it won't be any news to him. He's been rapped over the knuckles already. But I suppose he has some respect for my opinion, since he brought a patient to me, and I dare say he will believe that I am well disposed towards him."

"Very well," I said. "I'll tell him, and it's my belief that it won't make a pin's head of difference to him."

"Oh, that's very likely," grunted Dr. Habaden, and went on up to the billiard-room.

Chapter 2

I had expected that Myas would write beforehand to tell me when he would arrive. But it was not his habit to do what was expected. He called on me at my flat one morning early in the following March. He had already been in London some days, and said that he had got his work in Paris finished sooner than he had expected.

"At least 'finished' is not the word. I had gone as far as I could safely go there. There are some very brilliant gentlemen in Paris, and they have an inquiring turn of mind."

He still wore flowing and abominable neckties, and his silk hat had a perfectly flat brim. In fact, as I observed to him, he looked more like a French charlatan than an English gentleman.

"Possibly," he said, quite unperturbed. "I am thankful to say that I am neither."

He was energetic and vivacious, and there was a distinct note of triumph in his talk. When I asked him what he was so pleased about, he became vague in his expressions, and said that things had gone rather well with him in Paris. Then he changed the subject and began talking about the Hamiltons. They had received a serious blow. The Italian gentleman who played the 'cello like an angel had been shown to be a trigamist. Morals had triumphed over music, and the Hamiltons had blotted him out. They had now gone to Rome for Easter, he told me.

He refused to stay at my little flat. He said that his plans were too undecided, and his temperament was too erratic; and that he did not wish to make himself a perfect nuisance.

But," he said, I will come and feed, if you like. Food is the one subject to which you have given any serious study."

That statement, by the way, is, as I told him, a grotesque untruth. I took him off to the club with me, and gave him a quite simple and unpretentious luncheon. He was pleased to be enthusiastic about it, and I told him that he was making a deal of unnecessary and unseemly cackle.

"Don't say that," he said. "I know what the enthusiasm of your life is. You are not one of the illogical and nervous weaklings who are ashamed to eat and drink."

"Are there such people?"

"Of course, there are. They're a feature of the age. They browse on breakfast cereals and drink ginger-beer. The way the consumption of alcohol is decreasing in this country is perfectly appalling."

He paused to take a cup of black coffee. He refused the liqueur and proceeded—

"I have dined out a few times since I have been over here, and I have noticed things. One of the best wines is never drunk at all. It is always offered—apparently as a kind of ritual—and always refused. Although dinners have been made very much shorter, most women and some men refuse the joint. Dinner is becoming a farce. The really tragic thing about it is that these dyspeptic duffers seem to have the idea that their physical incapacity makes for refinement and mental improvement. It does nothing of the sort. Food for the body is food for the mind; the two are inseparably associated. Tell me now, what period in English history produced the finest men—the finest statesmen, generals, admirals, artists?"

"Well, I'm not an historian, but I suppose there is no dispute about that. Roughly speaking, the period would be the latter part of the eighteenth and the early part of the nineteenth centuries."

"Of course. And that was a hearty age. It was an age of beef and beer, and it was also an age of courage and inventions, which is precisely what one would have expected. Pitt drank his two bottles of port, went into the House of Commons, and spoke magnificently. There was oratory in those days, and there was consequent enthusiasm. The modern member of Parliament sips barley-water and stutters statistics, mostly wrong, and national enthusiasm is at a low ebb, which is also what one would expect."

"I wonder if there is anything in all this?" I said.

"It can hardly be otherwise. After all, the stomach is the one fundamental thing. It exists in the very lowest organisms, which have neither limbs nor brain. It is practically the first part of a man to get into working order. Its function is correct, before the baby can speak, or walk, or co-ordinate his movements. In fact, if I wanted to determine the Ego, I might be more likely to find the clue in the stomach than in the brain."

"Look here," I said. "What on earth do you mean by determining the Ego?"

"Well, in what does your 'self' consist? You would probably tell me that it consists in the association of your mind and your body. Now does it? When the mind has practically vanished, and no longer suffices even for a man's simplest needs, his life is still carefully preserved in an asylum. This would not be the case if it were not believed that the man's self was still there. When the man's body is dead and has decomposed, it is held by all religious people that the man's self still persists—that his personality is continued in another world; and perhaps science has rather more to say for this view than most men of science are aware. All of which is abominably dull talk after luncheon, isn't it?"

"Not to me," I said. "I have been getting rather interested in your work lately."

"You flatter me. And what do you know about it anyhow?"

"I know what that great and good man Dr. Habaden has told me."

"Dr. Habaden is a perfectly sound man in his own line, which is rather a terrific thing to be. It is quite detrimental to a sense of proportion. He sees a few blades of grass and he misses the landscape. I suppose my distinguished and learned colleague damned me as usual?"

"Oh, yes. Damned you very heartily, and told me to tell you so."

"Why?"

"He thinks you are a man of great ability, wasting your time out of perversity. He says you ought to be studying the aetiology of insanity, or the cure of cancer, or some other problem which really does need solution. He also suggests that you worry the last moments of dying patients, when they ought to be left at peace."

"Seems to have been saying a lot of sweet things about me," said Myas grimly. "Well, I needn't bother you with it. It's not your business. You belong to the leisured classes."

"You accused me of that before. It is true that I have no profession, and the only profession I ever wanted to have was not medical. But all the same I—"

"Hold on," said Myas. "What was it you wanted to go in for?"

"Army. The doctors wouldn't pass me. Ten years ago, my people tried to get me to go into Parliament, but I had no ambitions that way. Still, I've got lots of friends, and I'm keen on lots of things, and I do occasionally think. Of course, I don't know what your work is, but if it lies in the direction of the determination of self—"

"That is precisely it."

"Then it must be very interesting. Every man who thinks at all must ask himself sometimes, 'What am I?' And he has not got the answer."

"Look here, you should ask my esteemed colleague Dr. Habaden that. Put it in another form, and ask him what life and death are."

"I did," I said, "and he was pretty sick about it. He said that he knew when life ended and death began, and that was all we needed to know."

"Well, I deny that. I say there is no limit to what we need to know. I say, too, that the very first things which we need to know are the great elemental things. Let me know exactly in what 'self' consists.

173

Let me be able to isolate 'self' from its usual concomitants of mind and body, by which alone it has hitherto been cognisable. To isolate the 'self' is to add to the dignity of humanity; it is to exhibit humanity with the sources of all human frailty left out. You must surely see that this is fine work. If I can do that, then all the minor points, about which Habaden is so desperately anxious, will be added unto it. It seems to me that he wants me to begin at the wrong end of the stick. He calls my attention to details of more or less importance, when I am looking for first principles."

"Let me understand you," I said. "It comes to this. You are trying to comprehend—to capture—to isolate—the human soul."

Myas glanced at his watch. He shrugged his shoulders.

"That is the theologian's name for it," he said. "Names matter much less than facts. I've got my appointment at the hospital, and I must be off now. But if you are really interested, we can discuss the matter later, and I can tell you how the thing goes."

"Do," I said. "I want to hear about it."

CHAPTER 3

For a fortnight I did not see Dr. Myas, and heard nothing from him. I had not got his address, or I should certainly have written to him. I was extremely annoyed about it, and not merely because his neglect seemed to me unfriendly. He had promised to let me hear more of the very curious and interesting work on which he was engaged, and I was anxious to hear more. The matter had haunted my mind a good deal.

I am not an erudite man, and I am not a philosopher, and I had been puzzled by a point on which neither the erudite nor the philosophical seemed to help me at all. I refer to the way the mind acts on the body and the body on the mind.

A small piece of paper is placed on the hand of a man who has been hypnotised, and he is told that this will produce a blister. The blister does actually appear, but it is mind, and not a piece of paper, which has caused it. Every doctor knows how important in some cases the mental attitude of a patient is. With a fixed determination to recover, and a belief that he will recover, recovery does take place. Without this determination and belief, the man sinks and dies. The whole secret of the occasional successes of "Christian Science" lies here.

It is as true that body acts on mind. A certain state of the liver produces unfounded melancholy. A certain state of the lungs produces

174

an equally unfounded hope—the characteristic *spes-phthisica*. The hypodermic injection of a drug produces the full feeling of happiness. Everybody knows these things, but so far, I had found no satisfactory explanation of them.

I asked a physiologist what was the connection between mind and body, and where was the bridge between them. He told me that they were not connected in any way, but merely associated, much as the shadow is associated with the thing which casts the shadow.

I put this view before a well-known metaphysician, a man who spoke of all practical science with gentle contempt. "Yes," he said, "that is about right. But which is the shadow?"

This was not very illuminative, but if, as Myas had confirmed, both mind and body were but concomitants of the soul and self, it was easy to see how through the soul the one might affect the other. A man at Knightsbridge, wishing to speak to a man in the City, does so through the Telephone Exchange. It seemed to me possible that the soul might constitute a somewhat similar exchange. It might receive from the body and convey to the mind, or it might receive from the mind and convey to the body.

Of course, Myas had proved nothing, he had given me no details, he had narrated no special discovery of his which had led him to his conclusions. And there was one other point which made me cautious. Myas had already shown me, in the way in which he discussed the question of diet and in other conversations I had had with him, a distinct preference for the unaccepted view; and this preference was often a source of weakness. There is a type of mind which always falls in love with the minority, and suffers in consequence from that blindness to facts which is supposed to be incidental to those who fall in love. Still, I was intrigued. I wanted to hear what the man had to say. I wanted to go into the matter further.

I hope that the above does not give any false impression of myself. I am no profound student of such questions. I pretend to be no more than just an ordinary man of the world. But even to the most ordinary it seems to me that such things must occasionally offer both an interest and a perplexity. It does not destroy one's interest in politics or in bridge; it does not spoil one's fondness for sport, or upset one's convictions as to the way a man should deport himself; but it does occur to the mind now and again at odd moments. Ordinary men like myself rarely speak of such things, it is true, for we talk mostly trivialities. But I fancy that most of us do sometimes think of such things.

Consequently, I was rather glad, as I was walking down Piccadilly one Monday afternoon, to hear behind me the deep and sonorous voice of Dr. Myas calling me by name. He looked more abominably French than ever.

I shook hands with him, and told him—I trust with cheerfulness—that he had treated me disgracefully, and that on the whole he had better go to the devil.

"My dear Compton," said Myas, "if I have treated you badly, it is only because other people have treated me much worse. You see before you a martyr to science, or rather to the men of science. A grievance occupies one's mind to the exclusion of everything else. I confess that I had forgotten you, but I am glad to be reminded again. Now then, I am going as far as the fruit-shop, and then across the parks, and you may just as well come with me."

"I shall not," I said, "I am going on to Knightsbridge."

But as a matter of fact, I did go with him as far as St. James's Park Station. At the fruit-shop opposite the Green Park he purchased roses and strawberries. I heard the address to which they were to be sent, and I told him that he ought to be ashamed of himself.

"You have an absolutely evil mind," said Myas. "She was by way of polishing my nails, and incidentally she polished off the whole of the first joint of my fingers with wash-leather and pumice. If you like that kind of thing I don't. It hurts. I swore and she wept. Hence the strawberries."

"That's a very silly story," I said. "I'd sooner hear who has been ill-treating you scientifically, and how."

"You remember that when I last left you, I was going to keep an appointment at the hospital with which I was at one time connected. I wanted to obtain there, certain facilities for my experimental work. I was refused. At any rate I was so hedged in with conditions and qualifications that the thing became impossible for me. I have tried other hospitals with a similar result. That is the way the scientific investigator is treated in this rotten country."

"All right," I said. "If you don't like it, why don't you leave it? Who's stopping you? Skip back to Paris again. That hat of yours would feel a good deal more at home there, and so would your nostalgic necktie."

"No," said Myas decidedly, "I am not going. Here they take no serious interest in my work, but in Paris they take just a little too much. Everything I do is watched. Inquiries are frequent. If I went back to

Paris, some man would take advantage of my preliminary work and would possibly get to the goal before me."

"I wonder, Myas, that you have the cheek to talk like that. You were quite right when you told me that men of your profession were narrow-minded. You are a case in point. What on earth does it matter who makes a discovery, so long as the discovery is made? You are not a scientific martyr at all. You are only selfish and greedy. What do you say to that?"

"I don't pretend to transcend human nature. If somebody managed to sneak your watch, you would not say that so long as somebody enjoyed the watch it didn't matter who it was. You also would be selfish and greedy."

"But then I'm not posing as a scientific martyr. Hospitals are not established solely for research, and I have not the least doubt that you wanted something which was quite improper and illegitimate. I gathered from what your friend Habaden told me—"

"He's no friend of mine. Damn him, anyhow. He was one of the men who wanted to put the drag on the wheel."

"Well, what are you going to do about it? Have you got a plan at all?"

"I have—a very definite plan. Some time ago I made the mistake of showing children and fools, half-finished work. I think I told you about it. I published the results of some of my investigations and the deductions I had made from them. Really, I ought to have known my learned and distinguished colleagues better. I had broken the first commandment, which is that you shall make no new departure. You may continue work which has already been begun, and may make fresh discoveries in it, and be complimented and K.C.V.O.'d. But originality and imagination are the unforgivable sins. Very well, then. I shall publish nothing further at present. In spite of the hospitals, I have found a way by which I can continue my work here, and I intend to do it. But nothing more will be published until I can give an absolute demonstration of my determination of the Ego. The fact which they can see and test must convince."

"When you spoke of this before you said that mind and body were but the usual concomitants of self or soul, and that neither separately nor in association did they constitute self or soul."

"Something of the kind," said Myas. "Extraordinary that you should have remembered it."

Not at all. Now if science had chosen to deny, say, the existence of

177

sheep, I can understand that you could produce the sheep and demonstrate it. But I do not see how you are to demonstrate the existence of the human soul."

"Don't you? I have given up explaining my work now. I will be judged by results. And I tell you this definitely—before this year is out, I will demonstrate the existence of the soul to you personally."

"If you mean that seriously I'm quite content."

"I do. And here by the way is my station."

Before we separated, I asked him for his address. I was not quite sure which of our hotels could reach the high standard of luxury that Myas had habitually demanded. Myas smiled whimsically.

"I am living at 121 Knox Street. Know it?"

"Oh, probably, but I don't recall it for the moment."

"It is a back street in the Walham Green neighbourhood."

I said sardonically that he seemed determined to be right in the centre of things, and that I hoped he was comfortable.

"The place suits my purposes. I have four rooms over a little shop that sells newspapers and tobacco, and I have made them a little more possible than they were when I took them. The shop is kept by a widow, Mrs. Lade, and her daughter, and they wait on me—so far as a man of my simple habits requires any attendance at all."

I was astonished, of course. The best hotels of Paris had struggled in vain to be good enough for Dr. Myas. He had pointed out their defects to courteous and longsuffering managers. I had never known a man who required more attendance or was more particular as to the character of it. And now he had taken lodgings in a back street in Fulham, with a widowed tobacconist to wait on him. I supposed it was some fantastic whim of his, and I do not encourage fantastic whims. People who try not to be like other people are very tiresome. As I was sure that Myas expected me to ask many questions about his extraordinary selection, I would not gratify him by asking any at all.

CHAPTER 4

When I accepted Myas's invitation to dine with him at the Ritz a few days later, I did so with my eyes open.

"I ought to tell you," his letter said, "that I am bringing with me a Mr. Vulsame, a young surgeon who is in practice not far from here. He will be having a great treat, and I can remember that I once expressed agreement with your dictum, that the young man who is having a great treat is always a great nuisance. Briefly, Vulsame, though he is use-

178

ful to me, will not suit your fastidious taste. At the same time, I shrink from spending a whole evening with him by myself, and you can help me considerably if you will. I believe that under a highly conventional exterior you conceal some slight kindness of heart, or I would not venture to ask it. Do come and lend a hand with the beggar."

I replied that I should be charmed. One meets so many bounders that one more or less does not greatly matter. Besides, I was interested in Myas.

Myas himself was at his very best and perfectly delightful, but frankly, it was rather an awful evening. Vulsame had good looks, of rather a coarse and common kind, and his dress and manners were enough to make angels weep. He called me "Sir" previous to the champagne, and "old cock" afterwards. He bragged absurdly. Somewhere about nine o'clock we got him to some stupid music-hall, where he was particularly anxious to see that appalling abomination, a "female impersonator."

We came too late for this particular turn, at which he was very angry and I was very pleased. His comments on women and life were distinctly Rabelaisian, and Myas had to get him to speak in a lower tone. Throughout the evening Myas showed much tact in his management of the man. I think it was my good fortune to please Mr. Vulsame; at any rate, he asked me to drop in some evening in a friendly way. I cordially accepted the invitation, and to make the thing more realistic, put his visiting card in my pocket. But it can hardly be necessary to say that it was not my intention to let the thing go any further. I fully expected that that night I was seeing Mr. Vulsame for the last time. As it happened, I was destined to see him many times. Myas took him on to supper somewhere or other afterwards, but I thought I had done enough philanthropical work for one night, and pleaded an engagement.

During the whole evening Myas made no reference of any kind to his work, though he talked with a good deal of wit and acumen of most other subjects. I did not gather why he had taken lodgings in Fulham, nor why he was so desperately anxious to give this Mr. Vulsame a great treat. However, it was none of my business, and I made no attempt to get any information. It was for him to make the next move, if he cared about it.

One day in the following week, while I was at lunch in my rooms, the telephone bell went. My man, who attended to it, brought me word that Dr. Myers wished to speak to me. "I said I would inquire if you were in," the man added. He is a discreet fellow.

I guessed, of course, that Myers was telephonic for Myas, and went to hear what he had to say. He told me that he was very much depressed and worried, and that it would do him good to see some normal and commonplace person like myself. Would I come and see his new rooms?

As it happened, I had a blank afternoon, and I said that I would come with pleasure.

I had never seen Myas depressed or worried, and I gathered that information was awaiting me.

I told the driver of the taxicab to take me to Walham Green. There I dismissed him, and proceeded on foot in search of 121 Knox Street. I wanted to take a leisurely view of the neighbourhood, with which I was unfamiliar.

Knox Street is dull, and grey, and narrow. It contains many shops, and most of them look as if they were on the verge of bankruptcy. Everything in the windows seemed to be offered at sacrificial prices and far under cost. And apparently trade was possible in the things that one generally throws away. Curious and obscene rags were being sold as second-hand clothing. Soiled and aged back numbers of magazines had a price put upon them. As long as you got a lot for a penny, it did not seem to much matter what you got.

Each shop displayed notices of a familiar and even slangy character. "Stop that cough!" shrieked the chemist. "Here's a Sunday dinner for you," cried the butcher. Mrs. Lade seemed to be doing rather better than some of her neighbours. She offered for sale many different things. The solid basis of the trade was apparently penny novelettes and Woodbine cigarettes, but it also branched out into sweetmeats and mouthorgans.

There was no private door, and I entered the shop. Had I been dishonestly inclined, I might have snatched up a couple of mouthorgans and made a bolt for it. Nobody was there to prevent me. But from behind a door, which was half a window with a red curtain over it, at the back of the shop, there came voices. The first voice was, I diagnosed correctly, the voice of a fat and elderly woman.

"It may be all right, and I expect it is all right, for you're a good girl, Alice; but what I say is, that it don't look right, and sooner or later other people in the street will be bound to notice it, and if I was doing my duty, I shouldn't allow it to go on."

The second voice was much younger, and rather plaintive. Despite a London accent, it was not unpleasant in quality.

"I'm sure he always treats me with respeck—with most perfeck respeck. And why I should miss a chance of improving myself I can't see. It's most kind of him. And I can tell you this, he's not a gentleman that will stand much interference—not from nobody. If you want to lose the rent, paid regular as it is—"

"Setting up there for hours with him like that!" said the fat voice indignantly. "I don't call it—"

I thought the time had come to rap sharply on the floor with my umbrella. Through the red-curtained door came Mrs. Lade. She looked a conscientious, kindly, rather worried woman. She was fat and moved slowly. With a fold of her grey apron, she concealed her red hands from the glance of the curious.

"Dr. Myas?" I said.

"Were you wishful to see him?"

"Yes," I said. "That was the idea. I am Mr. Compton."

Mrs. Lade opened the red-curtained door again and called to an invisible Miss Lade: "Gentleman to see Dr. Myas. Just take him up, Alice, will you?" Then she raised a flap of the counter and turned to me. "If you'll step this way, sir."

I stepped that way, and behind the red-curtained door I found a very beautiful girl. Her hair reminded me of the days in my extreme youth, when I kept silkworms; it was just the colour of the natural silk, and she had any amount of it. Her eyes were a greyish-blue. Her face was well-cut and delicate. When she saw an actual stranger and spoke with him, it was apparently her habit to blush slightly. She was rather above medium height, with a slight graceful figure. Her dress was plain and quiet. She took me up some rather dingy stairs, and tapped at a door which had been newly painted. The deep voice of Myas bade us come in.

Myas flung down the book that he was reading, and shook hands with me. I noticed, by the way, that the book was *Alice in Wonderland*. I took one of his cigarettes, and sat down to talk to him.

"Before we go any further," I said, "tell me how is our dear friend, Mr. Vulsame?"

Myas grinned in a melancholy way. "I managed him beautifully. I gave him supper. I brought him back here in a taxicab. I kept him here for an hour, and took him to his own place in another taxicab. And it was really not until he reached home that he was actually drunk."

"It seemed to me that he was rather nearer that blessed condition than I cared about most of the evening."

"No, I assure you," said Myas. "Even when he got to his own home, he was not incapable, and he was very, very happy. Speaking seriously, I'm awfully obliged to you for helping me with him. He's rather a useful man to me."

"Useful? How?"

"Hadn't it occurred to you? I should have thought it would have been fairly obvious. I have still a little experimental work that I must do. And the hospitals refuse to give me the opportunities that I want. Vulsame has a practice—quite a large practice—in a poor neighbour-hood. You see he inspires no sense of shame, and people are sure they can tell him everything. Frequently he has cases which are of interest to me and have a bearing on my work. When that happens, he lets me know, and I come in as Mr. Vulsame's assistant. Mark you, I get none of the qualifications and conditions that the hospital wanted to lay down. As Mr. Vulsame's assistant, I do just exactly as I think right. Naturally I remunerate Mr. Vulsame. I also at times think it expedient to remu-nerate the relatives of the patient. When I came here, my friend, I did not do it merely to surprise you. It was essential that I should be liv-ing and working in a poor neighbourhood. With the expenditure of a very few sovereigns, I can get what I want. The relatives actually like it; it gives them so much money to spend on the funeral baked-meats."

"You're a gruesome beast, Myas," I said. "If you're not careful, you'll make this place too hot to hold you, and Vulsame's practice will go pop."

"Very likely," he said, with indifference. "At present I am being careful."

I looked round the room. The walls were newly papered in a flat tint. The furniture was all new, not strictly artistic, but fairly good and comfortable.

"You didn't find all these things here when you came, did you?" I asked.

"Lord, no! The rooms were empty. I went to Tottenham Court Road, gave them a rough idea of what I wanted and the price I would pay, and Tottenham Court Road did the rest. As long as the stuff was comfortable, and none of the things had any pattern on them, I did not mind much."

"What's your objection to pattern?"

"All pattern is an abomination. It annoys you because it is repeated. And then, where it has to stop because there is no more of the blessed curtain or wall-paper, it annoys you because it is not repeated. It reminds me too much of my fellow-men—so many of them and all just alike. Now you, of course, would suffer patterns gladly."

"I don't worry. I'm not particularly cracked about anything of that kind. Why should I enjoy patterns?"

"The thing's obvious. Your one aim in life is to resemble as closely as possible every other man in the same position in life, and their aim is to resemble each other and you. Any one of you would sooner commit a murder than wear the wrong necktie. Not cracked? Of course, you're cracked."

"And you're quite sane, I suppose."

"Absolutely," said Myas, with conviction.

"Very well, then. How's that girl getting on with her lessons?"

"Go to the devil!" said Myas.

"And I suppose the girl can go to the devil as well?"

Myas smote the palm of one hand with the fist of the other. "My word," he said. "How absolutely wrong you sordid and worldly people can get in your judgment. However, there is just this to be said for you. You live and learn. You'll get to know that girl better. Now then, let's speak of other things."

CHAPTER 5

"Look here," said Myas. "You must see the rest of my bachelor establishment." He opened the folding doors at the end of the room. "Here, for example, we observe my dining-room—furnished by Tottenham Court Road for £35, and looking exactly like a dining-room which has been furnished by Tottenham Court Road for £35."

"What do you want a dining-room for?" I said. "You can't possibly feed here."

"Can and do," said Myas.

I walked to the window, which opened down to the floor. From it an iron staircase led down to a narrow slip of ground, which was by way of being a garden. A gardener would call it a backyard. It was a weary, cat-haunted spot between high and blackened walls, but I noticed that there were two fine old mulberry trees in it. There was also a newly erected building, looking somewhat like a studio. This was raised a little from the ground, with three steps up to the door of it. I asked Myas what it was.

"That's where I do my work. That door in the wall at the further end of the garden opens into Durnford Place. Durnford Place runs parallel to Knox Street, and I'm not quite sure whether Durnford Place is at the back of Knox Street, or *vice versa*."

"Both, I should imagine."

"Anyhow, it's a very useful door, for it enables me, and incidentally my friends, to get up to my rooms without going through Mrs. Lade's part of the house. When you come to see me again, as I hope you will soon, you must come in that way. I've had a new lock fitted to it, and I'll give you a latchkey."

I pocketed the latchkey, and said that the confidence he showed in me was pleasing. "What I shall do of course will be to let myself in and burgle your workroom. There I shall reap the fruit of your researches, anticipate your discoveries, and subsequently enjoy the fame which you wrongly suppose is coming to you."

"You couldn't do it. You are far too much of a duffer at that kind of thing. What you found inside the workroom would be incomprehensible to you. For that reason, I won't trouble you with the workroom at present. Could you be bothered to climb up more stairs in order to see the most absolutely ordinary bedroom that Tottenham Court Road has ever achieved?"

"Certainly not."

"Well, there is one thing more you must see, just across the passage here." He opened a door. "This is my kitchen—electric as you observe."

"And does she cook here?"

"No, idiot. The cooking which is done here I do myself."

It was easy to believe this. Cooking was one of the things which he took seriously. He was doubtless acquainted with the practice as well as the theory of it.

"Well," I said, "I confess that I don't see your game. I suppose you built that place in the garden. You have redecorated these rooms. You have put in electric light and heating, and a telephone. You have filled them up with a lot of fair-to-middling furniture. Now in six months you'll be sick of this, and will start off on your travels again. Do you suppose you'll ever see your money back? There is probably nobody on the face of the earth, except yourself, who wants to live over a tobacconist's shop in Knox Street."

"No, my practical friend, I don't suppose I shall see my money back, but I wanted to live here for reasons which I have already given you, and I had to make the place possible; but it is by no means certain that I shall be leaving in six months, and I might quite possibly remain

184

here for the rest of my life. After all, living here is absurdly cheap. It cost me twenty times as much in Paris. Oh yes, I am quite satisfied with what I've done, so far as expenditure is concerned. I wish I had nothing else to worry me.

He seemed quite pleased with the electrical toys in his kitchen, and insisted on showing me how they worked, although I told him that he was talking like a man at an exhibition and becoming very wearisome. Then we went back into the sitting-room, and he rang the bell for tea.

It was Miss Lade who brought the things in and arranged them on a low table by the fire. She did not look once at either of us. Myas stopped her as she was turning to go.

"Do wait and pour out tea for us," he said. "I want to present to you a great friend of mine, Mr. Compton."

She murmured something unintelligible, and seemed a little in doubt whether she should shake hands. I settled the question for her. Her hands did not look as if she did much rough work.

I believe it is said to be the test of a gentleman that he is at ease under all circumstances and in all society. If this be the case, I am emphatically not a gentleman. At this extraordinary tea-party I was not at my ease at all. I did my best, but it was poor. I wanted to talk to Miss Lade—and not only because she was a very pretty girl—and the only mutual ground that I could find on which we might meet was the mulberry trees in the garden. At the time of the Revolution French exiles came to London and there planted mulberry trees, notably in St. John's Wood, and to a lesser extent in Fulham. So, I told her, and I dare say it may be true. I heard with great interest that the mulberries did actually ripen, and I made her promise to send me some of them in due season. She was certainly very shy, but I should say, appeared considerably less of a fool than I did. She poured out tea very nicely. Myas said little, and did not help a bit.

After a while, things went more easily, and I got her to talk about herself. She spoke of a theatre to which Myas had taken her. She told me that at one time she had been very fond of lawn tennis, but that she could not find time for it any longer. She had a very pleasant voice, and great simplicity—two things which I have always especially admired. She was absolutely free from affectation. There was not the slightest attempt to make an impression of any kind. I should think she was with us for about half-an-hour. Then she rose, and said that her mother was going out, and that she would have to attend to the shop. I tried to help her as she was taking away the tea-things, but she would not let me do anything. Myas did not even attempt to do anything. He had sat back in his easy-chair all the time, and watched us through the smoke of his cigarette, as if we were doing an interesting scene in a play for his benefit. It was scandalous behaviour.

"Well?" he said, when she had gone.

"Leave her alone," I said.

Then he spoke, with a good deal of emphasis, almost with excitement.

"Look here, my dear fellow, you misunderstand this altogether. I don't blame you for that. You take the ordinary view, and any other man of your blessed pattern would take the same. I'll go further than that. If you were in my position, I should give you exactly the same advice that you have just given me. But, as it happens, what you say is absolutely beside the point. The things that you imagine are not concerned in the question in the least. I'm not going to make love to that girl. Understand that definitely. I told you over the telephone that I was worried and depressed, and so I am; and that girl is principally concerned in it, but most emphatically not for the reason which you would suppose."

"I'm no good at mysteries," I said. "If the trouble is not what I think, I don't pretend to understand what it is. But I do profess to know something about human nature. Your intentions are excellent, of course. But in a case like this there is often a marked difference between a man's intentions and his conduct. I will flatter you so far as to tell you that you're not an ordinary man. Still, you're a human being."

"Admitted. I do not profess to have lived the life of an anchorite hitherto. But I am telling you the exact truth when I say that nothing exists now for me but my work, and that this girl troubles me only in so far as she is connected with my work. And if I do as I wish, she will be very intimately connected with it."

"Oh, very well!" I said. "But there's another thing to think about. For the last half-hour or so I have been watching that girl in here. If she is not very much in love with you. I'm mistaken, and I know nothing." Myas seemed to reflect for a minute. Then he said, with conviction—

"I hope she is. I hope to goodness she is. If she is not, she is not likely to be of much use to me."

"I give it up. I don't understand you."

"No," said Myas. "But you will one of these days."

"How?"

186

"How?" echoed Myas. "Well, you will understand, because either that girl or myself will give you the explanation."

As I rose to go, I pressed him to come and see me some time. He said that he would if he could, but that he was very busy now, and it was a long way to come.

"It is," I said. "But I should like to point out that the distance from Knox Street to St. James's Place is exactly the same as the distance from St. James's Place to Knox Street, which distance I have covered this very afternoon."

He said that I was a man of leisure, and that time, distance, and taxicabs were all as nothing to me. I was to come again. He generally knocked off work for an hour or two in the afternoon. I had my latchkey.

I left him with the uncomfortable feeling that I had been spending the afternoon with a friend of mine who was by way of being a blackguard. I did not suppose that he was a typical deceiver and seducer, but he did seem to me to be a man absolutely without scruple where his work was concerned. I did not like his business with Vulsame. I did not like the way he was treating Alice Lade. What business had he to make use of her fondness for him for his own purposes? That she was fond of him I had no doubt whatever. She looked at me with candid and friendly eyes, but when her eyes met his they became timorous and perturbed, and the long lashes flickered. The one saving grace of the man was that he was really worried about what he was doing. If he was indeed without scruple, it was with great difficulty that he had brought himself to that point.

About a month later I rang up Myas on the telephone, and suggested that I should come to see him that afternoon. He replied that he was very sorry, but that work which it was impossible to leave would occupy him the whole of that afternoon. He would come to see me.

But he did not come to see me. It was in June that I received from him a rather curious letter, in which he announced his engagement to Alice Lade.

Chapter 6

Myas said in his long letter that the news of his engagement would probably give me a comfortable feeling of superiority, I having always known, of course, what would happen. With this would be mingled a certain regret that he had not allied himself more advantageously from the world's point of view. And both feelings, he assured me, would be quite out of place.

"The fact is," he wrote, "that it had become necessary for the purposes of my work for Miss Lade and myself to be frequently together for long periods. Knox Street shook its respectable head, and Mrs. Lade did not like it. The proclamation of an engagement, and the purchase of an absurdly valuable ring, have changed all this. Knox Street smiles upon us, and dreams confetti. Mrs. Lade is quite happy. Briefly, the engagement is simply the price we pay to Knox Street for permission to continue our work as before. So, if you have any impression that you ever foresaw anything you should correct it. It is quite probable that we shall never be married, but that depends to some extent on the result of my great experiment.

"Meanwhile, as I require the whole of Miss Lade's time, I have provided a domestic substitute, to Mrs. Lade's considerable, but rather tremulous, satisfaction. For her Knox Street is the voice of society, and almost the voice of God. It is a street filled with people who have kept themselves respectable. Think of all the poignant meaning of that phrase. With insufficient means for the purpose, and with countless temptations to be otherwise, these good people are still respectable.

"Beside their hard-won respectability, your own, facile and cultured, is no more than sounding brass and a tinkling cymbal. Mrs. Lade is tremulous, because she has advanced one step up the ladder. There is a definite line of demarcation here, between the people who keep a girl and the people who do it all themselves. Mrs. Lade naturally fears lest she should be thought guilty of that quality, which the Greeks called 'hubris' and Fulham calls 'swelled head.' She therefore sighs, and explains to her friends that it was all on account of the lodger, and that she hopes it may be for the best.

"My work has gone on very rapidly, and the day is not far off now. I have little doubt that I shall be able to redeem a promise that I once made you. I wish you would come and see me tomorrow afternoon. It is too bad of you to have neglected me like this."

The man was astounding.

On looking into the matter, I found that I had made two appointments for the following afternoon. I had promised to go with the Hamiltons, who were in town for a few days, to the Queen's Hall, and I had also promised to play bridge with some other people. That made it all quite easy. I excused myself from the bridge-party on the ground that I had forgotten about the Hamiltons, and from the Hamiltons on the ground that I had forgotten about the bridge-party. These two appointments being safely and easily cancelled, I got into a taxicab and drove to Durnford Place.

I let myself in with the latchkey that Myas had given me, and went up the strip of garden. As I passed the workroom, I heard within a chink of glass and a light footstep. I hesitated a moment, thinking that Myas might be there; but I remembered that when he showed me the rest of his establishment, he had rather made a point of not showing me the workroom. So, I went on up the iron staircase, and tapped at the window. Myas himself let me in.

"Come to deliver your congratulations?" he asked, rather sardonically.

"No. I've come to ask you to explain yourself."

"But, my dear fellow, what is there to explain? It all seems to me so simple and natural."

"What do you mean by saying that it had become necessary for you and Miss Lade to be together for long periods? The thing is absolute nonsense. What possible use can she be to you in your work? She has certainly had no scientific education. She has probably had precious little education of any kind."

At this moment the door opened, and Miss Lade entered. She addressed herself to Myas, speaking eagerly and quickly: "The variation is three seconds and two-fifths."

As she spoke, she saw me. She greeted me cordially enough, and shook hands, but instantly turned back again to Myas.

"Yes," said Myas, "that's too much, isn't it?"

"I thought," she said, "of trying again with ether alone."

"Yes," he said, "you might certainly try that. Do. You'll be through with it by teatime."

"I expect so," she said, and went out of the room again. I think I have never before in my life experienced more completely the sensation that I did not matter in the least. I felt like a small boy who remains quiet and orderly, while his superior papa and mamma discuss questions of finance, or the morals of the parlour-maid, or anything else which is "not for little boys," in indifferent French.

"Let's see," said Myas, "you were beginning to talk about education, weren't you? Sorry for the interruption. I've got views about education."

"Oh, you've got views on everything under the sun."

"The London season's telling on your nerves, Compton. You incline to be irritable. I do not think, speaking quite dispassionately, that Alice Lade is exactly what you would have expected from her parentage and position in life."

"Obviously she's not. I admit all that."

"It is true, as you say, that her education was of the very slightest. That was all the better from my point of view. I had no rubbish to clear away. Nothing on earth is quite so easy to understand as what is popularly called Science. The only way that men have been able to make it at all difficult is by inventing a very frantic terminology which they habitually mispronounce, and by carefully suppressing all habit of simple and lucid speech. Education for the child means a march into the unknown. He is told that he has to do quadratic equations, but nobody ever dreams of telling him why. He has to know the name of the capital of Portugal. He has, in extreme cases, to know the names of the kings of Israel and Judah.

"The patience of the child is remarkable. He really does consent to lumber up his mind with all this nonsense, merely because papa, or the governess, or the schoolmaster wishes him to do it. It is a wonderful thing that any horse consents to draw any cart, but it is still more wonderful that any child consents to acquire knowledge, on the lines on which knowledge is now generally imparted. When you start on a journey, it is advisable to know where you're going, and you do not journey with much purpose or enthusiasm if you do not know it. One of the very first things I did with Miss Lade was to show her what I was aiming at, and how she could help."

"I see," I said. "You told her that you were aiming at the determination of the Ego, and she understood all that at once. Naturally, she would."

"Don't be an ass! That was, of course, what I told her, but equally, of course, those were not the words which I used. I asked her what she was, why she was here, and what would happen when she died. She told me that she was a girl, that she was here to do her duty, and that she would go to hell if she did not do it. As soon as I began to show her how far from satisfactory these answers were she became interested. These simple elemental things interest everybody, even you. We know of course very little about them at present, and the prospect that she and I would be able to discover more naturally attracted Alice. But I am not taking all the credit for my way of teaching. She is intelligent, plastic, receptive, to a very unusual degree. Many things she seems to acquire unconsciously. For instance, her talk—you noticed it?"

"Yes, I noticed it. The London accent has been eliminated."

"Yes, she now talks just as you do."

"There you are wrong. It is your own accent which she has copied. There is the faintest possible foreign note in it, which has come to you, I suppose, from the fact that you have been speaking French for so long. How did you get her to acquire it?"

"I did not. I have just told you that it was one of the things that she picked up unconsciously. I have never corrected her speech in any way. The fact of the case is that in some respects Alice is singularly childlike. If a child is given a nurse with a Cockney accent, the child will soon talk Cockney. If he has a French *bonne*, he will soon talk French. The influence of the person in authority, with whom the child is on intimate terms, always works, and always unconsciously."

"Well now, my friend, suppose we look at this engagement from Miss Lade's point of view. Does she understand that the whole thing is merely a farce, and that you have no intention of carrying it out?"

"But that is not the case. You must have misunderstood something I said in my letter. I have every intention of carrying it out, if it is possible. But the result of my experiment may make it impossible. It all turns upon that. I don't want to go into the question with you just now, but I admit there is a very grave risk in the experiment."

"And yet she is to take part in it."

"Well, yes. Why not? She wishes it. She is absolutely devoted to me, and for that reason alone she would do it, and by this time she is quite as keen about the work as I am. I own that I felt some reluctance at first. I was worried and depressed about it, as you remember. I still feel that I should be wrong if I put any kind of compulsion upon her—if, for instance, I told her that it was of supreme importance to me that she should take this risk. But I have not done that, and she is a free agent. What she is going to do, she has volunteered to do. And, mind, she runs no risk which I shall not share equally with her. That seems to me to make it all right. Don't you think so?"

"Of course, I don't. It's all wrong. It seems to me that what I ought to do is to go downstairs and have ten minutes' talk with the poor victim's mother."

"You can have ten minutes' or ten hours' talk with Mrs. Lade, if you like. It would make no difference. She is not the dominant factor, and Alice is. Of course, the consideration which you are leaving out in your own mind, is really the consideration which best justifies me. There is no advance without sacrifice, and in this case the advance is tremendous, and the sacrifice, if it is needed, is justified. However, the last thing I wish to do is to quarrel with you just now, more particularly as I want to ask a favour of you. I have just made my will."

"Don't for goodness sake say that you want me to be a trustee. I am trustee for three people already. They all liked me once, but they all hate me now. And they're all convinced that if I were not a curious combination of knave and fool, I could get them seven *per cent*, out of trust securities."

"Well, I do want you to be a trustee. I am leaving everything in trust for Miss Lade. I promise you that she will give you no trouble whatever. You will find her perfectly reasonable and docile."

After some discussion, I gave way and consented. And then Miss Lade came in again from the workroom.

"Well?" said Myas.

She shook her head. "No use at all. Worse than before." And then she turned to talk to me.

Certainly, the change in her in a very short time was remarkable. She was self-possessed, and only blushed once—when I congratulated her on her engagement. It was easy to talk to her. Her voice was pleasant and musical, and I thought her perfectly charming.

Myas came down the garden with me when I left. I said to him: "Do you mean to tell me that you're not in love with her?"

"Undoubtedly I shall be if all goes well. At present there is too much to think about. I haven't the time for love. Why, I've never even kissed her."

"If I were you, I should go back now and do it. Believe me, it doesn't take long."

"It would be absolute ruin," said Myas.

CHAPTER 7

During the next fortnight I saw a good deal of Myas and Miss Lade, and got to know the latter much better. I did not go to Knox Street every afternoon—Myas asked me to do so—but I went very often. One afternoon Miss Lade spoke with some interest of a forthcoming play. This seemed to me to offer an opportunity, and I asked her if she and Myas would dine with me on the first night and come with me to the theatre afterwards.

"I'm afraid I couldn't," said Miss Lade. "I have not got any evening dress. But it's very kind of you."

"That kind of thing must come later," said Myas. "When we've finished our work we'll come to you as often as you like."

"Good," I said. "I'll tell the theatre to postpone the production."

"Don't get angry with us," said Myas. "At present, except for an hour or two in the afternoon, we are horribly unsociable. There is a kind of interest in life, that shuts out all other interests. But the end will come soon now, won't it, Alice?"

"Very soon," said Miss Lade. She was standing against the window, and the pure beauty of her profile was a delight to one's eyes. Suddenly she exclaimed with ecstasy: "Carter Paterson! They've sent it at last."

"Good!" exclaimed Myas, and flew down the stairs.

Miss Lade turned to me rather apologetically. "It is some apparatus," she said. "We have been kept waiting a long time for it. Scientific instrument-makers seem to be the slowest people in the world."

Myas came panting into the room with a large box in his arms. They did not unpack it completely, but they took out one or two pieces and fitted them together. Miss Lade's joy over the contents of the box was quite real and unaffected. I doubted if her first evening dress would give her so much pleasure.

The more I saw of Miss Lade, the higher my opinion of her became. She had great abilities, but even so her acquirements and her advance during the last few months seemed to me miraculous. She still kept that almost childlike simplicity which from the first I had appreciated in her. Her devotion to Myas was obviously of the most exalted kind, and her enthusiasm in the work was not less than his own. I could understand now what he meant when he told me that it would be absolute ruin if he began to make love to her.

Afterwards, he would have been unable to continue his work, or to conduct any experiment in which the least risk to her was involved. Nature would have forced its way. Passion was not suppressed, but it was postponed. When the work was done, there would be dinners and evening dresses, and there would be time for love. I got an impression that she understood all this.

One afternoon I returned to St. James's Place on the top of a motor omnibus. On the seat in front of me were two old women with strident voices. They were discussing Mr. Vulsame. "I wouldn't go to him," said one of them, "and I wouldn't call him into my house, not if there wasn't another doctor in England."

"Bit too fond of lifting the elbow, eh?" said the other.

"Yes. That's true enough. But that's not all."

She became confidential and dropped her voice. I was not greatly surprised. I knew that Vulsame drank, and my curiosity as to what else he did was not very keen.

It was at the end of this fortnight, in the middle of the London season, and with countless engagements on hand, that I gave the whole thing up and went away. It was a sudden and overmastering impulse, which had occurred to me before, and will probably occur to me again. To my friends and acquaintances, I suppose that I seem a normal and cheerful bachelor of forty. That, perhaps, is what I am most of the time. Still, I have been through things of a kind that leave their mark. I was quite a young man when the doctors cut me off from the only profession that I could ever have loved. They stopped polo and hunting as well.

For a while I was a good deal of an invalid, and that, I dare say, was a sound enough reason for the girl who threw me over and married a better man. My health is fairly good now, and I do most of the right things at the right time. I enjoy the society of my fellow-men, and I think I can hold my own in any of the sports that my health has left open to me. I am not broken-hearted, and I am not a sentimentalist, but occasionally I get a sudden revulsion against the kind of life that I am leading. Its pleasures become an unmitigated bore. Its absolute uselessness and selfishness disgust me.

Then I remember that, but for a whim of fate, I might have been engaged in an active profession, and possibly doing some good in the world. Just at this time too, I recalled the girl who broke her engagement with me. Alice Lade reminded me of her a little. I was not in the least in love with Alice Lade, but yet I regarded Myas with envy. He had at any rate managed to make some woman care very much for him. My mood at such times is not cheerful, and there is no reason why I should ask my friends to put up with it.

Besides, I have found that quiet and solitude are the best cure for it. That is why some years ago I bought for half-nothing a little cottage far up on a hill in Gloucestershire, ten miles from the nearest railway station. When I find that solitude and the simplicity of life there no longer please me, my cure is complete. I can go back and mix with my fellow-men again.

I never take my valet down with me to the cottage. An elderly couple have the charge of it, and they can do all that I require. When I am down there, I want nothing that reminds me of London. I keep a small car, and have learned to drive it. The distance from shops and the station make it a necessity. I have the fishing rights over three miles of river. If I ever needed it, I could get some golf, but so far, I have left it alone. I go down to my cottage to avoid my fellowmen, not to mix with them.

It may have been partly perhaps because I had seen so much lately of the work which Myas was doing, that this fit of disgust of my own life came on me. I got tired of taking so much care of such unimportant things. I got tired of hearing so much worthless talk, and of contributing my share to the sum of it. For an hour or two I was busy with telegrams and telephone, and by that time my man had packed my things and the cab was ready to take me to Paddington. I did not, of course, let my friends know where I had gone. The cottage was my harmless secret. If I let my friends know, they would probably wish to come down and cheer me up, and that would be too depressing. I said that I was going to Paris.

I took with me two books, or rather pamphlets, which were all that Daniel Myas had so far published. The first of these was entitled *A Clinical Study of the Physical and Psychical Phenomena of Somatic Dissolution*, Myas had often laughed at scientific jargon, but he admitted that he was a master in the use of it himself. This work had appeared originally in the American *Journal of Abnormal Psychology*, and had attracted some little attention. The *Lancet* had dealt dutifully but severely with it.

Much of it was simply Greek to me. I was never taught any Science at school, and I did not know what a good deal of the jargon meant. But there were passages in it, notably where he summed up his conclusions in more popular language, which were wildly interesting. The other pamphlet had been privately printed since his arrival in England. It was called *Experimental Observations on the Continuity of the Ego*, I got on better with this. It was a most amazing little pamphlet. It was Science plus Religion, and Religion plus Poetry.

As any reader must have gathered, I am not much of an author myself, but I have read a good deal, and I think I do know good writing when I see it. I read that pamphlet more than once, and it increased my respect for Myas's abilities.

I had a week of the most delightful quiet at my cottage. I did a good deal of gardening under the direction of old Welsford. He is rather severe with me, and I think I like it. At any rate, it makes a pleasant change from the catlike obsequiousness of my man in town. Welsford is a great Nature student, too, and tells me and shows me much that is interesting. Everything in the garden has for him a distinct personality, and he speaks of flowers and vegetables very much as he would speak of human beings. I have heard him accuse potatoes of being obstinate.

At about eleven one morning, as I was working in the garden, a telegram was brought out to me which had been forwarded on from St. James's Place. It was signed "Lade," and there was nothing to tell me whether the mother or the daughter had sent it. It said: "Please come here at once."

I hesitated for a moment. I thought of telegraphing for further particulars, but the message seemed so urgent that I decided not to waste time on that. I sent Welsford to get the car out, and hurried indoors to change my clothes. There was an express that I should just be able to catch. I drove myself, and left the car in a garage near the station. Shortly after four I was in London.

I went first to a telephone office to tell my people at St. James's Place to expect me that evening, and then, as I had my latchkey with me, I drove to the entrance in Durnford Place.

My taxicab could not get quite up to the door, as a dogcart was standing there. It was a seedy-looking dogcart, and apparently had not been washed for a week. A wretched old horse stood dejectedly in the shafts. At the horse's head was a groom in dusty and ill-fitting livery. He was eating nuts, and he stared at me curiously, as if he wondered what I was doing there. Durnford Place was very quiet that afternoon, and the crack of the nutshells rang out loudly.

I was just about to pay my cabman, when it occurred to me that after all he might perhaps be useful. I told him to wait. At this moment the garden door opened, and Mr. Vulsame came out. He was drawing a pair of excessively ugly yellow gloves on to his fat hands. He had changed if anything for the worse since the night I met him first. His clothes were shabby, and he looked unwashed and unkempt. His expression was grave and troubled.

He spoke to me at once, without offering to shake hands. "So, you've come at last, Mr. Compton?"

"I came as soon as I got the telegram. It was forwarded to me from London. I was away in Gloucestershire."

"I see," he said. "Well, I suppose I had better go in with you."

"Can you tell me what is the matter, Mr. Vulsame?"

"Matter? I thought you knew. They should have told you in the telegram. Daniel Myas is dead."

CHAPTER 8

Inside the garden I paused for a moment. "It seems almost incredible," I said. "A few days ago, when I left him, he seemed in the best of health. When did he die?"

"I was telephoned for at a quarter to eight this morning, and was here by eight. So far as I can tell, death must have occurred at least six hours previously."

"And the cause of death?"

"The direct cause was failure of respiration under an anaesthetic. The anaesthetic was chloride of ethyl, and it was automatically administered. It was in his workroom there that he died. I gave notice to the coroner at once, of course. It will be for the inquest to settle whether the death was accidental or not."

I did not much like the man's tone. It was at once truculent and suspicious. "Dr. Myas was about the last man in the world to commit suicide." I said.

"I didn't say suicide. There's a sealed letter waiting for you up at the house. You would probably prefer to open it in the presence of the police, and to show them what it contains."

"Very well," I said. "And what about Miss Lade?"

"I haven't seen her. In fact, she won't see me. Well, I can understand that. She is shut up in her room alone, and I don't for a moment suppose that she will consent to see you either, Mr. Compton."

"I don't want to bother her," I said. "It is all perfectly natural. She was devoted to Myas, and this must be a terrible shock to her."

"Possibly. It may be so. Do you by any chance happen to know the terms of the will?"

"I do. Why?"

"Oh, nothing. Mrs. Lade knew them. I have had that definitely from her own lips. So presumably her daughter knew them too."

"I don't see what bearing that has on the question."

"Don't you?" sneered Mr. Vulsame. "Perhaps you will see it at the inquest. It is a point which will probably be raised. You seem to be singularly innocent for a man of your years."

I loathed the fellow, and I was getting more and more angry with him. "Wouldn't it save trouble," I said, "if you were to say quite plainly what you mean? Or are you afraid to say it? What is it you are trying to insinuate?"

"I am afraid of nothing, and I am not trying to insinuate anything. Perhaps everything is all right. There is no doubt whatever that Myas made frequent experiments upon himself. He had also experimented with Miss Lade. I found a record of many of the experiments, and I tell you frankly I cannot see for what purpose they were conducted." He jerked his thumb in the direction of the workroom. "I should say he had every known variety of anaesthetic in there, and some very neat apparatus for administering it. Clockwork can go wrong, and the medical man may make mistakes. That may have been the reason why, when already under the anaesthetic, he received double the amount of the chloride of ethyl that he intended. In that case I suppose the death would be considered accidental. I can't say. I have an open mind on the question."

I felt instinctively that this man might do some mischief, and that it would not do to lose one's temper with him. I decided to handle him a little more carefully. "I was told by Myas," I said, "that I was to be his sole executor and trustee for Miss Lade. Myas was a great friend of mine. You see I am very deeply interested in this, and I hope you will help me to get to the bottom of it. Could you perhaps spare me an hour or so at St. James's Place, if you are not too busy?"

"Busy?" he said savagely. "Plucky lot of business Myas left me! Well, he's dead. I'll say no more about that just now. Yes, I can come if you like."

"Thank you very much. Perhaps you would like to send your cart away. I've got a taxi there, and I don't suppose that I shall keep you waiting more than a few minutes."

"All right," said Vulsame. "There's the inspector, if you want him."

A friendly looking man in plain clothes had just come out of the workroom, locking the door behind him. I introduced myself to him.

"This is a terrible business," I said. "Have you any idea how it happened?"

"That's not for me to say, sir," said the inspector. "Not at present, at any rate. I'm just collecting the facts. So far as I have gone, I have found no motive for suicide, and it is quite possible that the death was accidental. I have been looking at the apparatus in there, and it's easy to see how a mistake could be made. It's a clockwork thing, actuating a little pump. You can set it to deliver this anaesthetic stuff once and then stop, or twice and then stop, or any number of times. He was playing a very dangerous game, and there is the evidence in his own writing that he had played it often before. I suppose he was studying the nature of these different anaesthetics. However, something else may turn up yet. Mr. Vulsame will have told you that there is a sealed letter waiting for you."

"He did."

"Well, we haven't been into that yet. Would it be convenient?"

"Quite. If you will come on up to the house, we can open it now."

We went up the iron steps, and Mrs. Lade's servant admitted us. She was a young girl—very frightened, stupid, and tearful. Somehow it seemed strange to stand there in Myas's rooms, and to know that he would never enter them again. What had become of his proud boast to me that he would demonstrate to me personally the existence of the human soul? The news of his death had been an unexpected shock to me, but I felt the necessity to put personal feelings aside and to keep very keenly on the alert. It was obvious that Mr. Vulsame meant mischief, and I had promised Myas, in the event of his death, to do the best I could for Miss Lade.

The letter contained Myas's will, properly executed, and a short note for myself. The note merely said that Myas was engaged in a line of research which presented certain risks, and that if anything happened to him, he wanted to take that opportunity of thanking me for my great kindness to him in the past, and for my promise to look after Alice for the future.

"Had he any near relations?" asked the inspector. "I see he leaves this girl everything."

"No, he had no near relations. He has told me so more than once."

"I see," said the inspector. He made a few notes, including one of my name and address, and then left.

I saw Mrs. Lade for a few minutes. The poor woman was rather incoherent. It was clear that she regarded the presence of any policemen on the premises as a disgrace, and an inquest as a stain on her own personal honour. On these points I did my best to console her. Of Myas she spoke with great enthusiasm.

"A better and a kinder man no one could wish to see, if only he could have been kept from messing with chemicals, as I often told him. And now I must look forward to seeing Alice go the same way, she being of age and with a will of her own."

"How is she?"

"Seems like a person dazed. She is alone in her room, and been there the best part of the day, and perhaps it's as well. But, oh, she's quite strange to me."

"How do you mean, Mrs. Lade?"

"Well, not like my daughter. That's the bitterness of it. It's no fault of hers, mind. It's just this education that's done it. I often think that girls nowadays would be happier without it."

"What did you mean when you said that you must look forward to Alice going the same way?"

"Well, she has told me already that the work must go on, and when she is once determined on a thing there is no moving her. But to my mind it is simply disregarding the warning that God has given us. Of course, she may still think better of it. We can but hope."

It was true, as Vulsame had told me, that she knew the terms of the will, and that Alice was now comparatively a wealthy woman. I will do her the justice to say this did not seem to affect Mrs. Lade in the least, except in so far as it removed the terror of funeral expenses. "By which so many have been crippled," she added feelingly. "The money will be little good to Alice," she said, "for she will never marry now. There never was but one man in the world for her, and that was Dr. Myas." I was entirely of her opinion.

I left word with her that Miss Lade could see me at any time. She had only to send a telephone message, and I would come at once.

I now went back to Vulsame. I found him seated in my taxicab, and smoking one of the very worst cigars I have ever had the misfortune to smell.

"You've kept me waiting a hell of a time," he said angrily.

"Sorry," I said. I persuaded him not to talk to me in the cab, on the grounds that the traffic made it difficult for one to hear, and while he remained silent, I could think over the situation and make my plans. I studied his physiognomy very carefully. It struck me that, if necessary, Mr. Vulsame would probably be purchasable at a moderate figure, provided of course that he was allowed to save his face.

At St. James's Place he watched me as I paid the cabman. "My word!" he said. "You toffs don't think much about keeping them waiting, ticking up twopences all the time. But it runs up, doesn't it?"

"Yes," I said, "it runs up."

"But I suppose," he added tactfully, "you take that out of the estate.'"

He accepted with alacrity the offer of a whisky-and-soda. "I don't mind admitting," he said, "that I'm simply parched. A thing like this knocks one over a bit too, though of course I'm a doctor and used to it. I can tell you, it wasn't a very pretty sight when I went into that laboratory early this morning."

I had the whisky left by Mr. Vulsame for purposes of reference.

The more talkative he was, the better he would suit my purpose. I told him that I should be glad to have his opinion on some cigars of mine. I struck a match and handed it to him. In fact, I waited on the beast. For a moment or two he jabbered nonsense about the cigars, and then I struck in.

"There was one thing you told me this morning, Mr. Vulsame, that surprises me very much." "Ah," said Mr. Vulsame complacently,

"I dare say. I've surprised a good many people in my time. What was it?"

"Well, I don't see how poor Myas can possibly have interfered with your practice. I should have thought that was quite secure. Myas always spoke of you as an able man; for that matter, I could see as much for myself. If I may say so, I am sure your genial manners would make you popular in Fulham or anywhere else. I was sorry as well as surprised to hear that business was not very good with you."

"The competition is pretty keen everywhere," he said. "It doesn't take so very much to put a man wrong. What I have told you is quite correct, and my books will show it. If you doubt my word, you can see them."

"But, my dear fellow, why on earth should I doubt your word?"

"Very well, then. I suppose you know the lines Myas was working on. I did permit him to make certain observations and carry out certain experiments with patients of mine. It was all quite legitimate, mind you, or I wouldn't have allowed it. Not for a moment. But it got talked about, and, of course, it got exaggerated, and it did me a deal of harm."

"By the way, do give yourself another drink, Mr. Vulsame. And it is solely to this that you assign the falling off in your practice?"

"Solely. I'm as good as ever I was. Better." He took the other drink.

"Well," I said, "this, of course, is a thing which ought to be looked into. If it's not too delicate a question, did Dr. Myas make you any payment for these important services that you seem to have rendered him?"

"If you can call it payment."

"Oh, I didn't want to know the exact amount. That, of course, I shall get later, because, as his executor, I shall have his bankbook in my hands." I wished to spare Mr. Vulsame the humiliation of telling lies which would afterwards be discovered.

"Quite so," said Mr. Vulsame. "I knew that. Well, as a matter of fact, he did pay me what was agreed upon between us, before I knew what the result would be. It is the result that makes all the difference. What we've got to look at is the injury to the capital value of my practice. You understand what I mean by capital value? Quite so, I thought you would. If he had left me in his will a matter of two hundred—or, say, three hundred—pounds, I should never have said a word about this to anybody. But I understand that I'm not so much as mentioned."

"You are not. And you consider that you have really a moral claim against his estate."

"Moral claim. You've hit the phrase exactly."

"Then, of course, it becomes my duty to consider this. I must turn it over in my mind, and see what ought to be done. Naturally, you wouldn't expect a decision offhand."

"Not at all. I'm a reasonable man. Your time is mine." And he took another drink.

"There's one other point," I said. "What is your real opinion about the death of Myas?"

"Between ourselves?"

"Quite."

"The thing's as clear as mud. It was murder. And either the old woman or Miss Lade did it, though almost certainly it was Miss Lade."

"This," I said, "is very interesting."

I was pretty certain that it was not a case of murder. I was absolutely certain that, if it was murder, neither Mrs. Lade nor her daughter had anything to do with it. But I did not want any suspicion of Miss Lade to be stated publicly. These things cling to one and do harm, even when the suspicions are shown to be baseless. There is always some idiot who has read half the newspaper report of a sixteenth of the evidence, and thinks himself justified in expressing his wonder afterwards whether there was anything in it. There are some offences, of which the mere accusation is enough to produce something like ruin. My interview with Mr. Vulsame began to be, as I had frankly told him, very interesting.

Chapter 9

Mr. Vulsame waved a soiled and impressive hand at me. "Now, Mr. Compton," he said, "I'm going to tell you. I'm going to put all my cards on the table."

"That's very good of you."

"I dare say you thought me a little short in my manner with you up at Knox Street just now. I have been a good deal worried of late, and worry—especially financial worry—gets on one's nerves. No offence was intended."

I murmured something consolatory.

"As a matter of fact," Mr. Vulsame continued, "I have very great confidence in you, Mr. Compton, and I'm going to be quite candid with you. I think you had a high opinion of this Miss Lade, and from something poor Myas once let drop, that was what I gathered."

"Quite correct."

"So naturally, you are not inclined to believe in her guilt. Still, one must do one's duty. One has got to face the facts."

"Undoubtedly. And the facts?"

"Some of them are known already. One of them—the most serious of all—is at present known only to me. I didn't mention it to the inspector, or to anybody else. I'm going to mention it now. Let us see what happened. Mrs. Lade, her daughter and her servant, all went up to their respective bedrooms at a few minutes past ten last night. They are agreed upon that.

They left Myas at work in his laboratory in the garden as usual. He often worked very late. It is said that they did not leave their rooms until the following morning. The servant, who rose at six, discovered that Myas had not been in his bedroom all night, and then called up Mrs. Lade and her daughter.

"Now, as it happens, I have got a latchkey to the garden entrance in Durnford Place. Myas gave it me at a time when I was seeing him frequently, and often had to fetch him away to cases of mine—sometimes after the rest of the household were in bed. For the last three weeks I have seen much less of him. He told me that he had completed his observations, and that he did not think I could be of any further service to him. When I met him casually in the street, he was rather inclined to snub me. And that's not a thing I take from anybody.

"Last night, soon after twelve, I was coming back home. I'd been spending the evening with a few friends in a convivial sort of way. That is a most unusual thing with me. Doctors have to be temperate men. But the fact of the case is that I had been a good deal bothered by a patient of mine—a woman. She jabbered about malpractice and neglect, and threatened an action. There was nothing whatever in it. I shall have her signed up and planked into an asylum in a week. But it was a disturbing thing, and when some of my friends thought that I wanted cheering up, I didn't say no. Well, let's see what I'm talking about."

"You were coming back after being cheered up."

"Exactly. I took Durnford Place on my way. It occurred to me that I might as well go and look up Myas, and have some explanation with him. I wanted to talk to him about the way my practice was going down-hill. He was a generous man, and I felt quite sure he'd be prepared to meet me. I don't mind owning that I wanted another drink too. And it doesn't do for a man in my position to be seen passing into a 'pub' just before closing time. People might think I'd been called in professionally, or they might not. See?"

"Naturally, Mr. Vulsame. You showed your customary good judgment."

"As soon as I let myself into the garden, I saw that the laboratory was brightly lit up. Funnily enough, Myas had never shown me his laboratory, though I had dropped a hint or two about it. He was secretive about his work. I don't know to this day what it was that his particular line of research was aiming at. That garden-path, as you may have noticed, is all grown over with grass and moss. Your footsteps make no sound upon it. I got close up to the window, which was partly open, and was on the point of calling to him, when I heard within the studio two voices. I could not catch what was said; but one was the voice of Myas, and one was the voice of a woman. What would any gentleman do under those circumstances?"

"Go away and hold his tongue."

"That," said Viseme, with conscious pride, "is exactly what I did. I put myself in his place. I asked myself how I should like it if I were sitting in there with a girl, all cosy and comfortable, and somebody came and interfered, or dropped hints about it afterwards. However, we needn't go into that. I suppose you see the point. If Miss Lade says that she went to her bedroom shortly after ten last night, and did not leave it till somewhere about seven this morning, Miss Lade lies."

"You are sure it was her voice?"

"Pretty sure."

"Do you think it enough to be pretty sure?"

"Well, there is what might be called corroborative evidence. What had Miss Lade to gain by the death of Myas? Absolutely everything— he had left her every penny he possessed, and she knew it. What had any other woman to gain by his death? Nothing. It can have been no other woman than Miss Lade, though I dare say her old mother is mixed up in it as well. We will go on a little further. This morning I am called in and find Myas dead from an anaesthetic automatically administered. Now no medical man in his senses would dream of giving himself an anaesthetic in this way without having somebody present qualified to watch him, and to do anything that might be necessary.

"Miss Lade had been working as his assistant for some time, and was fully competent. I have definite proof in his own handwriting that on another occasion he had placed himself under an anaesthetic with Miss Lade in attendance. This time, either she deliberately altered the regulator of that mechanical pump, or she saw that things were going wrong and did nothing. Murder in either case."

"Well now, Mr. Vulsame, I'll give you my point of view. I know that Miss Lade did not murder Myas. I know it definitely. I have seen them together frequently, and I cannot be mistaken. Miss Lade's devotion to that dead man was a very real and a very beautiful thing. She would have given her life for him cheerfully. If your evidence before the coroner is on the lines that you have just shown me, that is some of the evidence with which I shall meet it. You see, my friend, that it is of no use for you to say that no medical man would dream of administering an anaesthetic to himself unless there was some competent person with him.

"It is no use to say it, because that automatic pump proves you wrong. If Miss Lade were present and if she were competent to watch the process of anaesthesis, she was also competent to give the anaesthetic, and there was no necessity whatever for any mechanical apparatus. Myas had made many experiments upon himself with anaesthetics. You have told me there is a record of them. Probably he had found out exactly what he thought he could do within the limits of safety. He may have been exceptional in taking the risk, but the apparatus proves that he took it.

"You say that Miss Lade lied, and I fully agree with you. It was natural that any woman should lie under those circumstances. If she was with him alone in that laboratory so late at night, after the rest of the household had gone to bed, and this became generally known, her character would suffer for it—though in this respect as in the other I believe her to be entirely innocent."

"Put like that, it does of course look different," said Vulsame.

"Quite so. Now you and I are reasonable men, and can talk this over. You did not find me unreasonable when you spoke, for instance, of your moral claim against Myas's estate. I am somewhat more than the trustee for Miss Lade. I was asked by Myas to look after her. I give you my word of honour that I'm absolutely convinced of her innocence. If you mention before the coroner that Miss Lade was, or may have been, alone in the laboratory with Myas after twelve last night, I have no doubt that she will have an explanation to give. That explanation would go along with my evidence, which I tell you frankly would be dead against you.

"But though this preposterous charge of murder will be shown to have nothing in it, in the eyes of the pious and evil-thinking people of Knox Street Miss Lade's reputation will be gone. I do not think it necessary for you to tell the coroner anything whatever about your visit to the laboratory last night. Remember, I was more the friend of Myas than I was of Miss Lade, and I wouldn't say this if I believed there had been the barest possibility of foul play. The reasonable thing and the chivalrous thing for you to do is to say nothing whatever about this incident. And if you are reasonable, you will also find me reasonable."

"In what particular way do you mean?"

He shot one quick glance at me from his small and furtive eyes, and I saw that he understood exactly. I had to put the thing plainly enough, but not too plainly. I trust that I appeared to be more at my ease than was really the case.

"Reasonable in every way, I hope. To take one instance—the first that happens to occur to my mind—there is your moral claim against the estate of which I am trustee. You know, of course, that a moral claim is not a legal claim. I cannot pay you one penny out of the estate; if I had the best will in the world to do it, the law does not permit me to do it. This does not mean that I do not recognise the force of your moral claim. I am quite sure that Myas never wished you to be a loser by any transactions which you had with him."

"That's absolutely certain. If I had done what I intended to do last night, and what I was prevented by the natural delicacy of a gentleman from doing, I shouldn't be talking to you like this. As things stand, I am sacrificed to my feelings of chivalry."

"Well, now, Mr. Vulsame, the consideration of what Myas would have wished has great weight with me. If I wrote you a cheque on my account for, say, three hundred pounds—I think those were the figures—it would not inconvenience me in any way, and it would indeed give me a great pleasure to do this small thing for my dead friend. Naturally, I should not wish to act less chivalrously than yourself."

"If that is the way you look at it, I'm agreed—perfectly agreed. Why not? The reputation of the girl and the memory of the dead man both gain from the transaction. But if you put it to me that I'm to take three hundred pounds to hold my jaw—"

"My dear fellow, my dear Mr. Vulsame, please make no such pre-posterous suggestion as that. Do you think I'm not aware that I'm dealing with a gentleman? No, you may be assured that the arrange-ment between us will never be represented in that light. It is a matter purely between ourselves, and concerns nobody else. You will come to me after the inquest, and we will complete the matter, and not an-other word will be said about it."

"Very good. These cigars are first-class. I'll just take another and one last little drink, with your permission, and then I must be off. But I tell you candidly—there are some queer things about this case, and they beat me entirely."

"You are quite right. There are several things in it which I cannot understand in the least. What were you referring to particularly?"

"Well, I'll tell you one thing. In a corner of that workroom this morning there was a whole lot of apparatus. What it was I can't say, but it was a big elaborate thing, and must have cost a pot of money. I should imagine it was electrical. Now that was all smashed to bits, just as if it had been broken up with a hammer. What's more, I found a hammer there that might have done it."

"Yes, it's strange. But I can't see that such a thing should have any bearing on the death of Myas. For all we know, Myas himself may have smashed the thing. He had a nasty temper when his work disap-pointed him, and he was never very patient, with anything ineffective. By the way, before you go you might give me your latchkey to the garden in Durnford Place. I am returning my own key to Miss Lade, and I'll send yours with it."

"Myas gave it me—he didn't lend it me. Still, I don't want to make a fuss about it. Anything that you say is right is good enough for me. Besides, the damned thing is no use to me anyway. Here you are, Mr. Compton."

He laid the key down on the table. It appeared that he had his cigar-case with him, and was willing to pay me the great compliment of filling it with my cigars at my suggestion. He had not, however, brought his purse with him, and borrowed a couple of sovereigns for what he described as incidental current expenses. He then, to my great joy, drew on his absurd gloves, picked up his hat, and demanded a taxicab.

When he had gone, I reflected at length on my own position. I knew Miss Lade to be innocent. I knew definitely that she had not murdered Myas. I knew that if she was in the laboratory after twelve the night before, it was merely on account of the work that Myas was doing, and that she had made the visit secretly for obvious reasons—to prevent servants or Vulsame from misunderstanding her. This being so, it seemed to me the thing to do was to save her as far as possible even from the shadow of suspicion.

But one fact remained—I was about to pay a man three hundred pounds to suppress evidence at an inquest, and I did not quite like the thought of that when I went round to see my solicitor at his private house that night. I liked it so little that I did not say a word to him about it. Otherwise, it would have interested me to have asked him how many years' penal servitude I was likely to get if I was found out. Certainly, for a respectable, law-abiding, middle-aged gentleman I had gone rather far. But I thought the circumstances justified me.

Chapter 10

The coroner's jury returned a verdict of Accidental Death, and there was little or no suggestion during the inquest that any other verdict was possible. Mr. Vulsame was quite at his best. He had a frock-coat and his professional manner. He was omniscient, but he was also sympathetic. He spoke of Myas as a singularly gifted man, who had at one time come to him for advice. Myas, so he told us, was interested in medical psychology, and made many experiments upon himself; he (Vulsame) had given him a warning on this point on a previous occasion. In fact, Vulsame was very impressive and magnificent. Possibly with a view to earning his money, he mentioned that Myas was very happily engaged, and that Miss Lade's devotion to him was a real and very beautiful thing. The echo of my own words made me squirm.

I had not seen Miss Lade before the inquest. She was dressed entirely in black, of course, and kept her veil down. She spoke in a low voice, and seemed perfectly self-possessed. There was even a vague suggestion of dominance and decision about her which I had not noticed before. She was not required to say much. If Vulsame's story of the two voices in the laboratory was a true story—and certainly I believed it—then Miss Lade lied, and she lied simply, firmly and well.

My own evidence was merely to the effect that Myas had no financial trouble, and no other cause so far as I knew for taking his life. I confirmed Vulsame's opinion of the happiness of his engagement, and I mentioned that to my knowledge Myas had been anticipating a considerable success in his line of scientific research.

The coroner had a few wise words to say on the distinction between eccentricity and insanity. The jury might reasonably come to the conclusion that Myas was slightly eccentric, but they could not go further than that. Many medical men, he reminded them, had tried experiments upon themselves. Mr. Vulsame, who had given his evidence admirably, had told them that he himself had found a record of similar experiments in Myas's handwriting, and had given him a very proper and judicious warning against them.

Altogether it was a great day for Vulsame. As we left the court, I handed him an envelope, and he thanked me. "Pulled it off all right, eh?"

"I think you gave your evidence admirably, Mr. Vulsame."

He tapped the breast-pocket in which he had placed the envelope. Not a word about this to anybody, you know."

"Much better not," I agreed. "It could be so easily misunderstood."

The envelope contained three hundred pounds in Bank of England notes. I had not thought it advisable to pay by cheque. I had even taken the trouble to get the notes from four different sources. In fact, I was not prepared to trust Vulsame quite so far as I could throw him.

In accordance with the directions contained in his will, the body of Daniel Myas was cremated and no religious service was held over it, and I was the only person present. Mr. Vulsame had expressed an intention of being there, but was prevented by a professional engagement. I think it was Miss Lade who was responsible for the absence of herself and her mother. Old Mrs. Lade spoke to me about it and seemed to regret it. She had the deep interest in funerals which is characteristic of her class. "But we mothers have to do what we're told nowadays," she said. She also expressed a hope that friends in Knox Street would not think the funeral arrangements shabby. She admitted that Myas's directions for simplicity and his prohibition of floral tributes had to be observed.

That year, for the first time in my life, I spent August and September in town. I was engaged in clearing up all the business of Myas's estate. Fortunately, it proved to be a very simple matter; Myas had always been in the habit of consulting a solicitor as to his investments, and very few of them had to be changed.

I called at Knox Street on the day after the funeral, but Miss Lade was not to be seen. I did see her once in the following week, for a few moments only, at her solicitor's office, on matters of business connected with the estate. And I noticed then that her manner to me had changed completely. She said as little as possible, and she got away as soon as possible. She told me nothing as to her future plans. She asked for no advice. I noticed further that she avoided meeting my eye directly.

I met her again by chance, and rather curiously. I had received a letter from old Welsford. I was meaning to run down to my cottage for a week-end, and there were certain things which Welsford desired me to bring with me. He wanted a rain-gauge of a particular kind, and his letter reminded me that I had promised him his blessed rain-gauge. He also described the garden thermometer as being now "past work," and suggested that it should be replaced. That was how I came to visit the shop of Denville & Moore, the instrument makers in Holborn.

In the shop was Alice Lade, talking freely and even urgently to a managerial and dignified person on the other side of the counter. She had her back to me and did not see me. As I waited for an assistant at the other counter, I could hear what was said. People do not tell their secrets in the shops of the scientific instrument makers, and I felt no scruples about it.

"You must have got Dr. Myas's original specifications," said Miss Lade.

"We have, madam," said the man. "We always keep everything of that kind. Our difficulty is that while this piece of apparatus was being constructed. Dr. Myas modified those specifications and in some cases departed from them altogether. It was a very delicate piece of work indeed, and very complicated. We could construct the apparatus again according to the original specification, but we feel sure it would not give you satisfaction. He supervised every detail of the construction himself."

"That's all right," said Miss Lade. "I can understand that. Then let me see the workman to whom he gave his verbal instructions. Only an intelligent man could be employed for work of that kind, and he would be certain to remember any instance in which the specification was not followed."

"Probably he would. But there we are brought face to face with another difficulty. Dr. Myas's orders were given to our foreman. He was a very able and well-educated man, but unfortunately, he was intemperate, and for that reason we had to get rid of him. We cannot say now where he is."

At this moment my assistant produced rain-gauges, and my attention was for the moment diverted. But as he was packing up my purchases, I again heard Miss Lade—"That's what you must do, then.

You must advertise for this man. At any cost I must have this apparatus reconstructed." And then she turned and saw me.

She seemed startled and embarrassed, but what struck me most was that she looked very ill. She shook hands with me in a perfunctory sort of way, murmured a silly word or two about the weather, said good morning, and turned to go.

But almost immediately she turned back again. Her eyes beckoned me, and I followed her out to the cab which was waiting for her.

"Get in, please," she said.

As she spoke, I looked at her, and saw that her face was contorted with pain. She seemed suddenly to have grown many years older. I followed her into the cab. The driver apparently already had his directions. Alice Lade sat with her elbows on her knees and her hands covering her face. Then suddenly she touched my arm.

"Can you get me some brandy?" she said. "I have a kind of neuralgia that gives me such intense pain, that I'm afraid of fainting."

By the direction of my doctor, I always carry with me a tiny flask of brandy, though for the last two years I am thankful to say I have never wanted it. It was useful in this emergency.

She drank eagerly. Her colour returned slightly, and her face became more tranquil.

"Thank you very much," she said. "If you will stop the cab, I won't keep you any longer. I have to go on to some chemists in the City that are doing some work for me."

I was angry, of course, but I trust that I only appeared firm.

"You are not fit to go on to the City, or to do any further business this morning. Miss Lade. If you insist upon it, I shall certainly come with you. If you will promise me to go straight home, I will leave you. You will probably think me very officious and interfering, but you must remember that I promised to look after you."

"I don't think you officious or interfering. I am really grateful to you. It is only that just at present I cannot bear to have anyone at all with me. I must be alone. But I will do as you say, and will go home at once."

I stopped the cab and got out without shaking hands. As I stood with the door open, I said: "To Durnford Place or Knox Street?"

"To Durnford Place, please. Thank you again. One day perhaps—" She did not finish her sentence, and once more covered her face with her hands. I waited a second or two, and then closed the door and gave the driver his order.

I had a good deal to think of, as I sat alone after lunch that day. Try how I would to prevent it, Vulsame's suspicions of Alice Lade would come back to my mind. I told myself that these suspicions were unworthy of me. Miss Lade had seemed somewhat ungrateful; she had snubbed me and discarded me for no reason of which I was aware. Neither of those things should have made me suspicious, and I have always considered it rather low class to be wounded and resentful. But it was in vain that I tried to bully myself into a better frame of mind. The horrible and astounding fact was this—if Miss Lade had really been responsible for the death of Daniel Myas, I should have expected her to behave very much as she had behaved. She looked to me like a woman tortured with remorse and sleepless nights.

CHAPTER 11

Naturally, Myas was a good deal in my mind during these months. Again and again, I recalled his definite and boastful promise that before the year was out, he would demonstrate to me the existence of a human soul, of which mind and body were but the concomitants. Great had been his enthusiasm. Everything had been made to give way to his work. He had risked both life and love for it. He had looked forward with the utmost confidence to the day of his experiment. He had told me that it would revolutionize thought—that it would make a new heaven and a new earth. Had the experiment succeeded, his claim would perhaps have been justified.

And now all the years of work, all the ambition and ability, had ended in a little heap of dust in an oak casket. And things went on as before. I still insisted upon believing in Miss Lade's innocence; and if she were indeed innocent, then it seemed bitter that so much should have been wrecked by so little—by a flaw in a piece of mechanism, or by one careless moment in Myas himself.

One or two obituary notices had appeared. That in the *Lancet* was brief, but peculiarly admirable. Without taking back one word that had been said about Myas's pamphlet, it still found much to praise in him, and its expression of regret that he had not lived to complete his researches, seemed both decent and genuine. It has occasionally been my lot to read obituary notices of those whom I have known personally, and I have read them always with a kind of surprise. I have never recognised in them the men that I knew. This may be because it is the important part of them which figures in the obituary, and the characteristic trifles which one has grown to like or dislike are omitted. Certainly no one could have reconstructed Daniel Myas from his obituary notice. His work was there, but the man himself was not. After all, it would have been difficult to give a picture of him; the strange blend of serious strength and amusing weaknesses is common enough and human enough; but it is difficult to make it seem real.

There was much that was rather morbid in this business of Myas and Alice Lade, and I was not sorry when, early in October, another subject occurred to occupy my mind. An old friend of mine, coming rather late in life into possession of the family archives, chanced upon a manuscript diary relating in part to the Peninsular War. The rather absurd idea occurred to him that I was just the man to edit it for publication, and I'm afraid I was too vain to put the idea aside at once. I said that I would at any rate read this diary. I did read it, and I found it extremely interesting.

It was filled, however, with things which I did not understand, and allusions which I could not follow. I thought I had just an average knowledge of eighteenth-century history, but average knowledge was of very little use here. I was driven to the British Museum and to other libraries. I think I may say that I consider the joy of clearing up a difficult point in an old personal history to be one of the purest and noblest that I have known.

One sunny day, more like midsummer than October, I had spent the whole morning in the British Museum, and afterwards had lunched at the club. I had been rather successful that morning and had several excellent notes to add to my edition of that diary, if ever I undertook it. I went back to St. James's Place immediately after luncheon, in order to get to work again.

I let myself into the flat with my latchkey, and found on the table in the hall a registered letter in a foolscap envelope. It was addressed to me in a handwriting which, if I had not known him to be dead, I could have sworn to as the handwriting of Daniel Myas.

One obvious explanation occurred to me. It might actually be his writing; it might be some letter which he had left in the care of Alice Lade with instructions to forward it to me at this interval after his death.

I was on the point of opening it, when my man came out and told me that a person giving the name of Mrs. Lade had called to see me.

"Is she here now?" I asked.

"Well, yes, sir. She said that she knew you very well, and seemed so insistent that I allowed her to wait. Will you see her, sir, or shall I

213

send her away?"

"I'll see her. Show her into my study."

I put the letter down on the table in my study with the address downwards. Mrs. Lade would also have recognised the handwriting, and would probably have found it very upsetting. She was easily upset.

She was well-dressed in deep mourning, and seemed rather embarrassed by her clothes and by the situation in which she now found herself. As she struggled towards speech, I told her I was sorry I had been out when she called, and that she had had to wait.

"That did not matter in the least, sir. I had expected to wait. I have been made quite comfortable and had the *Times* newspaper."

"What's more to the point," I said, "is, have you had any lunch?"

"Oh yes, sir," she said. "Yes, Mr. Compton, I've lunched."

Here, suddenly and without warning, Mrs. Lade burst into tears. I dislike tears. I have the feeling, which is perhaps rather selfish, that people should not weep when I am present. However, I tried to be sympathetic and to find out what was the matter.

The flood-gates of her speech were now wide open. But some little time elapsed before I could rescue anything like a coherent story out of the torrent. She repeated over and over again that nothing had been the same since the death of Daniel Myas. She asked tragically what daughters were for. She said that she had always been respectable, as anybody in Knox Street would tell me. Friends in Knox Street had been kind to her under trying circumstances. She informed me that she was not a good sailor, far from it. She gave me, with more minuteness than delicacy, the details of the disease of which poor Willy's wife died, long before I found out that Willy was her brother in New York.

Gradually and patiently, I drew out all the facts and pieced them together. The thing which was affecting Mrs. Lade most was the great change which had taken place in her daughter. In the matter of money Alice was apparently generous. "I can buy what I like and go where I like. Cabs I take frequently. If it wasn't for this sacred time of mourning, I might be sitting in the theatre every evening in the week. And I should enjoy it too. For it takes you out of yourself."

But it appeared that Alice showed her mother very little affection, and was seldom with her. During the greater part of her time, she was shut up in the workroom in which Myas died. She refused to see any of her friends in Knox Street, and Mrs. Lade was tired of making one excuse after another to them. She spoke very little to anybody. And, although she caught cold, sitting late in that laboratory, and although it had affected her voice, she had refused to allow her mother to nurse her at all. "Different altogether, she is," sobbed Mrs. Lade. "And ammoniated quinine she simply refuses to look at."

At this juncture a letter had arrived from Mrs. Lade's widowed brother in New York. He had a house and children, and he needed someone to look after them. His experiences with paid housekeepers had not been encouraging. Some of them, he said, were sniffy and superior and incompetent, some of them drank, and some of them desired him to marry them. He appealed to Mrs. Lade and her daughter to come over and live with him. Mrs. Lade showed me this letter, and I was rather surprised that it could have been written by her brother. In spite of the fact that she was a bad sailor, the idea had appealed to Mrs. Lade. She had relinquished her shop now, because there was no necessity to keep it on. I should imagine the income derived from it had never been very attractive.

At the same time, Mrs. Lade was a woman who liked to have an occupation. "Added to which," she said, "they tell me America's a nice place." She had put the matter before her daughter, and her daughter's decision had grievously distressed her. Mrs. Lade was certainly to go to live with her brother. It was her duty. All the money that was wanted for her outfit and passage would be forthcoming, and on her arrival in New York she would receive a sufficient income to provide for her in comfort and independence. Thus, if she and the widowed Willy did not happen to hit it off together, she would be free to employ her activities elsewhere. Alice had urged—almost ordered—her to go. But at the same time Alice definitely refused to accompany her. She said that she was continuing the work which she had begun with Daniel Myas, and that this made it impossible for her to leave England. Tears and persuasions had seemed to have no effect on her.

I tried to get Mrs. Lade to see the thing from another point of view. Alice's resolve to continue that work was really a kind of loyalty to the dead man. But Mrs. Lade was not to be convinced.

"If she would promise to come out a year after me, or even two years, I could be satisfied. It's the separation for ever that is hard for me to face. But when I speak to her about it, she gives that quick little wave of the hand, same as the poor doctor always did when you annoyed him about anything; and I don't know that I've told you the worst yet."

The worst proved to be that for three days Mrs. Lade had not even seen her daughter.

"Do you know where she has gone?" I asked.

"Gone? She's not gone. She's still there. She has the rooms that were his now, and her time is spent between them and the workshop, and most of it in the workshop. Do you know, Mr. Compton, that I've had doors locked against me in my own house? Do you know that she doesn't even take her meals with anything like regularity? A few words scrawled on a scrap of paper—that's all I've had from her these last three days. I'll tell you what I think about it."

"Well?" I asked.

Mrs. Lade tapped her forehead significantly. "That, to the best of my belief, is what is the matter with her. There has been no history of it in my family, but, as Mrs. Porter was saying to me in Knox Street only this morning, grief may overturn the mind. If I had had any feeling of confidence in that Vulsame, I should have called him in, expense being no longer a consideration. But there, what use would it have been if I had? It's twenty to one she would have refused to see him."

I thought this extremely likely. The conduct of Alice was becoming more and more inexplicable to me. However, the absurdity of Viilsame's suspicions seemed to be demonstrated by it, and I was rather ashamed that the same suspicions had occurred to my own mind. A woman who had murdered Myas would not care to shut herself up in the rooms which he had occupied, and in the laboratory where he had died. Alice Lade had always had a simple natural affection for her mother; this had apparently vanished. The desire for solitude was remarkable. There were points in her behaviour when I met her at the instrument makers', which had seemed to me curious. I knew, too, how great her devotion to Myas had been. It was quite possible that, as a result of his death, her mind had given way.

I sympathized with the poor old woman, and did the best I could to console her. I promised that I would myself go and see Alice. I would talk things over with her, and, if I found that she was ill, I thought I could use my authority sufficiently to persuade her to see a doctor. I think that when old Mrs. Lade left me, she was much comforted by what I had said. In my own mind I felt far from sure that Alice would see me, and wondered what my next move ought to be in that case.

When my visitor had gone, I picked up that letter from the table and tore open one end of it. Something fell from it with a metallic little tinkle, and I picked it up. It was the latchkey to the garden entrance in Durnford Place.

The letter which accompanied the latchkey covered several pages of foolscap, and was written entirely in the characteristic handwriting of Daniel Myas. It seemed to have been written freely and firmly, and gave not the slightest suggestion of a laboured imitation of his writing. The sheets were fastened together by a staple placed, as he always placed it, in the middle of the top of the page—not in the corner, which is a more usual custom. My eye fell on the date under the address, and I was astounded. It was the same date as the postmark. I will give the letter in full—

Dear Compton,

It is not a coincidence, a chance similarity; it is I, Daniel Myas, who write this, though the hand that holds the pen is the hand of Alice Lade. And I shall redeem my promise to you—to prove by demonstration that the Ego, the soul, the self, exists independently of mind and body, though it is only by mind and body that it becomes cognisable by man under his present conditions. I had hoped to redeem that promise differently and more fully. I assure you I write now with no pride in what I have done, but even with an intense horror of it. I have reached the end to which I devoted so many years of labour, and I would gladly give all that I possess—yes, and life itself—if it could be undone again. I do not write to you to boast of any achievement. I write to ask your help.

Do you understand? I am supposed to be Alice Lade. I am possessed of her mind and her body, but with some modifications that have already taken place, and with others, I think, imminent. I am not Alice Lade and I am Daniel Myas. Yes, I know it is incredible, and I know what facile explanation will leap to your mind at once.

But that explanation of madness plus a considerable gift for forgery is wrong. I am Daniel Myas. I want your help. I want you to come to the laboratory in the garden. If you do that—if you see my face and hear my voice—you will need no other evidence. You will know that I am Daniel Myas.

At this moment the door opened. I was absorbed in what I was reading, and the opening of the door made me start up, but it was merely my servant.

"The gentleman who was with you here, sir, some months ago, Mr.

Vulsame, has called, and wishes to see you particularly."

The man hesitated. "Well?" I said.

"He is not sober, sir."

"Very well. I'm not at home. He is not to wait."

"Very good, sir."

I picked up again the pages in the handwriting of Daniel Myas, and I read on—

I have to tell you what happened on the night when my soul, the soul of Daniel Myas, became cognisable only through the mind and body of Alice Lade. I will tell it as clearly as I can. But you must make allowances for me. You saw what I was like at that shop in Holborn, and you can believe that I am rarely free from actual physical pain. For months too I have lived in an agony of fear and remorse, working without hope of success, and with the fixed intention to commit suicide if I failed. It was only a few days ago that something happened to make me give up that intention. I still suffer, though with a flicker of hope that I may yet undo the evil that I have done.

Remember, too, that the mind at my disposal is not my mind. There are things which I knew once and know no longer. There are abilities which I once had, but no longer possess. Some of these things may come back to me, for some of them have already come back. At the moment, for instance, I can write with equal ease the handwriting of Alice or my own. Other modifications have occurred. Still, I write as one not in full possession of my own powers, but limited by the medium through which my Ego becomes cognisable. The Daniel Myas of some months ago could have explained in the smallest detail what his intentions were, and how he proposed to carry them out. I have not these details, and am left with generalities.

I know that it seemed to me that there was but one way in which the independent existence of the Ego could be demonstrated, and that this was by a transference of an Ego to a mind and body other than that with which it had previously been associated. I put it clumsily. Simply, the aim was that Alice Lade and I should for a while exchange ourselves—or souls, as I think you preferred to call them. Many years of experiment and observation had convinced me that this exchange was possible. There were limitations, of course, and some of these I cannot

218

recall. But I know that the exchange could only take place between two persons of opposite sexes. I know that it had to take place when these two persons were anaesthetised.

I have a recollection of a piece of very complicated and elaborate mechanism. I know what firm made it for me. It was in their shop that you saw me. I recollect that there was the necessity for most accurate timing, and that the whole experiment hung, so to speak, on a sixth of a second. Further than that my memory has not helped me. I have seen the specifications of that mechanism written with my own hand, and I cannot understand them. I have by me many volumes of manuscript notes that I made from time to time for my own assistance, and they are as much Greek to me as if I were a first-year student. However, as I have said, a few days ago there came a flicker of hope that my knowledge will come back. In one particular it has already returned, and most wonderfully.

You noticed, when we met in Paris, that I spoke French just about as well as I spoke English. I knew the language thoroughly, of course, and therefore the compliment meant nothing to me. The only people who like to be flattered on their French are the people who cannot speak it. I am glad, though, that you noticed it, because it gives me further evidence with which to convince you. In my new incarnation, in the body of Alice Lade, I had practically no knowledge at all of French. I could not read a French book, though I knew what a word here and there meant. I knew what Alice knew exactly, and nothing more than that. A few days ago, quite suddenly, I found that I was actually thinking in French. The whole thing had come back to me. That is why I hope more important knowledge than that may yet come back.

I paused a moment as I read this. To say that the only people who cared for compliments on their French were the people who could not speak it, would be quite characteristic of Daniel Myas, but Alice Lade would certainly not have said it.

The letter went on:

On the night of my supposed death, Alice came secretly to the workroom, as she had often done before. The righteous and evil-minded people of the neighbourhood made such secrecy a necessity. An hour or more was spent in preparation for the

219

experiment, but I cannot remember in detail what was done. When I try to recall it now, I seem to see myself handling different pieces of apparatus, but I seem to see with the eyes of a person who does not in every case understand the why and the wherefore of what is being done. My last recollection of the moment when we both were passing under the influence of the anaesthetic is the tick-tack of the machinery, seeming to grow intolerably loud and then dying away as if it had vanished into some distant grey mist.

My recollection only becomes perfectly clear at the moment when I recovered from the anaesthetic. It was a sudden recovery. I stood up and rubbed my eyes, trying to recall where I was and what I was engaged upon. Then I looked, round, and saw, huddled in a chair close to me, my own dead body. I turned and looked into a mirror, and from the mirror the face of Alice Lade looked back at me. Half of the experiment had succeeded and half had failed. My own Ego was transferred to the body and mind of Alice Lade, but where was she? What had I done with her?

Then followed a short period of panic and madness. I had the feelings of a murderer, and was possessed with the idea that, to save myself, it was necessary to remove all evidence of the actual experiment which had taken place. I found a hammer and broke up the delicate apparatus which I had employed, and no longer understood. I burned in the stove papers which I think now should have been kept. Remember, I had become a frightened woman. I did things for which there was no reason whatever. I began to make everything neat and tidy. I put drugs away in their place. I swept the broken bits of apparatus into one corner of the room. I hid the little automatic pump which had administered the anaesthetic to the brain of Alice Lade. The other automatic pump I did not dare to touch, because it was too near to the dead body. That, perhaps, was as well.

I wanted to get out into the open air. I left the dead man lying there, closed and locked the door, and went into the garden. A breath of wind sprang up and shook the dark trees, so that they seemed to be living things that were trying to get at me. I fled up the staircase. The body and mind of Alice seemed to work automatically, doing actions which she must often have repeated, actions which were no longer controlled by the higher centres. I found my way in the dark through a part of the house where I had never been before. I stepped aside to avoid obstacles. At one point I was very careful to tread very quietly on tiptoe. I found the handle of the door easily, without fumbling for it, knowing just where it would be. It was Alice's bedroom-door.

It sometimes happens that one comes upon a scene which is really absolutely new, and yet seems familiar. On a road where one has never been before, one seems to expect every bit of it as it comes into view. It is, I suppose, the memory of a dream. My feelings in that room were very much like that. I slept there. It seems a wonderful thing, but for two hours I actually slept. And after that came hours of horror, on which I do not wish to linger. You are not an imaginative man, Compton, but I think you'll suppose pretty well what I went through. I was not able that night to make any plan of action for the future. All that I thought of was to keep the secret and to save myself at the inquest. I remained alone as much as possible, and said as little as possible. At the inquest, as you know, I lied.

After the inquest, I tried to get to work again. It was a hopeless business. I was working with the cortex of Alice Lade, not of Daniel Myas. At every step I found that I did not remember and did not know. I tried to get the apparatus reconstructed, which I had broken up in my panic. This has been done in some sort of a way, but I do not think it is right, and in any case, I do not understand its use. I suffered tortures from insomnia and from headache and neuralgia. I was filled with fears that Mrs. Lade, or someone else who had known Alice, would see something strange in me, and would guess my secret. Suicide appeared to be the only thing left for me.

Then, a few days ago, as I have told you, I suddenly recovered one branch of knowledge which I had lost. Who knows that in time the rest may not come back to me? The nature of Alice was plastic and receptive. The dominant force of my own Ego is even now working upon it. It has modified her mind. It has even produced physical changes. Let me become Daniel Myas with the knowledge that he had before, and with some of the ability that he had before, and I will undo some of the harm which I have done. The soul of Alice Lade shall once more become cognizable by her own mind and body. And my own soul shall go out into whatever it may be that awaits the lost.

I know that my own feelings before the experiment were feelings of triumph. I felt that I, and I alone, had the secret of life and death. As I write that now, with my present defective knowledge, it looks like the raving of a megalomaniac, but it all seemed logical to my mind then, based on science and working out inevitably. Is there not a faint possibility that I may find myself again in the same position, not with the same feelings of triumph, for these can never come back, but with the same confidence in myself and with the same certainty that what I have done I can also undo?

I cannot stop here. There are many people in this neighbourhood who knew Alice Lade, and will notice the changes that are taking place in her. Much of her special knowledge is slipping from me. Mrs. Lade speaks of things which she expects me to know all about, and I know nothing of them. The strain of fencing with this is becoming too much for me. An opportunity has now arisen to get Mrs. Lade away to America. I feel a great deal of pity for her. I want to spare her as much as possible, and for that reason alone it is best that she should go. There, perhaps, you will be able to help me. But there are many other ways in which I need your help.

I had intended to cut myself adrift from you altogether. You probably noticed that I had intended to let you think that Alice Lade still lived, and that I was dead. I was ashamed to let you think the truth. I am ashamed still, but I am compelled to appeal to you. What was done must be undone. You must help me to get away from Knox Street, and you must find for me some place where I can be absolutely alone. If necessary, you must help me in the work. I think circumstances will arise which will require me to give you a power of attorney to deal with all financial business. You understand what I am asking, Compton? I am asking you to help me to bring Alice back again. You must do it.

It cannot all be arranged by letter. You must come and see me, painful and shocking though this will be to you. I enclose the key of the garden entrance in Durnford Place, the key which you returned. Come tonight after ten, when there will be no fear of interruption.

There was no signature to the letter. By the time that I had finished reading it, it was beginning to grow dark. I switched on all the lights in the room. I locked the letter away in a drawer, so that I might not see it. I picked up a review and began to read, and found that the words meant nothing to me. I felt sick with horror and disgust. I could not bear to remain alone in my room. As I rose to go out, I heard a loud voice in the passage outside. It was the voice of Mr. Vulsame.

Chapter 13

I had never expected that I could hear with pleasure the voice of Vulsame, even in his more sober moments. But now this crude and material brute was almost a relief to my mind. My servant came in and appeared to be agitated. Mr. Vulsame had not only returned, but had definitely refused to go again. He was sitting on a chair in the hall, using the most awful language, and saying that if I was out, he should wait there till I came back again.

"I think," I said, "it might amuse me to see this man for a few moments. Let him come in here."

Mr. Vulsame lurched into the room. His gait was slightly more intoxicated than his speech, and his speech was not strictly sober.

"Glad to see you've got more sense than that damned fool of a servant of yours, Compton," said Mr. Vulsame aggressively.

"Sit down," I said, "and tell me what your business with me is."

"You'll know that fast enough, just when I like and how I like. You'll find I'm top dog this time. Don't issue orders to me, because I won't take 'em. I can sit and I can stand."

"The latter," I said, "seems to be an over-statement."

In illustration of my words, he sat down hurriedly and dropped his hat.

"Now then," he said, don't give me any of your damned superior airs, because I'm sick of 'em. I don't want 'em. What I want is a three-finger whisky and a little soda water."

"On a superficial observation I should say you are mistaken. But if you really think so, you had better go out and get it."

"Did I say something just now about your damned superior airs? because if I didn't, I meant to. Don't let me have to speak twice. If you offered me a drink, I wouldn't take it. I'd throw it in your face. I can buy a drink if I want one. I've got money, and I'm going to get more. I'm going to get it before I go home to my dinner tonight."

"Then I'd better not detain you. Go and get it by all means."

"That's where you slip up, my friend. That's where you come down and hurt yourself. I'm going to get that money out of you, unless you want to do time. You wouldn't look very pretty in a suit of clothes with broad arrows all over it."

"No," I said. "And what is it exactly that I'm going to do time for?"

"For bribing an honest man to suppress legal evidence at an inquest, and letting a murderer go free."

"I have no recollection of anything of the kind. There has been no murder, so far as I know. The last time I had the pleasure of any conversation with you, you pointed out that you were incapable of taking a bribe, but were willing to receive some slight compensation for damage to your practice caused by the late Daniel Myas. That is correct, isn't it?"

"It's your way of putting it. I've got my own way. Why are Mrs. Lade and her daughter going to bolt to America.? Does that look like innocence? You seem to think I know nothing. I was called in to attend a family in Knox Street this morning, and I picked up a thing or two, I can tell you. If I don't go straight off to the police and tell them everything I know, I run a risk of getting into a good deal of trouble myself, and I don't run risks for nothing."

"What is the figure," I said, "at which you do run risks?"

"One thousand pounds," said Mr. Vulsame solemnly.

"It is a large sum. I have not so much money at my bank at present. I should be compelled to realise securities."

"Can't help that," said Vulsame. "You've brought it on yourself."

"Suppose I paid you this sum, what security have I got that you will not come here tomorrow demanding another thousand?"

"You've the security of my word of honour. You're dealing with a gentleman. You seem to me to be continually forgetting that."

"Well," I said, "of course that would make a difference. If I could have your word of honour given me definitely in writing, I might be prepared to pay this sum, without admitting that I have been in the wrong in any way, but simply in order to save a public scandal."

"Quite so," said Vulsame. "I see your point. You're a sensible man, Mr. Compton. I said so when I came into the room, and I say so again. You don't want any public scandal. Give me this sum of money, and you'll get no public scandal. You'll never hear of it again. Nobody will. And I'll write anything you like. But as a matter of business, you don't get my undertaking in writing until I've got your cheque—see? You say you haven't got a thousand at the bank, but I suppose they might cash your cheque for that amount."

"Of course, they would. They hold my securities."

"Very good. Sit down and write the cheque now. Make it payable to G. W. Vulsame, Esq., M.B., or bearer. Not order, mind, and don't cross it."

I sat down meekly and wrote the cheque as directed. Then Vulsame came to the writing-table and gave me a receipt and his written undertaking that he would not molest me further, either with regard to the death of Myas or in any other respect. I locked up the receipt and the undertaking, and he put the cheque in his pocket and prepared to go. Really, it was all so easy that I was almost ashamed to do it, but the man was very drunken and disgusting, and had made me angry.

"One moment before you go, Mr. Vulsame," I said. "I do not recommend you to present that cheque for payment at the bank tomorrow morning, as the money will not be paid and you will be immediately arrested."

"What for? What are you talking about?"

"Don't be childish. You must see. You have threatened to charge me with being an accessory after the fact in the murder of Daniel Myas, and have withdrawn the charge in consideration of receiving a sum that you have demanded. You have given me evidence in your own handwriting that you have done this. If I remember rightly, this particular offence is punishable with penal servitude for life. The law does not encourage blackmail, you know."

This sobered him. He took the cheque from his pocket and tore it in half. "Give me back that undertaking of mine," he said.

"My dear Mr. Vulsame, you cannot suppose I shall do anything so silly as that. Behave nicely and you will hear nothing more about it. That's all I can do for you."

"I'm just going to tell you what I think of you, Mr. Compton. I'm going to say it in plain words. You've played a dirty trick on me. You—"

"Stop that," I said, "and get out!" Rather to my surprise, he did exactly as he was told. The alcoholic collapse had followed on the alcoholic courage. I congratulated myself that I had seen the last of Mr. Vulsame. I congratulated myself prematurely. As it happened, I saw him again that very night.

In one respect I felt grateful to the blackguard. For a few minutes, at any rate, he had taken my mind from that letter and the handwriting of a man whom I knew to be dead, summoning me to come and see him in a few hours' time. I was determined not to go to Durnford Place. I changed my clothes and walked round to the club for dinner. I had meant to look in at a telegraph office on the way and send my excuses. In my own rooms I had gone to the telephone, but had stopped short; I was afraid of what I might hear on the telephone.

I did not go into the telegraph office. It would be easy enough to send a telegram from the club. But of course, the thing that really stopped me was the conviction that, however much I might hate it and however great my horror, I should have to go to Durnford Place that night. There was the direct appeal for help. Whether it came from a man or from a woman, it came from a friend of mine, and to disregard it would have been to lose my most precious possession, my self-respect. Once I had determined that I should have to go, my mind became much easier. I played billiards for half-an-hour after dinner, and gave my whole attention to the game. And then it was time to have a taxicab called.

CHAPTER 14

I have occasionally seen, when for my sins I have been taken to a music-hall, a performance which is, I believe, intended to be amusing and funny—the impersonation of a woman by a man. It is a thing which always disgusts me. The more cleverly it is done, the more loathsome it is. If I happen to see that item on ahead in the programme, I take care to be out of sight and sound of it. I do not know if this is a special peculiarity or weakness of my own, but it helped to add to the difficulty of what I had to do. I had been the friend of Myas, and I had been the friend of Alice Lade. Whatever was waiting for me behind the door of the laboratory had a claim upon me. I, plain, conventional, and unimaginative man, as Myas had described me, had by sheer force of circumstances been drawn into a very whirlpool of horror and morbidity. I had to go through the mud.

Now that I had made up my mind to it, I went through the thing pretty steadily. There was an electric light in my taxicab, and on my way to Durnford Place I read the evening paper assiduously. Whoever this creature was that had appealed to me in the undoubted handwriting of Daniel Myas, it was a person desperately in need of my help and advice. Help and advice cannot be given intelligently by the perturbed and terror-stricken. By the time that I had read the last advertisement of the latest hair-restorer, I had brought myself, I think, to my normal frame of mind.

At first, I had some trouble with my key; the lock of the garden-door had not perhaps been much used of late, and had rusted. I began to think that I should have to go round to Knox Street, but at last the thing went back with a click and the door stood open. In a dark corner, from a mass of dusty laurels, a cat began to cry like a child. The place was very dark. The blinds were drawn down over the windows of the workroom, and only a faint glimmer of light shone behind them. I groped my way to the door and knocked—my usual brisk, social knock.

I had expected it, of course, and I think it should have had less effect upon me than it did. The voice which bade me enter was deep and resonant. It was the voice of Daniel Myas. I knew it to be his voice, and yet I had seen his dead body as it lay in the coffin. I'm afraid that I hesitated for a second or two before I could bring myself to turn the handle of the door.

The workroom was, perhaps, thirty-six feet in length. Near the door by which I had entered, there was one electric light, heavily shaded. I could see rows of bottles and retorts, and stands of test-tubes. Books were scattered about. The further end of the workroom seemed at first to be in complete darkness.

Then, as my eyes got accustomed, I could distinguish something moving. It came a very little nearer to me, and now I could distinguish a man's dressing-gown, with the sleeves turned back, because the arms within were too short for it. The collar of the dressing-gown was turned up, and there was a veil over the face.

Again, the voice of Myas came out of the darkness—

"I know exactly what you're feeling, Compton. You needn't shake hands. I understand."

"Nonsense," I said; and, advancing, took in my own the small hand of Alice Lade. Through the veil I could distinguish dimly the face of Alice Lade, but through her eyes the eyes of Daniel Myas looked out. That was, perhaps, the supreme touch of terror—the eyes of the man looking from the woman's face.

He thanked me for coming, and motioned me to a leather-covered chair by the lamp. I notice that I have written the word "he"—it conveys the impression made on me. He himself sat at some distance from me, in the dusk.

"My voice must have been a shock to you," he said. "You know, of course, that the organs of the voice are peculiarly susceptible of variation, and there my dominant personality has made a great change. I can still write in the handwriting of Alice—I made the experiment just before you came in—but I cannot speak with her voice. When I try to do it, I produce an absurd *falsetto*. There are other changes that you may have noticed."

"The colour of the hair seems to me darker," I said. "I noticed it when you came into the light just now."

"Yes, the pigmentation of the hair and of the iris of the eye have changed. Do you see what this means? Sooner or later, with all my care and precautions, Mrs. Lade will be definitely certain that there's something wrong. I only dare to speak to her in whispers, making a pretence that my voice is affected by a cold. But that kind of thing cannot go on indefinitely. This afternoon she knocked at the door and asked me if I would not see Mrs. Porter. I have not the faintest notion who Mrs. Porter is. Probably Alice knew her very well. You see the trouble, don't you? As I get back some of the knowledge that Daniel Myas had, I lose some of the knowledge that Alice had.

"The first thing I want you to do for me, the very first thing, is to get Mrs. Lade to go away to America. I don't want to be cruel to her, I want to spare her. If she found out what is going on in me, I think it would kill her. Can you get her to go?"

"I can," I said. "I think I can promise that definitely. I saw her this afternoon, and she made a suggestion then as to your mental state, which I shall be able to make use of."

He began to thank me, and broke off abruptly, and groaned as if in extreme physical pain. Then he took up a hypodermic syringe and I saw the heavy sleeve of the dressing-gown pulled back, and a small and feminine white arm.

There was a moment's pause, and then he apologised for the interruption. "Acute pain," he said. "It is part of the price I pay for what I have done. When the Ego of a man becomes cognizable by the body of a woman, that body must suffer. If it should happen again, don't take any notice of it, please. When can you get Mrs. Lade to go?"

"The idea that occurred to me was to make her believe that your restoration to health absolutely depended upon her departure. If she can be made to believe that, she will go by the end of the week. Can you get along until then?"

"Yes," he said. "I shall see her very little, and never in a room that is brightly lit. You will tell her not to prolong the last scene, when she says goodbye to me. You can say that the strain might be dangerous for me."

"Yes," I said. "I think you may consider all that as settled. But that

228

is only the beginning of things. What are you going to do, my friend, after she has gone? What is to become of you?"

I remained for over an hour longer, talking with this ghastly *hermaphrodite*. Part of the time he spoke in French, and I dare say he did this with intention. To me it was entirely convincing. Alice Lade may have known a few words of French, but certainly she could not have spoken it like that. Very few men in England could have spoken it quite like that.

He had his scheme quite ready. His one aim was to bring Alice Lade back again. It was to that end, and to his own self-obliteration that he now meant to devote himself. He believed, though the belief seemed to me instinctive rather than reasonable, that if he could recover the knowledge he possessed before the experiment, this would become possible.

As soon as Mrs. Lade had gone, he meant to get to some place where he was not known, and there to continue his work.

I told him of my little cottage, standing all by itself on a hill in Gloucestershire. I was ready to put this cottage and my two servants there at his disposal. He accepted this with great gratitude. When I warned him that the place was desperately lonely, for the first time he laughed—a short grim laugh. He wanted nothing better than to be quite alone now. Mrs. Lade was to leave for Southampton on the Friday, and on the Saturday following he would go down to Gloucestershire.

Then he told me something which, after all, did not greatly surprise me. He had made up his mind that he would no longer even try to pass as Alice Lade. He would not go down to Gloucestershire as a woman at all. Already, so he said, he felt it would be more easy to pass as a man than as a woman. As a man he would have more freedom and independence. He would be able to go about alone. He needed, of course, a complete outfit of man's clothes, and he had already taken all the measurements, so that I might get these for him. They were to be ready made, of course; there was no time for anything else. The power of attorney had also been prepared beforehand. He dealt with the necessary financial arrangements in a business-like matter-of-fact way. And somehow every one of these prosaic touches seemed to add to the ghastliness of the whole thing.

"I am taking a great deal from you," he said, "and I am giving you a deal of trouble. I know that the sight of me must disgust and distress you. If it can possibly be managed, we will not meet again."

"Don't say that," I said. "I am sorry for you and glad to be able to do anything for you. It does not amount to very much, when all is said and done. And certainly, I intend to see you again. I am not going to leave you to go mad in solitude. I admit that I find the whole thing horrible. You would not believe me if I said I did not. You have done something which is against Nature."

"That is it," he said. "That is exactly it. And Nature punishes."

I shook hands again with him when I left. I hope he did not feel how much I hated to do it.

Chapter 15

I had not kept my cab, and started to walk until I found one. I had only gone a few yards from the garden-door in Durnford Place, when I heard a man running after me, and turned sharply round. I found myself face to face with Mr. Vulsame. When he left me in the afternoon, he had been a collapsed wreck, but he had been drinking again and had recovered his spirits. He seemed to be extremely excited, but he was no longer unsteady on his legs nor thick in his speech.

"I've got you," he said, shaking a clenched fist. "This is a fair knockout. This explains everything."

"I don't know what you mean, Mr. Vulsame, and I don't want to know. I have had a great deal to try me today, and I do not think it would be wise for you to try me any further. You had better go home. If you want to communicate with me, you can write, you know."

But he would not be stopped. "I'll say what I've got to say. I'm not afraid of you nor of twenty like you. You were mighty particular that I should give back my key to the garden-gate, weren't you? You were ready to pay out your money to save the girl, and you did it. Now I know why. It's a bit indecent, seeing Myas has only been dead a few months."

"Well," I said, "if you will have it, you must." I gave him a good punch in the face, and he went down on the pavement. Very slowly, and breathing hard, he collected his hat, which had fallen off, and replaced it, and struggled to his feet. I had waited to see if he wished to attempt the usual form of retort, but as he did not, and merely babbled solicitors, I told him to go to the devil, and left him. Apparently, sobriety brought wisdom, for I never heard from Mr. Vulsame's solicitors.

I spent rather a horrible night. I slept, but the creature that I had talked to in the laboratory haunted my dreams.

Next morning there was a great deal to do, and no time to be lost. I went to see Mrs. Lade, going to the Knox Street entrance. I had telegraphed to her to expect me, and found her waiting and rather too well dressed. I said that I had seen her daughter, and I quoted the opinion of a non-existent medical man. I said that her own theory had been quite correct, that Alice's mind had been affected by her profound grief at her loss. The doctor recommended that she should be taken away into the country at once, and I undertook to see to that myself. It was expected that in time she would recover, and then doubtless she would regain her old affection for her mother and wish to go out and join her in New York. One has to tell these kindly lies, I suppose.

To Mrs. Lade the voice of a doctor was as the voice of a god. Once the medical authority was quoted, it was easy to do anything with her. When I left her, she was going round to fetch Mrs. Porter to help her with the packing. I was to book her passage, and I offered, if she cared about it, to see her off. But I was rather glad that the offer was refused. She said that Mrs. Porter had been a great friend to her in her time of trouble, and would expect to accompany her to Southampton. I gathered that, not only would Mrs. Porter be gratified by being able to render this service to her friend, but that also it would be to her somewhat of a jaunt at the friend's expense. My last words to Mrs. Lade enjoined her to make as much haste as possible, and to keep out of her daughter's way.

The doctor, I said, had insisted upon that. She might see her just for a moment, to say goodbye, but no more than that. I felt quite sure that Mrs. Lade would be far too agitated at this last interview to notice any of these slight changes which had occurred in Myas-Lade's appearance.

I cannot say that any of this was work which I liked doing. Frankly, I hated it, but it had to be done, and quite as much for Mrs. Lade's own sake as for the sake of Daniel Myas.

In the afternoon I went to the stores where I was to buy the outfit. I gave the assistant the measurements, and he found me at once some suits of clothes which would do well enough. The only trouble was about the boots.

"You see, sir," said the assistant, "it is quite an unusually small size for a man. Ladies' boots, of course, we could do in that size, but that's not what you require."

Ultimately, I succeeded in finding boys' boots which would do. The assistant's words had rather put me on my guard. I paid for the things, and he asked me to what address they should be sent. I was on the verge of giving the name, and then stopped myself. "I'll take them myself. I have a cab waiting outside. Let them be packed up and taken down to it."

In the cab I scribbled a brief note to Myas on a leaf from my pocket-book, telling him what I had done so far, and asking him to speak to me on the telephone at nine o'clock that evening. I stopped at a stationer's and bought an envelope for this. I addressed it to Miss Lade and put the note in the envelope underneath the string of the package. I drove to Knox Street and found that Mrs. Lade was out; she also had an outfit to buy. I directed her servant to take the things just as they were to Miss Lade, but I did not myself go in.

Punctually at nine o'clock that night my telephone bell went. I had a long conversation with Myas, pausing at intervals to prevent the exchange from cutting me off. We spoke principally about the house and laboratory. He wished these to be left exactly as they were. I was to find a caretaker for them, and it was to be a caretaker who had never seen himself or the Lades. He wanted me to order for him a portmanteau and a suitcase with the initials M. D. stamped on them. I asked him how he was going to pack the rest of his things, his books and his apparatus.

He surprised me rather by saying that he was not going to pack them at all. He was going to take nothing of the kind with him to the cottage. He gave me his reasons. His knowledge of French and his ability to speak it had come back to him quite suddenly, and without any effort on his part. He believed that his special scientific knowledge would come back to him in the same way without effort or struggle. All he had to do was to remain quietly up there in the cottage, reading my books, wandering over the country, trying to think of other things.

Somehow the voice no longer inspired me with any feeling of horror. It was exactly like the voice of Daniel Myas. It created the illusion that it was Myas himself, with no change in him, who was speaking. It struck me that as far as possible he avoided any but the most commonplace subjects. He took common-sense views about the house in Knox Street. He wondered if it would be worthwhile to let it, but on the whole decided that a caretaker would be preferable. He asked me, almost as if it were a matter of real importance, what I thought the wages of a caretaker ought to be

So little disturbed was I by this conversation, that I asked him to come and see me in St. James's Street on the Saturday morning before his departure. I went to bed, well satisfied with my day's work, and with my peace of mind restored to me. But no sooner did I fall asleep than the old horror returned to me in the form of a dream.

In my dream I was wandering very late at night over a Yorkshire moor. I knew the place well, I had been to a shoot there. It was a stormy night, and the violent wind tore my cap off. I could not find it, and I went on bareheaded, a few drops of cold rain splashing in my face. Already a feeling of imminent horror had begun, though I did not know what form it would take. Suddenly I saw a bright light. It was an electric lamp like those that they have in Hyde Park. I ran towards it as fast as I could go. I clung to it panting. I was glad to be there in the circle of light, and afraid to go out into the dark again.

Suddenly, at a little distance, where the light was at its faintest, I saw a figure moving. It danced about fantastically and came nearer. It was a small white figure of a woman, wearing a man's heavy dressing-gown. Her long hair streamed in the wind. The wind caught the heavy folds of the dressing-gown, and tossed them hither and thither. With a quick rush the figure slid up to me, and put two small and cold hands on my throat. It whispered in my ear, and the voice was a husky *falsetto*, as if Daniel Myas had been trying to imitate the voice of Alice Lade.

"That's exactly it," said the voice. "It is against Nature, and Nature punishes. It is said that there is no place for me, neither in this world nor elsewhere."

I woke with a start, and switched on the reading-lamp by my bed-side. I fetched a book from the library. It was one of the Badminton volumes. I got back to bed again and read, studying the subject of punt-racing, as though I were getting it up for an examination. I was determined not to fall asleep again. At last, there came the early morning sounds, the twitter of the sparrows and the clatter of a milk-cart. I felt with relief that after all the ordinary world was around me. I put down the volume, switched out the light, and almost instantly fell asleep again.

I got up at my usual hour, unrefreshed by the sleep, haggard and worn out, and depressed by the feeling that there was something to come—something hanging over me. I recalled what it was. Myas was to leave by an afternoon train from Paddington on Saturday after-noon, and I had asked him to come and see me in the morning. There would be time to stop that. I walked across to the telephone and took down the receiver.

"Number, please?" said the girl at the exchange.

"It's all right," I said. "It's a mistake, I don't want anything."

After all, I could not do it. It was too absolutely selfish and cowardly.

Chapter 16

"A Mr. Daniel is asking if you will see him, sir."

I knew that Mr. Daniel was Daniel Myas. He had told me of his intention to use another name. I directed that he should be shown into the library where I was sitting.

The first impression he made upon me was one of strangeness. I thought I had never seen him before, and did not know him in the least. There was really nothing about him which reminded me of Alice Lade. The hair had been quite short and was of a reddish-brown in colour. The eyes were the eyes of a man. Indeed, the general appearance, though it suggested an undersized and nervous little man, ludicrously out of keeping with the deep voice, had nothing that was feminine about it. His face was very white, and he looked as if he were ravaged by disease, but he no longer appeared, as on that night in the laboratory, to be in actual physical pain. His expression was one of distinct relief. He no longer inspired me with horror, but for the first few minutes, at any rate, I felt as if I were talking to a man whom I did not know.

He took a cigarette and began to say commonplace things. He had left his luggage at Paddington, where he would pick it up in the afternoon. He wondered how long it would take him to drive to Paddington. As he spoke, I noticed that his manner with the cigarette was that of Daniel Myas exactly. When a little ash fell on his coat, and he flicked it off, he swore just as Myas always did, with set teeth and without a sound beyond the initial letter. It was characteristic of Myas that the trivial things in life made him much more furious than the great disasters. I began to feel that, after all, I did know this young man in the blue serge suit, sitting opposite to me and watching me anxiously to see how I was taking it.

"How did you manage to effect this transformation?" I asked him. "I should have thought it was impossible for anyone anywhere in London to take on the dress of the opposite sex, without taking somebody into the secret, or without being found out."

"As it happens," said Myas-Lade, "it was simple enough. That old woman, the caretaker, wanted to go out to do her shopping. I told her that she could be away for an hour, if she liked, and that I should probably have left before she returned. I had everything ready in the laboratory. My clothes were all packed, except those which I meant to wear. The hair gave me some trouble. I cut it short myself, as well as I could, but not very short, and burnt it in the laboratory stove.

"After I had changed, I went first to Paddington, where I left my luggage, and then to the nearest barber. I told him that I had been living for months in a lonely spot in the West Highlands, away from the resources of civilization, and had to cut my hair myself. He seemed quite satisfied, and not much interested. Of course, someone who knew me might have seen me coming out with my luggage to the cab that was waiting in Durnford Place. Even if anyone did, it does not matter in the least. No one would have recognised me. You yourself, Compton, look as if you were hardly sure who it was who was speaking to you."

That is very likely," I said. "I knew Daniel Myas and Alice Lade. When I saw you that night in the laboratory, there was something of each personality in you. Now, in appearance at any rate, there is nothing that suggests either. Only the voice and the manner recall Daniel Myas to me. You look as though you were no longer in any pain."

"I am not," said Myas. "Last night, for the first time since the night of the experiment, I managed to get four hours' continuous sleep. Somehow it seems almost worthwhile to have suffered as I did, in order to get the ecstasy of being free from suffering. It is almost difficult for me to understand how it is, that people who are not in bodily pain do not experience constant and conscious pleasure from their freedom. I do not suppose that it is all over. On the contrary, the pain is almost certain to return, but that I do not mind. I have had my breathing-space. If it comes back tenfold, I can bear it now, and go on bearing it until the work is finished."

"Until the work is finished," I repeated. "You seem confident."

"I am confident. Yes, Compton, I shall not come to see you again, but Alice Lade will. It is only a matter of patience. What happened in the one case will happen in another. Because the knowledge of a language came back, therefore most certainly the other knowledge will return."

"And then?"

"That knowledge will form the means for my release. I use the word 'release' intentionally. My Ego, my soul, is detained here like some poor animal that has one foot caught in a trap. My body is dead. The apparatus of my mind contained in that body is dead. It is only, as it were, by murder and theft, that I, Daniel Myas, am cognisant to you now. I am due elsewhere."

I have known people who were very old or very ill to have that same curious feeling of being due elsewhere.

He told me much that was very curious. The knowledge which belonged specially to Alice had not entirely left him. Before the care-taker's arrival, he had gone through the rooms in the house in Knox Street, and in one of them had found the cheap foreign piano on which Alice used to play. To own a piano and to give Alice music-lessons had formed part of the laudable ambition of Mrs. Lade. Alice had some slight gift for music—nothing very remarkable. Myas was perhaps more of a musician *au fond*, but he played no instrument and had never had a lesson.

The sight of the piano seemed to awaken something which had been dormant in him. He sat down and began to play. What he played was part of a movement, very tinkly and simple, of one of Mozart's *sonatas*. Suddenly, he became conscious of what he was doing, and stopped abruptly in the middle of a phrase. He could not go on play-ing. The sub-conscious mind of Alice Lade made it possible. The con-scious mind inhibited it. He told me that when Mrs. Lade spoke with him about things that Alice would be supposed to know, he always found it easier to answer if he closed his eyes and tried to keep his conscious mind on some other subject.

In one trifling respect, he showed the personal taste of Alice Lade still. Daniel Myas had been an epicure and a judge of wine. Alice Lade hated the taste of it, and otherwise cared very little about what she ate or drank. I noticed that at luncheon Myas–Lade drank water only. He saw that I had noticed it.

"Yes," he said, "it is so. The other day I went into a confectioner's shop and bought sweets to eat. Perhaps after all it is not so strange that something still lingers, as that so much has already gone."

I did not go with him to the station. Much time is wasted in a very wearisome manner by kindly people in seeing other kindly people get into a railway carriage. I had promised to run down for a week-end at the cottage in a fortnight's time. Meanwhile I thought I was to have a rest from a trying and rather revolting business. I turned to that manuscript diary of which I have spoken, and resumed my work on it. I must have become rather absorbed in it. I have a faint recollection of telling my servant that I would not take tea and did not want to be bothered. It was seven o'clock before I finally put down the thing and went to dress for dinner. The window of my bedroom as usual stood open. Outside in the street I could hear the newspaper boys crying, "Disaster on the Great Western Railway."

CHAPTER 17

I could learn very little more that night.

I got all the evening papers, of course, but the notices were very scanty, and did not in details agree with one another. The train in which Myas-Lade had travelled had been wrecked. He might or might not be dead. My first impulse was to go off at once to Paddington and see what details they had, but I did not go, and I think my second thoughts were the wiser.

The morning papers gave fuller information. The accident had been due to the error of a signalman. The human machine, however near perfection, is never quite perfect. Considering the nature of the accident, the number of those actually killed was very small. Among the headlines of the account I read, "Sensational Discovery— Unknown Woman Disguised as a Man." Myas-Lade had been killed, his face being rendered unrecognisable. The railway authorities were doing their best to trace his identity.

What was I to do? Again, I did not follow my first impulse. My first impulse was to go down and claim the body and see that it had decent burial. Then I saw that would not do at all. In the trail of identification would come explanation, and the secrecy on which Myas-Lade had so strongly insisted would be lost. It seemed to me, right or wrong, that I carried out his wishes best if I did absolutely nothing.

The evening papers had further details of that sensational discovery. The handkerchief and linen of the dead girl bore the initials M. D. The man's clothing which she was wearing was absolutely new. There was a further supply of new clothing found in luggage which almost certainly belonged to her. It bore the same initials, contained clothes which would have fitted her, and had not been otherwise claimed. A later edition said it had been possible to find the stores from which the clothes had been bought, the name being on the buttons, and there was a short interview with the assistant who had actually sold the things.

He maintained stoutly that the person to whom he sold them was beyond question a man, and moreover a man who could not have worn those clothes himself. He gave a description of my personal appearance, which was flattering but inaccurate. So far as I was concerned, I felt no nervousness about being drawn into the affair. I have no eccentricities. I dress exactly like other men in the same position as myself. Myas used to chaff me rather bitterly about my passion for resembling other people. I had paid cash for the clothes, given no name or address, and taken the things away myself. Unless they found the cabman who had driven me on that occasion, there was no possibility that the true story would come to light.

The real cabman never came forward. Another cabman did provide a somewhat wild story. He had driven two people, he said, on that afternoon from the stores to a spot on Wimbledon Common. There he had been dismissed and had been paid double his fare. One of the two people answered to the assistant's description of myself, and the other was a girl. His story did not bear examination. It was excessively vague. The only definite thing about him was his desire to make a pound or two out of an evening paper.

I did not attend the inquest, but I was present at the funeral. The body was decently buried at the expense of the railway company, and was followed to the grave by a crowd of people who had never known Myas nor Alice Lade. The effect of a sensational story on an uneducated mind is really very astonishing. Some of these absolute strangers had even sent expensive floral tributes. I wrote to my servants at the cottage that my friend had changed his mind at the last moment and had decided not to go down to the country after all. Old Welsford still quotes this occasionally in his more pious moments on Sunday afternoon, as an instance of what he calls a special providence.

I wrote at the same time to Mrs. Lade in America, and gave her a very bad account of her daughter's health. I wanted gradually to prepare her for the news of the death. She wrote back that this was only what she had expected, and that she knew she would never see Alice alive again. It was a comfort to her that I was looking after the girl, and she was sure she could trust me to do all that could be done. She seemed to have grown very fond of her little nephews and nieces, of whom she gave me particulars. She added that she liked America, but that breakfasts there seemed to be a very different thing. It was a simple, kindly letter, and I liked it for its simplicity. Any fool can punctuate, and Mrs. Lade's pages were innocent of all punctuation, but that gift of simplicity is much rarer. It was the one distinguished thing about her.

Thus, in two graves many miles apart, lie the body of a man who loved knowledge and of the woman who loved that man. I do not know whether it is a vain hope that somewhere in the hereafter their souls have met and put old mistakes right again. It is not a thing that one can know, but I confess to the hope. And with that I close all that I can say at present of Daniel Myas and Alice Lade, and turn once more to devote myself to my more important historical work.

POSTSCRIPT

1

Four years have elapsed since I put down in a rough and ready way my experiences of Dr. Daniel Myas and Alice Lade. It seemed to me at that time that the problem was ended. The body and mind of both of them had suffered what is known as death; their souls were no longer cognizable on this earth.

But since I closed the record, I have been on several occasions tempted to reopen it. There was that extraordinary letter I received from Vulsame, and my strange glimpse of him on the beach at Brighton. There was the long and interesting conversation which I had with Dr. Habaden on the experiment of Myas and the part I had played in connection with it. There was the incident of the telephone message, which is still to me quite inexplicable. I have decided to make a brief note of these things, and there are reasons why it must be done at once. I have been suffering from a revival and extension of the old trouble, which many years ago shut me out from the profession of my choice, and from other things which would have made life more enjoyable.

Dr. Habaden and the other doctors whom he has seen in consultation take a serious view of the case and are in practical agreement about it. As I am not a particularly timid or hysterical person, I have persuaded them to speak quite frankly to me. Their verdict is that with care I may last for another six months. Old bachelors like myself are liable to acquire habits of almost absurd punctiliousness and tidiness. I have the feeling that I should like to leave this record finished as far as I can finish it. But I have no exaggerated ideas about it. I do not suppose that the facts with reference to Dr. Myas recorded by me would be of the slightest value to any scientific investigator in his particular field of research.

I deprecate research in that field altogether. I would prevent it as I would prevent a child from playing with fire. I have seen the horror of it, and I have grown to hate it. It is not only of the case of Dr. Myas I am thinking, as I say this. I have seen in other instances how that enthusiasm for the sealed and hidden knowledge has led to disaster—to madness and to suicide.

2

About six months after the railway accident, I received a letter signed G. W. Vulsame, which was rather surprising. Perhaps the most surprising point about it was that it contained a cheque to myself signed by him for the sum of forty-eight pounds ten shillings. He told me that he had disposed of his practice, and that he was now acting as assistant to a doctor in Whitechapel. He said that he had to acknowledge with the deepest shame and contrition that he had swindled me. It was to some extent true that the experiments of Myas had caused injurious talk in the neighbourhood, but it was also true that he had already received full compensation from Myas on this account. The decay of his practice was, he said, in reality due to his own drinking habits, which he had now happily overcome.

"But," he wrote, "I do not suppose for one moment that you were deceived. You did not pay this money as compensation, you paid it as a bribe to me to hold my tongue. You put temptation in my way and I fell. My conscience commands me to restore this money. I have not the sum of three hundred pounds at present, but I send a first instalment. I will send the rest, as soon as I can save it from the proceeds of my work. It is not for me to judge you for your part in this business, but if your conscience is not atrophied by years of the life of a selfish worldling, you will reproach yourself. Oh, my dear Mr. Compton, I do wish you would let me come and see you. Any appointment you like to make I would keep with gratitude. I am so anxious to bring you to the only true and lasting happiness."

There was another page or two of the same kind of material. I returned him his cheque, and wrote that my conscience did not trouble me in the least with reference to that payment of three hundred pounds, that I declined to receive any part of it back, and that he had better devote the money, if he wished to get rid of it, to some other object. I also said that I did not wish to see him, and that I had given instructions to my servants that he was not to be admitted. There was something about the man, whether drunken and ebullient, or sober and didactic, that annoyed me extremely. It was a positive satisfaction to me to be rude to him. He further infuriated me by a brief and unnecessary reply to my letter, in which he said that I had his full forgiveness.

In the summer of the following year, I had brought my car from Gloucestershire to London, and ran down to Brighton for a weekend. I had a friend of mine with me, a man who was a mighty walker, and on Sunday morning he made me walk over the Downs with him to Lewes. We lunched there and walked back by a different route. The weather was quite perfect, and if my friend had not bored me slightly by his insistence on the good the exercise was doing me, I should have enjoyed it extremely. As we came back along the King's Road to the hotel, I heard the usual cacophony that betokens that a section of the Salvation Army has got to work. They were perverting the beautiful melody of "Drink to me only with thine eyes" to the words of a hymn. As this finished, a voice that I recognised at once rang out in clear and commanding tones. I turned to my friend.

"I know that man who is speaking," I said. "I want to go down and listen to him. He interests me."

"By all means. You will excuse me if he doesn't interest me, won't you? I'll go on to the hotel."

"Right. We'll meet at dinner."

The little group of earnest people on the beach below me were mostly of a low type. They had the crooked faces and stunted frames of degenerates. Still, I want to be quite fair, and I must say that Vulsame, the speaker, seemed to me to have improved immensely. He had lost his bloated look, He had gained something which he had never had before, an air of sincerity. His face was white, his eyes were fanatical. I did not wish him to recognise me, and when I went down on to the beach, I took up my position behind him. He was giving, in much detail and with some self-complacency, an account of his own transgressions. This led him to speak of other sinners that he had known.

Soon, to my amazement, he was launched on a somewhat fanciful portrait of myself. He considerably overstated my income and my other worldly advantages. He imputed to me a villainy which would require far more of the romantic spirit than my very ordinary nature possesses. His final verdict that I must have led thousands astray was, I think, quite unjust. Every moment I expected to hear him roar out my actual name to the gaping housemaids in his audience.

But in this respect, he spared me. His moral was that there were many men like myself, not criminals in the eyes of the law, and on the contrary enjoying high positions and the respect of their fellows, who were none the less lost for ever. There was only one supreme satisfaction, and these poor wretches had never found it.

He said that he himself had sought that satisfaction in the pursuit of knowledge and in the pursuit of pleasure, and it was not there. He went on to make a fervent appeal to his audience, with no rhetorical skill, but with the most desperate sincerity. Perspiration streamed from his forehead, tears stood in his eyes. Presently, as the band showed signs of renewed activity, I strolled away. I have not since then seen Vulsame again, nor have I heard any further news of him. I have often wondered what became of him—whether, as seems more probable, he had a further relapse, or whether, as is not impossible, there was some further advance and he is now a good Catholic.

But the thing which struck me most—the thought which haunted me at dinner that night—was that here, by some magic touch, had come a change of personality. The Vulsame that I had just seen was not the man that I had seen before. It was a different being. I suppose that to some extent a similar change goes on in all of us. The tissues of the body waste and are renewed. The personality changes with it. What has the child of six in common with the man of sixty that he subsequently becomes? Was the miracle that Myas tried to effect any more wonderful than that normal miracle which is going on every day in all of us? It is strange how we cling to a belief in a permanent personality. Life everlasting means little to most of us, unless it be the life everlasting of the individual.

Can one believe in that? It may occur to my readers that at a later point an answer to this question was given me.

3

One evening in that year it happened that my old friend, Dr. Habaden, was dining with me alone and chanced to speak of Daniel Myas.

"You knew him, I think. What became of him?"

In answer I told him for the first time, very much as I have set it down here, the story of Daniel Myas and Alice Lade. He did not seem greatly surprised. I suppose that these accomplished men of medicine are rarely surprised. His attitude to me was rather one of irritation. He was angry with me.

"Really, Compton," he said, "it seems to me that you've been taking too much upon yourself. Self-confidence is all very well, but it has its limits. You are a layman, and could not be supposed to understand the problem that was before you. But why, knowing yourself to be ignorant, did you not apply to somebody with some knowledge of the subject? Putting it plainly, why on earth, when some appearance of the personality of Myas began to show itself in this Lade girl, did you not consult me?"

"Well, I did not consider it to be some appearance of a personality. I considered it to be the actual thing."

"Nonsense," said Habaden impatiently.

"Then again, it seemed to me to be a thing entirely outside your beat. If I were ill, I should come to you. But how does your special knowledge bear on an exchange of souls? I am an ignorant layman, as you say, but I am quite willing to learn anything that you can teach. What is your view of the case?"

"The only possible view. Myas was a clever man, as I have always admitted to you. And I have no doubt that he was sincere. He probably did believe that by some fantastic method of his own—some weird game with electrical apparatus—this exchange of personalities could under certain conditions be accomplished. Anaesthesis was one of the conditions. His ideas were quite wild and undisciplined, and he was trying to do a thing that is not possible and never has been and never will be. He died in the attempt. Make no mistake about that. Myas died from the effects of the chloride of ethyl. It is dangerous stuff. We use it as a spray to produce local anaesthesis mostly. His soul, if he had a soul, may have gone through various adventures, of which neither I nor anybody else can possibly know anything. But the one thing which is quite certain is that his soul did not enter into possession of the mind and body of Alice Lade."

"Very well. And now, perhaps, you will account for Alice Lade as I saw her in the laboratory that night."

"Certainly, I will. What you witnessed was very much less unusual than you think. There are many similar cases of double personality on record, though I admit that the case of Alice Lade has its peculiar and interesting features. There is nothing surprising in the fact that she should have suffered from mental disorder. You know, as well as I do, that every anaesthetic produces a temporary disorder of the mind. This disorder may become in part, and sometimes does become, permanent and persistent. It was not the first time that Myas had given an anaesthetic to that poor girl. On your own showing he had done so frequently.

"The shock of his death provides another possible cause, especially when one considers the circumstances of it and her devotion to him. The person you saw in the laboratory that night was Alice Lade and nobody else, but it was Alice Lade with a fixed delusion that she was Daniel Myas, and with some very curious but quite unconvincing physical evidence to show for her belief. As I have said, it was a case of double personality."

"You have come across such cases before?"

"They are not in my line. They would not be brought to me. But I have read of them, and I know doctors who have seen them. For instance, a girl who is morose and well-educated wakes up one morning as a totally different person. She is now very cheerful, but absolutely ignorant of the things she knew previously. Sometimes the two states alternate. Sometimes in one state the subject has no memory whatever of what has happened in the other. The thing is explained to my mind by the theory of complete somnambulism. Alice Lade was a case for medical treatment. In fostering her delusion, and in allowing her to dress as a man and to go off by herself, you did very wrong."

"Habaden," I said, "the fact that there have been similar cases and that they have been classified, does not impress me very much. Classification is not explanation. You talk about absolute somnambulism. That is, I suppose, the regulation thing, the accepted theory, but I cannot see that it removes the difficulty. When science cannot remove a difficulty, it invents another name for it and is quite satisfied. I almost wish now that I had brought Alice Lade, if it was really Alice Lade, to you. Previous to the death of Myas, Alice Lade knew little or no French. She did not speak it at all. She could not understand it when it was spoken. After the death of Myas, that night when I saw her in the laboratory, she spoke French fluently and perfectly, as Myas himself did. Does somnambulism explain that?"

"No, my dear fellow, but unconscious memory does. There seems to be practically no limit to what the unconscious memory can do. I could give you twenty recorded cases of it, which to you or any other layman would seem almost miraculous. Alice Lade had heard you and Myas talking French together. She had unconsciously remembered the sounds she heard."

"Afraid it won't do, Habaden, unless she also unconsciously understood the meaning and the grammar. The French she spoke to me that night was not a repetition of sounds which she might have heard before. She was expressing her thoughts at the moment correctly. However, I need not labour that point. Do you suppose that Myas and I would ever have spoken French in the presence of that girl, knowing that she did not understand it? Can you suspect us of anything so vulgar and barbarous?"

"Very well. Either you or somebody else must have spoken French in her hearing, because that is the only possible explanation."

"And that," I said," is about the least logical observation I ever heard from you, and a man of science should be ashamed of it."

"I know what I know," said Habaden dogmatically. "You can give me no other explanation that is as good. For that matter, how do you know that Myas himself did not teach the girl French? He was educating her, you say."

"I am sure that if he had been teaching her French, he would have mentioned it to me. He was educating her only for his own special purpose. And for that special purpose the usual routine of a girl's education would have been quite ineffective."

"Oh, well, it is not only from the medical point of view that you have been wrong, Compton. You have been too sure of yourself. You have taken your own way in a manner that seems to me almost unscrupulous. What right had you got to bribe Vulsame to suppress evidence at the inquest? Why did you lose your temper with him and assault him? What business had you got to allow the body of Alice Lade to go unclaimed and to be buried like the body of a pauper? And what about her money? I suppose you have found some equally highhanded way of dealing with that."

"Well, I think I can give an answer to all your questions. I suppose it was illegal to bribe Vulsame to suppress evidence. All I can say is that I don't care. It was the right thing to do. I knew perfectly well that Alice Lade did not murder Daniel Myas, and I was determined that she should not suffer from the suspicion of it. Nor am I in the least ashamed that I hit the man. If he ever repeated that swinish innuendo to me, I should hit him again. The body of Alice Lade went unclaimed, because I felt certain that it would be in accordance with her wishes and the wishes of Daniel Myas, and I did not see that anybody else was concerned in the matter. It is not true, by the way, to say that she was buried like a pauper.

"As to her money, I suppose you will think that my way of dealing with that was high-handed. It seems to me to be all right. She left no will, and as sole trustee for her and with a full power of attorney from her, I exercised my discretion. Everything was realized, and the money sent out to Mrs. Lade in New York. I have her receipts and the trust accounts, if you care to look at them."

"Don't be an ass. You know perfectly what I am accusing you of— of taking too much into your own hands, and overriding the law of the land. How did you manage about the Chancellor of the Exchequer? Have you sent conscience-money?"

"I have not, and I intend to send none. If, as I believe, the person who died in that railway accident was Daniel Myas, the duties are already paid."

"But it was not. It was Alice Lade and nobody else."

"There we are back again at our first point of difference. I do not believe it was Alice Lade. It was the body of Alice Lade, if you like. It wrote with the hand of Myas. It spoke with the voice of Myas. Its actions were guided by the soul and personality of Myas. That is what I believe. You, of course, consider it a fairy tale."

"Frankly, I do. But it is no use to discuss it. You have come to a pig-headed conclusion on a subject you have never studied."

"Nor have you ever studied it, my friend—for the simple reason that you have never had the chance to study it. This is something which has not occurred before in the world."

We went on to speak of other subjects, and perhaps it was just as well. Neither of us had made the least impression on the other.

4

I have the habit of sitting up late at night, and have always had it. It is, I believe, generally supposed to be a bad habit, but I have never found out on what grounds. Probably the supposition is that it is invariably accompanied by dissipation and excess, but in my case that supposition would be incorrect. I do not want to be self-righteous. The simple fact is that dissipation and excess have never amused me at all. I appreciate the good things of life, and know that too much of them spoils the appreciation. In my library at St. James's Place, I have a telephone extension. It can be disconnected or connected at will from the main instrument. After ten at night, I have this extension connected up. My servants go to bed, and if the telephone rings I can attend to it myself.

Some months after my conversation with Dr. Habaden I dined one night at the club, played three rubbers afterwards, and walked back to my rooms. I changed my coat and sat down by the reading-lamp with a bundle of documents to examine. They had been sent me by the same man who sent me the Peninsular-War Diary, and consisted principally of letters of the same period. Many of these letters were extremely difficult to read. They were written on both sides of the sheet in faded ink. The paper was thin, and the writing was often crossed. When I found any letter which seemed likely to be of some use for my purpose, I made a rough transcript of it in pencil. I had to work with a magnifying-glass, and one may readily believe that my attention was entirely absorbed. I may add that at this time I was in fairly good health, and so far as my memory serves me, no thought of Myas or Alice Lade had entered my mind that day.

As I was working, the telephone bell began to bother me. It did not ring outright. It gave a faint *tink-tink* at intervals. It had happened before, and I had been told that it was due to wires touching, and that consequently a high wind often caused it. But I personally know nothing whatever about these things. I picked up the receiver, because this continuous *tink-tink* annoyed and interrupted me. I wanted to complain to the exchange. For twenty seconds, perhaps, I heard nothing whatever, and was irritated by the delay, and then came a gentle sound as of someone sighing.

"Look here," I said. I want to complain about this telephone. Are you the right person to attend to it?"

The answer came very slowly, with a long wait between the words. It was a voice that I knew perfectly well.

"I am Alice Lade."

"Yes. Go on, please," I said.

She told me that it was only with extreme difficulty she managed to make words and get them heard by me. She thanked me for what I had done. She told me to worry no longer about the difficulties of the case, and that in a very short time I should understand.

"Tell me of Myas," I said.

The voice became so faint that I could hardly hear it. It is my impression that the words were these: "I am Daniel Myas and I am Alice Lade." After that there was no sound at all. I tried to call the attention of the exchange and failed. Suddenly an idea occurred to me. I went out to the telephone in the hall. I saw then that the extension in the library was disconnected. My servant on going to bed had forgotten to switch me on.

I left it disconnected and went back to the library. I put away my papers, mixed myself a brandy and soda, lit a pipe and sat down to wait. For nearly an hour everything was quite silent, and then very faintly the bell sounded twice. I lifted the receiver and heard a sound like a woman sobbing. The only word that I could catch was "Cannot" twice repeated. The sound broke off suddenly, and after waiting a few seconds I hung the receiver up again and went back to my easy-chair. There I waited for another hour with no result, and then went to bed.

It is difficult to describe exactly what my sensations were. Certainly, they had in them nothing of the horror tinged with disgust that I had experienced that night in the laboratory in the garden. They were not feelings of fear exactly, but rather of awe. Later, as I was undressing, together with that awe came something like a feeling of triumph. What would my friend Dr. Habaden have to say to this? What would be his facile explanation? How would he classify it?

I wanted to be quite certain that I had made no mistake and had observed correctly, so as my man was putting out my clothes next morning, I said, "You forgot to connect the telephone up to me last night."

"Yes, sir," he said. "Almost the first thing I noticed this morning. Sorry, sir. Don't think I ever missed that before." That morning, as it chanced, I met Dr. Habaden in Albemarle Street and stopped him for a moment. "I want to have a talk with you some time," I said.

"Right," said Habaden. "I've got a couple of doctors dining with me tonight. You had better join us. They will probably talk their own shop a good deal, but you won't mind that. They always leave early, and then we can have our talk."

It was rather a nuisance. I had asked a man to dine with me at the club that night. However, it would be easy enough to telephone that I had given him the wrong date by mistake, and I accepted Habaden's invitation.

It happened very much as he said. When dinner was over, these men, who were keen on their profession, did begin to discuss a medical question. To be precise, they were discussing whether the accepted view as to the normal position of the human stomach was really correct. It always interests me to hear people talking when they know what they are talking about, and I listened with interest. It was while Habaden was speaking that the light suddenly broke in on me.

"Well," he was saying, as he described a case, "we percussed him out, marked with the blue pencil and filled him up with *bismuth*."

Suddenly I saw the whole uselessness of it. I got his special matter-of-fact way of looking at things. I knew beyond a shadow of doubt what his explanation would be. He would simply say that I was suffering from an auditory delusion, and would make wise recommendations.

When the other two men had gone, he turned to me and said, "Now then, Compton, what was it you wanted to ask me?"

"Nothing really of very great importance, and, as it happens, it no longer matters. It was about a young chap who has been trained as a chauffeur. Some friends of mine are interested in him and asked me if I knew of a berth. He seems to be a first-rate man, and I thought perhaps you or some of your friends in Harley Street might take him on. However, just as I was starting for dinner tonight, I heard on the telephone that he has already got a situation."

"A pity," said Habaden. "I could have placed him. There are not so many really good drivers. By the way, Compton, any further news of the mysterious Myas?"

"No," I said. I am not going to worry about that any more. My historical work takes up most of my time now. I have got some mighty interesting letters of the Duke of Wellington's that I should like you to see."

It was later that night that I fell ill again.

5

I write these last few pages at my cottage on Consay Hill. I have got rid of my flat in St. James's Place, sold the furniture and even sold by far the greater part of my library. When the doctors say that a man has only a few months to live, property presents very little attraction. It seemed best to turn it into money and leave it on deposit at the bank, and in this way to save my executors some trouble. I saw the collections of many years dispersed in the auction-room in one afternoon, and watched it all without the slightest pang. Man wants but little here below."

It is quite with the approval of the doctors that I have given up London and come down into the country. So far as anything can be good for me, I suppose the quiet and the purer air are good for me. But I have come here much more to please myself than to please the doctors. The fact of the case is that the ordinary routine of life—especially when it has been such a worthless and useless routine as in my case—is not endurable in the face of death. I came here by easy stages, taking three days to do it, in a luxurious car with old Habaden to accompany me. I got through it all right, and now that I am here, I really suffer very few limitations.

I am not confined to my bed. I can walk in the garden, or even take a short stroll across the common land beyond it. Nominally the number of cigarettes that I may smoke *per diem* is very strictly limited. In practice I do not worry very much about that or any other medical limitation. I smoke when I want to smoke. The time is very short in any case, and one does not want to be grasping about the last moments.

In one respect my illness has been rather a revelation to me. I knew that I had many acquaintances, but I had not the slightest idea that I had so many friends. I am by no means left continuously alone here. Busy men waste their time by coming down from town to see me. Sometimes they bring with them suggestions for a change of treatment. They tell me wonderful stories of unexpected recoveries. They are uniformly and horribly hopeful. Old Habaden has been among the best of them. He has discovered suddenly that it is good for his health to spend the weekend here. He has acquired quite a new manner of talking to me. He treats my opinions with deference. He no longer lectures me. It is really rather pathetic, because, of course, where he disagreed with me before he still disagrees with me. Only he thinks it might annoy me if he said so. Neither that nor anything else will annoy me anymore.

The weather has been very good this spring. There have been many warm and sunny days, and I have spent most of them out of doors in the garden. A long-terraced walk gives me a fine view of the valley below. Down there among the trees an excellent trout stream runs. I have the fishing rights over some miles of it, and I shall never throw a fly there again. However, it gives my guests from London something to do, and saves them some hours of their self-inflicted boredom. Old Welsford has made this garden very charming. I like his high walls and archways of clipped yew.

"What are you going to do with that bit you've left sticking up there?" I asked him.

"I'm working on that, sir," said Welsford. "It's coming into shape already. In a year or two that will be a peacock."

It really seemed rather absurd that I should not see that peacock. I think if I had my choice, I would sooner die out here in the garden than in my bed indoors, and it is quite probable that the end will come as I desire. It will be quick. I shall just throw up my hands and drop. And yet this is not a subject about which I think very much. Far more often I find myself still acting and speaking as if I had a year or more before me. For instance, I find old Welsford working in the garden and give him directions. I watch carefully to see them carried out, and feel glad that the result will be good in the flower or fruit. It will perhaps not be till some minutes afterwards that I will suddenly burst out laughing at my own silliness.

Of course, whatever the result is I shall not see it. I often wish now, that I had spent more of my time in this garden. During the greater

250

part of the week, I am alone, but I never find myself bored here at all. I have more books than I shall have time to read, and I have this writing to finish. It even pleases me to sit on the terrace in the sun and to do absolutely nothing— except to watch the cloud-shadow's chasing one another over the pale bracken, or the sparkle of light on the water below in the valley.

Dying men are made much of. They get the idea that they matter. Perhaps that is the reason why I have been so egotistical. Yet it is not my own story that I wish to tell here.

It is an old idea that at the approach of death one may become endowed with spiritual powers of perception, of which one was previously unconscious. It may be—and I suppose it is more likely—that when the body is ill, the mind is no longer to be trusted, and that one has illusions. I write down quite simply that I have seen within the last few days Daniel Myas and Alice Lade, but I have not said a word to anyone about it. I can imagine too vividly what would happen if I did.

I can see old Habaden stroking his pointed grey beard and saying humbly that my experience is really very extraordinary. And I can imagine tactful questions which would follow, in order to find out if I had suffered from any other form of illusion. I cannot say myself what I actually believe about it. My opinion changes. At times I seem to know definitely that I did see them, and at other times I can put the thing aside and call it, as Habaden would probably call it in private, merely symptomatical.

It was early in the morning between five and six o'clock. Unable to sleep any longer, I had got up and dressed and gone out into the garden. A great deal of mist hung over the hill, not in one unbroken mass, but in flying patches. Sometimes they melted and joined together. Sometimes they seemed to open out like a flower and then vanish in the sunlight. I stood watching the scene for some time, and then I made my way slowly up to the top end of the garden. There is a door here in the high wall, which leads out on to the common. It is kept locked at night, of course, but I had my keys with me. I opened the door, and immediately, within five yards of me and standing with their faces towards me, I saw Myas and Alice Lade.

I saw them for a few seconds only. They had not the appearance of ghosts—filmy things. They looked solid and natural. Afterwards, when I tried to recall everything that I had seen, I noted one point particularly. They were exactly as they had been when I first saw them. Myas was bareheaded, but he wore that flowing necktie which I persuaded him to abandon when he came to London, and looked as young as on the day when I saw him at the Hamiltons'. Alice Lade was in a poor sort of grey dress. It was the dress she had worn when I saw her in the little room behind the shop in Knox Street. The sunlight shone on the red-gold of her hair in a way that lent realism to the picture.

The expression on the faces of both of them was similar, and was moreover rather curious. It was the expression of someone who welcomes a person with a smile. The effect upon myself was rather curious also. I had not the slightest feeling of fear. I walked rapidly towards them with my hand outstretched. It was only when they vanished that I began to be afraid. Close to me a couple of sheep moved among the bracken, hidden from sight by it, and their movement startled me. I went back into the garden to my seat on the terrace.

It was impossible for me at first to believe that I had suffered from any delusion, or that my imagination had shaped the flying mists on the hill-side into human forms. I told myself that it was delusion, but I could not make myself believe it. Her hair had caught the sunlight just as it would have done if she had been actually there. Their bodies had not been transparent and had shut out what was actually behind them. That expression of welcome was to me consolatory. I liked it. It seemed to approve of all that I had done. After I had rested for a few moments, I once more went out on to the common, in the hope that I might see them again. I even called to them, not loudly, by name. But that morning nothing further occurred.

Since then, I have twice thought that I saw them, but never with the same clearness or with the same feeling of certainty as on that early morning. I have seen them as figures at a distance in the dusk of the evening. I have seen them amid the trees of a wood on the hill-side. In both these cases I could readily believe it to be a mistake of my senses. But on that early morning it still seems to me at times that there was no mistake, and that I did in reality see them.

This view is strengthened by a conviction for which I can give no reason. It has been born in me and it grows stronger every day. I believe in it, as I believe in my own existence. It is a conviction that the story of Myas and Alice Lade is not yet finished, and that at some future time I shall take part in that story.

I suppose no man goes through life without at some time trying to picture what happens after death. Because we do not know, we take an analogy and make a guess. For a long time, it satisfied me to think that just as all the rivers run into the sea, so all the personalities are hereafter merged into that of a Supreme being. I find myself unable any longer to hold that theory. It had its philosophical consolations for me. I had missed most of the best things that life holds. My own personality had been baulked and insignificant. I believed that death ended it, partly, perhaps, because I wished death to end it.

As I have said, I can no longer hold that belief, though I can give little plausible reason for the change in me. The fact remains that I face death with some of that feeling of pleasurable excitement with which one starts out on a journey that promises new sights and new adventures.

What awaits me on that journey must necessarily be beyond my power to imagine. The souls of the dead are cognizable, not by body nor by mind, but in some way beyond human experience or thought. It was, I think, with great difficulty that these two people, whom I shall shortly rejoin, sent me any message from the life beyond. The message came in a form that science would call illusion. It may be. It does not necessarily seem to me to condemn it. It does not lessen in the least the hold it has upon me, and my conviction that I shall now begin rather than end my story.

Thus, then, I start out with pretty good hopes—*per iter tenebricosum unde negant redire quemquam.*

Going Home

CHAPTER 1: POMMES SOUFLÉES

You may possibly remember the remarkable trial of George Overman for conduct likely to produce a social revolution. George, who was of lowly origin, had by ability, force, work and dishonesty, become the sole proprietor of every fashionable restaurant in London. It was claimed that he maintained in these restaurants a Lucullan luxury, calculated to infuriate everybody who for financial or moral reasons was unable to partake of it.

The prosecution was strangely lukewarm and apologetic. Its case was badly put.

On the second day of the trial the evidence of the tramp was taken. He said that while lying on the grass in the Green Park, hungry and disconsolate, he had observed a party of wealthy people lunching expensively at a table in the window of the Ritz. This had so greatly exasperated him that he had immediately assaulted a policeman as a protest against the existing order of things and the capitalist system in particular. He made various exaggerated and conflicting statements, and was completely pulverised in cross-examination by Sir Harshiall Maul, K.C. his evidence really told in George Overman's favour.

And then Albert Smith was called, a man of the industrial classes, decently clad in blue serge. The report in the daily Press ran as follows:—

'What is you occupation?'

'I was till recently a sorter of *pommes soufflées* at Claridges.'

The Judge: 'What is Claridge's?'

Counsel: 'I am informed, M'lord, that it is an eating-house in Duke Street.'

The Judge: 'And these *pommes soufflées?*'

Counsel: 'Certainly, My Lord, I will put the question to the witness—What are they?'

'*Pommes soufflées* are slices of potato, cut thin, and then blown out. Same as the tyres of your motorbike.'

'Is the work of sorting them dangerous?'

'Dangerous? You believe me! Them *pommes* won't stand the pressure, not with any certainty. The man who had the job before me had his hand blown off through one of them exploding. He was compensated and the thing was hushed up. I nearly lost the sight of my right eye myself from a flying splinter and was in hospital for a week.'

'Why is this work requisite?'

'Because, however clever the cook may be, accidents will happen. Some of these *pommes soufflées* are blown up too much, as I've said, and explode, and they have to be cleared out. Sometimes the gas pressure fails, and they're not inflated enough, and these have to be cleared out too. Then they all have to be graded to size, so as to look neat and uniform in the dish.'

'And what impression has this made on your mind?'

'Me with the Mons riband sorting ballooned potatoes for profiteers, while thousands is out of work and starving! The impression it's made on me is that we want a change.'

'What change?'

'Bloody anarchy!'

(*Sensation in Court.*)

One strong point that Sir Harshiall Maul was able to make in cross-examination was that the management did provide the *pommes soufflées* sorter with a metal mask and that, through his own negligence, Albert Smith was not wearing the mask at the time of his accident.

"How would you like your beer poured into you through a bit of perforated zinc?' said the witness.

The judge rebuked him for this observation, but it may possibly have reminded him of something, for the luncheon-interval was then taken.

Dora Muse rose from her place in the public gallery, from which with sleepy wondering eyes she had been watching the proceedings. And now as she went out, a beautiful idea came to her. But she was not going to carry it out at Claridge's or at any other fashionable restaurant; her clothes were charming but not good enough. She walked northward.

And presently she saw a little restaurant, and the foreign proprietor's name which was painted up was rather like Angina Pectoris, but not quite. She went in and sat down. An elderly waiter, whose feet hurt him, shuffled up and handed her a gelatined bill-of-fare, and she handed it back without looking at it.

"Bring me," she said, "in her soft-music voice, "some *pommes souf-flées*."

"Sorry," the waiter said, "but we do not 'ave them. We 'ave boilt—masht—fryte—sooty. Tey some nice sooty potatoes."

"There's many a true word spoken in Swiss," said Dora gently, and went out immediately.

The waiter stared with his mouth open at the place where she had been, as if wondering what would happen to it next.

Dora tried another restaurant but here she also failed.

"The chef can do them special for you of course," she was told, "but that takes rather some long time."

"And, you see, I don't" said Dora, as she passed out. And one more waiter suffered from dropped jaw.

Her next attempt was at a larger restaurant in a street of superior tone. Here her order was accepted at once.

"Certainly, mees," said the waiter. "And with them?"

"I don't know yet. Get me the *pommes soufflées* first."

The waiter dashed off with young alacrity and enthusiasm.

"Success the third time," said Dora to herself. "Always the third time. Dear number three, if you were a kitten, I'd kiss you!"

And then the waiter came back, looking years older, a haggard and broken man.

"I am ver' sorry," he said with despair in his voice. "The last portion of *pommes soufflées* is just gone."

"Who's got it?" said Dora impatiently. "Tell me who's got it."

"See. It goes just now to the gentleman sitting alone at that table."

Dora looked in the direction indicated. The gentleman sitting alone was a man of the industrial classes, decently clad in blue serge. He was, in fact, the sorter, and Dora recognised him.

"But this is infamous," she said, hurriedly collecting her gloves and handbag. She sped up the room and seated herself at the sorter's table opposite to him. "Oh, Alfred Smith," she said eagerly, "how can you? How can you?"

"I beg yours," said Alfred Smith icily. His eyes had suddenly become glassy.

"I was in court just now," Dora went on impetuously, "and I heard every word of your evidence. It impressed me so much. You said you fought at Mons, and your work as a *pommes soufflées* sorter made you long for bloody anarchy. And now you're eating *pommes soufflées*. At any rate you're going to. It seems so wrong—so cynical—so false—so inconsistent—so hypocritical."

"Excuse me again, but you're wrong. I'm in favour of destroying the capitalist system by force, and of depriving the rich of their luxuries by force. But am I going to take what I don't want? Not likely. And this dish that you see before me was not bought with the blood and tears of the swindled and downtrodden. No, indeed! It was bought with the sweat of my brow. And if you've ever been cross-examined for twenty minutes by Sir Harshiall Maul K.—blast him!—C., you'd know what that meant. In other words it came out of the expenses allowed, on a liberal scale, to witnesses. Be just. Be reasonable."

"I wish to be," said Dora. "I was perhaps too hasty. You see, I'd ordered *pommes soufflées* myself, and I was told you'd got the last portion."

"Ah! That's a different matter. (Another plate, waiter, and get a move on you.) I'm a practical Socialist, I am—not all gas, same as some. There you are." He pushed the dish across the table to her. "Help yourself. Within reason," he added though dully.

"It's very kind of you," said Dora. She helped herself absent-mindedly, and then looked at her plate. "Is that about half?" she asked.

"Quite," said Alfred, hustling the rest on to his own plate, where they could enjoy the society of a loin chop. "Judging by your words—and actions—these are a favourite dish with you, Miss."

"I've never had them in my life before."

"You won't find they make much of a luncheon—taken alone like that."

"They're not luncheon: they're an experience."

"And what do you make of them? I may tell you that they're pretty fair but not up to Claridge's."

"They're pure, and exalted, and delicate, like Walter Pater's prose. They taste a little like success."

"And what's that taste like?"

"Dust, of course."

He looked puzzled, and told the waiter to bring him another pint. He watched her with his mouth full. She had finished the potatoes, and sat with her hand resting on one hand.

"And what might you be thinking about?" he asked.

"Were you ever at Mons?"

"Oh, well. Picturesque little trick. Public speakers—they have to do it. You should come and hear me one Sunday. You've got to hold the attention, and if you can't do that, you're nowhere. You begin: 'Last night I stood by the bedside of a dying woman' and you've got 'em. And you've got to get 'em, or your arguments are all lost. It's not bragging, or lying, or anything of that sort. It's just an ordinary oratorical device. Suppose you was to find yourself in—"

And here he pulled up, realising that the girl had suddenly and noiselessly departed.

Somewhat sulkily he called for his bill, and the waiter presented it.

"The lady who has just gone out," he said explanatorily, "she pay me herself for the half of the *pommes soufflées*."

CHAPTER 2: THE BOOK OF EXPERIENCES

No, Dora decided. She could not go to the studio. There were still some hours of light, and the chances were that Kate Mason would have a model. If not, it was probable that Kate (gaunt and merciless) would make Dora sit, and Kate talked but little and poorly when painting. Later, perhaps, she might visit Kate but not now. Besides, Dora had entries to make in her *Book of Experiences*. So she went, with the assistance of an omnibus, to her little flat in Hampstead.

A few words with Jane in the kitchen—Jane seemed preoccupied. A few minutes in a snowy bedroom. And then Dora sat down at the writing-table in her one reception-room, a room that was neat and carefully ordered.

The *Book of Experiences* had been in process of compilation for nearly a year, and was already in its second large manuscript volume, all indexed and cross-indexed.

Dora opened the book and first of all made the following entries under general Observations.

"Because one side is all wrong, it does not follow that the opposite side is all right."

"There are no class-viced but only human-vices. Dives and Lazarus are the same man. Apparent differences are merely the result of opportunity on the one side and lack of opportunity on the other."

She made three other entries which were indexed thus:

Anarch, bloody.
Oratory, public, effect on orator.
Sorter, pommes soufflées.

These were new subjects. She also made a note under *Sex-Attraction, influence of.* But there were already one hundred and seventy-eight entries under this head.

And the Jane came into the room. She was cleanly attired in grey and white for the afternoon; her eyes were pathetic. And Dora knew that another confession was coming. Jane had a perfect passion for confessing.

Jane was a year older than Dora, but none the less reverenced her as an elder, a superior, an employer, and a person to be adored. Some people thought that Jane was a treasure, and in so many respects she was. Others said she was a perfect scream, which is as it may be. Dora, who knew her better than anybody else, was very grateful for Jane, but could imagine her in tragedy. Indeed, Jane possessed a blend of sentiment and animal passion which often tends in that direction. Jane was a beautiful girl. Her eyes were exceptionally dark—darker even than Dora's—and her complexion was a warm dusky cream. Her mouth was quite large, yet well-shaped, and her full red lips did not get their colour out of the handbag.

"I'm sorry, miss," said Jane, with desperate resolution, "but I have to tell you that this morning I kissed the milkman."

"Jane, you said you never would!"

"I know I did, miss. And in a manner of speaking, I didn't do it. It was like as if something inside me that was not myself did it. I know it left me all of a tremble."

"How did it happen?" said Dora sternly, and conscious of a faint reminiscence of Sir Harshial Maul.

"I was up early as usual. Sunny morning, but a little chill. Birds all at it, and green trees showing aver across the Heath. So, he came—and very nice he looked in his gaiters and all. I hung back a bit, knowing what he was. And the 'Bit fresh this morning, Janey,' he says. 'Give me a good cuddle to warm me.' And next moment he'd got me tight in his arms and I was—"

"I don't want to hear about it. You're a disgusting pig. I suppose you'd better go and marry him."

"Married already. Four children and another expected. Misfortune for everybody."

"Well, I don't see how I can keep you here after this."

Large tears came into Jane's solemn eyes. Her rich bosom heaved. A part of her nature was enjoying every emotional moment of this, but she was not conscious of it.

"Don't say that, miss. Please, don't say that. I've got nobody in the world but you, and one cousin not on speaking terms, and a few chance acquaintances. I'd work my fingers to the bone for you, yes, and drop dead for you, and be glad. Truth, I would. If you only knew how it happened. It was like as if there was nobody but him and me in the world just then, and I did but kiss him once—three times at the most. That's all it was. And I've never had a moment's happiness since, nor fancied my dinner neither, nor couldn't till I told you. Do forgive me this time!"

Now Dora could not help forgiving anybody who pleaded for forgiveness with tears in their beautiful eyes.

"Well, I shall arrange that we get our milk elsewhere in future—I'll see to that on the telephone. And nothing of the kind must happen again. And this time, because you're sorry and are a good girl generally, I will forgive you."

Suddenly, impulsively, without the least bit of acting, Jane flung herself on her knees and kissed Dora's arched instep.

"Get up, Jane," said Dora. "Don't go on like a silly baby." But for just a moment her hand rested gently on the girl's head.

Jane retired to the kitchen and instantly, without ceasing to sob, began to clean silver. She seldom wasted time, and, when possible, did two things at once.

Dora paced up and down the room, not in the least angry with Jane, but quite angry with herself.

Taken by surprise by Jane's confession, she had been false, unfair, and conventional. She had pretended a horror of nature which she had never really felt. She had said none of the things she should have said.

"Made for love" was written on Jane's face. And what chance had she of a love worthwhile? Most days she saw no man, except the representatives of tradesmen that called in a hurry for a few moments, but did dull work well in solitude. On her holidays she tasted the emotional joys of the cinema, but made no men friends. She was as shy as she was passionate, as not infrequently happens, and an approach by a stranger merely frightened her. She had got slowly used to the milkman—a lusty good-looking young man—and no doubt he had been fascinated by her. It was summer-time and the birds were singing—the chance for a moment of sweetness. The man was married, but Jane was herself the illegitimate child of a married man; it would affect her views.

Yet it was on this point, Dora felt now, that she should have talked. It was not wrong to feel lonely—to long to love and to be loved—to give oneself to the embrace of the beloved. That was all in nature, and there was nothing disgusting about it. But she might have asked Jane if she thought it fair to the other woman—if the man who had cheated the other woman might not also cheat her—things of that kind.

Well, there was no serious harm done, and she could talk to Jane later. Meantime she could prevent a renewal of the temptation. She went to the telephone, and with two consecutive calls changed the source of the milk-supply. And when she had vowed that she would talk to Jane like a woman and not like a little tin goddess, Dora felt much better.

But here was material for the *Book of Experiences*, and she returned to the writing-table. She wrote slowly, as she always did, choosing her words, trying to make sure that she was saying just exactly what she meant. She filled a page or so with an accurate record of direct observation. The deductions made were, however, open to criticism. The entire entry was classified in the index: "*Milkmen, exceptional opportunities of.*"

Then she locked the book away in a drawer. It was a book that had to be locked away. For it aimed at the whole truth and no shirking, and some of it was—well, very detailed and very intimate. No one but Dora had ever seen a line in it.

It was just then that her clock struck four. And it was then—and not till then—that Dora realised that her luncheon had been distinctly sketchy. Her body followed her mind, and instantly became hungry. She rang the bell.

Jane appeared, exhibiting no trace of tears but with just a touch of fallen-angel lingering about the expression.

"Tea as soon as you can," said Dora. "And—"

An impending order dealing with potted-meat sandwiches was arrested by sounds (*prrrring*, also *rat-tat*) from the exterior of the outer door of the flat.

"Just see to that," said Dora.

Dora could hear the voice of a man in the passage. There were a few seconds delay, and then Jane brought in a visiting-card on which was written in pencil:

"Business of the utmost importance to me but very little to you. Can you possibly spare me half-an-hour?"

The name on the card was that of the sole owner of London's fashionable restaurants, at whose trial Dora had been present that morning, George Overman.

This was unconventional, but conventionality had already failed Dora once that afternoon. The message on the card had a candour that appealed to her. The risk seemed slight, and her curiosity was aroused.

"I will see the gentleman, Jane. Bring tea in just the same—two cups of course."

"Certainly, miss."

It was with no trace of fallen-angel but with a high and ceremonious manner that she showed Mr. Overman into the room.

Chapter 3: The Master

Mr. George Overman was tall and of a good figure. His pale blue eyes had an almost superhuman steeliness and force. His lower jaw was excessive. Yet his clean-shaven face was not ill-looking at this period of his career—he was still in his thirties. He was dressed well, carefully, and quietly.

"Good afternoon," said Dora. "Won't you sit down and tell me what it is you want? Your visit is—well, rather a surprise."

"I am sure it must be, Miss Muse," said George pleasantly. "Your kindness in receiving me at all in this way is more than I should have hoped—though I knew of course that you were kind."

"I was present at your trial this morning."

"My trial? Oh, yes, a trumpery affair. But it was there that I saw you for the first time in my life."

"A trumpery affair, Mr. Overman? But you must know that for conduct likely to provoke a Social revolution a man may be sent to prison."

"No doubt. But this is a Government prosecution, and the Government wishes heartily it had never embarked upon it, and the prearranged result will be a wash-out. I will tell you how I know this later, if you like, Miss Muse."

"What's puzzling me at the moment is that you know my name, my address, and take it for granted that I am kind, and yet you say you saw me for the first time in Court this morning."

"I will explain all that, though there are things in it that you may find it hard to forgive. I'm afraid too that it's a long story."

At this moment Jane with suggestions of a Vestal virgin engaged in some high temple ritual, brought in tea.

George took one cup of tea—nothing more. Dora who wanted

to listen more than she wanted to talk, and wanted to eat even more than she wanted to listen, took up a strategic position from which she could attack any dish on the table without stretching, and said she was eager to hear his story.

"Well," said George, "I'm going to talk about myself, but then I've been an egotist all my life. Some people would tell you that I was a bad man. That would be untrue, but it would be equally untrue to say that I was a good man. Power interested me and morality did not. I was ready to do anything, good or bad, that would lead towards power. I was always intelligent of course. I would break any law if I were sure of escaping detection, but not otherwise. For example, take my first important *coup*. I saw when I was quite young a thousand *per cent*. Opportunity. It was not a speculation—I never speculate—but a certain opportunity with no chance about it. I put all that I had saved into it, and all that I could borrow, and also all that I could borrow, and also all that I could safely embezzle—what ordinary men would call a considerable sum. I knew that before this money could be missed, I could replace it and could render any detection in the future impossible. Everything happened exactly as I had planned it."

"Suppose it had not," said Dora with one hand flickering over those chocolate cakes.

"I should have been ruined of course. But the chance was too remote to be worth consideration; as far as anything in this world can be certain, my success was certain. To this day I use any effectual means to an end, without regard to their morality, if I can do so without impunity. Take my case in the Courts at present. The public supposes that I am defending myself in the usual way with eminent counsel and so forth. And no doubt, for the look of the thing, I am playing that farce. But as a matter of fact, I settled the whole thing before it ever came into the Courts, and I settled it by blackmailing the prime minister. That's what it amounted to."

"Do tell me about that," said Dora.

"As soon as I heard that they meant to go for me, I drove straight to Downing Street and saw Sainton Mackworth himself. There was no difficulty about that—he knows me. I asked him what the game was, and he told me what the solicitor-general had said, and what this, that, and the other had said, and was very high-horse. So, I got up to go. 'Very well, Sainton,' I said, 'I see I shall have to sell my restaurants. And when I do, I'm going to buy newspapers.' He begged me to sit down again."

"I don't think I see. Why?"

"Sainton doesn't want to lose his job. Like every other politician he sneers at the Press openly and is very secretly afraid of it. This government is no better and no worse than any other government. It has made mistakes, as all governments do. Some of the mistakes might, if they were generally known, be called by harsher names by the vulgar Press and the ignorant voters. Do you see now?"

Dora paused in the act of taking the jam sandwich. "Yes, I think I do. But go on."

"Well, Sainton Mackworth got off the high horse and more or less fell in the mud. There was not the slightest intention of forcing me to sell my restaurants—they could not be in better hands. It had been already decided that the utmost consideration was to be shown me in the conduct of the case—and as a matter of fact I have enjoyed unheard of privileges—and he was sure that the result would not be a prejudicial to me in business or in any other way. The whole thing was really an object-lesson to let the public see that the new Act would be administered without fear or favour.

"He's kept his promises. In some indirect way the word has gone round. Why, today we had the cleverest lawyers in England putting into box witnesses who—as those lawyers well knew—would damn any case. A farce to end in a washout. I've never been in prison, Miss Muse, and I'm not going now. I've never incurred social ostracism. Of course, modern society is very lenient to millionaires, but I think I may say that I am almost a favourite. At the same time, I have never—until this morning, I have never loved good because it was good. I have never, until this morning, hated evil because it was evil."

He looked up suddenly at Dora. It seemed to her that he always looked up just at the moment when she was helping herself to another; it might have been coincidence.

"Why do you say 'till this morning'?" said Dora. "What happened this morning?"

"That," said George, "is what I have come to tell you. It frightens me because it is very personal, and you may resent that, and refuse to help me. I can only pray that you will forgive me and hear me to the end before you refuse."

Dora, her mouth being but partially full at the moment, was able to say that she would hear him to the end.

"This morning," he continued, "I looked up and saw you in the public gallery. I looked long. Don't misunderstand me. I did not fall

265

in love with you. I am not in love with you now. I shall never marry you. '*He rideth the fastest who rideth alone,*' as the man said who did not take his own hint. I shall never marry anybody. Crude instinct I know, but not love sentiment. It is Greek to me. No, what happened was this—stated quite simply. As I looked up at your wonderful eyes and pale face—with an expression on it that was all new to me—I knew suddenly what was meant by the beauty of holiness. The expression is there now. The ordinary things of life do not affect it. Tea cannot drown it; jam sandwiches—"

"I know," said Dora, "but I had hardly any luncheon."

"True. Half a portion of *pommes soufflées*—in the opinion of an intelligent observer not quite half."

"Oh, how do you know that. You were not there."

"No, I was not there. I will tell you how I know it. But let me preface my confession with my excuse. To realise what was meant by the beauty of holiness was to know that the prizes for which I have struggled so hard, so infamously, and so victoriously, are dust and ashes. The inspiration that filled me at the sight of you seemed to open just a little way a door through which I could see far better things than what the world accounts as prizes. Whither that inspiration will lead me I do not know yet. Bit I did know at once that I must never lose it. Without a moment's hesitation I sent a messenger to fetch Beaver."

"Beaver?"

"Beaver—the best private inquiry agent in London. I have employed him frequently and he has reason to value my patronage. I indicated you to him and said: 'I want the name and address of that lady. You are not to cause her the slightest annoyance. She is not to know that she is followed.'"

"I certainly did not know it."

"You were followed by eighteen of Beaver's women-detectives. One was always near you, and the rest were grouped at intervals some way behind. Whenever you turned a corner the one next to you dropped back, and one of the others took her place. If you had looked back—and I understand you did not—you would always have seen a woman a little way behind you, but at the next corner she would have been out of sight and another would have taken her place. You would not have guessed that you were followed. After you had been tracked to this flat it was child's play to get your name from the porter. Every stage in your progress was reported to me over the telephone, and the moment I knew your name and address I got into the car which I had in waiting and drove here. It was no doubt a great liberty."

"It was cheek," said Dora thoughtfully, "but you're like that. You must know you are. I don't believe I'd have seen you if I'd known that at first."

"I began my story at the right end. And why did you see me?"

"Curiosity, I suppose. I'd read about you in the newspapers. I'd been at you trial. I didn't see how I, being what I am, could possibly be of any importance to you, being what you are. Even now I don't know what you want."

"And to me it seems so obvious. I want you to continue the great work that, all unconsciously, you have begun today. I want you to let me see you—as often and as much as possible. You may make the conditions of our meeting what you will, and whatever they are you may be sure that I shall always treat you with the utmost respect. I'm not going to trouble you for spiritual advice and suggestions as to my better conduct. Your conscious self cannot help me a bit; it is the unconscious and unreasoning you that I need. Indeed, reason means little to a man who has always reasoned—has always achieved that much. No, it is by my eyes that I am healed—by my vision of you. The strayed angel in your eyes looks at me and calls me to better things—I've no idea what they are as yet. But I shall know if only you will let me see you. It is for you to say whether you will save me or let me be lost."

"It all sounds like madness," said Dora.

"Madness? Today for the first time in my life I have been sane. When I sought for power, and wealth, and nonsense of that kind, I was mad indeed."

Dora rose and walked up and down the room, deep in thought.

"Very well," she said at last. "I will see you again. I do not know how often—that will depend a good deal on you."

"I have no words to express my gratitude," said George. "I wish you wanted, say, the Savoy Hotel and a cascade of diamonds that I might give them to you."

"I don't. And don't talk like that please."

"I know it's hopelessly clumsy of me. But do remember that if ever I can be of service to you, all that I have is absolutely at your disposal." He picked up his own visiting card and wrote a telephone number on it. "If you wish to speak to me at any time, please ring that number. If you took the telephone numbers in the book, your call would be filtered through clerks or servants; with the number on the card, you will get straight through to me myself at once. When may I hope to

267

hear from you?"

"I don't know. Perhaps—when the trial is over."

"Thank you. It's all I can say, but I at least mean it. Goodbye Miss Muse."

He shook hands rapidly with her and departed. She rubbed her eyes and wondered if she could be dreaming.

Jane came in to clear away the tea things. And Dora for a whim suddenly asked her what she thought of that gentleman.

"He's the master," said Jane firmly and without a moment's hesitation.

"What do you mean?" said Dora almost irritably. "The master? Master of what?"

"Well, miss, you've only to look at him said Jane feebly.

She carried the tray through into the kitchen, set it down, and said aloud to nobody:

"And he ain't half in love with her neither."

He was not. He was not in the least in love with her.

Chapter 4: The Strayed Angel

Kate Mason came to see Dora at nine that evening. Kate stood nearly six feet high, and was plain and angular. Her dress was careless and without any artistic pretensions. She smoked too many cigarettes and frequently used strong—not to say bad—language. She was a hard worker. She had never said a sentimental thing in her life, always spoke of her art as her job, lived solely for beauty and would have been angry and surprised if anybody had told her so,. She painted classical nudes with great dexterity and knowledge, and there was a tone of suppressed poetry about her work. She was successful.

"Doing anything tomorrow morning?" said Kate.

"Why?" said Dora suspiciously.

"I'd like you to come over to the studio. Just for the feet. It will only be for an hour or so."

"Look here," said Dora. "You make lots of money with your pictures. Why can't you employ professional models, instead of pestering all your friends to sit?"

"Pestering all my friends. Well, of all the damned lies I have ever heard! I've had Cicely twice for hands, and you for everything, and I may have picked up a background head here and there. That's the lot. Then you talk about professional models—they're enough to break your heart. I thought I was fixed all right when I got Annie Marks, and so I was for a time; and then the selfish beast got fat and sagged. And after that I was on to a damned spoiled hussy who kept about one appointment in every three, and was generally an hour late for that, and objected to my language. Besides, good feet are pretty scarce anyhow. You won't be later than ten sharp, will you?"

"Sitting with bare feet is chilly."

"I'll have the studio as hot as Gehenna. I swear I will."

"And you don't talk when you're painting, and I get bred stiff."

"Oh, well, you can do the talking."

"To a woman who doesn't listen? No. but I'll come. I knew this would happen. I was coming to see you this afternoon, and didn't because I had the feeling that you were going to get me."

"Well, I'm tremendously grateful and all that. Good. Now I can see my way through tomorrow's work."

She had been standing as she spoke.

Now she lit a cigarette and dropped—a mass of untidy comfort—into an easy-chair. "What have you been doing all day?" she asked.

"Getting experiences—rather a lot of them, as it happens—and entering them up in my book. I've been followed through the streets of London by female detectives, and a millionaire, whom I'd never seen in my life before, had tea with me here."

"Great Scott! He'll marry you."

"He says he will never marry. He's not even in love with me. He told me so."

"I want to hear all about it."

Dora told her some of it, but not all. She described George and said that he was wicked, but wanted to be better, and thought there was something in her that helped him."

"It's all impossible," said Kate bluntly.

"Don't say impossible when you mean unusual—so many people make that mistake. Now you're an artist and can see—tell me if there's anything strange about my eyes."

"Well, there is," said Kate meditatively. "And it's damnably annoying too, because I ought to be able to say what it is and I can't. I know the construction of the eye absolutely and yet I can't get it. I shall get it in time of course, but at present it beats me. And the funny thing is that I once did get it unconsciously and accidentally. Remember that part-draped full-length I did from you? I was to put another head on it, and I saw a girl in a teashop who would do for it. So, I persuaded her to let me make a sketch of her head."

"I'm sure you did," said Dora with conviction.

"Why not? You've got to take what you want when you find it. She wasn't a bit like you, and my sketch was all correct, of course. And yet somehow or other I'd given that girl's eyes the look that I've seen only in yours. I must find up that old sketch and analyse it out. It's absurd for a woman who knows her job to be beaten by a childish thing like that."

"Still, if you recognised the look when you painted it accidentally, you must know what it's like."

"It's not normal human," said Kate decidedly.

"What animal does it remind you of?"

"None. If it didn't sound so damned silly to say so, I should say it was the kind of look you'd expect in an angel. Mind, I'm not saying that you're angelic or any rot of that kind. It's a sort of provisional description until I spot what the thing really is. I say, why don't you let me see that book of yours?"

"I sit to you for my body, but it's only to myself that I sit for my soul."

"Well, you're going to publish it one of these days, aren't you? Else, what's the use?"

"I'm going to use it very much as you use studies and sketches for your pictures."

"So, I shall see the story you make out of it."

"If it turns out to be a story. I don't know yet what it will be. I want to know the real things—and then make them lovelier."

"Funny job, writing," said Kate. "Can't even spell, myself. Well, I must be off if I'm to be ready for you in the morning. Ten sharp, mind."

"Kate, you can't go into the street smoking a cigarette."

"Can't I?" said Kate grimly. "Guess again, my dear. I'm old enough and ugly enough for anything. Goodnight."

When Dora went to bed, she looked at herself in the glass, long and critically. George Overman had spoken of the "strayed angel" in her eyes. Kate Mason had found herself reluctantly compelled to use the word "angel" to describe the same thing. And Dora admitted that she herself had had strange feelings at times, explicable perhaps on some "strayed angel" theory. They had already been recorded in her *Book of Experiences*.

These feelings were not quite that wave of *desiderium*—that longing to fly away and be at rest—which comes at times to all those who love and are sad. At such times the longing of Dora's heart was always to return, to go back again, like a child that is homesick. it would come suddenly to her, without the spur of beauty to provoke it, when she was doing some quite ordinary and commonplace thing. That very morning it had come to her as she tied her shoes. Tears filled her eyes, and she had found herself saying aloud "Oh, to be there again!" There? Where? She did not know. But from time to time a memory of the peace, deep and warm, seemed to reach her.

Sometimes she would wake in the morning, and, though she could not recall her dream in any way, yet be sure that in the dream she had gone back and drunk of ecstasy. And when that happened all through the day she would be filled with happiness and content, and all through the day her most beautiful thoughts would come to her. Those were days when Jane looked at her with awe, and spoke to her in a hushed voice, and did not know why.

Dora turned away from her mirror, perplexed, and began to undress. The wonderful dream did not come to her that night.

It was while she was at breakfast next morning—half an hour later than usual—that the messenger arrived from the Piccadilly florist with the big box of red roses. No card was enclosed, but Dora knew they had come from George Overman. She did not want him to give her things. But the colour and the scent of the roses were beautiful, and Dora took care of them.

Outside in the street she found a motorcar waiting. The driver stood beside the door with a letter in his hand. The moment he saw her he stepped forward, asked if she were Miss Muse, and handed her the letter.

"You don't let me give you presents—flowers don't count, of course—but do let me have the pleasure of lending you something. I have more motorcars than I can use, and I have given orders that this little car and its driver are to be at your disposal at all times. Please use them often."

Thus wrote George Overman, adding the telephone number of the garage, and an assertion that he had that day for the first time in his life been moved by unmixed compassion and had saved a man with a large family from financial ruin.

Dora hesitated. If she walked to Kate's studio, she would be late for her appointment; if she used the car, she would be punctual. The driver, a pleasant-looking young fellow, stood now holding the door of the car open, obviously expecting her to enter.

She yielded, giving the man the address of Kate's studio as he put the rug over her knees. But she said to herself that George Overman was making her do things, and she did not wish to be made to do things. For a moment she thought she would never use the car again, never see George again, write to tell him so, and forbid him to send any more flowers. But she had rather an uncomfortable conviction that it would be no good if she did, and that George was not so easily managed. A millionaire was a power. He had been a power for evil and she could change him into a power for good. Indeed, if what he said was true her spell was already working on him. Also, he was not in love with her—and that was a very great consideration.

So, when she reached the studio and the driver asked at what time he should return for her, she said that he was to be there at twelve.

"Now," said Kate, when Dora had slipped off her shoes and stockings. "Flat on your back on the long cushion and you can stuff the small one under your head. Now draw the left leg up. Not quite so much. Right. Cross the right knee over the left. Further over. Perfect. Is that comfortable for you?"

"Absolutely. I could sleep like this."

"Do, if you can do it without losing the pose. The skirt gets a little in the way—I want from the knee down. Thanks. Now we're off."

Kate picked up her palette, took a long look, and for half-an-hour worked eagerly without speaking to Dora, her lips tight together and her eyes intent.

The studio was very hot. For a while Dora looked upward, and saw a fly going through physical exercises. Then the fly went away and Dora closed her eyes. Her mind was drowsy, half awake and half asleep. Suddenly and poignantly her nostalgia was upon her—the blind instinct to return. She was lost in this world—lost and lonely. It was with some difficulty that she remained motionless. She wished that Kate would swear again—Kate swore softly to herself when working—for that might break the obsession. It seemed to her to last a long time.

Then she heard the scratch of a match. Kate was lighting a cigarette. "We'll rest a bit," said Kate.

Dora stood up, stretched herself, thrust her feet into her soft suede shoes, stepped down from the throne, and joined Kate on the hearthrug.

"Can I see the picture?" asked Dora.

"When it's finished. You know I never—Dora, you've been crying."

272

"N'no. I don't think so."

"You have. Your face is all wet. What's the matter?"

"Nothing," said Dora, taking her handkerchief from her bag. "It's just that every now and then one gets the kind of thoughts that brings tears into the eyes. Everybody does."

"Do they? I'll take my Bible oath I don't. Eat chocolates." She took a package from the mantelpiece and handed it to Dora.

"Thanks," said Dora, pulling open the band of gold thread. "That's a beautiful idea of yours."

"Went out myself and got them for you this morning. I hope you'll finish them—they're not things I ever eat myself."

"I'll try hard. Kate show me the head you did of the teashop girl, when you made her eyes look like mine."

"Can't. That went into the coke-stove last night. I got it out to try to spot the angel-effect. I came to the conclusion that it was not the result of a single subtlety but of a combination of perhaps twenty or thirty. I might have found some of them, but I was fed up with it. And the sketch wasn't good either and that annoyed me too. So, I made an end of it, and that's that."

She paused and said awkwardly: "About this weepy business. If you're tired, or seedy, or worried about anything, and would rather not sit any more this morning, you'll have the sense to say so, won't you?"

"I'm all right. It was just a passing thin. I shan't be silly anymore."

"Then, if you're ready," said Kate, and Dora took up the pose again, placing the chocolates by her side for purposes of reference.

CHAPTER 5: "PURCHASE, CONSUMPTION, AND ASSIMILATION"

Warm in bed on Sunday morning Dora read the closing scene of George Overman's trial.

The judge said that he could not but suppose that these proceedings had been taken on sound advice and with good reason; but he confessed that he had been quite unable to discover what the reason was. Defendant's counsel had stated—and the other side had fully admitted it—that Mr. Overman employed large staffs, male and female, working under very good conditions, and extremely well paid—in some cases paid considerably above the rates demanded by the Trades Union. Was this conduct likely to cause a social revolution? Was it not rather conduct that tended to cause contentment and social stability?

This being so, plaintiffs had attempted to show that Mr. Overman had committed a technical error and asked that a suitable penalty should be imposed. And for this purpose they had relied mainly, if not entirely, on Section 3, Sub-section 2, Clause 109 of the Act. Now he would say that he thought that the Act as a whole was well drawn; on the contrary there was much in it that was ambiguous, loosely-worded, and likely to cause trouble. But as to this particular clause there could be no doubt whatever. It dealt with out-of-season and other delicacies and imposed certain penalties on anybody harbouring and exposing such things—to give the exact words—"in a manner provocative of their purchase, consumption, and assimilation."

It was to be noticed that the Act did not say "purchase, or consumption, or assimilation." Had it done so, it would have been sufficient for the plaintiffs to have shown that the defendant had harboured and exposed anyone of the scheduled delicacies in a manner provocative of anyone of the three. But the act said distinctly "purchase, consumption, and assimilation." All three must be proved. If for instance it were shown that the defendant had exposed a scheduled delicacy in a manner provocative of purchase and consumption, but that by the action of the chef, or by any other reason, assimilation had rendered difficult, or impossible, then in that respect the case against the defendant failed.

Now had all three been proved? He would turn to the evidence of Mrs. Bumpingham. She was a credible witness, and he wished he could say as much for some of the other witnesses that had been heard. She might be thought simple and uncultured, but she had given her evidence in a manly and straightforward manner, and was obviously speaking the truth. She said she was the widow of a man who had purchased a row of eight cottages and eight pig-styes in January, 1914, had sold them in June, 1919, and had then expired, leaving his widow a large fortune. The fact that the late Mr. Bumpingham had converted each pig-stye into two maisonettes had been brought out, to cause prejudice. It had no bearing on the case and he dismissed it from his mind. This Mrs. Bumpingham was a regular patron of the defendant's restaurants, and had frequently partaken of the scheduled delicacies. She said that the very sight of them fairly made your mouth water. This seemed to him conclusive. It showed both an incitement to consume and an incitement to assimilate, the secretion of the saliva being the first step in assimilation. Mrs. Bumpingham's statements had moreover, been confirmed by the evidence of eminent medical men.

Incitement to consume and to assimilate had been proved. But had an incitement to purchase been proved? A line in defendant's advertisements said:

"Everything the little Mary needs at London's highest prices always."

Mrs. Bumpingham herself had said the defendant's charges for these delicacies were "enough to frighten you," and that on two occasions she had preferred to do without forced strawberries rather than pay the price demanded for them. He could only hold that no incitement to purchase had been proved, but rather the reverse. The case against the defendant therefore failed.

In conclusion he could only say that he thought it would be a sad day for England when—

But here Dora threw down the newspaper, took the bell-push from under her pillow, and rang.

"Jane," said Dora, "I'm disgracefully late this morning. Please get the bath ready, and then I want you to telephone for me. You will find Mr. Overman's card on the writing-table. Ring up the number that is on that card, say you are speaking for me, and ask Mr. Overman if he would like to see me today and, if so, what time."

"Very good, miss," said Jane, picked up Dora's breakfast tray—Dora breakfasted delicately and continentally—and went out.

Dora heard the water gurgling in the bathroom. Now she would really have to get up and no nonsense. So, on went the rose silk dressing-gown.

From the bathroom she could hear Jane at the telephone: "Is that Mr. Overman? Miss Muse's maid speaking. Miss Muse wishes to know if you would like to see her today, sir, and if so, at what time.....Very good, sir, I will ask Miss Muse, if you will kindly hold the line."

Jane stood outside the bathroom door and called: "Mr. Overman thanks you very much, and says he would like to see you now"—Dora smiled—"if he may come along in his car."

"Say I shall be ready for him in half-an-hour."

Could it be done in half-an-hour? It could, with a little assistance from Jane. In fact, it was done. When George Overman arrived, Dora was meekly clad in blue serge and seated in her sitting-room

George was in country clothes. He had been intending to play golf that day, he explained, but had cancelled all his engagements on hearing from Miss Muse.

"I wish you wouldn't do these things," said Dora. "They make me feel dishonest—as if I'm pretending to an importance that I certainly have not got."

"I am quite certain that I am of considerable importance," said George. "And as you influence me in a most extraordinary and unprecedented way, I think your importance must rank even higher. Did you read the result of my trial?"

"I did. I thought the judge was quite right."

"That's curious, because I know that he was quite wrong."

"Wrong? In what way?"

"In the way he dealt with purchase, consumption, and assimilation. I own restaurants. It is therefore necessary for me to provoke purchase and consumption in every possible way. It is part of the business and I do it. But I am not in the least concerned with assimilation, and it is probable that I have overworked and consequently wrecked, more digestions than any man in London. The judge argued that high prices for scheduled delicacies were a deterrent. On the contrary, they are an attraction. The majority of my clients have no palate and none of the knowledge of the epicure. Price is their one criterion. The dearer the thing is the better it must be. If I were to content myself with a reasonable profit, I should lose all my best clients. They like to feel that they are doing what very few can afford to do. They like to brag afterwards about the prices they paid."

"How terrible!" said Dora earnestly.

"It is terrible. It is also disgusting. Here in your presence, I realise it for the first time. I knew it before but could always dismiss it cynically from my mind. As long as I made money, I did not care who suffered. I even took over a large pepsin factory in order that I might derive further profit by curing the disease which I myself had caused. I must think what can be done. If I simply sold my restaurants, others would buy them and continue to run them in the same way. If I closed them all, I should cause much unemployment and distress, and other restaurants on similar lines would be opened for a certainty. When I look at you, I wish to do good, but it is very difficult to do good, without causing a lot of harm by it."

"Yes," said Dora, "but then we don't get much practice, do we?"

"True. And some of us—myself, for instance, take up the game rather late in life."

"Tell me about that first attempt—the deed of compassion?"

"It was a man—quite in a small way—whom I've come across once or twice in the course of business. He came to me, he said, for advice: what he really wanted was money. He'd had bad luck, but not quite so bad as he made out. He's made errors, and tried to minimise them. His business, if he could hold on, had fair prospects, but not quite so rosy as he wished me to believe. Just the kind of thing that the world's much too full of. The kind of thing that I turn down whenever it comes up. He was getting some papers from his pocket-book and a photograph fell out. 'My second daughter,' he said, and that started him talking like a sincere, sweet-natured imbecile. He said she was beautiful, forgetting, I suppose, that I had just seen the photograph.

"He said she was very intelligent. 'And she's devoted to me,' he said, 'and believes that I can do pretty well everything.' I believed that absolutely, partly from the sheepish half-proud way in which he said it, though it through doubts on her intelligence. She was a girl of about your age. I did not care two straws about the man, but I wanted to save that girl. So, I told him what to do and lent him the means to do it; the fact that the cheque carried my signature won't do him any harm with his bank by the way."

"That was good."

"I'm not sure. I told him not to talk about it, but he may. If it were generally known, quite a number of wicked people would think that I was easily deceived and would try to deceive me. Thus, my act of compassion would be transformed into an incitement to crime."

"And is that really the only time that you have been moved by compassion?"

"I won't say that. When Mrs. Honor's scandalous husband died, I was sorry for the old lady and provided for her quite liberally. But then she was a distant relative of mine and I knew what would be said about me if I did not. Also, I foresaw that she would occasionally be useful to me, and she has been—it is a great pleasure to her to do anything for me."

"Anything else?"

"It reminds me of another case, because the boy—he's a man now—went to live at Darkwood under Mrs. Honor's care and is there still. I found him at a fair in a village just outside Brussels—can't remember the name—and I rescued him from a brute of a Belgian showman who was treating him very badly."

"But surely that was pure unmixed compassion?"

"I'm afraid not, Miss Muse. I was sorry for the boy, but I acted as I did from another motive. I am abnormal."

"I know."

"You don't know the full extent of it yet. At the time I was much interested in abnormality of every kind and was making a study of it. This boy was abnormal—so far as I know, his abnormality was and is quite unique. The blackguard he was with, made money by exhibiting it."

"What was the abnormality?"

"He had wings."

Dora rose with wonder in her eyes, her hands involuntarily clasped over her bosom.

"Oh!" she said. "Wings, wings! Will you take me to him?"

CHAPTER 6: "NOW WE'RE OFF!"

"I am glad," said George Overman, "that I can gratify your wish. I can promise you that tonight you shall see the man with wings. But, you know, I had no idea this would make such an impression on you."

Dora sank into her chair again, and looked at George Overman almost apologetically.

"Have I been—silly?" she said.

"No, I did not think so."

"Wings! You can't think what they mean to me. They've been so often in my dreams. They're bodily hope and prayer. I've always believed that if I had but wings—real wings, not an engineer's dodge—I could get home."

"I wonder," said George, "if you have any conception how amazingly and spiritually beautiful you are." He paused, and added prosaically: "May I use your telephone?"

"Of course, you may," said Dora. "I'll go into the next room till you've finished, shall I?"

"Please don't. I'm only going to fix things up for tonight, and I want you to hear what I say. Besides, it's a trunk-call, and we can talk while I'm waiting to get through."

After the telephone interlude, as they sat and waited, he added;

"It would really be possible for you to see Eagle before tonight, but—"

"Eagle? Is that his name?"

"I've no idea what his real legal name is. That Belgian blackguard said that he was his son, but that was proved to be a lie. I could get no history of him at all. He was called *Aiglon* for the purposes of the show, and so I called him Eagle. Mary—that's Mrs. Honor—always calls him punctiliously Mr. Eagle. As a matter of fact, the name's not very appropriate. His wings are not in the least like an eagle's wings. They are more like the wings of some gigantic bat."

"I see. You were saying that there was some objection to my seeing him before tonight."

"Oh, yes. You see, it's like this. When I first saw Eagle, his wings were rudimentary and he did not attempt to use them. Since then, they have grown very considerably—for the last year, when fully outstretched, they have measured nearly twelve feet from tip to tip. It was Mrs. Honor—an extraordinary lady—who first persuaded him to try to use them, and now he flies with ease, moreover flying is about the one thing that he seems really to care for. But he is very sensitive—more sensitive than most girls. He cannot bear to be treated like a freak or a human curiosity—his early experiences might partly account for that. In consequence he has become a night bird. He flies secretly and in the darkness.

"Perhaps that's just as well, because he wears no clothes or next to none when flying. He's lean, muscular, and strong, but when he comes back from these long flights by night, he is generally exhausted. He sleeps from eight in the morning till four or five. Then he gets up, but he prefers to breakfast alone in his rooms and does not join the rest of the household till dinnertime. Still, I could fetch him out of his bed. He obeys the unseen whip of benevolence just as he formerly obeyed the cruel whip of a cruel master.

"He's always sullen about it but he obeys. In fact, he's generally rather sullen and does not talk much. He never forgets that he owes everything to me and—perhaps for that reason—he does not like me, though I think he tries. He has real affection and respect for Mary Honor. Well, Miss Muse, what do you say? Shall we insist on his coming down a few hours earlier today?"

"No, a thousand times! It would make him hate me. I'd sooner wait for days, excited though I am."

"Very good." The telephone bell rang. "Ah, there's my call."

George had a special voice for use over the telephone—low and very incisive.

"Mr. Overman speaking. Will you ask Mrs. Honor to be kind enough to come to the telephone? Thanks . . . Hullo, Mary, good-morning. How are you? . . . I'm glad. And Eagle? . . . That's right. . When am I coming to see you? Funny you should ask me that. I rang up to suggest that I should drive down for dinner tonight and bring with me a girl whom I'd like you to know. . . . I'm no good at descriptions. Besides, you'll see for yourself in a few hours what she's like. But I

279

know you'll be fond of her and she has the eyes of an angel. . . .Now, Mary, I knew you'd say that. You're an incurably romantic. But as a matter of fact, I am not—not in the least—and I've even told her so. . . Yes, I think we could. . . .Thanks, very much. Then if it's no trouble to you to put us both up we will stay the night. . . .Yes. . . Certainly. Very kind of you. . . .Don't think so, but she's here and I'll ask her."

He turned to Dora. "Mrs. Honor is asking if you'd like to take your maid down with you. No? I thought not."

He finished his conversation with Mrs. Honor. As he hung up the receiver, Dora said:

"How did you know that I could or would stay the night?"

"I didn't know. But I knew that you would correct me if I were wrong."

"I wasn't sure whether you were wrong or right. I'm not sure even now. I can't make up my mind very, very quickly, as you do."

"Well, we'll settle it this way. It takes about an hour and a half to drive down to Darkwood. I'll be here in the car at three. I hope you'll be ready the to stay the night. I know Mary will love you and take the greatest care of you. But, if not, there is still the telephone and you can modify the programme any way you like. And now I must be off."

"You're very good to me."

"One has to be as good as one can with you looking on."

"I did write—but I must thank you again for the flowers and for the car."

"I hope you'll use it often, *Au revoir*, Miss Muse."

And, again with a very brief shake of the hand, George departed.

Dora felt rushed and bewildered. She felt it was wonderful that she had remembered to say anything about the car or about the flowers. And what was she to do about this visit to Darkwood?

At a superficial glance it was all wrong.

A man whom she had seen but twice in her life—a man moreover who on the first occasion had tracked her down by detectives and the introduced himself—proposed that he should drive her off in his car to stay for the night at the house of an elderly female relative whom she had never met. The inducement was a promise that she would meet a man who had wings.

Now on the film this could only mean abduction. Mrs. Honor and the man with wings would of course, both turn out to be mythical. George Overman would drive her to some lonely spot and on the plea of an accident to the engine pull up before a tavern of dark and sinister aspect. She would be lured within. George would instantly lock the door, turn on her with his arms over his blown-out chest, his mouth in a spasm, and his eyebrows gong like skipping ropes, and say—or, preferably, hiss: "In my power at last!" (End of Part Three. Part Four will follow immediately.)

Dora laughed at her thoughts. It was all right of course. There is nothing so incredibly false as a good American film story; nothing happens in film land as it happens in real life. There would be no abduction. It was she herself who had suggested that she would be taken to see the man with wings. The telephone conversation had been genuine. And what abductor who knew the barest elements of his business would suggest that the victim should take her maid with her. And, above all, there was the fact that Dora was conscious down to the tips of her pretty toes that George reverenced her. It was going to be unusual, and even a little adventurous, but it was not going to be abduction.

And she had to be ready by three. She had the lucky chance to find a taxi and drove to Kate Mason's studio; and, as usual, Kate was quite glad to spend the night at the flat while Dora was away.

Kate had a considerably larger income than Dora, but—except where her work was concerned—Kate had no energy at all. She still slept and fed at the same unclean lodgings she had occupied as a student, and was still the prey of the same dishonest landlady. She simply could not bring herself to face a change and the effort of housekeeping. She said that the only times when she had any comfort were when she was doing the caretaking job for Dora; and Dora said very sternly that it was all her own fault.

Dora got back to the flat just in time for luncheon, and told Jane as much as she thought Jane should know, being aware that if she had told her the whole truth it would have created a quite false impression in Jane's mind.

Jane said it was very good, and she had no doubt she could make Miss Mason comfortable as she had done before, and she hoped Dora would enjoy her visit.

"But," added Jane (of Arc) in her military way, "you mustn't think I'm afraid of burglars. I could manage here quite alone."

"But I'm afraid of burglars," said Dora. "Also, of milkmen."

And Jane (no longer of Arc but simply Jane) blushed and smiled rather winsomely.

After luncheon, Jane—now a somewhat authoritative expert—did the packing under Dora's direction. And that direction was not much more than an appeal that she might have all her very nicest things. The decision as to which was the nicest was mostly made by Jane.

And at five minutes past three Dora, seated in the car beside George Overman, leaned back and said with great contentment:

"Now we're off."

Cautiously and sedately the car glided through London streets. Then on the great road, with fields and trees on either side, it woke up and began to show its strength. It flashed up hills and came quietly down them, speeding up again on the level and roaring an occasional warning in a deep and haughty bass.

Chapter 7: Darkwood

"Have any doctors or other men of science seen your winged man?" asked Dora, as they sped along.

"They have not. Naturally, the thing has not been kept entirely a secret. The servants at Darkwood know of it and servants always talk. Mary has had letters from eminent men, stating they have heard a rumour and asking permission in the cause of science to come and examine the goods. Permission is always refused, firmly and even curtly. Eagle would hate anything of that sort. So, science, which always believes that which it cannot see is not true., thinks the rumours baseless. I suppose if he fell ill a doctor would have to be called in, but he does not fall ill. I've seen him myself of course, many times. Apart from the wings, but connected with them, he has a whole array of muscles on his back and shoulders which are not to be found in a normal man. He is also abnormally light. He weighs only seven stone and looks as if he weighed twelve."

"Tell me a little about his appearance. I don't want to be surprised when I first see him."

"He'll be wearing ordinary evening things, except that he has a short-sleeved cloak instead of a dinner-jacket. Seen from the front, he's a fine-looking boy, very well built, slender, graceful in every movement. His face is classical, but his expression is rather sullen. He's got absurd yellow hair, very frizzy—but Mary Honor likes it, and thinks it a pity he keeps it short. Seen from behind, you might think him slightly hunchbacked. His great wings pack into an extraordinarily small space when they are not in use, but still they make a distinct protuberance. When he is stripped for flight, with nothing on but a pair of rowing shorts, and with his wings fully extended he looks magnificent. Then he gives not the slightest impression of freakishness or deformity; on the contrary he makes one think the rest of mankind deficient."

"I believe it is not easy to be very tactful when one is very excited," said Dora, "but I am goung to try."

"I've great confidence in you."

"You said didn't you, that Mrs. Honor was an extraordinary woman?"

"She is in some ways. She's without sense of wonder or any tendency to speculate. For her, whatever is, is, and there's nothing more to say about it She is impervious to surprise. When her husband died and left her destitute, I—a distant relative whom she had never met—came to see her. I think I may safely say that I read character quickly—it is an essential quality in business. Before I had been with her ten minutes, I knew she was straight, kind, and capable. Before the interview was over I had told her that I should give her Darkwood absolutely and also a annuity on which she could live there in comfort, and that I should ask her to take the entire charge of a boy nearly sixteen who had wings and spoke very little English. She was grateful for the gifts—and still is—but I am sure it has never occurred to her to ask why on earth I should have given them. As for the boy, she said she would do her best, though, as far as she could remember, she had not met one of these winged cases before—those were her exact words."

The car had slowed down, and was now expressing its intention of turning down a narrower road on the right in several deep, authoritative blasts.

When the last of them had died away, Dora said: "If I—or most people had acted like that, it would have turned out badly. But you can do these things. The experiment succeeded."

"I should hardly call it an experiment—I neither experiment nor speculate. I observe and deduct. Mary captured Eagle at once, perhaps because she was no more surprised that he had got wings than that he had got eyes. She never had children of her own and she became a mother to him. She has also been his governess—she's a well-educated woman—and has taught him what he knows. By the way don't speak French to him. He has been speaking English for the last five years, and today you'd hardly know that English was not his native tongue. He always thinks in English now, he tells me.

"Well, his wings grew very rapidly—perhaps the result of good food and a healthy life. Mary said in her commonplace way that it had always seemed to her a pity that a boy who had wings should not make proper use of them. Of course, he would have to learn—even the birds had to learn. He did learn. He got on very slowly at first, and had some nasty falls. But he got keen on it, and today he can go for miles and do practically anything in the air."

The car stopped definitely before iron gates, and an old serving woman with a prehistoric curtsey emerged from a lodge and opened them.

George held up the car for a moment while he asked about the rheumatism, recommended a liniment, and bestowed excessive *largesse*.

Then, as the car climbed a steep and winding avenue, George said:

"I like people to seem pleased to see me here, and I can buy it. It's a country luxury. In town I'm hated, feared, and respected by those I employ, and intend to be. Even here I'm not fool enough to suppose that I'm loved. Love can only be got for nothing or debt. You'll have it all your life, Miss Muse."

From the shade under the trees on the left the deer rose up and went away at a moderate pace, expressing no panic but complete disapproval. And now the car reached the end of the avenue, and Dora saw before her a wide terraced garden with velvet lawns and clipped yews, and above that, halfway up the slope of a hill, a grey stone house was almost white in the sunlight. Behind and above the house, extending beyond it on both sides, was a great plantation of dark conifers with red beeches interspersed.

"How lovely," said Dora. "And now I see why it's called Darkwood. But it's not English in tone. It's Continental. I think it's Spanish."

"Good shot," said George. "A Spaniard built it, and it was on his death that I bought it."

As they neared the pillared entrance, there came out a short and rather fat lady, expensively and very plainly dressed in black, with a face that was at once shrewd and kindly, and with beautiful white hair.

She welcomed Dora bestowed on George the kiss of cousinly affection, and turned back to Dora, talking fluently the pleasant commonplace of a first meeting. Servants came out and carried in the luggage—George had a word with each of them. And then Mrs. Honor turned back to George.

"George, I think you're simply a fool."

"Oh, don't say that, Mary. Why?"

"You told me over the telephone you were not in the least—"

"I know. It's true."

"Then that's why I am—and I've lost no time. You've got your old room, George, and now I'm going to show Miss Muse hers. And don't go far away, George, because we are going to have tea on the terrace directly."

Dora was charmed with Darkwood, and saw she was going to be quite fond of Mary Honor. When one acts on an impulse and all turns out well, that has a special charm that is not obtained by the successful result of discreet planning.

Dora was soon downstairs again, and joined Mary and George on the terrace outside. From the terrace broad steps led down to a lawn. George pointed them out to her.

"That was where Eagle learned to fly. He used to jump off those steps."

"Poor Mr. Eagle!" said Mary. "I'm afraid he often hurt himself. But that's all over now, and I'm sure that he's glad that he took your advice and persevered. He really enjoys flying, and it must be a satisfaction to him to feel that he is doing something which quite a number of people cannot do."

"Quite a number," said George gravely, but with a twinkle in his eye.

"I wish I had wings!" said Dora wistfully.

And then George and Mary both spoke together.

"You have had," said George.

"You will have." Said Mary.

They sat talking for a little while after tea, and then George rose. It was wicked to do business on Sunday, but he had three trunk-calls to get through, and would have to spend the next hour in the telephone room.

So, Dora was left alone with Mary Honor.

"I wish you'd tell me," said Mary, "what you've done with George."

"I—I've only known him a few days. I can't have done very much. But why?"

"I don't think he looks quite so wicked as he used to. Mind, he has been goodness itself to Mr. Eagle and to me, but the newspapers have said very unpleasant things about him. And he certainly did look—well, fierce—as if he'd twist the neck of anything that got in his way. Today he's gentler and more human than I've ever known him to be. Oh, there's no doubt that you influence him. Why today he was engaged to play golf at Northwood with Sainton Mackworth, and the moment he found he could see you instead he cancelled the engagement. He told me that just before you came down. Think of it—throwing over the prime minister. But George never did seem to take these politicians seriously."

"Which were the newspapers that attacked him?"

"Most of them, I'm afraid. It was when he bought the Hotel Cecil, and apparently, they didn't think that everything was as it should have been. The *Morning Light* was the worst. In fact, I asked him why he didn't bring a libel action against them."

"And what did he say?"

"He said that he thought it would suit him better to wipe that paper out; so of course, it doesn't appear any more now."

"How did George do it?"

"He said it was a series of coincidences. One after the other, all the best men left them. Then the advertising dropped to nothing. George said that advertisers are very sensitive and suspicious. Now I want to hear a great deal about you, Miss Muse."

They strolled through the garden till it was time to go up to dress for dinner.

And when Dora was dressed for dinner, she looked lovely, but a shade more sophisticated than usual. Mrs. Honor's capable elderly maid had seen to that. Dora herself was excited almost to torment at the thought of meeting the man with wings.

Chapter 8: Dora at Dinner

When Dora came into the drawing-room George and Mary Honor were seated on the couch. The man with wings stood in shadow at a little distance. Dora dared but one swift look at him, and recognised that George's description of him was correct as far as it went; but was insufficient. His beauty was virile, and the frizzy golden hair did not seem to her at all absurd. His expression might have been described as sullen, but she saw in it rather a gentle submission. When Mrs. Honor presented him to her, Dora held out her hand and he took it. His hand was hot and dry like the hand of a man in a fever. He said something correct to her in a mechanical way, and Dora knew that he was merely repeating what Mrs. Honor had taught him.

And then dinner was announced and they passed into the dining-room. It was a large room, with a semi-circular recess halfway down on one side of it. The recess was brightly lit, and here a round table was laid for dinner; the rest of the room was dim and shadowy. George sat on the right of Mrs. Honor, Dora opposite to her, and Eagle on her left. In the middle of the table was a tall vase of salmon-coloured carnations, and Mrs. Honor had them removed at once.

"I wanted to see Miss Muse," she said explanatorily, and the carnations were replaced by a low bowl of white roses.

"You like white roses very much," said Eagle to Dora. It was said not as a question but as a statement of fact.

Dora had just time to reply when George, who was continuing with Mrs. Honor a discussion that had started in the drawing-room, turned to Dora.

"Miss Muse, we want your opinion. We were speaking of my trial, and Mary says that she hopes I shall not cause a social revolution, because she is very well satisfied with things as they are. I tell her that as a business man I should hate social revolution—security of property, stability, and confidence, are the backbone of business. But that as a moralist I see hardly anything which could not be altered for the better. What do you think?"

"What I'd really love is anarchy."

"Do you mean that?" said Mrs. Honor. "Lamp-posts and guillotines?"

"Oh, no," said Dora. "Not that kind. But all government is a confession of weakness by the governed. It means that they are not good enough to be trusted. If we need penalties to enforce law and order, that's because we do wrong and use violence, I want the anarchy that would become possible if so many people had good feelings that those who wanted to do a wrong would not do it, for fear of the social disgrace and ruin."

"You want the millennium," said George. "Your kind of anarchy could never be possible."

"But it already happens—in a very limited way. It happens at any sort of social function. I wonder how many dinner-parties are going on in London at this moment."

"Well, my restaurants are responsible for a good many. We will call it thousands."

"Very well. At these dinner-parties strangers meet. They act and talk as if they were well-disposed towards one another. Nobody tries to grab all the food or wine for himself. Women wear costly diamonds and pearls, and nobody tries to steal them. Nobody tries to annex the table silver."

"I'm not so sure," said George. "The souvenir-hunters have had a good many of my forks and spoons."

"Yes, yes, but that is an offence against you, who are not of their party. Within the limits of their own party—temporarily no doubt and in a very small society—they do behave well and no compulsion by any government has anything to do with it."

"But, Miss Muse," said Mrs. Honor, "at the fashionable wedding reception is it not found necessary to have detectives to look after the wedding presents? The men are disguised of course."

"I know," said George. "Disguised to look just like detectives. I've seen them."

"That is true," said Dora, "but I should think in most cases the detectives have nothing to do, and where they do have anything to do it is because a thief—not invited—not one of the party—has managed to slip in. But I am generalising, of course—I do not say there are no exceptions."

"Then," said George, smiling, "your idea of heaven is a series of dinner-parties and wedding receptions, with etiquette superseding the Ten Commandments."

"I don't go to wedding receptions if I can help it." She looked at Mrs. Honor. "But if all dinner-parties were as charming as this little one I should want them to go on for quite a long time."

"Ah, there I'm entirely with you," said George with conviction.

"How nice of you both," said Mrs. Honor. "But do go on, Miss Muse."

"I think I was going to say that I won't be frightened by a word. We jeer about etiquette, but it's based on good feeling and useless without it. And there is the same good feeling in the social gatherings of the poor as in those of the rich—indeed, there is more. I know I can't have my anarchy, but truly there are some of the materials for it sometimes."

"I wonder why we can't have it," said Mrs. Honor. "I should like your kind of anarchy. It seems a pity."

"Class hatred is one reason," said George.

"And the rich are responsible for it," Dora said earnestly. "Years ago, the rich tried to crush trade unions, paid wages on which a man could not subsist properly, and ground the face of the poor, and treated them like dogs. Even today some of them are trying to do it. You're not one of them, Mr. Overman. The case showed that you always treated your people generously."

"Yes," said George. "I tried the other way, but I found this paid me better. If you keep the class placated you have more freedom in

288

dealing with the particular individual in that class who happens to concern you. Hence, the Overman Homes for Those Past Work, and various other things."

"Are you sure they do any good? The working man today looks on the kindness of the capitalist as sharp practice, bribery, or funk."

"True enough," said George, "but I'm very careful."

"I'm not pleading for one class or another. I'm pleading for man. A sure fact is that some of the worst treatment the poor have received has come from those who, once poor, are now rich themselves. Dives and Lazarus are the same man after all."

This was not the first time, nor was it the last, that Dora that evening quoted from her *Book of Experiences.*

"If the classes were suddenly transposed, I believe each would act very mush as the other is acting now. It's rather sad. Go right back to the Great War. One of the very few good things that came out of it was that rich and poor got really to know one another and to respect one another. And then we slipped back again into the old bad way. I'd like to go to the workers and say: 'you were wronged, and perhaps in some ways you still are. It's natural for you to want to get your own back. But if that's all you want, you'll be making one mistake worse by making another. No final good ever came of vindictiveness.'"

"If you want to make a labour leader laugh heartily," said George, "talk to him just like that. There is vindictiveness, of course, in labour writings and in park oratory. But you'd be told that labour was working for better economic conditions and that the capitalist system is economically unsound. Labour's out on economic stunt, and when it finds that it knows less of economics than it thought we may get a bloody revolution of one person against ten. In that case it's bad for the one. We're a law-abiding nation. You don't quite know the facts, Miss Muse., but you've got a beautiful mind."

"I know," said Dora disconsolately, helping herself to caramel pudding. "I feel all the time that I don't know enough—that somebody who knows a little more is sitting on my head and sniggering. But I think my general idea is right. After all, we're all human."

"We have that disadvantage," said George grimly. "Eagle, you gay young chatterbox, what are you thinking about it?"

Eagle flushed slightly. "I'm sorry, Mr. Overman," he said. "I was too much interested to wish to interrupt."

All through the dinner he had gazed at Dora as one spellbound. Both George and Mrs. Honor had noticed this, and Dora had not noticed it at all.

"Why do we worry so much?" said Dora. "This is not the only world."

"Ah!" said Eagle, suddenly, involuntarily, as with instant agreement.

Dora turned to him and looked in to his fine grey eyes for the first time, and began to talk about white roses. He chatted with her, no longer sullen boyishly, freely, animatedly.

And George and Mrs. Honor talked about the local rates, which were wide open to criticism.

Then the cigarettes came round. They were Russian cigarettes, and everybody smoked them except George, who wielded a capitalistic Havana. George drank no wine after he, or anybody else in the room, had begun to smoke, and at Mrs. Honor's suggestion the two men followed the women back into the drawing-room.

In the drawing-room Mrs. Honor opened a window wide. The garden was bathed in bright moonlight. From a copse nearby, full and rich, came the song of the nightingale.

"It's Paradise," said Dora. "I must go out there. Mr. Eagle, will you take me?"

"I'd love it."

"I must rush up and get a wrap of some sort. Please don't ring, Mrs. Honor. I'd like to get it myself."

The wrap was flimsy, but it was not a cold night. When Dora came back into the drawing-room she was instantly conscious that Mrs. Honor, and George, and Eagle had been talking about her.

The window opened to the ground Eagle followed her through, out on to the terrace.

Chapter 9: The Man with Wings

The air was still and cool; the nightingale no longer sang.

"I liked listening to you tonight," said Eagle. "You said some things that have been in my own mind, but away at the back where I couldn't get at them."

"I think I talked too much," said Dora, "but you all led me on. This place is lovely tonight, isn't it? Silvery grey and velvet black, and peace and quiet. And tomorrow in every city in the world the silly cutthroat game of man against man will begin again. If only one could do anything!"

"Maybe the world's only half-grown and will come all right when it's older. And after all, you said that it was not the only world, and I think you know more than you said. You know that this is not your own world—nor is it mine."

Dora became a little breathless. "How do you mean?" she said in a low voice.

"I don't think I can be wrong about it. There are times when you long so much to get back, and seem to hear so clearly the call homeward, that you become perplexed and very sad. Tears come into your eyes."

"Yes, that's true. I think it has been happening more often lately. It's recorded in a book I keep—a sort of journal—but nobody has ever read a line of it. I've never spoken of it to anybody either. How could you know it?"

"I knew it as soon as I saw your eyes. For I have seen eyes just like yours before, but never in this world."

"What are you saying? Never in this world? Where then? Tell me."

"It has happened sometimes when I have been flying at night. Suddenly I am in that other world for a little while. At the time I don't know how it happens. I know what I experience. But I have to return, and when I touch earth all memory of it goes. But when I saw you one flash of memory came back. I knew that your eyes were just like the eyes I have seen over there."

He spoke simply, earnestly, and without excitement.

"Well," he went on, "I felt that I could tell you about it. I've told nobody else. I don't want to be regard as a lunatic as well as a freak. But you belong to that other world as I do. We're exiles together. We must help one another."

"Yes," said Dora. "I want to hear everything. I want to ask you a thousand questions. I am too much amazed to know where to begin. And now we must go into the house again, and tomorrow I leave."

"Perhaps you will not leave tomorrow—or will return very soon. I know Mrs. Honor will try to persuade you. She wants to see much more of you. You've won her heart. But even if you do not return, remember I can come to you any night. It cannot end like this. I shall never let you go. I must always be at your command. I wish that even tonight there were something I could do for you."

"Do you? There is. I long to see you fly."

Eagle smiled. "You ask a little thing. I've done as much for Mr. Overman, whenever he has required it, and for Mrs. Honor many times. By now it is a commonplace performance to both of them. Of course, you shall see it. How shall we arrange it? Come out on the balcony of your room at eleven. I will be waiting on the terrace below. When you wave a white scarf or handkerchief, I will go up."

She bowed her head in acquiescence and almost whispered conventional thanks. She was terribly excited.

But she re-entered the drawing-room as a calm normal girl, and Mrs. Honor immediately annexed her. George Overman approached Eagle with a sort of sub-acid geniality. Once or twice, Dora glanced at them. Eagle spoke deferentially, briefly, constrainedly. There was no doubt now about the sullenness of his expression. Dora recognised that George had told her the simple truth—Eagle did not like him, but never forgot how much he owed to him.

"If I might ask," said Mrs. Honor, "have you many engagements in London this week?"

"I have none," said Dora. "I know very few people in London."

"Then perhaps you could do me a very great kindness. Don't go tomorrow. Stay for a week at least. George says that if you do, he will come down again next weekend. You've not really seen Darkwood yet. I'm alone most of the day and should love to have you with me. It would be so good for Mr. Eagle too, to have a young companion."

"I should love to come," said Dora. "But the kindness is all yours. This place seems very beautiful to one who has been for months in London. Are you sure you really want me? You've known me such a short time—you might find me very disappointing."

"I'm absolutely sure I want you—and equally sure that the longer I know you the fonder of you I shall become. That's settled then. I'm so glad."

"But I've only brought things for one night with me. And I must arrange for somebody to take charge of my maid and my flat. If you don't mind, I'll go back with Mr. Overman in the morning and return in the evening."

"As you please—return as soon as you can, and don't bring any very elaborate dresses, for we shall probably be alone all the time."

"I've not got anything very elaborate, and I think I shall like it best if we're alone."

"George," Mrs. Honor called, "come and congratulate me. You too Mr. Eagle. I've secured Miss Muse for a whole week and perhaps longer."

"You're a fortunate woman, Mary. And will Miss Muse let me come down again for the next weekend?"

"It would be delightful," said Dora. "But why ask my permission?"

"Perhaps for the delight of getting it."

Shortly after ten Mrs. Honor said that Miss Muse must be tired, and that she was going to carry her off to bed. George and Mr. Eagle must do as they pleased.

"I shan't sit up long," said George.

Eagle and Dora said a formal goodnight to one another in words, while their eyes said *au revoir*.

And now Dora's excitement became almost torment. She could get rid of the maid—that would be easy enough—but suppose Mrs. Honor wished to sit and talk in her room for an hour. Dora could plead weariness after her journey, but she felt that it would be ungracious to her new friend and hostess. Then it was possible that Mr. Overman might detain Eagle, or might himself wish to watch the flight that night. She might miss it after all—after all, when it seemed so near.

And in a flash, she was angry with herself. If it could not happen tonight, she had only to wait, it was absurd for her to have the thoughts of an impatient child. Would anybody else make such a fuss about a man with wings? Mrs. Honor had taken him for granted. Mr. Overman had been interested about it, but she felt sure that he had been perfectly dispassionate. Really, a person of her age ought to have some sense of proportion.

But it was in vain that she argued thus; for wings meant far more to her than in others, and instinct is stronger than reason. Hers was no common eagerness to see a show; it was more like the passion of the devout for invitation.

And, since it was to happen so, tonight all went well. Mrs. Honor remained only for a few minutes in Dora's room, and then kissed her and said goodnight. Dora undressed quickly, tied back her hair, put on the rose-silk dressing-gown, and then switched off the lights. She drew back the curtains from the window on to the balcony—the window itself was already opened wide.

Then she stepped back and sat down. There must be still some minutes to wait. She would take her time from the distant clock in the church tower; she had heard it already that night.

Suddenly she sprang up. What was she doing? She was to wave a white scarf. She must get it at once. She hunted eagerly for it in the dim room, and—since tonight it was to happen so—she found it easily at once.

Yes, that was the sound of a footstep on the terrace outside. It was not immediately under her window; it sounded rather distant and to the right. And there was no sound of talking—George Overman was not there then Eagle was alone—alone and waiting for her.

Would the church clock never strike? Could something have happened to it? Would it be better to switch the light on for a moment and glance at her watch? Would it—

"*Boom!*" said the church clock, not even troubling to introduce an acrimonious tone into it in consequence of her doubts. "*Boom!*" with the boredom of a timepiece to whom time is merely monotony but dust in the works an event. "*Boom!*"

But already breathless Dora was out on the balcony, straining her eyes. Yes, there he was, standing on the middle of the top step of the broad flight that led down to the lawn below. She could just distinguish that he was facing her and that he wore a long black cloak.

The white scarf fluttered and leaped out—again and again.

A bare white arm came from the black cloak in an answering signal—curiously zigzag, it seemed to Dora.

Then he turned his back on her, detached his loose shoes with two swift movements of his feet, let the cloak drop in an inky pool about them, and spread his wings out to their full extent.

Dora had a momentarily glimpse of him thus. It was like the dream of some old Greek Sculptor, filled with strength and grace. The slender muscular body was ivory; the wings in the moonlight were ivory and silver with touched of dusky bronze.

He crouched low for an instant, and then sprang high into the air, the wings making a mist before Dora's eyes with the swiftness of their movements. But these movements grew slower and slower, and soon there was no more than a regular easy beat as in a wide spiral the ivory figure climbed the skies. She watched him till he was out of sight.

And all her heart went with him up into the skies. All her desires went with him, back to the other world which she had lost. She struck the stone balustrade of the balcony in impotent agony.

She went back to her room, dropped her dressing-gown, and groped her way to her bed. And there she lay, with her face to the pillow, trying to choke the sound of her furious sobbing.

Chapter 10: Dora Cannot Tell Kate

As George Overman and Dora drove back to town together, he took the opportunity to assure her once more that he was not in the least in love with her, and this annoyed Dora.

"Mr. Overman," said Dora, "I know you're not in love with me. If I thought you were I should not be with you now, and I should never see you again. But don't keep on repeating that. It looks as if you thought I might be under some delusion about it—and that's insufferable."

"Sorry," said George, "but I don't like unexplained things, and I was trying to explain my feelings towards you by a process of elimination. I began by eliminating human passion. To proceed, I should think your experience of life is almost negligible, and though you have a nice fresh little mind, there is nothing very exceptional about it. It must be your soul, mirrored in your wonderful eyes, that I adore. It's that which conquers—that which uplifts."

"You talk in an exaggerated way," said Dora. "You saw me most of yesterday. I am with you again this morning. Tell me what I have done for you in that time. You show me great kindness—and would show me far more if I would allow it—but what have I been able to do for you? Whatever it is. I am unconscious of it."

"I can tell you that. I told you that I should never love and should never marry. I thought I was too hard for love's delusions. You have changed all that. I know now that life without sentiment is a picture without light, and that there are delusions far more to be valued than the cold scrap-iron that we call truth. Yes, I know now that I shall love—and that, if my love be returned, I shall marry. '*He rideth the fastest who rideth alone.*' Not a doubt of it—but whither? He rides to hell, *via* considerable success. He soareth the highest who soareth with love. The unspoken sermon of your eyes has taught me."

"You mean that?" said Dora, and felt that it was feeble. She was somewhat taken aback. She had not expected that man to speak in that way.

"I mean it."

"Whom will you love?"

"I don't know. It won't be one of the greedy harpies who have hitherto attracted the animal side of me. Last Sunday at Brighton—"

"I think I don't want to know what happened last Sunday at Brighton, do I?"

"Of course not. But that was before I'd met you, remember."

They went a little while in silence. Then a shameless fat bird, flying low, lolloped across the road at a little distance, and screamed a hoarse derisive cuckoo. Dora woke up, and began to speak animatedly of the sweetness of Mrs. Honor and the beauties of Darkwood.

"By the way," said George. "What did you think of the flight?"

"Very, very wonderful. More than that. Oh, but how did you know?"

"It was quite clear that he was spellbound. You didn't even have to be very tactful, as you threatened. You and he are for one another. There's a curious thing about that flight."

"What is it?"

"Well, I know nothing of mathematics or physics. Occasionally I need them in my business, and then I buy what's wanted. It's very cheap. One does not make money by being an expert but by employing experts. But Mrs. Honor became proficient in these things in her younger days at Girton. She taught Eagle. For the last three years he has been mad keen on the subject of flight from the scientific point of view, and had been studying hard. He gets every new work of importance on the theory of flight. Mind, he learned to fly as a child learns to walk—by practice, without any theory about it. His investigations came later. Well, he's come to the conclusion that he actually does things in the air which can't be explained by our present knowledge."

"So does the albatross," said Dora.

"Does it? I didn't know. And he not only achieves the demonstrably impossible, but the achievement is conditioned in an inexplicable way. He tried to tell me about it one day but I couldn't make much of it. You ask him."

Dora said she would, and that it was very interesting.

A few minutes later Dora reached her flat, and received a beaming welcome from Jane, at the door.

"I suppose Miss mason has gone," said Dora.

Jane dropped her voice.

"Still in the sitting-room, miss, and says she is never going. But she may not mean it," she added encouragingly.

Dora, knowing Kate Mason's little ways, smiled. "I'll go and talk to her," she said.

The atmosphere of the sitting-room was blue with smoke. Kate lay on her back on the couch, reading the newspaper that insured Dora's limbs and life.

"Morning," said Kate. "Would you like my beastly lodgings, or would you rather doss on the floor of the studio. Make your choice. I've given up art and taken to comfort; so I'm going to stay here with Jane. I asked her to tell you so."

"She did. That's all right. That's what I want you to do."

Kate sat up suddenly. "You knew I was rotting, didn't you? Of course, this is heaven on earth after those God-forsaken rooms of mine, but still—"

"Of course, I knew you were rotting, but I'm not. They want me to go back to Darkwood till next Monday. If you'll care-take till then, I'll be thankful."

"You bet I will. And that rather relieves my conscience."

"I doubt if you ever had one. But what do you mean?"

"Well, Jane, your priceless treasure, has got a good head on her."

"Yes, she's intelligent about her work and learns a new thing quickly, but—"

"Oh, who cares about the inside of the head! What I mean is that she's jolly paintable. So, I fixed up with her to sit for me. And afterwards I had a twinge of remorse, because she'll come to me in the mornings and you might be wanting her for other things."

"You needn't have worried," said Dora. "You'd have been the only person inconvenienced. Kate, I wish you weren't such an imbecile; you make me laugh when I'm doing my best to be angry with you. Well, you can do Jane's head while I'm away."

"Not a doubt of it. I believe she'd be good for the figure too. I'll—"

"No, you won't," said Dora with sudden seriousness. "I won't have it."

Kate looked aggrieved. "Well, I like that from you, Dora. You've sat to me for the figure yourself—many a time."

"You understand, and I do too. Jane doesn't. Oh, can't you see?"

"I see things as form and colour."

"I know you do. But what's the use of talking to Jane like that?"

"What a world!" said Kate with disgust. "Well, I suppose I ought to be getting on to the studio."

"Kate, chuck it for this morning. Do stay and have lunch with me. Just for once."

Kate meditated and yielded.

"Oh, all right. I mean, many thanks and all that sort of thing. After all I've just read three-quarters of a column of art-criticism, and that's enough to make you forswear painting for the rest of your natural."

"What's the matter with it?"

"Lies, ignorance, and pontifical shibboleths. He's raving about Peveril James's show—more especially the little 'Dryad'—speaks of the 'typically Jacobean treatment of the flesh.' Jacobean, by the way, is the very best pontifical jargon. I was at the show and looked at that

'Dryad' from the other end of the room. At that distance I can see the colour but lose the outlines. I said to myself: 'What the deuce is Peveril James doing with a still-life of cold boiled salmon against Cos lettuce?' Then I went closer and saw that it was a woman of sorts among ferns. She must have had a goitre on the back of her neck the size of an orange, but still it was a woman. And her flesh was simply cold boiled salmon—and Canadian at that."

"I thought you'd a great opinion of Peveril James."

"Oh, he's all right—masterly, in fact, when his cranky side doesn't get the better of him. And that's just the side these fools encourage. The Lord knows I don't want a literal rendering, but what's the sense in being deliberately and damnably wrong?" .

Dora showed a decent interest, but she was not deeply concerned with art-criticism at the moment. Her mind was filled with wings. She believed she wanted to tell Jane about Eagle. Yet every time the opportunity to start the subject arose, Dora let the opportunity go past.

The same reticence hung over her at luncheon. She did not think that she was secretive—she had been in the habit of telling Kate most things. But not one word about Eagle could she say. Did she fear Kate's question? No, she did not believe that was the reason. She had a dim idea that she did not know enough—that there was more to come—that it would be like telling a story of which she did not know the end. She would put the whole thing out of her mind.

"Kate," she said, "be a good woman and imitate your Mrs. Atkinson for me."

Mrs. Atkinson was Kate's abominable landlady. Kate was an excellent mimic. She did some quick touches to her hair, made her lips thinner, twisted her mouth to one side, changed the expression of her eyes, and looked ten years older. Her voice became acidulated; her manner of speech suggested imperfectly-fitting teeth.

"So, I said to the girl: 'Another time,' I said 'if a haddock or anything slips off on to the stairs while you're carrying it up don't just put it back on the dish. You blow the dust and fluff off, or give it a wipe on your apron before you take it in.' Maybe I'm particular but cleanliness is what I was brought up as a child, and to this day there's scarce a morning passes that I don't wash down to the waist line. And that's what reminded me, Miss Mason, that there was a new gas-mantle not charged in your last week's. Was charged, was it? Yes, but that was a different one on the other gas. No wear in them. Gone in a minute like pearls before swine, and sometimes can be commonly honest. An aunt of mine—in Kensal Green now—used to—"

Kate Mason dropped her impersonation of Mrs. Atkinson suddenly and became Kate Mason again.

"I'd like," she said viciously, "to make that art-critic take rooms at Mrs. Atkinson's, and take them for life. I could come here."

"Of course," said Dora lightly. "Now do some more Mrs. Atkinson."

Chapter 11: Goodnight

Dora returned to Darkwood in the car that George had lent her. The car and its driver were to remain at Darkwood during her visit' George had pointed out that Mrs. Honor had no car of her own and might like to use it sometimes.

Half-an-hour before dinner Dora was dressed and came down into the drawing-room. It did not surprise her to find that Eagle also had dressed early and was there waiting for her.

Soon they were speaking together of that world of theirs.

"Yes," Eagle said, "when I went up last night, almost immediately I was there. I remained there longer than ever before. When I became conscious of this earth again, I was hovering over the wood at the back of the house and the sun was warm on my wings. It must have been nearly six, and I seldom return so late on these light mornings. I flew off to the top of the hill—I've got a sort of shanty there where I can dress before coming back to the house. It's a desolate spot at most times, and this morning there was not a soul about."

"Can you tell me nothing—nothing at all about this other world?"

"Always as I touch the earth the memory of it goes. But all today I've had a feeling as if last night I'd heard some great news."

"Where is it—this new world?"

"Sometimes I fly in one direction, and sometimes in another, and sometimes for many miles and sometimes a very little way. It does not seem to matter. Suddenly I am there. I don't know. I think really that it's everywhere—not very far from any one of us. Only, for almost all, the way to it is hidden. I believe that one day you will find it."

"But how? I have no wings."

"Yet I must believe it, since you have the eyes of those who are there. Every hour I grow more confident. I no longer try to explain. There was a time when I worried. I couldn't make the accepted theories of flight fit in with my own flight."

"Mr. Overman spoke of it. Tell me."

"To start with, it ought not to have been possible for my wings and muscular apparatus to raise my body; yet they did it for many hours with no more effort than I could command, and now every time my flight seems more effortless. And also, if my wings were capable of that, then weight, other than myself, should not retard and pull me down as it does. I assure you that even one extra ounce of clothing is very appreciable. I know that here on earth I am submitted to the same natural laws as everybody else. But in the air, there is a new command—there is a force which draws me upward, and counters the force of gravity which draws me down.

"Apparently, it is unknown and acts selectively. It has selected me and will help me, but it will do nothing for anybody else. The mechanical aviator, climbing three times higher than I ever go, with his cartloads of metal and material feels nothing of that force. It will help me, but it will do nothing for any dead matter I carry with me—for that I must fight with all my strength. Well, what of it? There is evidence of my abnormality on my back, and never yet did an abnormality go single. Where there's one there's two and sometimes more. I don't begin to understand but I do know; and I take what's given me."

The placid tone of Mrs. Honor was heard without, speaking to a servant.

"Quickly," said Dora. "I want to see you fly tonight. Can I?"

Eagle smiled. "Mrs. Honor goes to bed early. Be on your balcony at eleven again; and this time if you will let me, I will come and say goodnight to you."

"Do!" said Dora fervently.

"And," he added "I want to try something. May I? You won't be frightened? I won't hurt you."

"Anything you will," said Dora, with perfect confidence in him. She could not have told you why she felt that confidence—could not have justified it—but there was no doubt about it.

She did not in the least know what was going to happen, but she was no longer excited. That confidence was the root of her placidity. She had become passive. She was content to be led, not asking how or whither. Already before the sun is fully up the gold touches the clouds; the first rays of a great and wonderful happiness had already fallen upon her.

Mrs. Honor was made to talk quite a good deal at dinner that night, she spoke from a full mind. Dora recognised that the old lady's simplicity and *naivete* were misleading; they were in reality accompanied by wide knowledge and good abilities. She seemed, as George had said, to be without wonder and incapable of surprise. She recognised marvels, but the word "marvellous" was not in her dictionary. To her nothing that happened could be a miracle, but was merely one of the things that happened. It might possibly by inexplicable, but that merely meant that in our present state of knowledge the forthcoming explanation had not yet arrived.

Eagle talked too and with far greater freedom than when George Overman was present. It chanced that they fell into a discussion of reality—old as the hills, of course, but new to Dora.

How do we know anything is real? On the evidence of our senses transmitted to the brain. Can we trust them? Generally speaking we can, so far as we are concerned here and now. Beyond that we have no reason to trust them at all.

With different senses and brain, we should come to different conclusions. Would these be correct, or are the conclusions to which we come by our present apparatus correct? Nobody can say. There may be beings with more and higher senses than ours and with minds beside which the human brain is a poor limited toy. The whole universe as we know it may be no more than a puff of smoke—an illusion. Time itself may be an illusion.

And then Mrs. Honor, who made the descent from speculation to firm earth with ease and rapidity, asked Dora if she would take her to London in the car one day to do some shopping.

"I'd love it," said Dora. "Tomorrow?"

"Tomorrow's Tuesday. No, my dear, I couldn't manage it tomorrow. I always write my letters and do my accounts on Tuesday. Only the strictest allegiance to method saves me from being quite unmethodical. But Wednesday has always been a shopping day with me. I've bought a lot of things on Wednesdays. Would that day suit you?"

"Any day would suit me," said Dora. "And I'll put on my noblest rags, and take you to lunch at one of Mr. Overman's best restaurants."

"What shall we have for lunch?"

"*Pommes soufflées*," said Dora without hesitation.

"And. . .and one or two other things?" suggested Mrs. Honor meekly.

Dora laughed. "Heaps of other things. I said that because it happened to be the first name to come into my mind."

Then they went out on to the terrace for their coffee, and there they remained talking animatedly and not at all seriously until Mrs. Honor thought it was time to go to bed.

Alone in her room Dora partly undressed, put on her dressing-gown, and then lay back in an easy chair, and let her thoughts go free.

Was it possible? Was this world that at times seemed to her a prison-house, keeping her from her home, itself nothing but an illusion? And was that other world the world that seemed to be calling her back, the one reality?

Suddenly she was roused from her reverie. Through her open window she heard the church clock striking the hour of eleven, and instantly she stepped on to the balcony. She looked down, but Eagle was not on the terrace. Then she looked upward and saw the winged figure of silver and ivory gliding gently down towards her. In a moment he alighted and stood by her side on the balcony.

"May I lift you in my arms?" he said. "I want to fly with you for a little way—for a minute."

"Yes," she said. "But I'm heavy—terribly heavy. It's not possible."

"If not, then I shall be borne quite slowly and gradually to the ground. You shan't be hurt."

He picked her up with the utmost care, and stepped lightly on to the flat top of the low parapet, holding her close to him as one might hold a little child. She heard the roar of his wings above her as he crouched and sprang.

For some seconds it seemed to her that they were sinking slowly. And then the wings prevailed. Upward they went. Dora saw dark treetops flicker past her and a bright star dancing in the sky. The wings beat regularly and more slowly now.

Dora closed her eyes. "Oh, if only I could die like this—just like this!" she said to herself.

Then she no longer heard the wings, and opened her eyes again. They had circled round and were gliding down toward the house again. He came gently down on to the balcony, and put her on her feet again.

"It's no good," she said in a piteous whisper. "I can't talk about it tonight. Tomorrow."

He bent over her.

"Goodnight, my dear, my beloved!" he said. Her eyes closed again, her head fell backwards, their lips met—again and again.

Then once more he sprang on to the parapet and up into the air.

A little later Dora lay in her bed in the dark room. She was not in the least cold, and yet at intervals she shook and shivered. She was trying to be very firm with herself.

"Dora Muse," she said in a low accusing voice, "what was it you said to Jane about the milkman? Face it. What did you say about the milkman?"

She recalled what she said. And then up in her heart flamed her triumphant defence.

"But this was not the same. This filled me with awe. This—this was almost sacred."

CHAPTER 12: JANE IN THE CONFESSIONAL

On Tuesday morning Mrs. Honor went into the library to do her accounts with the meek reluctance of a lamb led to the slaughter. Being a real mathematician, childish arithmetic bored her horribly. As a rule, if she added up the same column of figures three times she got three different results, and it was by no means certain that anyone of the three would be correct.

But this morning as she laboured it chanced that Dora in the garden strolled past the library windows. Instantly Mrs. Honor ran out and requisitioned her. Dora had not Mrs. Honor's familiarity with $\sqrt{-1}$, but the addition of pounds, shillings and pence had no terrors for her. By twelve the accounts were finished, the tradesmen's books were checked, and the baker was found guilty of an error of fourpence to his own disadvantage.

"And now," said Dora firmly. "I must leave you to write your letters."

"Letters don't run away," said Mrs. Honor. "Next week you won't be here. I'm coming out."

"You won't be happy if you do," said Dora.

But Mrs. Honor came out on the plea that there was always the afternoon for letter writing. And at five that afternoon Eagle came down, unusually and unexpectedly and took Dora out with him through the wood and up to the top of the hill. So, the letters were really written.

Dora found herself with so much to say to Eagle that she hardly knew where to begin.

"You must be very strong to have carried me in your arms like that."

"I don't know," said Eagle. "It seemed to me that the same force that draws me upwards drew you also. It was only the weight of clothes

303

that seemed to be pulling against me. Still, I could not have taken you very far like that. I must think of a better way."

"Where did you go when you left me?"

"I was flying for hours. Between two and three I was over London, where there are always lighted windows. I followed the river eastward, and then came down and rested for a few moments on the dome of St. Paul's. It made me dirty, but it was rather impressive."

"Did nobody see you?"

"I think not. People in towns seldom look upward. Besides, at that height the figure of a man looks very small. If I had been seen it would not have mattered much."

"And afterwards? Did you find that other world of ours?"

"No. Many nights I never get there. I used to long to be there, just as you do. But now I'm afraid."

"I don't understand. Why?"

"Lest I remain there—and lose you."

"Yet you might be happy. In the other world you might have no recollection of me at all. It is I who should be unhappy, left here, alone and remembering, until I could come to you."

They stood now on the flat top of the hill, looking down into the valley on the other side, on red tiled roofs and a white road along which heavy sheep pattered slowly. The evening light was soft and mysterious.

"I've found you, my beloved," he said. "I can never leave you."

That night for the first time for many months, Eagle remained on earth.

Next morning soon after breakfast Mrs. Honor set out for her shopping expedition in London. Dora accompanied her as far as her flat, and there got out. It was arranged that Mrs. Honor would investigate Bond Street alone, and that Dora would rejoin her at the Ritz at one.

As soon as Dora entered her flat it was apparent to her that Jane had something on her mind. Jane did not look penitential, but she did look solemn. Kate Mason had already gone to her studio.

"I'm glad you've come, miss," said Jane. "In a sense," she added. "Everything has to be known sooner or later. It's better to have a little courage and get it over."

"Come into the sitting-room," said Dora firmly, "and tell me what the trouble is."

Dora sat down with her hat on and looked searingly at Jane.

"I think you ought to know," said Jane, "that I was out with him on Monday in the afternoon and again yesterday in the evening."

"Oh, Jane! What was the good of my ordering milk from a different shop? You told me you were going to give up that milkman altogether."

"So, I have, miss. Whatever I could have seen in him with his nasty gaiters and common ways I can't think. I wasn't speaking of him."

"Then who was it?"

"It was the Master," said Jane reverentially.

"I still don't understand. What master?"

"The first time he came here you asked me, and I said you'd only to look at him to see he was the Master."

"Good Heavens, Jan! You don't mean to tell me that you're speaking of Mr. George Overman."

"Yes," said Jane, "I'm speaking of George. It was only last night—after I'd become engaged to him—that I began to call him George."

"You're going to marry him?"

"It had to be. There was never any way out of it, not that I wanted one. He gets what he wants."

"Jane, this sounds like madness, but I suppose you know what you are saying. And don't stand there, looking as if you'd broken a teacup. Sit down and tell me all about it."

Jane sat down, encouraged by Dora's smile, yet not unmindful of the first law of the self-conscious—that the moment of chair-seat actually occupied varies inversely as the respect felt. At first Jane only occupied the extreme edge.

"It was like this, miss. Monday, as soon as you'd gone, Miss Mason said I could go out, being back in time to do the dinner. She's a kind lady, and it's a pleasure to wait on her—once you get used to the language. And as I was going out up came George in a motorcar. He took off his hat and said: 'Good afternoon, Jane. I was just coming to see you. Where are you off to?' I gave a gulp twice before I could say that I was going to the pictures. 'So, am I,' he said, 'and I'd like to take you with me. Get into the car, won't you?' So, I got in for the sake of the ride, though it was no distance to go. We'd the best seats and me with a box of chocolates on my lap—more like a dream than anything else. And all the time he was talking."

"What did he talk about?"

"He talked about you, miss, a good deal. He said that until he met you, he had done nothing but run after things not worth having. He

305

had despised most people, and hated quite a few, and never loved anybody. But you had shown him what was worthwhile and what wasn't, and made him want things that are not to be bought worth money, such as real love. And he said that was why he had come to see me."

"And what did he say about you?"

"I hardly like to repeat it, miss, because it sounds as if I were singing my own praises. He said he had read me same as a book, and that he knew that I had beauty, intelligence, passion and devotion."

"And what did you say to that?"

"I think I said: 'Oh, you do exaggerate.' It was something like that., but my head was all aswim. There was the Fourteenth Episode of *The Black Pearl* going on all the time, which I'd been looking forward to, but I couldn't tell you one blessed thing that was in it, and that shows you. He said a lot more about me and all very grave, nothing larky about it. I do hate larkiness—that milkman used to be full of it. Then we'd tea and scones at the corner shop, and he drove me back here. So, I got Miss Mason's dinner, which was curried chicken and an omelette, and took it in, and she said to me: 'Jane, what the hell have you done to your eyes to make them shine like that? And I said I supposed it was standing over the fire. But I was aglow all night."

"And last night?"

"I had the evening, for Miss Mason was out, and he came in the car to take me to dinner. We went to a place that was more like a king's palace than anything earthly, and he said it went by the name of Carlton. Oh, it was easy to see there that he was the Master. It was just as if they couldn't do enough for him. There were lots of people in evening dress, and of course, I'd nothing of that kind. But that didn't matter, because we didn't dine in the same room with them, but had a little room all to ourselves. There were flowers—biggest carnations I ever saw in my life. I used to think I could cook, but the cook there could cook my head off and then not think he'd started."

"And what happened then?"

Jane blushed. "Nothing wrong, miss, but it's as if I couldn't tell anybody. It's as if I didn't know myself what happened. He was talking, saying he'd live wholly for me and not for himself, and that he hoped one day I would love him enough to marry him. And somehow next moment he was holding me in his arms and kissing me, and I was crying—though what there was to cry about I can't tell you."

"Then you do love him, Jane?"

"I hope so, miss, though I've not had the experience and education to say for certain. I'm his. He can do anything he likes with me for evermore. There isn't anything except him, you see. The rest has stopped. When he took me in his arms, it was death and the life everlasting rolled into one. Oh, I dunno! If it isn't love, I hope it'll grow in time."

"I think," said Dora gravely, "it has already grown into it. You're going to be a happy woman, Jane. When is it to be?"

"Any time he says. But he doesn't want you to be inconvenienced, for he says you've made him. And I think my sister, Lucy Ellen might suit you, miss. She's not my sister strictly speaking—same father, different mothers, and not married to either. She's more refined than I am, having always gone to classes in anything as the chance came along. Working in a boarding-house at present but not satisfied. If you'd try her, she'd jump at it."

"Right," said Dora. "I'll try her."

But, as it happened, she never did.

Chapter 13: The Voice in the Dream

When Dora reached the Ritz, she found Mr. Overman in conversation with Mrs. Honor, and she was compelled to abdicate her intended role of hostess. He had already conveyed his astounding news to Mary Honor, who was not in the least astounded.

"I always thought, George, that you would marry one of these days. You've never been hampered by conventional ideas. You've judged for yourself. You've taken the opportunities that ordinary man may have been too blind to see. It's exactly what would be expected by anyone who really knows you, and I am very glad of it."

Dora spoke with enthusiasm of Jane's many high qualities, maintained that she could perfectly well do without her, and—having the cleverness of her kindness—made all that was superficially contradictory seem fundamentally convincing.

It transpired that George had been at Kate Mason's studio that morning to buy the forthcoming portrait of Jane, and that this had been arranged. He was more quiet and subdued than Dora had ever seen him, and was quite obviously deeply in love. He spoke of Jane as of a deity. At one juncture he said to Mrs. Honor: "What would you advise?" This was probably a phrase that he had never used in his life before. He had never asked people what he was to do; he had frequently told them what they would have to do, unless they wanted to be badly hurt. In fact, as he talked now, one hardly noticed his chin. There were men to whom that chin had seemed as it were a flaming sword.

It was settled between them that the marriage might just as well take place in a week's time.

"Subject to Jane's approval," said George. It was the first time that he had desired to be subject to any approval—and almost the first time that he could have obtained any.

Dora had no doubts now. Mysteriously, without her will, without any knowledge of how she had done it, she had changed this man. Sex attraction had nothing to do with it. She would have known in a moment if that had been the cause. He had said truly that he was not in the least in love with her. There was a possibility that he might regard her as his saint and saviour. He said that he did.

Dora had observed that he had been very rapid—two days.

"More than that," said George, and glanced round to see that there was no waiter present in the private room in which luncheon had been served. "I fell in love the first time I saw her—the first time she came to the door of your flat. But I was not able to read my feelings correctly then—the illumination came later. It is to you that I owe it, as I have been telling Mary."

Here he turned to Mrs. Honor. "Here's a problem for you. Suppose that apples are not to be got for money or by barter. I owe Miss Muse some apples; I cannot get them. I can buy tons of bananas, But Miss Muse detests bananas. The debt is in apples, and must be paid in apples. What am I to do? What would you advise?"

Mrs. Honor laughed. "But that's quite easy, George. You must plant a tree, grow your own apples, and ask her to be patient."

"That's very wise. Miss Muse, the spiritual debt is not to be repaid in any material currency. I can only promise that I will begin my spiritual orchard, and ask you to be patient."

Dora's only answer was a little laugh, rather shy and rather friendly. She liked what he had said. He had understood her.

Dora had time to pay a flying visit to Kate Mason before returning. Kate was cheery.

"Well," said Kate, "anything can happen now, can't it? Any old damn thing. My engagement to the Prince of Wales or the Archbishop of Canterbury may be announced any minute. First time I ever took a commission for a portrait of my cook to be paid for by my cook's young man. I asked him three hundred and he said it seemed very little, and wrote the cheque there and then because trifling sums escaped his blessed memory. Dora, my dear, what the devil are we coming to? And incidentally how are you going to get on without your priceless Jane?"

"She recommends her half-sister, and I'll probably take her on. Seriously, what do you think of it?"

"He's making no mistake. The wise would say he was. But then the wise are scratch and he's plus three. She's my loaned domestic servant, for the moment, but in three months the duchess will be afraid of her. He'll teach her about one *per cent* himself, and she'll do the other ninety-nine on her own, and do them quickly. She has a flair. She told me she didn't like American films of English life. She said that they didn't look at all like it, and were always doing things that English people didn't do. She observes. She's got a heart of gold—and most people who can observe have got no heart at all. She's all right. Don't you worry about Jane. All you want to do is to freeze on to the half-sister. Follow the breed. As a rule, when you get much intelligence the conscience ha to leave to make room for it."

"You've got a cheek," said Dora, "advising me about my domestic arrangements. What sort of a mess have you made of your own?"

"Oh, damn! Don't remind me of Mrs. Atkinson. To think that in a few days I've got to go back to those filthy rooms!"

"You needn't. You could perfectly well get a flat for yourself."

"You could: I can't. House-agents, and solicitors, and decorators, and furniture dealers, and the whole army of the devil! They frighten me. I could drop into something that suited me readymade. Sell me your flat and get another."

"Can't do that, but I'll leave you the rest of the lease in my will."

"Good," said Kate. "I'll do it with poisoned chocolates."

On her return to Derwood that evening, Dora found Eagle in rather a restless frame of mind.

"You must never go away again," he said. "I've been imagining motor accidents—all kinds of horrible nonsense. I never knew before that I had got nerves."

"But I'll have to go away again," said Dora. "You will have to get used to it, and won't be anxious anymore."

"I don't know. All day I've been in a state of excitement—and I've not the slightest idea of the reason. I feel as if something were impending."

"I know," said Dora. "I've had it too sometimes. Nothing ever comes of it."

Naturally, there was a good deal of talk at dinner about George Overman's forthcoming marriage. It struck Dora that such interest as Eagle showed in this event was politely simulated, and that in his heart he did not care one straw what happened to his benefactor.

After dinner Mrs. Honor, who was really tired after her day in London, was persuaded by Dora to go early to rest. Dora remained a few minutes still in the drawing-room with Eagle.

"You will fly tonight?" said Dora.

"I'm not sure. I'm far too excited to sleep. I think I shall wait and see if I feel any strong impulse. Some nights, you know; it is like that—as if I were being called up into the air. If that came tonight, I should have to go. And if I never returned—if I lost you!"

"It won't happen," said Dora. "We belong to one another. More and more I feel that."

It was almost as if Eagle's excitement had affected Dora. For hours she could not sleep. But it was an unhappy excitement. She was quite content to lie still and to listen. Her rose-coloured dressing-gown and white slippers were ready to hand. If she had heard a step on the terrace, she would have gone to the window at once to see Eagle make his flight. But no step came, and she heard nothing but the love-song of the nightingale in the distant wood.

And at last, she fell asleep, and in her sleep, there came to her a dream that was not of this earth. When she woke suddenly at dawn, she was conscious only that it had been strangely and wonderfully beautiful and remembered nothing more except the words that the voice had just spoken to her, and those words came to her again and again like a peal of bells.

"Your eyes shall be his eyes," said that voice, "and his wings shall be your wings. Not as two but as one shall you who have strayed return home. Hope then and trust."

Suddenly there came a faint tapping at her window. She put on her dressing-gown and slippers, drew back the curtain a little way and looked out. There on the balcony stood Eagle, his wings widespread in the cool grey light of the dawn. A mist was over the garden below, whence came the rippling blended music of many waking birds. In an instant she had passed through the open window, and looking up at him read the joy and exaltation in his eyes.

"I had to come to you," he said. "Tonight, I have brought back one memory to earth. At last, at last! On Friday night, between sunset and midnight, you and I go home together. It is sure. It is certain."

"But I knew it!" said Dora. "I knew it!" And she told him of the voice that had spoken in her dream.

And then, sitting side by side on the flat low parapet of the balcony, they made their plan together. And since they did not know whether this last flight would be brief or long, they settled how he should take her up with him. For more than half-an-hour they talked earnestly, and then the sun was well up and it was time for Eagle to go.

"I shall sleep well," said Eagle, as he kissed her. He leaped from the balcony, and flew upwards towards the hilltop.

Chapter 14: The Last Flight

Early on Thursday morning Dora went off to London again. She instructed and perplexed her solicitor. At first, he had some doubts of her sanity. But she was quite matter-of-fact, not in the least excited, seemed quite aware that the course she was taking was extraordinary, and expressed regret that though she had a full explanation there was private reasons why she could not give it. In the end he prepared the simple deed which she required. She executed it, and was back at Darkwood for luncheon.

It was at that luncheon, at Mrs. Honor's suggestion, that the two called one another by their first names.

"And I hope, Dora," said Mrs. Honor, "that you won't think me too impulsive and gushing. I dislike anything of the kind. But from the very first I was strangely attracted by you. Perhaps I should not say 'strangely.' We are too ready to call a thing extraordinary when all we mean is our experience has been limited and deficient. But I was attracted by you, and I hope I am going to see a great deal of you."

And Dora could only say that this was very kind. She knew that on the following night they would be separated—that she and Eagle were going home, and that no one living could follow them.

"There's no effect without cause. All works out according to the laws. An earthquake is less common than a sunrise, but both are the result of natural laws. In fact, there's nothing supernatural and never will be. What is, is nature. I do wish people would see that—then they'd give more time to study and less bewildered gaping."

Dora took her part in the conversation quite easily, and this surprised her. She had expected to be preoccupied and excited. And she was calm and content to be able to fix her mind on what she was doing or saying. She had noticed the same thing when she was talking to her lawyer that morning. But when she was quite alone, she had only to close her eyes, and then she seemed to hear once more the words that the voice in her dream and spoken.

"Your eyes shall be his eyes, and his wings shall be your wings. Not as two but as one shall you who have strayed return home. Hope then and trust."

After tea that afternoon Eagle came downstairs to take Dora out. Once more they went through the wood and up to the hilltop. And as Dora spoke of what she would do on the next night, Eagle said:

"And you don't mind—anything?"

"Why should I? Not as two but as one shall we return home: we shall become one in soul and body."

"It's the dream of all lovers, and for us the dream comes true."

When Dora went up to her room that evening, she wrote the first of the farewell letters that she was to leave behind her. It was a long letter to Kate Mason. And on the next day she wrote letters to Jane, to George Overman, to Mary Honor, and to other friends. She had no near relatives living.

And at last, the end of the day came. All ready, up in her room, Dora waited. Her heart was beating fast now. The house grew quite still. And now it was time for her to go.

She crept stealthily and noiselessly down the darkened staircase and out through the side door that Eagle used at night. A faint breeze ruffled her rose-silk dressing-gown. The thought crossed her mind that the heavy night dew would ruin her white slippers. And then she smiled, for what would it matter? She would never want them again.

She went out through one of the upper gates of the garden, and took the track through the wood. Here and there some shy little thing of the night hopped and scurried at her approach. And then suddenly overhead the nightingale broke into a full tide of song. For a moment she listened entranced, her clasped hands pressed against her bosom.

These magic lines came back to her memory.

"Now more than ever it seems rich to die,

To cease upon the midnight with no pain."

And now she passed out on to the flat hilltop. And there before her, with his back towards her, his wings widespread, crouched Eagle, like a steed awaiting a rider, an ivory statue on the scented thyme of the hilltop.

"I am here," she called softly.

"Come then, beloved! Come quickly."

She stood by his side. "We're going home, dear—home! She said drowsily. "I'm so happy."

And then the last flight began.

★★★★★★★★★★★★★★★★★★

312

Those who searched for the missing two the next morning found on the hill the little white slippers and the rose dressing-gown circled about them. But Eagle and Dora came no more to earth.

Did anyone behold them in their last flight? It may be. The statements of Mr. Percy Handcock and his wife Julia must at least be taken into consideration.

Mr. Handcock of the High Street, Orple, was a dealer in second-hand and antique furniture. He did not make a fortune by the business but he made sufficient for the support of himself, his wife, and three small children. He was a rubicund man of middle-age. Julia looked after him well, but was sometimes eluded. He was a man of generous girth and there were things that he liked to put inside it. But he was not a grossly immoral man; on the contrary he was a regular church goer and fond of his family.

On the evening of Friday Percy Handcock went to the village of Newfield five miles away to inspect certain furniture and to make a sufficiently low offer for it. He got a lift in a friend's car, most of the way, and walked the last mile.

He bought the furniture advantageously, had supper at the inn in Newfield, and there met a friend with whom he had some discussion. At ten he started to walk back and took the short cut—a foot track which runs along the side of Darkwood Hill. He had told Julia that he would not be later than half-past eleven.

Now as Percy Handcock was dressing on Saturday morning, he became aware that he was in disgrace. Julia's demeanour, before she went to look after the children, had most clearly indicated it. At first, knowing his own moderation on the previous evening, he was inclined to be aggrieved. And then he made a horrible discovery. He could remember everything up to the time when he started along the Darkwood track., but from that moment till the following morning he could remember nothing whatever. Anything might have happened.

At breakfast he tried to be facetious with the children, but his heart was not in the work, and a glance from Julia checked him. After breakfast she sent the children into the garden.

"I want to speak to your pa," she added ominously.

"Now then," she said, "what did you have last night?"

"Let's see. Usual pint with my supper. Another after. Then I happened on Atkins and he gave me a drop of whisky as I was leaving."

"That was all?"

"Absolutely."

313

"Then I can't make it out. You were home a few minutes before your time. You walked all right, and there was no thickness of the speech. But you were white and trembly, and such nonsense as you talked, I never did hear in all my born days."

"Why? What did I say?"

"Said that as you came over Darkwood you saw a man with wings up in the air, and a girl sitting astride his back and her hair flying in the wind. And as far as you could make out, they'd little or no clothes on."

"Don't recall it," he said heavily. "Did I say anything else?"

"Bless you, yes. You said those two figures seemed to melt into one, same as the dissolving views of the Holy Land in the parish room. And all of a sudden, the whole thing vanished, like blowing out a candle."

"Well, if I said I saw it, I saw it. But I don't recall it."

"Then it must be some sort of brain-mischief."

"Some sort of stuff and nonsense," said Percy, waxing courageous. "You dreamed I said it—that's what it was. Here I must go down to the shop."

And when he got there, he sat down and for some minutes was lost in thought. Glimmerings seemed to come back to him. They filled him with disquiet.

★★★★★★★★★★★★★★★★★

A year later in the flat that had once been Dora's Kate Mason sat and pondered. By deed of gift Dora's possessions had come to her, and it was Lucy Ellen, the half-sister of Dora's maid, who looked after her. Lucy Ellen was not so pretty as Jane had been. She was firmer, more decided, more angular. Men did not attract her. Even her affection for Kate Mason was tinged with severity, but she recognised that it was her life's mission to take care of Miss Mason. For Miss Mason was a child, and not always a very good child, and needed supervision.

Kate held in her hand the last long letter she had received from Dora. She had carried out every request that Dora had made in it. The string of small pearls had gone to Mrs. Honor, the watch to Lady Overman—George had acquired his baronetcy a few days after his marriage—and the two precious volumes of the *Book of Experience* had been burned unread. Kate had read that letter many times, and now on the anniversary of Dora's departure she had read it again.

Presently, she locked the letter away in her desk, lit a cigarette, and paced up and down the room. Lucy Ellen came in to lay the table, and looked at the cigarette with disapproval.

"Would you like me to keep dinner back, miss, until you've finished smoking?"

"Never. Go straight ahead with it. If I don't get something to eat soon, I shall probably bite you."

Lucy smiled faintly, and as she went on with her work said:

"I had a telephone message this afternoon, miss, while you were out. Her ladyship gave birth to a son shortly after three. Both doing well."

"What? Jane got a kid? Well, I'm damned. However, I suppose something of the sort was likely to happen. We'll both drink to their health tonight."

"Thank you very much, miss. It's a coincidence that her child should be born on the anniversary of poor Muss Muse's death."

"What are you talking about?" said Kate fiercely. "I'll die. You'll die. But Dora Muse never died—never! Damn it, I painted her eight times and I ought to know!"

Back in her kitchen Lucy Ellen raised her eyes to heaven and murmured in tones of pious resignation:

"These artists!"

And then she carried in the soup.

LEONAUR

ALSO FROM LEONAUR
AVAILABLE IN SOFTCOVER OR HARDCOVER WITH DUST JACKET

THE COMPLETE FOUR JUST MEN: VOLUME 2 *by Edgar Wallace—The Law of the Four Just Men & The Three Just Men*—disillusioned with a world where the wicked and the abusers of power perpetually go unpunished, the Just Men set about to rectify matters according to their own standards, and retribution is dispensed on swift and deadly wings.

THE COMPLETE RAFFLES: 1 *by E. W. Hornung—The Amateur Cracksman & The Black Mask*—By turns urbane gentleman about town and accomplished cricketer, life is just too ordinary for Raffles and that sets him on a series of adventures that have long been treasured as a real antidote to the 'white knights' who are the usual heroes of the crime fiction of this period.

THE COMPLETE RAFFLES: 2 *by E. W. Hornung—A Thief in the Night & Mr Justice Raffles*—By turns urbane gentleman about town and accomplished cricketer, life is just too ordinary for Raffles and that sets him on a series of adventures that have long been treasured as a real antidote to the 'white knights' who are the usual heroes of the crime fiction of this period.

THE COLLECTED SUPERNATURAL AND WEIRD FICTION OF WILKIE COLLINS: VOLUME 1 *by Wilkie Collins*—Contains one novel 'The Haunted Hotel', one novella 'Mad Monkton', three novelettes 'Mr Percy and the Prophet', 'The Biter Bit' and 'The Dead Alive' and eight short stories to chill the blood.

THE COLLECTED SUPERNATURAL AND WEIRD FICTION OF WILKIE COLLINS: VOLUME 2 *by Wilkie Collins*—Contains one novel 'The Two Destinies', three novellas 'The Frozen deep', 'Sister Rose' and 'The Yellow Mask' and two short stories to chill the blood.

THE COLLECTED SUPERNATURAL AND WEIRD FICTION OF WILKIE COLLINS: VOLUME 3 *by Wilkie Collins*—Contains one novel 'Dead Secret,' two novelettes 'Mrs Zant and the Ghost' and 'The Nun's Story of Gabriel's Marriage' and five short stories to chill the blood.

FUNNY BONES *selected by Dorothy Scarborough*—An Anthology of Humorous Ghost Stories.

MONTEZUMA'S CASTLE AND OTHER WEIRD TALES *by Charles B. Cory*—Cory has written a superb collection of eighteen ghostly and weird stories to chill and thrill the avid enthusiast of supernatural fiction.

SUPERNATURAL BUCHAN *by John Buchan*—Stories of Ancient Spirits, Uncanny Places & Strange Creatures.

www.ingramcontent.com/pod-product-compliance
Lightning Source LLC
Chambersburg PA
CBHW030406030726
47497CB00002B/506